Death by Chocolate Chip Cupcake

Sarah Graves

Kensington Publishing Corp.
www.kensingtonbooks.com

KENSINGTON BOOKS are published by
Kensington Publishing Corp.
119 West 40th Street
New York, NY 10018

All Kensington titles, imprints, and distributed lines are available at special quantity discounts for bulk purchases for sales promotion, premiums, fund-raising, educational, or institutional use.

This book is a work of fiction. Names, characters, businesses, organizations, places, events, and incidents either are the product of the author's imagination or are used fictitiously. Any resemblance to actual persons, living or dead, events, or locales is entirely coincidental.

To the extent that the image or images on the cover of this book depict a person or persons, such person or persons are merely models, and are not intended to portray any character or characters featured in the book.

Special book excerpts or customized printings can also be created to fit specific needs. For details, write or phone the office of the Kensington Sales Manager: Kensington Publishing Corp., 119 West 40th Street, New York, NY 10018. Attn. Sales Department. Phone: 1-800-221-2647.

The K and Teapot logo is a trademark of Kensington Publishing Corp.

ISBN: 978-1-4967-2924-8 (ebook)

ISBN: 978-1-4967-2923-1

First Kensington Hardcover Edition: April 2022

First Kensington Trade Paperback Printing: December 2023

10 9 8 7 6 5 4 3 2 1

Printed in the United States of America

One

If I'd known right up front that so many dead bodies would be involved, I'd have vetoed the chocolate pizza. Besides, I was already busy reinventing the chocolate chip cupcake.

And then there was the earthquake. "Did you feel it?" my friend Ellie White wanted to know when we arrived that morning to our small, chocolate-themed bakery, The Chocolate Moose.

The brief, gentle shaking had happened at four a.m., just in time for me to not be able to get back to sleep.

"Yes," I said, "but I doubt it really was one." Everyone knew Maine didn't have earthquakes.

"The U.S. Geological Survey thinks it was," Ellie countered. "It was on the radio. A two-point-four, they said."

Okay, so I'd been wrong. As it turned out there was a well-known fault line not far from us at all, along the shore on the mainland near the St. Croix River.

Well known to geologists, anyway. It seemed that a Maine island town could get as shook up as anywhere else, just not as often.

"That's all news to me," I told Ellie when she'd filled me in on the details.

Still, the event was over and likely wouldn't happen again. So we dropped the subject, and it wasn't until later that afternoon that she mentioned another thing she'd been mulling.

"I want," she began, "a . . ."

You guessed it. ". . . a chocolate pizza," she finished.

"Do you, now?" I answered cautiously as I glanced out the shop's front bay window. On that damp, late-September afternoon, shadows had already begun gathering between the two-story brick or wood-framed storefront buildings on Water Street, across from the harbor in the remote island village of Eastport, Maine.

"To sell by the slice, you mean . . . ?" I let my voice trail off into deliberate uncertainty.

We'd closed early, due to not having even one customer all day. I was scrubbing out the drinks cooler and thinking about how the cupcakes I was inventing had to have real whipped cream filling, not the spray-can kind.

"Both," she called from back in the kitchen, where she was baking chocolate pinwheel cookies. "Slices, or whole pizzas."

Drizzle streaked the window looking onto the gray, empty street. On a day like today it was good to be warm and indoors. Too bad everyone else thought so, too; see *not even one customer,* above.

"Also, it has to be *great* chocolate pizza," said Ellie.

Due in part to the treasured old baked-goods recipes that Ellie's grandmother had passed down to her—the other part was plain hard work—the Moose had an excellent reputation and we didn't want to risk damaging it.

"Not too sweet, though, not cloying," Ellie said, tapping a wooden spoon into the palm of her hand. "With hazelnuts, maybe?"

For our work that day she wore a white cotton turtleneck,

red quilted vest, and denim jeans, with a blue chambray smock top pulled on over all of them, plus white Keds. In that outfit I'd have looked like somebody getting ready to clean out a bunch of stables; she looked like a million bucks.

"Hazelnuts sound good," I said, a little less skeptical. After all, we already sold cakes, cookies, pies, pastries . . .

So why not a dessert pizza? Except . . .

"But, Ellie," I said, "we've already got cupcake invention in progress."

The cream-filled ones, I meant. Chocolate chip batter with chopped cherries would make fine surroundings for the cream.

But I hadn't even run a test batch yet. "Maybe with winter coming we should wait on another new recipe? At least until we've got more money?"

Ingredients were expensive, after all, and the empty street outside wasn't due only to the drizzly weather. It was also because we were nearing the end of tourist season now, and the people who'd flocked here all summer had mostly gone home.

That left only a thousand or so year-round Eastporters to buy our high-quality but also more expensive bakery items. Not only that, but they had to come downtown just for them instead of getting cheaper packaged things at the IGA.

I sprayed my towel with our own homemade cleaning solution, wrinkling my nose at the pungent ammonia smell, and began wiping down the front of our glass-fronted display case.

"We could wait," Ellie agreed. "But I've been thinking it over, Jake, and I feel we need something new right now."

She'd stuffed her strawberry blond hair into a hairnet but soft tendrils curled from it, framing her heart-shaped face. Blowing strands away impatiently, she flattened the cookie dough with quick, deft strokes of her rolling pin.

"We need it *because* of winter," she said. "For the variety, see? So people *will* keep coming to the Moose."

She had a point. Winter in Eastport is a cheery, life-affirming combination of sleet, snow, wind, ice, and the kind of dense, energy-sapping gloom that closes in on you at three in the afternoon and doesn't let go again for sixteen hours.

Also, Eastport really is remote—three hours from Bangor, light-years from anywhere else—and when the fog freezes, it puts another ice layer on the roads, iron hard but slipperier.

That's why in winter some Eastporters get so desperate for entertainment that when it snows they take their lawn chairs and cocktails outside and sit watching the snowplows go by.

Not me, of course. Well, hardly ever. Anyway:

"But the truth is that mostly the idea came out of the blue and now I can't stop thinking about it," Ellie said.

"Ohhh," I breathed, my interest suddenly piqued; that made a difference. When Ellie got an idea for a new chocolate treat, it bounced around in her brain for a while until finally it went away. That is, unless it became an obsession, in which case she nurtured it stubbornly through test batches, taste surveys, and careful ingredients-tinkering, followed of course by new batches, tastes, etcetera.

Her venison jerky in bitter chocolate went through twenty-two revisions, as I recall. But then came the result: tender but chewy, mind-bogglingly delicious, and delivering a really quite noticeable jolt of energy.

Customers had loved it. Now: "I suppose it could work," I said, meaning the pizza.

In our display case right now were batches of peanut-butter-and-chocolate cookies, mocha fudge brownies with a broiled pistachio crumble topping, and a chocolate-cherry cheesecake with our special, super-secret ingredient (hint: it's a dollop of Hershey's Syrup) in its chocolate-wafer crust.

Fortunately, all these items were special ordered, paid for, and waiting to be picked up; no way would we be able to sell it all at this time of year, otherwise. But these and many more of our most popular offerings were the result of Ellie's creative streak, and I had no reason to think chocolate pizza would be different.

"It's not like we're new at this," I added.

We'd been in business for five years already, so we weren't poorly equipped. We would have to buy ingredients and a couple of kitchen tools—we did not, for instance, have a pizza stone and we'd be needing one of those—but now that I thought more about it, what better thing to bet on than Ellie's great track record?

"All right," I said finally, pulling chairs back one after another from our quartet of black cast-iron café tables.

"You may be on to something," I said, "so let's go ahead and try this. How can I help?"

Saying this, I looked around for my next cleaning task. When we'd first rented it, the shop space had been filthy and in need of repairs, but now we owned the narrow, two-story wooden building, and after our improvements The Chocolate Moose boasted a slate tiled floor, handsome exposed-brick walls, and a large, late-nineteenth-century wooden-paddled ceiling fan, which slowly stirred the sweet-smelling air under the vintage pressed-tin ceiling.

"You can think about toppings," Ellie replied as I got the broom and dustpan from the utility closet. "Jalapeño, maybe?"

Or maybe not. Ellie is brilliant, daring, inspired, but she goes a little far in the surprise combinations department.

So I didn't answer, just began sweeping silently, watching the fishing boats motoring into the blue-shadowed harbor with their running lights glowing. As they glided up to the finger piers, their captains shut their engines down just as the last light drained from the sky and the night took over.

Ellie's boat was there, too; I spotted the black canvas Bimini awning that shaded the helm and the small porthole in the boat's little cabin, lit by the dock lamps on the breakwater nearby.

Soon she'd be wanting me to go out for a last, chilly ride with her before winter, and although I was a landlubber through and through, I would agree; it was important to her.

Happily for me, though, it was the last thing on her mind right now. "I'd like the crust to have a plain, saltine flavor," she mused aloud.

On the breakwater, the dock lights shed glowing yellow cones hazy from the drizzle falling through them. "With the salt sprinkled on top, you know?" she went on. "Like the cracker."

Chocolate where you don't expect it, such as on a saltine, can be either a triumph or a complete flop. But I'd begun thinking already that we might have a winner; well, minus the jalapeños.

At last I set aside my broom. The clock over the counter said half past four, and now the boats bobbing at the dock were black cutouts under a nearly full moon.

While I watched them, a long, dark limousine glided up to the curb outside our shop.

"Um, Ellie?" The street was painted for angle parking. The limo parked unapologetically parallel to the sidewalk. Its windshield wipers beat back and forth over the tinted windshield to sweep away the thickening mist.

"So if you can come up with more toppings, I'll get to work on the crust," Ellie went on, pleased that I'd agreed.

I glanced back into the kitchen, where she'd spread the flattened cookie dough thickly with a layer of melted chocolate, rolled it up again, and sliced the roll into neat, thin rounds.

Then I stared out at the dark limousine some more. Maybe it was a Fig Newton of my imagination, as my son, Sam, would say.

"Ellie?" I repeated, turning to her again. With her fine, regular features, gold-dust freckles, and a mouth almost always curved into a smile, Ellie was as delicately pretty as a fairy-tale princess.

But she was as tough as an old boot when she had to be, which I hoped wasn't right now. We didn't get many long, dark limousines around here, and so far I wasn't at all sure how I felt about this one.

"What's in a saltine, anyway?" Ellie wondered aloud, still unaware we were being visited by the Longest Car in the World.

She slid the cookies into the cooler; tomorrow she'd bake them and—voila!—warm cookies for morning customers.

If we had any. Outside, the newly arrived vehicle just sat there, radiating vague menace. "Ellie, come look at this."

The limousine's headlights lit the street all the way to the big granite post office building on the corner of Washington Street. The tint on the windows kept me from seeing inside.

The wipers kept flapping. I was about to call Eastport's police chief, Bob Arnold, and ask him to just casually stroll down here from his office half a block away, and find out what cooked in the unfamiliar vehicle department.

But just then the driver's-side door opened and a man in a cream-colored fisherman's sweater, chauffeur's cap, and brown leather jacket got out and peered carefully around.

"Ellie," I repeated more sharply than before. "You really should come and . . ."

She emerged from the kitchen, still not listening to me at all. Rain tapped the window glass, slid down in shining trails.

The limousine driver unfurled a black umbrella as he stepped briskly around to the curb side of the car, then opened its rear passenger door. The car's overhead light went on and something big moved inside. Big and . . . *hairy*?

I squinted, but whatever it was had moved out of sight.

"The obvious choice is still hazelnuts. Or maybe walnuts," Ellie said. "Pizza crust is already fairly chewy, so no pecans. We could use hickory nuts, but . . ."

We'd driven all over downeast Maine looking for a hickory grove but had no luck.

"Look," I said, turning her by her shoulders.

The limo driver was extending a hand to whoever was in the rear passenger compartment.

"Who . . . ?" Ellie began, her eyes widening as the vehicle's occupant emerged from the backseat.

Which was when I saw who it was, and so did Ellie.

"Oh my goodness," she said as the world-famous swirls of pale blond hair appeared, followed by a face that had launched a string of Hollywood hits, back in the day.

"That's Ingrid Merryfield," said Ellie wonderingly.

"Yep," I said. "It certainly is."

In her final film, *Call Me*, a scam artist and a woman who's gathering evidence against him fall in love. She'd been gorgeous then, twenty years ago, maybe, and now in a tailored white pants suit and jacket she still looked fabulous, darling.

Leaning back, heedless of the rain, she peered up at the sign over our door. It was a big, wooden cut-out moose head with branching antlers, googly eyes, and a toothy grin.

Ingrid Merryfield grinned back up at it just as a kid on a bike pedaled past on the pavement behind her: sandy hair, flat brown cap, tweed jacket. Then she *actually entered our shop*, the door's little silver bell jingling over her blond head as she swept in.

"Hi," I murmured, suddenly not knowing what to do with my hands; at last I stuck them clumsily into my apron pockets.

"Can I help you?" I asked, only stuttering slightly.

At close range, the film star had soft little jowls under her jaw, and her hair looked more gluey than glam now that it was wet. But she still had that zillion-watt smile, the one that made you think the sun had suddenly come out just for you.

And it worked even better in person than it had on the silver screen. "Hello," she said pleasantly, looking around, and gosh, wasn't I glad I'd just finished cleaning the place up?

"I'm Ingrid Merryfield," she said, offering her hand.

"Yes, you are!" I blurted, taking it. Then, "Oh gosh," I added, a flush of embarrassment warming my neck.

I hadn't thought I'd be star struck. But she just laughed, the same peal of friendly amusement that I recognized from her films, and suddenly it was all fine again and I was fine, too.

"Welcome to Eastport and The Chocolate Moose," Ellie said.

"Why, thank you." The blond head tipped slightly. "What a sweet little bakery," she said including me in her glance.

"Thanks," I replied. *What are you doing here?* I wanted to add, but I didn't because with her next words she explained.

Sort of. "I'm from here, actually. Eastport, I mean. Why, when I was a little girl, this was the drugstore."

She glanced around nostalgically. "The soda fountain with red leather stools where we sat and drank Cokes and read movie magazines was right over there."

Ellie and I glanced at one another. Ingrid Merryfield had it right about our building's history, but . . .

The aging film star looked up at me, her large, beautifully made-up blue eyes softened with memories. "At the back of the store was the phone booth, and on the counter were those little jukeboxes, remember?"

I didn't. All that was before my time here, back when the city was busy with its two main industries, ships and sardines.

"It sounds wonderful," I told Ingrid Merryfield as Ellie emerged from the kitchen with the tea she'd gone back there to make. "I didn't know you were from here," I added.

The star's merry laugh rang out again as she accepted the mug and Ellie's invitation to sit by the window.

"No one does. I've kept my own name—no stage name for me, thanks! But other than that, I've kept my personal life to myself, and somehow no one's managed to track me back here."

She inhaled the tea's fragrant steam. "Thanks, this is good of you."

Reflected in the darkened window glass behind her, she reminded me of a rose just past its prime, no longer perfect but still lovely and fragrant.

And hiding sharp thorns, the thought popped unbidden into my head, and where had that idea come from, I wondered?

Then her driver came in, raking the shop with an assessing glance and even peeking into the kitchen, then approaching Ingrid Merryfield. Before he could speak, though:

"Bryan," she said, "have one more look around outside, will you? Make sure there are no predators."

I must've looked puzzled. "It's what I call the paparazzi," she said, hissing the final word unpleasantly as the driver went back out. "That's Bryan Dwyer, by the way. My driver and right-hand man."

Ellie caught my eye. *What the heck?* her look said, and I agreed; we were on an island seven miles from the mainland, and any paparazzi we got way out here were probably lost.

Then Bryan returned, and now I noticed that although his waistline was trim, his shoulders bulked his jacket out in a way that pretty much yelled, "regular workouts."

One of those shoulders also yelled "don't mess with me"; it was the one with the bulge that even his well-cut leather jacket didn't quite conceal.

He saw me looking, shot me a tight smile; I shrugged back because, hey, what did I care? Whatever made him think he needed a gun was none of my affair.

Or so I thought at the time. Ellie spoke up. "Anyway, it's lovely to see you. But what can we do for you, Miss Merryfield?"

Bryan had found no paparazzi on Water Street, I gathered. Now he eyed the display case's content hungrily, and I realized that the two of them had probably just gotten into town.

"Listen," I said quietly, sidling over to him. "If you're staying here in Eastport and you want to get dinner . . ."

I glanced up at the clock. Somehow it had gotten to be a little past five. "You will want to visit the IGA," I finished.

Three of the four restaurants in Eastport were already closed for the season, and the fourth, the Busted Flush, was mostly a drinking establishment.

"The IGA closes at seven," I added. "Or you could drive back over the causeway and north on Route 1," I said. "There'll be something open somewhere up there, I imagine."

Bryan was about sixty years old, I estimated, with short salt-and-pepper hair, a ruddy complexion, and bushy eyebrows on a prizefighter's crumpled-looking face.

"Okay," he exhaled resignedly, possibly contemplating the unhappy prospect of a grocery store delicatessen dinner heated up in a motel room microwave.

"Ma'am," he said, turning to his boss. "This nice lady here says if we want something to eat tonight, we'll need to—"

"Wait, though," I cut in as a new thought hit me. After all, here were a real, no-kidding movie star and her driver, just in off the road to Eastport.

And here *we* were, able to help them. Meanwhile, I had a stepmother at home who was right now getting a delicious dinner on the table, and who would skin me alive if she didn't get to meet them.

And there were always plenty of leftovers. "Come on up to the house," I said. "You can freshen up and have dinner there. And maybe a drink?"

Ingrid Merryfield's bright-blue eyes brightened even more at the mention of refreshments. Still:

"Oh, no, we couldn't possibly impose on you to—"

"Ma'am, we don't even know if there's pots and pans at the house," Bryan interrupted. "And has the power been turned on?"

Ingrid got up, looking vexed. "Well, I don't know, Bryan, I'm not the one who's handling—"

I got the strong sense that Ingrid Merryfield rarely handled the troublesome details. She had people for that.

Bryan, here, for instance. "But you're right," she added to him, "we should go there first and check things out, at least."

Ellie stepped quickly between Ingrid and Bryan. "You should go with Jake," she told the movie star kindly but firmly.

Meaning me: Jacobia Tiptree, Jake to my friends.

"Even if you buy food for dinner," Ellie went on, "it seems like you're not even sure that you're going to be able to cook it."

Bryan nodded at this but Ingrid Merryfield still looked stubborn, and now, to tell the truth, I was getting a bit tired of these perfectly pleasant people who nevertheless couldn't figure out what they wanted, or how to say it if they did figure it out.

Or maybe I was just getting hungry, myself. Silently I eased them toward the door; Ingrid didn't seem to mind and Bryan couldn't do much about it because she was his boss.

Outside, he glanced up and down the dark street again as he moved toward the car. No one had told him, I supposed, that in Eastport you could walk stark naked down Water Street with the Hope Diamond in your hand and nobody would bother you.

"Call if we can help with anything," I told the film star as we stood together on the sidewalk. The rain had stopped for the moment, leaving the pavement gleaming.

Then Bryan helped her back into the car, and did I catch another glimpse of someone—or something—in there with her?

Maybe, but before I could look again the long, dark vehicle was pulling away from the curb, then driving off into the night.

"They're not headed toward the IGA," Ellie pointed out; she'd overheard me mentioning it to Bryan, earlier. And on an island only four miles wide and seven miles long, it's hard to get lost.

"They'll find it sooner or later," I said. Then we went back inside and for the next hour worked steadily, knocking off our remaining baking and cleaning chores.

Grating ginger and shaving long curls off a block of dark chocolate, for instance, or mopping off the metal top of the drinks cooler, which I'd discovered, to my horror, that persons standing more than six feet tall could actually see.

Finally Ellie gave the whole place a last looking-over while I snapped the fan and the lights decisively off and pulled my key from my bag.

"Why do I feel like we haven't heard the last of them?" she said as I turned the key from outside.

Across the dark bay lay the Canadian island of Campobello; lights were on over there in the little windows and I could see the bluish glow of TV screens through their open curtains.

A car went by, its tires hissing through the puddles. "Of Ingrid Merryfield and Bryan? Oh, I'm fairly sure we haven't."

As I crossed the sidewalk to Ellie's car something else occurred to me. "Are you hauling your boat soon?"

Each autumn the vessel got pulled from the water and stored at the boatyard for the winter, and the sooner it happened the sooner I could quit stressing about boat rides.

But: "No." She dug around in her bag for the keys to her old Honda. "I'm going to keep it at the dock until Thanksgiving, try to go out a few more times."

"Cool," I told her, lying through my teeth as I got into the car, then fastened my seat belt and rolled down the window.

In the distance a foghorn honked. Down in the boat basin, the bolts and chains on the floating dock sections creaked.

"Anyway, why not?" asked Ellie, backing out. "Why don't you think we've seen the last of them?"

"Well, for one thing," I said, "can you imagine either one of them cooking anything like a decent dinner in the kitchen of some empty, unheated house they'd just walked into?"

"No," she said with a smile from behind the steering wheel. "Neither of them looked very domestic."

She didn't ask the other reason I thought they'd be back. But from the way he'd glanced around and the weapon he carried, I was pretty sure I'd identified Bryan's real profession.

So just before he left the bakery with Ingrid, I'd quietly mentioned one more thing to him, since in a world full of convenience store coffee and vending machine sandwiches I knew that what a bodyguard always wanted—

"We're having stewed chicken with garlic mashed potatoes," I'd told him, and heard his stomach growling in reply.

—was a home-cooked dinner.

"Jake, what're you up to?" Ellie asked. I'd just told her about tempting Bryan with dinner deliciousness.

"First of all, Bella will kill me if I let Ingrid Merryfield get away without giving Bella an autograph."

Bella was my stepmother as well as my housekeeper. She'd worked for me at first, then married my father, and now we all lived together in my big old house on Key Street, along with my husband, my son and his young family, and various pets.

Lots of pets; right now they included a cat, two hamsters, and ten neon tetras in a tank with a heater, an aerator, and a red plastic diver who bobbed up and down, expelling bubbles.

Also there was a parrot who sang "God Save the Queen" in a voice that was eerily like a small child's, but never mind him; I certainly tried not to.

"Besides, we can't just let them wander off on their own with nothing to eat," I said, because you didn't treat strangers that way here in Eastport, you just didn't.

"But," Ellie pointed out, "you *did* just let them . . ."

"Like I say, they'll be back. Just in case, along with a preview of tonight's dinner menu I gave Bryan directions on how to get to my house."

And he hadn't refused them, instead visibly committing them to whatever was inside that blocky salt-and-pepper head of his. So maybe he and I had the same idea, that with just one end run around Ingrid Merryfield's stubbornness, they both could get fed.

"I bet you can manage to find out what they're doing here, too," said Ellie as she drove past the long, wooden fish pier with the tugboats hulking against it. At the pier's far end a single street lamp stood like a beacon against the night.

Lobster traps, large brightly colored wire crates baited with dead fish or pig hide that the tasty crustaceans crawled into but couldn't escape from, stood stacked under the street lamp.

"I am sort of curious about why Bryan keeps peering around like he thinks something's getting ready to pounce on him," I said. "Not to mention why he's carrying a gun."

I went on to describe the shoulder holster as we passed the old Frontier Bank building, then turned by the red-brick library with the cannon on its lawn.

"And from the way he was carrying himself when he came into the Moose you'd have thought he was walking into the O.K. Corral," I said.

"Oh good, just what we needed," Ellie said, "a nervous guy with a weapon."

Over the years we'd met more than a few of those. Something about Eastport just brings out the murder in people, it seems, and it had brought out the snoop in us: together, Ellie and I had nosed into quite a few of the deadly crimes, sometimes with Eastport police chief Bob Arnold's approval and sometimes not.

Ellie switched the wipers on again as we drove up Key Street, under the maples, whose orange and yellow leaves shone wetly. From the windows of the small wooden houses we passed, warm, golden lamplight poured out onto the neat front lawns.

"Maybe it's routine," said Ellie, meaning the gun. "A big star like Ingrid Merryfield must attract plenty of unwanted attention."

A cat streaked suddenly across the street right in front of us. Ellie hit the brakes and we held our breaths until it shot up onto the opposite sidewalk unharmed, then glared at us.

"From fans. And from crazies, too," Ellie added as we crested the hill and my big old house came into view.

It was an 1823 white clapboard Federal with three full stories plus an attic, six fireplaces, forty-eight old wooden double-hung windows with the original wavery glass mostly still in them, and a two-story attached barn, where my husband, Wade Sorenson, had a gun repair workshop.

"Maybe," I said as Ellie pulled into the driveway behind Wade's old pickup truck, Sam's new pickup truck, Bella's little VW, my daughter-in-law Mika's Prius, and my own car, an elderly orange Fiat currently on the disabled list.

Farther out on the back lawn were a flatbed trailer with an assortment of yard care machinery on it, a massive yellow plow attachment that belonged to Wade's truck, and, lit up by Ellie's headlights, a blue plastic barrel lying on its side in a wooden cradle made of sawhorses.

CAUTION—FLAMMABLE read the stenciling on the barrel in letters so big I could read them in the gloom, and I happened to know the barrel held gas mixed with oil, for the lawn machines.

Then as Ellie pulled alongside the Fiat, headlights turned in behind us. I recognized the limo as it rolled to a stop and an interior light went on dimly, showing people shapes inside.

Two—no, three of them, as I'd thought earlier. Bryan got out, stretching in the chilly darkness before opening the rear door, and Ingrid Merryfield emerged.

Letting her head loll back in a way that looked unnervingly as if her neck had been broken, she spoke: "Home," she breathed nostalgically. "Oh, that *smell*."

The mixed aromas of woodsmoke and seaweed, the tannic scent of wet leaves and pine sap mingling in salt air . . . she was right, nothing else was like them, especially if you were from here.

Suddenly the limousine's third passenger leapt eagerly from the limousine's backseat, then trotted past us out onto the lawn to lift his leg. Brown and shaggy, he stood three feet tall at the shoulder and had a head the size and shape of a concrete block.

The difference of course being that there are no big, white razor-sharp choppers in a concrete block. "That," said Ellie in a wondering tone, "is an Irish wolfhound."

The dog finished his errand and loped to Ingrid's side. Bryan looked sideways at the animal as it went by, and from his face I gathered that he and the dog weren't exactly bosom buddies.

"We're so sorry to bother you," Ingrid said. "But we went to see the house and you were right. It's a bit of a shambles."

The house they were renting here in Eastport, I supposed she meant. Ellie got into her car once more, waving a farewell as she backed out past the limo and drove off down Key Street.

"And I wonder, if it's not too much trouble," Ingrid said, "if we might take up the invitation we turned down earlier."

"Oh! Of course!" I turned to include Bryan. "Let's all go inside and warm up and get dinner, then, shall we?" I said, and they both seemed to think that this was a fine idea.

So we did. Get supper, that is. Drinks, too; several of them.

And that's not all we got.

My beloved old housekeeper-slash-stepmother, Bella Diamond, had frizzy dyed-red hair, big grape-green eyes, and a jutting jaw that she generally kept clamped shut around strangers. But that night for Ingrid Merryfield Bella made an exception, and for Ingrid's dog, too.

Especially for the dog, actually. "Igor," Bella crooned,

crouching arthritically to put her face practically right up against its big white teeth.

Around her my big old-fashioned kitchen was filled with delicious smells: chicken cutlets simmering in mushroom gravy, garlic potatoes mashed with pepper and sour cream, and sliced red tomatoes picked green in September from the brown paper bag of them still ripening in the butler's pantry.

"Oh, aren't you a good dog," Bella sweet-talked the enormous canine, who seemed to melt into a puddle of brown fur at her words.

I sat at the big, round kitchen table, which was covered with a red-and-white-checked cloth and had a red chrysanthemum plant in a blue-glazed pot sitting at the center of it.

"So it's not too much trouble?" I asked.

Bringing two dinner guests home without calling her wasn't my usual habit, mostly because she'd have murdered me the first time I tried it.

But: "Oh, no," she replied, "not when it's —"

Not when it's Ingrid Merryfield. When they came in, a "How d'ye do?" and a stiff handshake were all she'd had to offer.

But the small, secret smile playing around Bella's lips now said it all: this was the most excitement she'd had since the Campobello ferry lost power in the middle of the bay, and Wade had to take a skiff out to fetch her.

"Excellent dog," she said, fondling its shaggy ears. She'd set out a bowl of water and fed it a Ritz cracker, which it seemed to enjoy.

Meanwhile, I unfolded a sheet of paper that Ellie had given me on our way home. On it was a quick-and-dirty cost/benefit analysis of a new bakery item, the chocolate pizza.

On the plus side, we'd done well over the summer, selling enough macaroons, dream bars, and biscotti to float a barge, as Bella would've put it. But there'd also been big expenses; the floor, for instance, which had begun falling into the cellar.

One day it was level, the next badly slanted, and on the third day the floor dropped six inches while I was standing on it. Fixing it had cost a fortune but we'd had little choice, and now as I frowned down at Ellie's numbers I couldn't imagine how we'd develop anything without running out of cash this winter.

But this was no time to try figuring it out; I had guests, and perhaps even more interestingly, my elderly father, Jacob Tiptree, had discovered these guests and in response had gotten out his fancy martini-mixing kit.

"Hello, Jake," he said, beaming at me while coming into the kitchen to spread the kit's parts out on the counter.

"Hi, Dad," I said a little nervously as he poured clear liquid into a thick-walled glass mixing jar that he'd filled halfway with ice. A dash of vermouth from a pale green bottle came next; then with a long glass wand he stirred the mixture.

The wand clinked against the glass; after pouring the mixed drinks through a metal strainer into chilled martini glasses, he finished each with a rim-rub of lemon peel and an olive on a frilly toothpick.

"Voila," he pronounced when he'd served our guests, and the three of them raised glasses together.

"Great, Dad." Although I wasn't so sure. A bony old guy with long, stringy gray hair pulled back into a leather thong, he wore a black turtleneck, baggy jeans, and leather sandals. Ordinarily he drank water jazzed up with a lime slice.

But the look of pure bliss on his liver-spotted old face kept me from issuing any warnings as he sipped his potion again. Our guests, newly returned from freshening up, drank happily, too, and even Igor appeared cheerful, which on a dog that ferocious looking was quite some trick.

Although the marrow bone Bella had given him to gnaw once he'd finished his Ritz cracker may have lifted his mood. It surely helped mine, since whenever he was biting on it, he wasn't biting on me.

"What a lovely space!" Ingrid exclaimed once drinks were

over and we were gathered in the dining room. Gazing around, she took in the gracefully green-draped windows, old gold medallion wallpaper, and the cut-glass cranberry lamps on the tables by the hearth, where the fire crackled pleasantly.

"And that looks delicious," she added as Bella set down the big blueware platter heaped with chicken and vegetables.

"No kidding," said Bryan, picking up his napkin eagerly. With his prizefighter's face freshly scrubbed and his collar buttoned, he looked more gentlemanly than before. He still wore the gun, though, I noticed, and he had turned down a second martini.

"So you have a house here?" I asked Ingrid Merryfield when we'd finished sending around the gravy.

It was just us five tonight, with no husband, children, or grandchildren in evidence; Wade and my son and his family were all out for the evening, and all had been picked up by friends; thus, all the cars out in the driveway.

"Yes," Ingrid said, answering my question about the house, and was about to go on, but just then Bella offered her another biscuit while I helped myself to more gravy, rich and flecked with delicious chicken bits and browned pan scrapings. Finally, though:

"Yes, I do have a house here," Ingrid said. "I bought it sight unseen, if you can imagine such a thing."

I could, actually. I'd bought my own house here in Eastport about twenty minutes after driving into town for the first time. But she kept talking so I didn't say this.

"I needed to find a getaway place," she explained.

Her hair in the firelight was the color of spun gold. "A peaceful place where I could relax. And I found it, too, right here where I was born," she finished proudly.

"How nice for you. Where is the house?" asked my father pleasantly.

"Oh, didn't I mention?" The film star looked bemused. "It's

Cliff House," she said, and right then I should've realized that we were in trouble.

"Not that it matters where," she added, "as long as it's in Eastport. Driving over the causeway to the island, the weight of the world comes off your shoulders, doesn't it?"

In her well-tailored white pants suit and soft, white shoes, and with a pair of large round diamonds glittering in her earlobes, she didn't look as if she knew much about the world's weight any more than she did about troublesome details.

Still, I gave her the benefit of the doubt as she went on: "When the house came up for sale I was already watching the listings here in town, and of course I recognized it!"

Bella's voice was like the creaking of an old screen door. "Wait a minute. You're from Eastport?"

"Born and bred!" said Ingrid, and here I should explain that to be a real Eastporter, you had to be born one. I couldn't be, nor could anyone who hadn't been physically produced right here on the island, ideally in the hospital that was here then; thus Ingrid's clear pride.

"And now," she finished, "I've bought Cliff House."

In the silence that followed Bryan popped a green bean into his mouth and chewed it. Bella got up hastily, gathered the plates, and took them to the kitchen, where I heard her getting the apple pie out of the warming oven.

"How lovely for you," I managed to tell Ingrid as, out in the kitchen, Bella gave the oven's door an uncharacteristically hard slam.

"I've never been there," I went on, "but the view must be spectacular."

Perched on a bluff high over the water, Cliff House looked out onto channel-like Passamaquoddy Bay to the east and Cobscook Bay, its shoreline squiggly with so many coves and inlets that a child might've scribbled it, to the west.

"I just can't wait to start fixing it up," enthused Ingrid in the same breathy, girlish voice I remembered from her films. If you looked away you'd think you were listening to a shy twelve-year-old, and she seemed thrilled with her purchase.

Maybe that's why I still thought that all this was mildly interesting, nothing more.

Nothing worse. Then my dad took charge, making the guests laugh, telling funny stories and asking questions that made them feel interesting and important. The earthquake came up, of course, our recent minor jiggle paling by comparison with the ones Ingrid and Bryan had experienced in California, and Ingrid charmed the socks off Bella by asking for the chicken recipe.

Finally, though, Bryan got up. "Ma'am," he said to his employer with a glance down at his watch. "Ma'am, we might want to get back to the house."

The look on his face was all business. It made me decide I'd rather not tangle with him, and what, I wondered, had sent that notion popping into my head?

She got to her feet. "You're right, Bryan. We'll need to put some heat on, or a fire in the fireplace or something."

She turned back to me. "I tried hiring someone to get the place ready," she went on as I followed her to the kitchen.

"To turn on the lights and stock the fridge and all," she said. "Put clean sheets on the beds."

Bryan had already found his way outside. Igor, still the size of a small pony, grinned toothily at me.

"But I couldn't get anyone to do it," Ingrid said. "I can't imagine why."

Bella ruffled the big dog's ears; in reply he butted his head against her hip. The dog had a sweet side, it seemed; I just hoped he didn't use it to lure unsuspecting prey. Still, I'd probably never see the animal again so mostly I didn't care.

"Thank you for everything," said Ingrid as we crossed the shadowy front lawn under the maple trees together, toward the driveway and the long, dark limousine waiting in it.

Bryan stood by the open rear door. Inside it was all plush white leather and carpet trimmed with hints of gold. Igor waited for Miss Merryfield to get settled before jumping in behind her.

Then they were gone, gliding off down the foggy street until their taillights dissolved in the murk, and by the time I got back into the house I'd half-forgotten about them.

In the kitchen, Bella was washing dishes, plucking them out of a sinkful of billowy soapsuds and rinsing them under a spray so steaming hot that it fogged her eyeglasses.

I fetched a dish towel. Neither of us spoke for a while, content in one another's silent company.

But finally, "I suppose if you've money enough you could get that house livable," Bella allowed grudgingly.

Cliff House, she meant. Perched on a bluff overlooking the water, on a moonlit night the place stood outlined against the sky, its gables and turrets and the cupola with the widow's walk all aimed sharply heavenward.

But heaven was not the location most closely linked with Cliff House. *Oh, wait until I tell Ellie,* I thought as my dad came through the kitchen again.

"Nice work with the drinks," I told him, and he twinkled at me; he'd had a pair of those martinis, himself.

"Liquor is quicker," he agreed owlishly while carrying the drinks kit tipsily to the laundry room; moments later I heard the faucet go on in the sink out there.

Bella frowned studiously into her sudsy dishpan, seeming to disapprove, but her lip twitch gave her away. Once upon a time he'd been young and strong, but now fun was harder to find.

And she'd never deprive him of any. "They do seem like nice people, though, Miss Merryfield and Bryan." She emptied the dishpan.

"And Igor," I reminded her, folding my towel.

"Yes, and Igor." Her smile faded. "But whoever sold Cliff House to that poor woman should give her her money back."

Because it was a murder scene, she meant; everyone in town knew it. Ever since a long-ago survivor staggered out of it, screaming, the place had stood empty; now it had been deserted for so long, hardly anyone even thought much about it anymore.

But when they did, they knew it was haunted.

Two

Early the next morning when I got downtown to The Chocolate Moose, Bryan's limo was parked in the broad, paved lot by the fish pier. *Darn*, I thought; I was in a hurry. But then I saw that he'd already gotten out, crossed Water Street, and walked out onto the fish pier, so I made it past him without being spotted.

In the harbor, boats motored out of the boat basin, their prows lifted jauntily to meet the waves. Flocks of crying gulls flapped and settled behind the boats, waiting for edible morsels to be washed overboard when the decks got sluiced.

After slipping into the shop, I locked the door behind me. Ellie was in the kitchen, preheating the oven and dissolving yeast in warm water.

"Morning," I called to her, then filled the coffeemaker, turned on the cash register, and stocked the soft drinks cooler with Moxie, a venerable old Maine beverage that tastes just like roots stewed in swamp water.

I don't know why I enjoy it so much. "Listen, Ellie, about the money," I called.

Overnight my feelings about Ingrid Merryfield, her driver, and especially about Cliff House itself had all crystallized. I wasn't sure why, but I wanted nothing to do with them.

And I had other things to think about. "The money we need to create the chocolate pizza that people will buy," I summed up the project Ellie wanted badly to do.

"Mmm." She didn't look up from the ball of dough she was kneading for chocolate swirl bread. The chocolate was on the stove in a double boiler, sending sweet fragrance into the air as it melted with a lump of butter.

"We could just go for it," I said. "Spend whatever money it takes to make sure that it's fabulous, then see if it sells."

Ellie kept kneading. But she was listening. I already knew that this was the plan she liked best; it always was.

"Or," I took a deep breath, "we could close the Moose for the winter," then quickly amended at her look, "part of the winter."

We'd always meant to stay open year-round but there'd never really been enough business for it. In fact, maybe we didn't have cash for new products *because* we were here all winter.

Ellie frowned. "I don't want the Moose to be a hobby. And it shouldn't be just for summer visitors, either."

"Of course not, but . . ." But from the numbers I'd seen the night before on her notebook paper, staying solvent any other way was about as likely as us walking on water.

Ellie caught my tone. "I know," she agreed resignedly. "I mean, it's expensive just keeping the doors open at all. Lights, phone, and don't even talk to me about heat—"

I cringed inwardly at this unwelcome reminder of our next big expenditure. Every winter our poor old furnace wheezed and juddered its way through so much fuel oil that we might as well have burned hundred-dollar bills.

"However. It seems to me those things cost nearly the same whether we're in here or not," she said.

"Huh," I said thoughtfully; yet again, Ellie had a good point. We needed the furnace to stay on or the pipes froze. Then there was insurance, mortgage, the security monitoring service we hired after a burst pipe nearly finished us off. . . .

She was right, I realized. For our long-term survival as a going business, we needed to take in more money, not spend less. Because for one thing, upon close inspection there didn't really seem to be any way that we *could* spend less.

Which brought me back to Ellie's chocolate pizza again, but right now it was time to open the shop. A couple of customers wanting peanut butter kisses cheered me briefly; it's always fun watching people eat peanut butter kisses.

Then Tillie Jones from the high school came in for the refreshments she'd ordered. She'd promised a party to her junior math class if they all passed a fractions test, and they had, and Tillie was over the moon about it.

"Look," I said to Ellie when the little silver bell over the door had signaled Tillie's departure.

"How about we just take a little vacation right after Thanksgiving?" I said, moving another dozen peanut butter kisses from the kitchen cooler to the display case.

"We'll still do pies, of course," I added. Pumpkin was still the go-to for the autumn holiday, but after our chocolate cream pies debuted at a few Thanksgiving tables, the news of them got around.

"But after that—" I slid the display case door shut.

Silence from Ellie. Then: "Okay," she breathed reluctantly. "But how about *during* the break is when we'll develop the recipe for the pizza, then?"

As a compromise that sounded reasonable, and if by some chance we really didn't reopen until spring, we could always eat the pizza ourselves. But before I could answer, Bryan the driver came in, looking as if he'd had a sleepless night.

"Miss Merryfield wants to know if you can visit," he announced after we'd taken pity on him with coffee. "Not a social visit. She's planning an event and she'll need—"

"Catering?" Ellie asked alertly from behind the counter.

This could be just what we need, her look said. *A catering job, and maybe a big one.*

So much for having no more to do with Ingrid Merryfield and Bryan, I thought.

"We do events, don't we, Jake? Snacks, desserts . . ."

Ellie wanted it so much, I couldn't say no. "Yes, we do," I said. "And we'd love to come out to the house and discuss it."

Considering which house it was, maybe *love* wasn't the right word. But it was true that a job like this just as winter loomed could be helpful. It might even keep the Moose open, and Ellie knew it.

"At the moment, though, we're busy running the shop," I said.

I waved around at the burbling coffeemaker, the glass-topped café tables with their paper doilies and vintage napkin holders nicely arranged, and the display case, now holding only three dozen chocolate-frosted graham crackers destined for the Senior Center, where they were always a big hit.

"We could visit later, though," I added. I didn't want Ingrid Merryfield thinking she could just summon us on a whim. That, anyway, was the reason I gave myself for not wanting to visit Cliff House immediately.

"Jake," Ellie suggested sweetly, "I can handle things here. Why don't you go talk with her right now?"

"I'll be at the car," said Bryan, heading out as Ellie's eyes gleamed mischievously at me.

Once I got there, she knew, a deal would almost surely be made. All we really needed was to agree on a price, and to her even that wasn't a big sticking point.

"Just get us closer to keeping our doors open over winter if you can, and I'll be satisfied," she said.

Minutes later I found myself sitting in the plush, white-leather-upholstered backseat of a fancy limousine, feeling like Cinderella as it whisked me away.

The glamorous Cindy, I mean, not the pumpkin one.

I hoped.

Soon we were passing between two huge stone gateposts whose black iron gates Bryan had to get out of the car and open, then haul closed again when we were through. Next, we rolled down a long, graveled driveway and around a circle drive to . . .

Cliff House. Sitting at the end of a peninsula so narrow it was barely wide enough for a driveway at all, it hunkered under trees so gnarled and decrepit that they looked ready to topple.

"Wow," I said into the silence when Bryan helped me out of the backseat.

Corbels, dentils, and curlicue-carved wooden moldings of all types and varieties, check. Leaded-glass windows, mossy old stone steps, and damp, roof-rotting front porch, check. I stared up at the turret with the weather vane atop it.

"This house is really something," I said, still gazing. No ghosts or other weird otherworldly beings presented themselves, but if there were any I thought they'd feel right at home.

No dog appeared; looking around, I wondered where Igor was and hoped the big canine was (a) romping happily on the property somewhere and (b) not about to pounce.

With the gate closed at least he couldn't get lost. Besides the driveway there was no way off the narrow peninsula unless you wanted to jump off the cliff that the house was named after, and I assumed the dog didn't.

When I turned, Bryan was already driving the limo toward the garage building behind the house. Meanwhile, no one had come out to greet me so I invited myself in, crossing the porch with the feeling that my foot might go through it at any moment and pulling open the massive old wooden door.

"Hello?" The entry hall was gloomy with dark wainscoting, crumbling pink plaster the exact same color as Pepto-Bismol, and a ceiling festooned with cobwebs.

No sound. A spider crept across one of the webs. Swallowing hard, I ventured down a black- and white-tiled hall toward the back of the house. Maybe in the kitchen I'd find someone.

Ideally it would be the someone who summoned me here, I thought, then realized that irritation wasn't the only thing I felt.

Or even the main thing. Suddenly in the silence the chilly, tiled hallway smelled stale, like a long-unopened cellar.

Stop that, I scolded myself as I turned and fled back to the front hall. But it didn't help: *Out, out, OUT*, a voice in my head repeated insistently as I hurried toward the door.

Just as I was about to fling myself out, Ingrid Merryfield appeared, hurrying down the front hall's wide staircase.

"Oh, apologies, apologies," she breathed, hands fluttering dramatically. "I'm so sorry to make you wait."

The bad feeling vanished abruptly. *Silly*, I thought as she led me down a different hallway than the one I'd tried; drawers, closets, and cupboards with glass doors lined the dim passage.

Once, crystal and china would've filled them, with silver and linen packing the drawers and closets. But now they were empty.

"You and Bryan were all right here last night?" I asked.

"Oh, yes," Ingrid Merryfield trilled, hurrying ahead of me. "No disturbances at all. Of course, by then we were both so tired that you could've sent a marching band through here and it wouldn't have bothered us."

Which I thought was a funny way to put it. Who'd said anything about disturbances?

As I followed her to a cavernous kitchen I ran my hand

along the radiator and found it was warm. So they'd gotten the furnace going, anyway, I thought.

"Beautiful, isn't it?" said Miss Merryfield quietly as I paused in the kitchen doorway.

"Yes," I breathed, taking in the old-fashioned room, which I guessed must have been unchanged since the 1940s. An elderly gas stove flanked a round-shouldered old Frigidaire. A vintage Formica-topped table and four matching chairs stood in a corner.

The wallpaper was a grid pattern of grape leaves and berry clusters; soft morning light slanted in through the windows over the sink. Beyond them a lawn sloped gently away, then came to an abrupt stop.

I turned from the window as Miss Merryfield poured coffee from an old-fashioned electric coffeemaker. Then she led me through a wooden screen door out onto a stone terrace.

Someone—Bryan, probably—had set out high-quality patio chairs that must've been in storage somewhere. Cream and sugar were on the low, glass-topped table and a green braided indoor-outdoor rug completed the ensemble.

"Bryan made an early run to the store," Ingrid explained. "And we'll still have to do some straightening up, but at least the gas and power were on when we arrived."

"That's good." I drank some coffee, tried to relax. The scene was inviting, with last night's rain gone by and the sky a pale, pearly blue overhead. So why did I wish again that I were somewhere else?

"At any rate, to business," Ingrid said, not seeming to notice my discomfort. "Bryan has told you what I'm looking for?"

When I said that he had, but only generally, she went on to outline the event she had planned: the number of people, the menus each day, and so on. "You'd be doing desserts," she said.

I listened, impressed. Not many people would have thought to list the whole menu for the dessert caterers, to be sure all the edibles complemented each other. Clearly, she was a planner.

But what she said next didn't please me so much. "You and Ellie will need to stay the night with your helpers, if any."

I started to object, but she was firm on this. "Guests will be up late. You'll need to be here to keep the serving platters orderly and attractive, and to refill them in case anyone wants second desserts. And cleanup afterward, of course."

Those didn't sound like good reasons to me. We lived only a couple of miles away, for heaven's sake. But:

"Naturally I will make whatever inconvenience this may cause either of you well worth your while," she went on, sounding accustomed to papering over any little objections with money.

Then she named an amount that could've papered over the Grand Canyon.

"Th-that sounds fair," I allowed, still trying to catch my breath. "Divided between Ellie and me, it works out to—"

"Oh no," she corrected smilingly. Her eyes really were the most astonishing shade of turquoise. "That's for each of you."

"Each," I repeated stupidly as she held two checks out to me: one with my name on it, one with Ellie's, each for a truly remarkable amount of money.

"I've taken the liberty of making payment in advance. I hope that's all right?"

"Y-yes," I replied, still staring at the paychecks. They bore today's date; Ellie and I could deposit them today, if we wanted. But why?

And then I got it. The size of the checks and the payment in advance was to make her job offer—and its inconvenient stay-overnight terms—irresistible.

She didn't only want us to bake chocolate dessert items, or serve and clean up after them, or even to help handle guests who got rowdy, or homesick, or whatever.

No, she wanted us to be here with her all night.

The Chocolate Moose ladies, I mean.

Who were also the town snoops.

* * *

Half an hour later, Bryan dropped me off on the sidewalk in front of the shop.

"Mom!" called my son, Sam, as the limousine pulled away, and I looked around to discover him striding jubilantly down Water Street toward me. "Mom! We found it!"

He was a tall, slim young man with dark curly hair; a long, narrow jaw; and a smile that could light up the whole East Coast. In the crook of his arm rested my year-old granddaughter, wrapped in a quilt Ellie had made for her. Tugging Sam's sleeve, whining, was my toddler grandson, Ephraim.

"I'm tired," Ephraim moaned. His cheeks, plump and rosy, were shiny with tears.

"I'm hungry," he added as Sam scooped the kid up into his free arm. Ephraim promptly buried his face in his dad's neck.

"Mom, we found a place!" Sam went on. "A house! Mika and I went over there just now, and . . ."

"Oh, Sam," I began, and then I shut up, not wanting to spoil his happiness.

I should've been glad, and not only for his family. My house was so crammed absolutely full of us all, it was a wonder people weren't tumbling out the upstairs windows.

"Three bedrooms," he enthused. "*Two* baths. And a yard."

They'd been talking about getting their own place for so long, I'd let my guard down. Now the wind coming off the water was cold; I tasted snow, or imagined it.

"Sam, that's great!" I said, although it wasn't.

". . . fenced yard, washer, dryer, garage," he was reciting.

"Wonderful," I lied heartily. "When are you moving? After the holidays, I suppose?"

Christmas, I meant. Even New Year's, maybe. But I supposed wrong.

"Uh, no," he replied. "You're not happy about it, huh?"

I was the one who'd tried telling him when he was little that spinach was just green whipped cream, and he'd seen right through me then, too. But I was so miserable at the news he'd delivered that it was probably oozing visibly from my pores.

Lucky for me, just then Ellie stepped out of The Chocolate Moose.

"Hi!" She looked uncertainly from me to Sam and back.

"Hi," I responded, eyeing another torn-open yeast envelope in her hand and knowing what she must be up to, despite saying she'd wait: chocolate pizza.

"So anyway, if you go to check it out, it's the house on the corner of Chestnut and Pine," said Sam, jouncing the baby, who'd begun fussing.

As he spoke, he was backing away from me, knowing that the sooner he was gone, the faster I'd be able to digest what he'd just told me: that very soon, and for the first time since he was born, my kid wouldn't be living with me anymore.

"Come on," said Ellie, guiding me inside.

They won't be far away, I assured myself. *We can be close without living in each other's pockets. It'll be better for everyone.*

Right now at my place, space had gotten so tight that Wade had begun drinking his morning coffee while leaning on a wooden pallet in the garden shed, just for a moment's peace.

Still, by the time I'd gotten myself seated at one of our café tables and swallowed the glass of water Ellie brought me, I was crying so hard I could barely see.

"Jake," said Ellie, looking concerned, "are you okay?"

I pulled out a tissue. "Oh, I don't know. I felt glum out at Cliff House. Then Sam showed up, and—"

Fresh tears threatened. You'd have thought they were all moving to Australia. "This is ridiculous," I grumped, wiping my nose.

Then, giving my big-girl pants a yank, I reported on the meeting with Ingrid Merryfield, leading with the big-money part and following up with the us-staying-overnight portion of the program.

"We can make desserts here, deliver them before the guests start arriving, and—"

"Um, why are we staying the night, again?" Ellie asked.

Trust Ellie to get right to the heart of the matter. "I'm not sure. She gave me some reasons."

But they still didn't hold water. We could leave plenty of late-night snacking material, and our reputation as snoops could not possibly have anything to do with it, I realized on second thought; after all, how would she even know?

"Whatever, though," I finished. "She wants it and she'll pay." But then my earlier thought returned naggingly.

"Ellie, what are the odds that she'd drive into Eastport and immediately find her way straight to us?"

To The Chocolate Moose, I meant, and to its proprietors, who had a reputation for being diggers into bad deeds.

"Because I'm wondering if maybe she didn't just come to us by accident. What if instead she already knew about us somehow?"

Ellie's eyes narrowed skeptically. But we had been in the local papers and even the *Bangor Daily News*, on account of some deadly shenanigans we'd sorted out a year earlier.

"Maybe she read about us and decided to check us out when she arrived?" I mused aloud.

Ellie looked doubtful at this, then glanced at the yeast packet she still held and hurried to the kitchen, where a bowl of dough was rising prettily atop the gas stove's hood.

As I suspected, it was pizza dough, much sooner than I'd expected; I could tell by the bottle of olive oil out on the table. But for all I knew, next year we'd be rich on account of it, so I didn't say anything about it when I followed her to the kitchen.

"I didn't tell her for sure that we would do it," I went on. "I thought I'd better talk to you, first."

Ellie punched the dough down, turned it out on our butcher-block table to knead it briefly, and put it in the cooler.

"But for what she's offering I'll sit by her bed and read her a story," I finished. The amount mentioned wouldn't just fund chocolate pizzas; it would replace our furnace, and that, despite my unease, had changed my opinion.

"Yes," Ellie said quickly. "We should do it. And how about Mika for a helper?"

"Fine with me." I knew my daughter-in-law would want the job; moving is expensive, and before she came to Eastport and married my son she'd been a pastry chef.

"So it's settled, then."

"I guess so," I sighed, feeling another twinge of the odd uneasiness that had assailed me at Cliff House.

But then a sprightly, musical sound burbled from my purse. My cell phone was ringing.

Minutes later we'd closed up the Moose and were on our way out to Cliff House, this time in Ellie's car. As we passed the IGA, the firehouse, and Bay City Mobil station heading for the long curve past the airport, I put the window down and let my head fall back onto the seat's headrest.

Yellow leaves on the birch trees along the road fluttered vividly against the cloudless sky. Apples shone red from the gnarled branches of abandoned orchards and the fields rippled golden.

"Why exactly do we need to go back right now?" Ellie asked.

"She called to find out if we've decided. I told her that we had, and that the answer's yes."

Ellie steered expertly around a slow-moving truck hauling a flatbed trailer stacked with lobster traps. "And?"

"And they're out buying more household supplies right now, so she thought—"

A couple of young deer stepped unexpectedly from a roadside thicket. We slowed, letting them cross, and soon afterward turned down the narrow road leading to the Cliff House driveway.

"So she thought now's a good time for us to check out the

kitchen some more and pick out which rooms we want to stay in," I finished.

We left the narrow road and drove through the iron gates, which had been left open for us. "She also said the party's this weekend," I added.

It was a tiny detail that I hadn't mentioned before. Ellie looked sideways at me. "So, three days away?"

In other words, it was desperately short notice. "Yep. But we can do most of it in advance," I assured her.

I hadn't realized before how much I wanted to give Ellie her wish and keep the shop open. And even though the event was insanely imminent, this job would do it.

Ellie knew it, too, and was probably about to say so as the house came into view. But instead she gasped faintly, fingers tightening on the wheel as on either side of us the earth sloped sharply away from the driveway.

"Yeeks," she breathed. Waves glinted below. From the limo's backseat earlier, I hadn't seen it, but this rocky peninsula really was narrow, so much so that I thought a person on foot could tumble off.

Luckily its steep slopes were also thickly overgrown with brambles, so that would be impossible.

I hoped. "This business of Ingrid Merryfield being from here, though," I mused aloud. "Wouldn't you think somebody would've mentioned that Eastport had produced a movie star?"

Ellie shrugged as well as she could while still hanging on as if she were already down there in the water and the steering wheel were a life ring.

"Maybe no one knows it," she said. "If she was young enough when the family left, and no relatives are here anymore."

"Mmm. Maybe." It still didn't seem likely; if Eastporters are alive and awake, they are talking.

"What I think, though," said Ellie, "is that probably a few

older people do remember. They haven't had time yet to recognize her and gossip about it, is all."

We pulled at last into the white-graveled circle drive in front of Cliff House. Through its tall, mullioned windows the old dwelling seemed to be inspecting us with slit eyes.

"I suppose if we really wanted to find out, we could ask Nanny Jackson," said Ellie.

The town's elderly historian was famous for knowing whole genealogies by heart. "Or look in the graveyard register," she added. "See if her last name's there anywhere."

"Mmm. If she uses her real name. Not a stage name, I mean."

We parked under an enormous old tree whose roots were half out of the ground, a victim of windstorms and the thin layer of soil here atop the granite cliff.

Suddenly the other thing that I'd been worrying about all morning burst out of me. "I'm worried about my dad," I said as Ellie shut the car off.

Ellie's hand was on the car door. "How come? I thought you said he had fun?"

I'd already told her about last night, the martinis and so on. "It was fun," I said now, "but today he's tired. Quiet. I asked Bella to call me if he doesn't perk up."

"Maybe he's hung over," Ellie suggested, and this idea seemed possible enough that I could let myself feel reassured.

"Maybe." As we crunched across the pea-gravel circle drive, the house peered down at us. *To see if we're good to eat*, the thought popped into my head.

Then: *Don't be silly*, I told myself yet again. "You think the car will be okay there?"

All I could think when I glanced back at the old tree was that it could crash down any time. But now I was just borrowing trouble, and Ellie's look at me confirmed this; those roots had clearly been exposed for a long while and would probably go on surviving, maybe even for longer than I would.

Buck up, I ordered myself as we climbed the mossy steps to the porch. Ellie ran her hand along the old wooden railing, then yanked it back. "Ouch!"

"You all right?" I opened the heavy old front door.

"Fine. Just a splinter."

Ingrid had told me we should go in and look around, so we stepped inside.

"Wow," Ellie exhaled as we made our way along the cavernous front hall.

She was right about that, too, though I'd been too nervous to notice, earlier. The woodwork was varnished walnut, the hallway's smart-looking black and white floor was real tile, and the vintage gas stove in the kitchen wasn't at all the junk that I'd first thought it was.

Old, yes, but it had everything we needed, and when Ellie turned a knob and struck a wooden match from the box of them on the mantel, a burner ignited with a blue-flamed *whoof*.

"Okay," I said, but then I opened the round-shouldered old Frigidaire. Its tiny interior featured an open freezer that was approximately the size of a box of tissues.

"She'll do something about this, though, I hope." You could get an appliance delivered fairly pronto around here.

"She's buying the ingredients, right?" Ellie asked as she peered past me into the refrigerator's interior.

"Uh-huh," I said distractedly. For the number of guests and elaborate menus she'd described, I hoped Ingrid Merryfield had a plan for provisioning the place, too. You could certainly get racks of lamb, fancy cheeses, and beef tenderloins in Eastport, but it was always a good idea to order them in advance.

Thinking this, I closed the refrigerator just as something sizable fell with a crash, somewhere upstairs.

I looked at Ellie, and she looked at me. "Jake, don't let it spook you," she said, eyeing an open doorway. Beyond it, a set of steps led up from the kitchen.

"We're going there next anyway, to inspect the bedrooms," she reminded me. "Probably a piece of the old plaster ceiling or something," she added, crossing the kitchen.

"Of course it was," I agreed stoutly, not fooling her a bit. For that, action would be required.

"She did say we should pick the bedrooms we want," I added as we started up.

The stairs were steep and narrow. "Hello?" I called when we reached the door at the top. No answer, though, so I reached for the doorknob.

Then as my hand moved slowly toward it, the door unlatched itself, and drifted open to reveal a long hallway with a faded Oriental runner stretched out along it and doorways at regular intervals piercing the walls.

"Hello?" I called again. The doors, which I assumed led to bedrooms, were closed, and the hallway was deeply gloomy except near the window at the far end.

Opening doors as we went, we found the rooms empty except for the usual bedroom furniture. Then we hurried down the hall toward the far window from which sheer panels billowed inward.

As we neared it, we saw that the window was broken, with glass scattered across the rug.

"So that's where the crash came from," I said.

"Not broken from in here," said Ellie, noticing the glass on the floor. "From outside. But this is the second floor."

"Maybe a bird hit it?" I knelt on the cushioned window seat and peered down to where a small patio, brick paved, and grown over with dark green moss, hid in the shade.

Then I used my shoe to punch out more of the broken glass, stuck my head through the resulting hole, and peered upward. An attic window, directly above me, was unbroken, and nothing else looked unusual.

I pulled my head carefully back in. The few shards I hadn't knocked away looked as sharp as steak knives.

"Okay, so a bird probably hit it," I said even though no dead bird was visible below. But when I turned, Ellie had gone back down the hall to start looking into bedrooms again.

"This one," she said, looking into another room as I joined her, and it did look quite habitable.

A braided rug, green pinch-pleat curtains, a white chenille spread all promised quiet comfort. There was a good-looking bedside lamp beside the old iron bed, too, and a pitcher and basin on the dresser.

A connecting door linked this bedroom to the next; Ellie went through it and I heard her sound of disappointment.

"Hmm," I agreed when I followed her in; stained wallpaper, elderly venetian blinds, and sections of fallen ceiling plaster dangling by threads of horsehair were like the *after* picture to the previous room's *before*.

The rug by the bed was so grimly unattractive, the thought of stepping on it made my feet want to crawl up inside my pants legs. "We'll share," I said firmly, and Ellie agreed.

I twitched aside one of the slats in the blinds. The limo hadn't yet returned. Then another crash, this one from the floor above us, sounded almost taunting.

"Drat," said Ellie, and that was my reaction, too. I felt like we were being lured. And since I had absolutely no intention of staying the night without knowing what was doing the luring, I stomped back out into the hall.

"All right, damn it," I said. I get mad when I get scared. "Let's just see about this."

The back stairs went up another flight. We climbed them; me to punch someone or something in the nose and Ellie to help me, or at least that's the role I'd mentally assigned her.

At the top, the stairwell door opened—not by itself this time; we had to turn the knob ourselves—onto an enormous open room whose ceiling was held up by equidistantly spaced posts.

"Goodness," I breathed. The room's hardwood floor gleamed. Paper lanterns, faded with age, hung limply from the posts.

"It's a dance floor," Ellie realized. "For parties."

Suddenly I could almost hear toes tapping and a dance band tuning up, ice clinking in glasses and champagne corks popping while long-departed musicians bantered among themselves.

But then all at once the room's gaiety dissolved and a chill went through me. Dust motes twinkled in the bright, still air, but everything else felt silent and dead.

"Let's get out of here," I breathed quietly, not wanting to be overheard, and the two of us quick-stepped right back down those stairs so fast that it was a wonder neither of us—

Broke your necks.

Ellie stopped in the kitchen. "Did you hear that?" she asked, meaning what we'd both just perceived clearly: a voice.

A voice where there wasn't supposed to be one. Without any discussion we hurried on to the front hall, raced out onto the porch and down the mossy steps, and hustled across the driveway.

"Okay," I said when we were in the car. "I personally think this house needs to fall off the cliff that it's named for."

A car was coming in, its tires crunching gravel. "But never mind that," I went on as Ellie turned the key. "For now what we need to know is, are we still doing this?"

Because if it meant having the spit scared out of us the whole time we were here, was it worth it?

The familiar dark limousine pulled up to the porch, but the big old tree's sagging branches hid our car so well that Ingrid Merryfield went in without seeing us, Igor pacing beside her.

Bryan hadn't looked our way, either; he'd gone on around the side of the house to the garage, then disappeared inside.

"Because if we are still doing it, we'll need to wrap our heads around this."

The fright part, I meant. "But if not, we should let her know." Not right this minute, though, since we weren't yet quite sure what we'd say.

The car was quiet enough not to alert them, and we got down the narrow drive and out past the gateposts without any trouble.

"I think we're still doing it," Ellie said after a moment.

The shoreline here had once bristled with docks on twenty-foot pilings. Now the pilings' ancient stumps were blackened and weed streaked, and each had a seagull perched on it.

"We need the money if we're keeping the Moose open, there's just no two ways about that," she said.

Along the road, crimson sumac and bittersweet flared among green cinnamon ferns. A vee of south-flying geese arrowed over, honking.

"So we'd better get used to the notion of maybe not being *comfortable* doing it," Ellie finished, turning toward town.

On High Street we passed Spinney's Garage, its windows full of red geraniums, and the white-clapboard Baptist church, now home to the Eastport Arts Center. At the old granite-block post office building we turned onto Water Street and parked in front of the Moose.

That's when I spotted Bryan in the limo, a couple of cars back. While I watched, he turned in at the municipal building parking lot and maneuvered the oversized vehicle into a spot.

"Huh," I said. Could he have been following us?

"So we are, right?" Ellie asked as she unlocked the shop's door. "Doing this catering job, that is."

Inside, I started snapping the lights on, along with the fans, the radio, the cash register, and the credit card reader.

"Jake? Are we?" Ellie got a bowl of puff-pastry dough out of the cooler and began to do whatever it was she so expertly did;

if I even looked at puff pastry, it collapsed like a pin-stuck bal-loon.

"Yes," I said reluctantly. "I'm sure we can both survive a creepy atmosphere and a few weird noises for a night."

Because for that kind of payday, and considering what was at stake, of course I had to say I thought we should do it.

Even though I definitely didn't.

Three

When I first came to Maine I was driving a brand-new red Mercedes that belonged to my then-husband, Victor. I'd taken Sam, too; Victor had shown all the fatherly care you'd expect from a cold-blooded, swamp-dwelling reptile, which he resembled in most other respects as well.

He was a brain surgeon, the kind you go to when the others have already smiled sadly at you and sent you home. Also, he was the kind of philanderer who looks puzzled when you catch him.

I mean, in flagrante. No denials are possible, and he stares at you like *Well, what did you expect?* And it turns out there's a limit to how many black, lacy lingerie items you can find in your husband's coat pocket without losing your cool.

Still, getting out wasn't easy; for one thing, back then I worked as a money manager for guys in black topcoats who would murder you, no problem. As long as I saved them money or found ways to make more, things were good; if ever I didn't keep my mouth shut about it, though, or tried to quit . . .

Well, that was another story, and it was why on the day I grabbed Sam and shoved us both into my soon-to-be-ex-husband's expensive car, I'd signed documents confessing to the felonies I'd committed during my work.

Tax crimes, mostly, the kind that earn federal prison time. Also, I implicated my bosses in worse misdeeds, then sent the documents to an attorney with orders that if anything happened to me, they'd be opened and read.

Whereupon they'd become evidence in a criminal trial that would hollow out mob families in the city for generations; it wasn't a guarantee, but it was the best I could do, and funnily enough it also helped twelve-year-old Sam during our escape.

He was in the backseat having a meltdown and probably it says something about me that my supply of bland chatter began and ended with why mobsters weren't going to kill me.

But the facts calmed him down; it says something about me, too, I fear, that at his age he knew all about the guys in the topcoats, and had been worrying about them.

But the conversation didn't end there. After I'd promised him that we weren't about to be slaughtered by tommy-gun-firing wiseguys, Sam had blinked owlishly at me and crammed a handful of Cheetos into his already orange-ringed mouth.

"How come Dad hates us?" he blurted.

I'd have liked to pull over but just then we were entering a road-construction-related underpass lit by flickering smudge pots whose smoke thickened the murk.

I fumbled for the headlights. The smoke thickened, with a rank, oily taste riding on it.

"Mom?" said Sam. "Mom, why—"

How come Dad hates us. It occurred to me that I could just step on the gas, drive the car into a bridge abutment.

"Sam," I said quietly as we exited the tunnel. Sunshine, jack-hammers, and the mineral smell of concrete dust slammed my senses all at once, not pleasantly.

"Sam, just shut up and ride, okay? I'm gonna tell you all about everything—"

He looked frightened at this, but he needed to know why we were leaving his father and why I wasn't going back.

"—as soon as I'm not so busy driving," I said, and this satisfied him; traffic around Manhattan was hellacious as usual, and he didn't feel like getting smeared across the road any more than I did.

Past Mamaroneck the cars and trucks thinned out a little, though, and by the time we reached Long Wharf outside New Haven he'd been listening to me, transfixed, for over an hour.

"Wow," he exclaimed over one of his dad's exploits, "what a douchebag!"

I hadn't realized he even knew the word, and I wouldn't have encouraged him to say it, either, under normal conditions. But it didn't hurt my spirits even a little bit to hear it used about Victor.

"Listen, Sam. Your father's who he is, he's a—"

"It's okay, Mom." He settled back on his seat. The Cheetos bag was empty. I started looking around for a place to get lunch but didn't see any exits that had food at the end of them.

"—a different breed of cat," I finished, not wanting to sound as mean as I felt.

Sam just snorted. "Yeah, an alley cat," he scoffed. "I knew all this, you know," he added.

I glanced back at his dark hair, hazel eyes, and lantern jaw that were all just like Victor's.

"You did?" I asked, but Sam had already dropped the subject in favor of the golden arches on a sign by the next off-ramp.

Minutes later we were happy with our salty, greasy lunches, with the sugary soft drinks that washed them down, and with the glazed crullers that we got at the Dunkin' drive-thru across the street afterward.

"Okay, then," said Sam, settling into the backseat again.

He was feeling extremely grown up, I realized, after all I'd confided in him. But what he said next surprised me.

"So listen, how about from now on I don't lie to you and you don't lie to me?" he said.

Meeting mine in the rearview mirror, his gaze was open and full of hope, for once, and for the first time I knew I was doing the right thing.

"Sounds like a plan," I told my son. "So let's not."

Lie to each other, I meant, and from then on we didn't.

But now, all this time later, I would have to find a loophole in that old promise; Sam and his family would have their own home, soon. I should be happy for them instead of hating the idea.

I mean *really* hating it.

Which I did.

And I couldn't very well say that.

If there's any better place to perch chocolate kisses than atop bite-sized peanut butter cookies, I don't know about it.

"We could put some kind of sleeping potion into the Cliff House desserts," Ellie said, creaming together the peanut butter and brown sugar for the cookies.

The library had ordered them for a meeting with county officials; the job meant our heat bill was paid this month.

"So we could get the guests to bed early and then we could go," she added.

The notion of going home from Cliff House appealed to me more than the thought of being there in the first place.

I mean by orders of magnitude. "We *could* get something to help them relax from Nanny Jackson," I mused aloud, "while we're asking her about people from here named Merryfield."

Besides being the town historian, Miss Jackson had been a school nurse here in Eastport for forty-plus years, then retired to pursue her first love: herbal remedies made from things she grew in her own garden.

A short laugh came from Ellie. "Good luck. I've heard she's getting grouchy, won't let anyone in her house anymore at all."

I'd heard that, too, plus some other, less savory things. Little old ladies who don't suffer fools and have solitary, even reclusive, habits have always had to contend with rumors, and Nanny was no exception.

"I think we're just going to have to suck it up," I said, "and stay as long as our employer wants us to."

As I spoke I was mixing up some ginger blossoms: same basic recipe as the one Ellie was using, but with regular butter and candied ginger instead of peanut butter.

"Rum balls?" I suggested after a while. "Those chocolate drops with the fruity liqueurs injected into them?"

Getting the Cliff House guests tucked in and asleep as early as possible was still a good plan, even if we did stay.

"A breeze is coming up," I said, glancing out the front window after getting no reply to my earlier remark.

By now it was nearly noon and the bright weather had turned unsettled. Past the breakwater where tugboats bumped the dock, a thin mist blew off the waves' foamy tops, while the few boats that hadn't gone out today bounced hectically at their berths.

Ellie looked up. "Sorry. I was thinking about what we heard back there. The voice."

So Cliff House had gotten to her, too. I mixed freshly minced bits of candied ginger into the cookie dough, then sighed and put the spoon down.

"It wasn't a voice. We heard something," I added at her look, "but not what we thought."

A bird, a branch scratching against a glass window . . . it could've been anything. "For all we know, the pipes make that sound when someone flushes a toilet."

Which of course no one had been doing, either. "Anyway, if nobody was there, then nobody said anything," I added. "There could be plenty of explanations."

Ellie looked knowingly at me while sliding her cookie dough into the cooler to chill. "You don't like the place, either."

"No. That's putting it mildly, in fact. But nothing has happened to make me think we can't spend a few hours there, or that Miss Merryfield's guests won't have a perfectly fine time."

If nothing terrifies them, I was about to add. But instead the shop door flew open, the little silver bell over it jangled, and Eastport's police chief, Bob Arnold, hurried in, turning to force the door closed against the rising wind.

"Man," he said, pushing his thinning blond hair back from his high, wide forehead. "That breeze's blowin' hard."

Hahd, the Maine way of saying it. He spied a plate of broken cookies that I'd set out atop the display case for people to sample, and chose one. "So, this Bryan fella."

Ellie and I looked at one another. "What about him?"

Bob searched the plate for another chocolate snickerdoodle fragment but settled for chocolate chip. "Came in the cop shop to see me earlier, says his boss bought Cliff House."

So that's what Bryan had been doing. I felt a little better now that I knew he hadn't been following us after all.

Meanwhile, Bob thought people should have to live here for a while before buying houses; for one thing, it would cut down on the noise complaints from folks who thought boat engines, bell buoys, foghorns, and seagulls all had volume controls and didn't like learning otherwise.

"So I said that's nice, thanks for letting me know, and he said he'd heard that the place had a history, and could I tell him about it," said Bob.

He ate another cookie piece, then went on. "I gather you two are catering a big bash she's having this weekend, bunch of Hollywood friends going to come and stay in the house?" Bob asked.

With his pale-lashed blue eyes, pink rosebud lips, and a general air of being related to the Pillsbury Doughboy, Bob didn't look like a police officer at all, much less a good one.

But he could get a bad guy locked in his squad car before the guy got rowdy, and in a place where help might not arrive soon this was an advantage. Also, not getting pepper-sprayed or clobbered made even bad guys appreciate Bob, and that helped.

"That's right," I confirmed about the party, and I could see from his look that he didn't approve of that, either.

"Bryan," he put a skeptical twist on the name, "also told me he's this movie woman's bodyguard, and on account of that he carries a gun. A concealed," Bob specified, "weapon."

Bob's own belt held a baton, keys, a mace canister, cuffs, a whistle, his radio, and a phone; he was the Swiss Army knife of cops.

"Did he have to?" I asked. "Tell you he's armed, I mean?"

A requirement to report that you're carrying a concealed weapon was a new one on me, and an unwelcome one, too, since I did this occasionally, and staying innocent of as many felonies as possible is a sort of guiding principle with me.

Bob shrugged. "No. He didn't have to, but it's polite. A pro with a gun, new in town, a certain amount of professional courtesy is always appreciated."

He took one last cookie piece, chomped it. "Also, let's say Bryan gets his tail in a sling somehow, he needs to call me. Came in here first, introduced himself, now he's not just Joe Schmo anymore, see?"

I took his point.

"Anyway, why don't you come on and take a ride with me?" Bob invited. "You can tell me about this catering job you've signed on for."

Me, he meant, and he no more wanted to know about our catering job than I wanted to walk out to the far end of the fish pier and jump off.

I put my cookie dough in the cooler. He made an after-you gesture at the door. "And I'll fill you in on what all I told Bryan about Cliff House," he said.

"Oh, Bob," Ellie protested, looking up from the puff pastry

she was working into layers with her rolling pin; her daughter's cross-country running team all loved our éclairs, and she had promised them some.

"Jake and I are awfully busy," she said, "and anyway I don't see why she needs to hear all that unpleasant old . . ."

Clearly she didn't want me hearing more upsetting things about Cliff House. But Bob was insistent, so I went out past him to his car.

The black Crown Vic with the cherry beacon on the dash and Eastport's sunrise emblem stenciled on its doors was immaculate inside, as usual. "Where are we going?"

The car's dashboard had a radio handset hanging off it, and a double row of red plastic rocker switches mounted on it. The perp screen was freshly sprayed with black Rustoleum; you could still smell the paint fumes even over the pine-tree-shaped air freshener dangling from the rearview mirror.

He didn't answer my question about our destination. "How about you do me a favor, and in return, I'll tell you a story?" he suggested instead.

It wasn't quite what he'd promised, but never mind; he'd done me plenty of favors over the years we'd been friends.

"Fine, but what's the favor got to do with Cliff House?"

"Not a thing. I just need a little assistance, is all." He drove us out Route 190 past Redoubt Hill and Carryingplace Cove, until we reached the turnoff to Quoddy Village.

I wished he needed his assistance elsewhere. Quoddy Village was where Sam's newly rented house was located, and I'd been trying not to think about that.

Bob took the turn. "There's a place back here that I want you to have a look at from the inside."

The warren of narrow, curving streets and small houses set on irregularly shaped lots had been built in the 1940s during a then-urgent wartime construction project. Eighty years later the project was long abandoned but the dwellings still remained inhabited, many rehabbed by younger people in creative ways that were beginning to make the area trendy.

I didn't see Chestnut or Pine on any of the street signs as we wound our way around them; finally Bob pulled over.

"Here," he said, gesturing out at an antique center-chimney cape with a few of its old windows intact. But the sagging roof-beam said they wouldn't be for long, and the walls had started bulging out from the downward pressure.

"Okay," I sighed. "You want me to go in there. You know it, and now I know it. But what I still want to know is why."

That he was reluctant to go in himself was also clear; if he hadn't been, he'd have done it already. But he wasn't usually deterred by an empty old house even if it was dark and creepy-looking, the intact windows opaque with grime and the graffiti scrawled inside visible through the fallen-in front door.

"So tell me what's in there that's so important and why you can't just go get it for yourself," I told Bob, "and then start telling me about Cliff House."

Because that was still the deal, even if it had been modified a little: I helped him in some way that he hadn't yet clarified, and he divulged Cliff House details to me.

His hands stayed on the wheel. I'd seen him use them to lift a squalling drunk off her bar stool and set her feet on the floor, whereupon she promptly went home. I'd watched him tame a pack of brawling longshoremen, too, and he'd captured a rabid skunk using only a snow shovel and a burlap bag. But now:

"They're gonna tear it down. I want something from in there but I'd rather not go in. You gonna need more reason than that?"

He knew I didn't. Sam had endured a couple of rough years as he hit adulthood; without Bob, I wasn't sure my son would be alive.

"Nope," I said. "But your Cliff House tales had better be good ones," I warned, just as a kid on a bicycle pedaled by.

Then I got out of the car and made my way through dry

weeds and overgrown grass to the old structure. A sagging wall had twisted the front doorframe, forcing the door inward. The wall had been helping to hold the roof up, too, but now not so much, and as a result I thought habit was all that held it.

Bob lumbered behind me. I'd expected that he would stay in the car. But never mind, having him nearby made complaining to him easier.

"Whole thing's going to fall on me," I said dourly. "What's so important in there, anyway?"

"It's not going to fall." Bob wiped his pink forehead with a handkerchief. "I grew up here, did you know that?"

I hadn't. The bright autumn trees shed red leaves that fell slowly, like drops of blood. When I turned back to the house, a graying curtain flapped through a broken pane.

I hadn't figured him for the sentimental type, either. Still, I guessed that if it were my childhood home, I wouldn't want to go in any more than he did.

"Okay," I gave in. "Just tell me what to look for."

Probably he wanted his memories kept free of black mold, fallen plaster, and bathrooms out of his nightmares, I decided. He told me what he wanted as I put a foot on the rotted front step, shuddered as my sneaker went through into whatever soft stuff was below. And then whatever it was *moved.* . . .

"*Yeagghhh!*" I remarked calmly, then yanked my foot up out of there so fast I nearly dislodged the cat now clinging to my ankle with all of its sharp claws.

The cat sprang away with a yowl and streaked off across the lawn. Meanwhile, I fell right on into the house through the broken door and landed on the debris-covered floor, whereupon the smell in there nearly propelled me back out again.

Mold, wet mattresses, cats, a fouled drain, all mingled in a horrid stench. The broken windows had let animals in, just not their stink out. Not much light came in, either, through the grimy windows.

Luckily, I always had a small LED flashlight in my pocket; that and a thin current of fresh air led me to a kitchen window, its glass shattered across the floor.

Or what had been the floor. Bob stood nearby outside.

"Maybe I should do this after all," he said after seeing my face; window or no, the smell in here was still eye watering.

"No, I'm in now, I'll do it. But can you tell me a little more about what I'm looking for, please?"

The ruined kitchen featured a sinkful of beer bottles, a tiled backsplash that years of moisture had soaked off the wall, and linoleum whose few small unruined areas showed a multicolor-splatters pattern on a background of light cream.

"A little notebook," he repeated what he'd told me outside. "Spiral. Blue cardboard cover."

"Wow, so it's really going to stand out, huh?" I queried sarcastically, then aimed my flashlight around some more.

A shiny brown beetle skittered through one of the bright spots the flashlight made. I yanked open a cabinet drawer and emptied its contents into the terrible floor.

And there it was, first place I'd looked: blue cover, wire spiral binding. Dampness glued some pages together but they separated easily and the childish writing inside hadn't smeared.

The entries in the notebook were kids' names; beside them were the words *AMT OED*, which, after a moment, I figured out was how Bob must've spelled "owed" in those days. The sums scrawled by the names went as high as two dollars; there was a column for "PAYED" amounts, as well, and one headed simply "%."

It might've looked cryptic except that my whole working life was once spent figuring percentages like the ones in this book. They indicated the interest that Bob had been charging.

I couldn't help chuckling. "You were a little loan shark, weren't you? When you were a kid, you—"

No wonder he'd wanted the book; it had his name in it. And

once the place fell down, which I still thought it might do any minute, he'd never get a chance to retrieve it.

Someone else might, though, I thought, while they were clearing the debris or just picking curiously through it. Then the jokes about Bob's youthful crime history would begin.

Mine included. But my amusement evaporated promptly when a skunk waddled into the kitchen with its black nose twitching and its bright, beady eyes angrily alert.

"Yeeks," I whispered. Its striped tail waved dangerously.

"Jake, you okay?" Bob chose that moment to call to me.

"Beat it," I said. The skunk had noticed me.

"Huh?" he asked. The top of an old stepladder appeared in the window, and soon his round, pink face loomed there, too.

"Oh," he said, understanding the situation swiftly when he saw me and the skunk. Creases appeared above his sparse, blond eyebrows as he thought it over.

"Skunks don't want to mess with you unless they feel forced into it," he said finally, "so you just take a slow, easy step to your right. Toward the door."

I stuck my tongue out at him. "Toward the door? Wow, that's helpful. How about if you and I just trade places instead?"

Because, for one thing, this skunk did want to mess with me. From the look blazing in his eyes it was clear that he wanted to rip my lungs out but he'd settle for gassing me to death. In fact, on second thought, Bob's advice sounded eminently correct.

All but the slow part. The skunk curled his lip at me; his yellow incisors curved behind it. Then he turned ominously, and don't you just hate it when a skunk turns his back on you?

I flung myself across that kitchen so hard that when I hit the back door it broke outward, I burst through it, and the door and I just kept on going together out into the backyard.

"Hey," said Bob as I careened past. Then came the face-plant in the yard's dry grass and weeds. When I got up, fallen leaves clung in my hair; some had even gotten inside my sweatshirt.

"This what you wanted?" I held up the notebook with the names and numbers in it. The amount of interest that Bob had been charging his young pals for loans would have made my old crime-boss clients blush.

He grabbed the notebook from me, gazing fondly at it, then went back and got far enough inside his old home to shove the front door as far shut as it would go.

Then we kicked our way back through fallen leaves to his car. "Bobby Frenkle," he said reminiscently, a half smile on his round face. "You old welsher, you still owe me half a buck."

We got into the squad car just as the kid riding the bike came by again. This time he was near enough for me to see his newsboy's cap, tweed jacket, and corduroy overalls.

Wait a minute, I thought as he swooped by on the bike. The kid had sandy hair, a pug nose, and lots of freckles.

Wait a minute, that kid looks familiar.

"The story," I reminded Bob as we drove back into town. "I help you, then you help me, remember?"

Now that his initial pleasure over the notebook had faded, he seemed subdued; it would've been better if he could remember his old home the way it was, I thought.

"Cliff House," I reminded him firmly again, and finally he gave in.

"Right after World War II," he began, "this old retired Hollywood movie director built the place."

He steered the Crown Vic into the long, swooping curve at Redoubt Hill. "Guy was getting over what they called a nervous breakdown back then," said Bob. "He'd seen wicked bad fighting, saw wounded men and worse, when he was overseas."

The Crown Vic took the turn as if it were a bathtub mounted on bedsprings. "He brought his wife here, a kid, and a bunch of servants," Bob went on.

Cook, housekeeper, driver, maid, an outdoor caretaker, and

the caretaker's helper, I counted the likely staff on my mental fingers.

"Everything seemed fine at first," Bob went on, "and the grocer and butcher and the other Eastport provisioners were all happy with the amount of food and drink that got bought. Clams, champagne, fish and meats, all got delivered on the regular."

"Until gradually they didn't," I murmured. That's why Bob had mentioned the food deliveries, I felt sure.

He glanced at me. "Yup. Dozen eggs less one week and two dozen less the next. Bread, coffee, sugar, salt, groceries, and supplies of all kinds all trending downward."

"And you know this how?" We passed the old power generator, already resembling some nineteenth-century scientific artifact.

Bob nodded. "My old man was the caretaker's helper when he was a kid, also the cook's pet. He was there for it all."

We slowed for the sharp turn into town. "He said the place was first class all the way. Latest stuff in the kitchen, wired for electricity in the whole house, all parquet or tile floors. They even had a boat, a nice little open cruiser, my dad said, and a dock to tie it to."

At the fire department building the fire truck was getting washed, foamy white suds flooding the garage's paved apron.

"But then, my old man said, things started getting odd," Bob continued. "The retired movie director would go down in the cellar, sometimes for days, and there'd be building sounds down there. Or digging. My dad didn't know for what."

"Huh." I paused. "I'd heard there were . . . uh, deaths."

Not *murders*. On account of some previous snooping we'd done into a number of violent demises that had happened around here, Bob was alert to signs that we might be planning to nose around in more; he was, as if I needed to say so, against the idea.

"Finally," he went on, ignoring my comment, "no one from outside got let through the gates anymore, not my dad nor any supplies, either. So the town sent some men to see if the folks in the big house out on the cliff were okay."

"And were they?" We passed the Catholic church, with its lovely old perennial garden surrounding the rectory.

Bob laughed humorlessly. "Not so much. The Hollywood guy they found in the cellar, dangling from a rope."

He frowned. "The rest were worse. Knives and so on, and tools from the garden shed, had been used on them. Ten in all, the police thought, six of the staff, a couple of their children, and a couple that never got identified. Though, to tell you the truth, the bodies were in such bad shape they never knew how many for sure."

Of course; forensic medicine wasn't as advanced then as it was now. We rolled down Washington Street while I averted my mental gaze from the scene Bob's words conjured.

"But why'd they stay? They must've known he was getting, uh, unstable. So why didn't they just all get out while they still could?"

Eastport's police chief shrugged as he slid the squad car into an angled parking space in front of The Chocolate Moose.

"Nobody could say. Some of them they found in their beds, still alive. But they were too badly injured to talk, and none of them survived."

We rode in silence until he held up the notebook again. "So that's what I know, and now you do, too. Thanks for this."

"No problem. Thank you." For the story, I meant, not that I'd enjoyed it. But I'd rather know one bad true story than let my mind go on and torture me with a lot of imagined ones.

"I'm gonna go now, and collect from these guys in my book. They still live around here, most of 'em."

"Not so fast," I said. There was one more question I still hadn't asked. "So why'd you really send me into your old house just now? You could've done it. Or"—I pointed at the notebook I'd salvaged for him—"Or one of the old buddies whose name is in there could've gone with you."

He frowned slightly. "Yeah. Well. Thing is, I didn't want to go in. And . . . well . . . I didn't really want to admit that to any of 'em."

I digested this for a moment. Like I said, we were friends, Bob and I, and over the years I'd depended on his friendship more than a few times.

But I hadn't realized that he also had decided he could depend on me.

"Fair enough," I said, and started to get out of the car.

Then a question I hadn't thought of before hit me. "So no one escaped? All the ones who were still working or living out there, they all ended up dead?"

I opened the door and got out. Bob put down his window as I reached the sidewalk.

"His wife got away. Their kid, too, I heard. But they were back in California pretty quick, from what my dad said, and I don't know what happened after that," Bob said.

On my way into the Moose I stopped once more. "Bob? Did you happen to recognize another kid, the one who went by on a bike a couple of times just now out at your old place?"

Bob looked away from his rearview mirror; he'd been in the act of backing out. His pink forehead crimped puzzledly.

"What kid?" he said.

Four

Three days later I'd tried all I knew to keep whipped cream from liquefying inside a cupcake. A chocolate cupcake, to be precise, with chocolate chips plus chocolate frosting spread lusciously atop it, and the first problem was just getting the cream in there.

My pastry needle took care of that, along with a syringe so big you could probably use it to wash your car. That cream, though, went fluid in under an hour, and it turned the cupcake around it to something more like a soupy pudding.

And since I was too proud of these otherwise drop-dead-good little morsels not to show them off at Cliff House, I'd decided to whip the cream on-site and inject it just before serving.

Now, though, the time had arrived, and the cupcakes weren't the only thing worrying me. "I'm telling you, I saw him."

We were unloading plastic platters, paper plates, plastic cutlery, and plastic drinking glasses from the back of Ellie's car. To my surprise, Ingrid Merryfield wasn't a snob about such things, so the event wasn't ecologically correct but at least we wouldn't be fouling any water with dish detergent.

"I'm serious, Ellie," I said, grabbing a carton of napkins. I carried them and another six-pack of paper towels to the Cliff House service entrance, which accessed the cellar via slanted metal doors at the rear of the dwelling.

"I didn't think anything of it at the time, but it was the same kid," I said. "On a bike. First in town the night Miss Merryfield and Bryan arrived, and then out at Bob's old place. The kid was dressed kind of funny, too."

"Uh-huh." Ellie hoisted two satchels full of aprons, hair covers, latex gloves for food-handling, and our own personal things in two canvas duffel bags, for staying the night here.

Which I still didn't like the thought of, but as time went on I'd begun feeling even sillier about getting all spooked over weird sounds and a broken window. Besides, tomorrow it would all be over.

I grabbed more bags, hauled them to the cellar opening, then with both hands full picked my way down the concrete steps to push an old wooden door open with my foot.

Inside, cobwebs brushed my face as I hauled the bags across a packed-earth floor. Dark, heavy beams crossed the low ceiling, supported by massive posts made of tree trunks with their bark still mostly clinging to them.

A square-headed nail speared a dusty swatch of deer hide to a beam.

". . . if you say so," Ellie was replying as she came down the concrete steps behind me.

About the kid on the bike, she meant. Four bare lightbulbs dangled on cords from the ceiling beams, illuminating the spiderwebs draped there.

"But I can't help thinking you're mistaken," Ellie said.

"What?" I demanded as we unfolded the metal legs on our card tables. "What do you mean, I'm . . ."

Never mind spacious kitchens, what you need when you're catering is another space, your own space, where things you put down will still be there when you need them instead of getting filched by some guest who just wanted to lick the spoon.

"... mistaken?" I finished indignantly.

Upstairs, footsteps crossed and recrossed the kitchen; besides us, a mother-and-daughter team of cooks from Cherryfield was prepping for the main course, while another pair of kitchen staffers they'd brought with them got ready to serve appetizers and drinks.

"Now, now," said Ellie, laying out the clear plastic trays on which we meant to serve the dessert items. "Calm down."

I just love being told to calm down. "Fine. But it's still weird, though. Just remember I said it was odd."

"Extremely," Ellie agreed seriously, "weird." But she used the tone I knew meant that she was humoring me.

I squinted darkly at her. In reply she just smiled, which on Ellie is really saying something; you could heat whole houses with the warmth of that expression when she's beaming it.

I stayed stony for two seconds, all I could manage. Then:

"Okay," I laughed, "I give in. If there's a ghost around here, it's probably just Casper and I hope he likes chocolate."

Besides, we had work to do. Platters, the cake servers, confectioner's sugar for the chocolate doughnuts we meant to set out for late-night snack food, all had to be organized.

Bella would arrive soon with foam coolers full of cupcakes; it was imperative that they stay chilled. We planned to serve them with ice cream, and I was hunting around for the ice cream scoop when a face appeared in the cellar doorway.

"Hi," said the new arrival, peering down at us.

"Hi." He was a slender man in his twenties with wavy pale blond hair, very pale blue eyes, and the kind of angelic face that used to get painted onto cathedral ceilings.

"Main door's around front," I called out, perhaps a touch crisply. I was here to feed guests, not socialize with them.

Undeterred, he took the steps two at a time, landing with

practiced lightness on both feet at the bottom. His offered hand was clean and well manicured.

"I'm Gilly Blaine," he said. "How d'you do?"

He looked around. "Man, this is a creepy old place, isn't it?"

Raising an expressive blond eyebrow, he indicated the beams draped with cobwebs, the tree-trunk support pillars, and the narrow flight of steps leading upstairs.

Dusty steps, dark and steep, curving up and out of sight. I'd seen cobwebs there, too, and with my luck they were *inhabited* cobwebs.

"Makes a guy think he should've brought his rosary," Gilly said, and of course I had to like him a little bit after that. Laughing at whatever I'm scared of is always a key to my heart.

"Go on, now, we're busy," Ellie told him, making a shooing gesture toward the outdoors, and he danced back up the cellar steps again like he was in an old Fred Astaire movie.

Then from outside I heard Ingrid Merryfield say his name, not sounding pleased. "Gilly, honestly, must you always be so early? I invited you for dinner, not lunch."

As they moved away I could hear him soft-soaping her about how he couldn't stay apart from her any longer and she laughed, forgiving him.

I'd have liked hearing more—we were snoops, remember?— but instead Bella and my daughter-in-law, Mika, arrived with the cupcakes and I forgot all about Ingrid and Gilly.

The next few hours went by in a flash, getting the food into the house and refrigerated, doing the many last-minute preparations for serving and plating, and getting utensils and the plastic dessert trays and so on all set out in the kitchen.

Speaking of which, the pastry needle I'd planned on using to inject the cupcakes could've been bigger. It had the diameter of a drinking straw, but that cold whipped cream was thick and a needle the size of a railroad spike would have been better.

Still, I got the stuff in there and the cupcakes were very pretty, all gussied up with candied violets and raspberries on top of the chocolate frosting.

A couple of the guests did look worriedly at the pastry needle when they peeked into the kitchen. But we promptly shooed them out again along with whatever—glass of water, a Tylenol for a headache, or whatever—they'd come in here for.

"Back to the peanut gallery," Bella said approvingly when the last of them had scuttled back to where the rest gathered in the parlor, and I agreed. We didn't need an audience getting in the way of our dessert-finalizing assembly line.

"Don't sound like much of a party, though," she added, sifting powdered sugar onto the doughnuts by rubbing it between her thumb and forefinger.

No music, for one thing, and the murmurs of talk drifting from the parlor sounded subdued, despite the drinks being drunk out there. But the dinner being cooked smelled divine: sirloin tips with caramelized onions, mushroom pilaf, and the kind of homemade rosemary biscuits that rise up like saints and taste like heaven.

If that didn't make them feel better, then nothing could, I thought as I set filled cupcakes on their platter and slid it first into a two-gallon storage bag, then into the refrigerator.

They'd replaced the old one with a fridge whose insides looked big enough to garage a truck in. I checked to make sure the plastic bag wasn't smearing the frosting; when the door closed, it made a sound like an expensive car's door slamming.

"Your dad feeling better?" Ellie asked. She was wrapping spoons and forks in paper napkins; then Bella sealed the napkins with circles of paper tape.

"Bright and chipper." I glanced around. Chocolate jelly beans in bowls, check. Tiny chocolate chip ice cream cannolis, check. Anxious forebodings . . .

Stop that, I told myself yet again. "This morning he seemed to have bounced back from all the excitement," I said.

Or as far as a very old man like him could bounce, anyway; Sam and my grandchildren were staying with him for tonight, and Sam would call me if things didn't go well.

"Looks like it's almost showtime," said one of the cooks from Cherryfield, gesturing at the windows looking out over the dark lawn and the darker water beyond. I spotted the Cherry Island Light, its beam a long ghost-white bar sweeping across the waves.

Then as the guests were being summoned to the dining room, we dessert folks—me, Mika, Bella, and Ellie—went upstairs to the rooms Ellie and I had chosen, to eat our own dinners.

No crashes this time, no broken windows or strange voices. Still, I practically vibrated with nerves; perched on a chair edge, I tried to relax, imagining myself in some more pleasant situation, like the dentist's chair.

But Mika was charmed. "Oh!" she breathed, brushing back her black hair to gaze happily at the bedroom's vintage details: fringed lampshades, brocade upholstery, finely worked doilies on the tables and on the arms of the old-fashioned furniture.

For work tonight she wore a frilly white bibbed apron over a black turtleneck leotard top and black yoga pants, and black flat slippers. Weighing only a hundred pounds or so, she looked doll-like but after living with her I knew she was as strong as a steel cable.

"This," she breathed, "is lovely." Which it was, I admit, but *Here's where he caught her* was the thought that bubbled up in my mind without my wanting it to.

Oh, did I ever not want it to. But who knew, I thought hopefully, maybe Miss Merryfield would change her mind and send Ellie and me home at midnight, when Bella and Mika would go.

For now we ate sandwiches and drank seltzer water or Moxie:

Ellie in the overstuffed chair, Bella on the bed, and me on the footstool. Mika sat limberly cross-legged on the floor, leaning against the room's old cast-iron radiator.

"Funny bunch," said Bella. She'd met some arriving guests out in the driveway when she'd been carrying in more cupcakes.

"All dressed in new L.L.Bean stuff," she said, this being a sure sign of newbie-ness in Maine.

I'd seen them, too. Four came in their own cars, which they'd parked in the driveway and meant to drive out in tonight, back to Portland or Boston where they were from. The others, all Los Angelenos, had come in by plane from Bangor and been driven here; they were the ones who'd be staying in the bedrooms.

Miss Merryfield, I'd gathered, had her room at the other end of the house. Ellie stood by our little bedroom's window.

"Pretty out there," she said, and I went to join her.

"Yes, it is." The window looked out over the driveway. A fat round moon was on its way up, and in its light the white pea gravel seemed to give off its own pale glow.

Which was how I could see the shadowy figure skulking under the evergreens between the house and the garage.

"Ellie. Right down there." I pointed, then realized there was no longer anyone to point at.

The figure was gone, vanished among low evergreen branches whose shadows in the stiff breeze still blowing out there seemed to dance on the gravel. Or had anyone been there at all?

Maybe not. "Sorry," I murmured, still peering. But there was no one to be seen.

Bella got up and rolled her sandwich wrappings into a ball. Mika's glossy black hair, cut in a blunt bob, swung forward to hide her face as she pushed herself up off the floor.

"Time to go," she exhaled.

Oh wonderful, I thought.

Ellie shoved all of our trash into a plastic bag; neither of us wanted to come back here later after we were done cleaning up downstairs only to confront another mess.

I took a last glance outside, saw nothing more to give me pause, and left the bedroom behind. But as I went, I couldn't help also giving that long hallway a last looking-over.

The broken glass was gone, cleaned up by Bryan, who, for tonight, anyway—after taxiing the overnight guests here from Bangor—had also become the man of all work.

Everything else seemed ordinary, now, too, if a bit dusty and outdated. Perfectly fine, I told myself; no problems whatsoever. Except maybe that old hallway carpet. Frowning, I stared at it.

Red-patterned, it was still nicely fringed at the ends, and had a vaguely predatory-looking design of entwined vines running through it. And those vines . . . oh, come on, were they *wiggling*?

No. They most certainly were not. I turned my back on the rug and the hallway and all of it, and followed the others back down to the busy kitchen.

"Grab that pan before it boils," said one of the cooks from Cherryfield five minutes later.

Luckily, she didn't mean me; as the younger one hurried to obey, I went on down to our worktable in the cellar.

"Yes, like that," I heard Mika directing as I descended the stairs. Bella grumbled in reply, but she only grumbles if she loves you and she feels well, so this reassured me.

Then we all worked steadily for a while on the rest of the desserts: chocolate cookies, petit fours, and those cupcakes, of course. I'd found half a dozen that hadn't been filled in one of the coolers, so I hurried to finish those.

"Darn," I said impatiently, nearly stabbing myself with the pastry needle.

"Maybe a sweet cream injection wouldn't hurt you," Ellie said mildly.

"Sorry." Despite the lectures I'd been giving myself, now that the night of the event was really here I felt sour as a pickle.

"But I can't help it, this place gives me the screaming meemies."

Bella looked dourly at me. She didn't like it here, either—I could tell by her face, which is not exactly an oil painting at the best of times; now it looked like she'd bitten into a lemon.

"I'm telling you, that woman should get her money back for this place," she muttered as I finished the last cupcake.

Just then one of the cooks leaned into the cellar doorway. Besides plenty of staff, they'd known enough to bring their own pots and pans, I'd been happy to see.

"We're clearing," the aproned young woman announced, which meant that the dessert course should happen soon.

So we each took a plate, platter, or tureen—for the home-made chocolate sauce, naturally—up to the dining room, where I got my first look at the guests Ingrid Merryfield had invited.

The dozen of them had left the table and gathered in the parlor, which was sparsely furnished with a lot of elderly settees and armchairs, and more of those unpleasant red rugs.

Now the company stood around chatting with after-dinner drinks in their hands; among them I spotted Waldo Higgins, who'd played Sam's favorite alien in *Space Wars* back when Sam was little. Beside him stood the actor—now, what was his name again? I searched my brain—who'd played the fellow who got axed in that well-known cult classic *The Hurr-Durr Murder.*

Of the women in attendance, none had Ingrid Merryfield's grand Hollywood status but two of their faces were familiar. I was puzzling over why I knew them, and what the pale, wan-faced third one standing with them was doing here, anyway, when Bryan appeared beside me.

"Having fun?" His mashed-in prizefighter's face looked out of place among the guests' expertly snipped-and-tucked ones.

"Or are you strictly a worker bee like me?" He was wearing a blue blazer with a light blue shirt, dark slacks, no tie. In his hand was a glass of milk.

"Working." His eyes met mine briefly, then ranged back over the guests again. I didn't see the gun; he had better tailoring in his dress-up clothes, maybe, or maybe he just hid the weapon better on social occasions.

"You always stick this close to her?" I asked.

Nearby, my three coworkers smiled and chatted tirelessly while using tongs and cake servers to dish out the sweets.

"Not always," he said, smiling, but the smile didn't reach his eyes, and he kept glancing across the crowded room toward Ingrid Merryfield.

Raised voices came from the area of an old upright piano, hideously out of tune, as I'd learned earlier when Gilly Blaine had sat down to try playing it. Now I recognized him again—blond, slender, with a dancer's toned body and a dancer's unconscious physical poise—standing by that same piano but this time looking like he wanted to fight somebody.

"... hell of a nerve," his voice came through clearly, then faded, blending with the others' chatter. I turned curiously to Bryan, but he was crossing the room toward Miss Merryfield, who stood by a pair of doors opening onto the terrace.

But it was time for me to get back to business. The chocolate chip cupcakes with the dark ganache frosting and the candied violets and raspberries on their tops had already nearly vanished from the platters. The ice cream was a hit, too; I'd had my doubts about whether it was just too over the top or not, but now I was glad.

The folks here tonight all seemed a little over the top to me, as well, the men's hairlines augmented with transplants that looked like thin crops in poor soil, the women in full makeup plus plenty of leopard print, brightly dyed leather, and suede boots.

Ellie waved from across the dining room where we'd set up the second dessert station. "Fill 'er up!" she mouthed smilingly at the fast-emptying trays of dessert items.

I nodded back at her. Despite my unease and the ongoing lack of hilarity here tonight, all seemed well.

But then Bryan caught my eye again. Beyond the opened pair of glass doors he had found something interesting to watch, out on the terrace. Someone had lit tiki torches out there though the night was too breezy for them, the yellow, red, and orange flickers dancing eerily over the flagstones.

His rough face smoothed purposefully as he put his glass down and started for the doors. A few guests glared affrontedly at him as he elbowed past them.

Then someone in the torchlit gloom on the terrace screamed, and went right on screaming.

I hurried out there. A woman lay on the terrace, one of the guests whose name I hadn't recalled. Now it popped into my head just as someone nearby murmured it.

"Audrey Dalton . . . is she all right?"

Somebody got a lamp from inside and someone else found an outlet near the terrace doors to plug it into.

"Get back, everybody," said Bryan, and I'm pretty sure he threw an elbow to enforce this, but the torches were sputtering and the night seemed to swallow the light so I couldn't be sure.

"Give her some room," another voice said, and the horrified Hollywood people backed off except for Gilly Blaine, kneeling by the fallen woman.

"What happened?" I asked him. The woman moaned and shifted unhappily.

Gilly didn't look up. Waldo Higgins, who stood behind me with a drink in his hand, answered instead.

"Seems she's passed out," he said. "Again," he added.

He sipped his drink. "I warned her not to overindulge, but that's Audrey."

And now it came back to me: Audrey Dalton had been a film critic for decades, then become a newspaper columnist focusing on the entertainment industry. Her face was familiar because I'd seen it in print so often.

I now recognized the man talking to me as more than a star warrior, too: he'd also been a crusading lawyer in a series of films based on popular crime novels, and his familiar voice was like honey with grains of brown sugar in it.

"Don't get loaded with your enemies is a rule I thought everyone knew," said Waldo, and of course I'd have questioned him about this, but just then Audrey Dalton sat up and looked around peevishly.

Once upon a time she'd been a full-figured redhead whose glamour was equal to that of the stars she wrote about. But now she seemed smaller and thinner than she'd been in the photos I recalled, her hair still bright red but cut short in a pixyish style that didn't suit her.

Also, she hadn't passed out just now, not from drink or anything else. While I watched she touched her head gingerly, then grimaced at the red smeared on her fingers.

"One of you hit me," she accused, looking around. Gilly Blaine had gotten up and slipped off somewhere while I was talking with Waldo.

"Audrey," said Waldo, setting aside his glass. Crouching, he tried helping her up, but she wasn't having any.

"Don't *touch* me," she said, slapping his hands away, then began to weep softly into her own.

No one moved, everyone unsure what to do. But Bella had been watching, too; now, after stomping across the flagstones in her bib apron and flowered hairnet, she pushed the actor aside.

"Come on, dear," said my bony old stepmother to Audrey; *deah*, the Maine way of saying it. "Let's just get you inside, now, and have a look at that poor head of yours."

The other guests moved away, trying, it seemed, to revive some party-like mood. "More drinks! More desserts!" one of the guests called out merrily. Then one of the cooks brought out a radio and music began, finally; it was jazz night on Eastport's local radio station.

I stayed on the terrace until the rest were all inside but for Bella and Audrey. From out there I could see Bryan standing by Ingrid Merryfield, alone together in the parlor.

He slipped his arm around her waist, saying something to her in a voice too low for me to overhear from where I stood. With a nervous glance around, she stepped away.

"Come on, now," Bella told Audrey again. The fallen woman's pale leggings and embroidered tunic were stained with moss from the terrace stones.

"You just lean on me, dear," said Bella, "we'll do it together."

Good advice; I'd been leaning on Bella for years. I followed the pair inside, closed the doors, and drew the pair of floor-length red velvet draperies together.

Then I hurried to the kitchen where a first aid station had been hastily set up and put to use: ice in a wet towel on Audrey's head, gauze and tape from the first aid kit we always brought to catering venues.

Just as I went in I saw Gilly Blaine ease quietly out the door that led to the patio and the backyard. Once I'd made sure that Audrey's wound wasn't serious and that Ellie and Mika were okay without me for a little while, I followed him.

The wind gusted purposefully, smelling like rain, and the full moon had gone beneath clouds. Waves crashed in the cove below the cliff's edge at the far end of the yard.

"Gilly?" I whispered. "Are you out here?"

No answer. "Gilly, I just want to ask you—"

"What's going on out here?" Bryan's voice came suddenly from behind me.

I jumped. "You scared the daylights out of me," I said, but in the glow of his flashlight his face looked friendly enough.

Well, except for his eyes, which were dark, thumbed-out hollows. *Shadows from the flashlight*, I told myself.

It was plausible. Likely, even, that the eerie lighting effects were coming from the flashlight. Only the fire-siren alarms blaring from my nervous system said otherwise.

"Just getting some air," I said, and if his look tightened at the sound of the lie, I couldn't help it. It was the best I could do with a heart rate gone suddenly through the roof.

He lit a cigarette, stared at the dark sky. A few drops of rain spattered down; he cupped the smoke.

"Seen Gilly Blaine?" he asked casually.

Why, what a coinky-dink, as my son, Sam, would've said. I turned toward the kitchen door. "Nope. Why, is something wrong?"

I may resemble a mild-mannered bakery lady—well, not with a pastry needle in my hands, but you know what I mean—but I didn't work for all those mobsters without learning some things. You want information from me, be ready to give back.

Besides, the minute Audrey Dalton's bleeding head hit those flagstones out on the front terrace, I'd stopped trusting anyone here. Bryan flicked the cigarette away.

"If you do run into him again tonight, let him know I'm looking for him."

That's another thing I don't run, a free messenger service. But: "Sure, I'll do that." Which I might or might not. Another thought struck me. "Where's Igor?"

I hadn't seen the dog since we arrived. But now, as if in answer, the animal burst out of the bushes dividing the yard from the massive old evergreens growing thickly beyond it.

"Wuff," Igor uttered as he loped past me, negotiated the open cellar doors, and vanished into the gloom down there.

The enormous canine didn't need a fence, I gathered, which was excellent because I couldn't imagine any that would hold him except maybe the raptor paddock at Jurassic Park.

"I guess Gilly will show up eventually," I said.

"Yeah," Bryan said, not sounding convinced, then turned to cross the driveway toward the garage. "Well, off to bed."

Now I wasn't convinced. "You're staying up there?"

He nodded, not looking back at me. The black metal fire-escape-type stairs leading up to what I guessed must be his room gleamed wetly.

"G'night," I called, but he just climbed the stairs and went inside without answering, and lowered the shades at the two uncurtained windows up there.

I guessed his job description didn't involve night work. Although maybe he wished it did; that grab he'd made at Ingrid Merryfield's waistline had looked pretty heartfelt.

But then again, so had her quick step away from him, as if she didn't want anyone even thinking they might have more than a driver-employer relationship.

I looked again down the long, dark lawn to where it ended against an even darker swathe of sea and sky. The wind blew in bullying gusts and the waves sounded angrier, exploding on the rocks below.

"Gilly?" I whispered once more, but got no answer.

Not unless you count a spatter of cold rain hitting me in the face.

The squall hit suddenly; by the time I got inside, it was raining so hard that silvery columns seemed to march across the pea-gravel driveway.

"Was this forecast?" Mika asked. She was stuffing used paper plates into a trash bag.

"Not that I saw," Ellie spoke up, returning to the kitchen for more ice. By now it was past eleven-thirty and the guests were in the parlor again; the ones who weren't staying the night were saying their farewells.

"Well, I hope it stops soon," I said. Through branches thrashing in the downpour, from the kitchen window I could see that Bryan's lights over the garage were out; by then, the cooks and their helpers had already packed themselves, their equipment, and their paychecks into their van before trundling off into the night.

"What are they doing in there, anyway?" I angled my head toward the parlor, where laughter had just suddenly erupted.

Bella sighed. "They found a Ouija board in the drawer of an old desk."

"And they're playing with it," added Ellie. "Which I think is a bad idea."

She thought no-kidding ghosts were about as likely as unicorns. But in this house we'd both heard and seen enough already to leave well enough alone, summoning-spirits-wise.

I grabbed another bucket of ice and used it as an excuse to check things out. By now the departing guests had actually departed; Waldo, Miss Merryfield, and Audrey Dalton sat on chairs pulled up to an old coffee table with half the veneer chipped from its top.

With them were two others: Maud Bankersley's pale elfin face, short-cropped black hair, and petite frame were famous from the series of blockbuster fantasy-adventure films she'd done a few years earlier. Tilda French, the plain, dowdy woman whom I'd seen earlier and wondered about, was beside her; I still didn't know why she was here but I'd overheard one of the other guests mentioning her name.

Most of the table was covered by a game board with the familiar letters and symbols on it. The planchette was a flat piece of wood, mostly oval but with a point at one end.

"Go on, ask it," Maud urged Waldo, so they all put their hands lightly on the planchette and he spoke:

"Oh, spirits," he intoned, "will I live a long life?"

The planchette didn't move at first. But then it jerked a little and began sliding in circles under the fingers touched lightly to it, finally resting on "Maybe."

Laughter greeted this. "Not very specific," Waldo grumped.

"Maybe we should introduce ourselves," Miss Merryfield suggested, "before we ask questions. Jake, turn the lights down, will you please?"

There was a dimmer switch on the wall, so I did, and they tried again. "Is anyone here?" Maud inquired into the darkened room.

Nothing. "Cat got your tongue?" asked Audrey, who was still in a foul mood after her head bump. Still drinking, too.

"Oh, this is a waste of time," said Waldo, getting up.

The planchette sailed across the room, bounced off the wall, and hit him in the chest. He caught it, frowned at it, and placed it very gently back onto the Ouija board.

"And that," he pronounced, turning away from the table and the women still at it, "is enough of that."

Suddenly, "Oh!" exclaimed Maud Bankersley. Her hands, along with Tilda's, were on the planchette again.

D-I-E-D-I-E-D-I . . . The planchette zipped quickly from one letter to the next.

"Dydeee-eyedee-eye?" Looking over Maud's shoulder, Tilda sounded it out puzzledly.

"No." Audrey got up quickly, her face so pale that the gauze pad Bella had taped to her forehead barely stood out.

"It says, 'Die.' Over and over, it says . . ."

Her voice broke. "We need to get out of here. Something is happening, we need to . . ."

Whirling, she ran unsteadily from the parlor, through the dining room and into the kitchen.

"Poor dear. She really did hit her head hard," Miss Merryfield said sympathetically as she got up, too. "Let me just go see if I can help."

But soon she returned. "Audrey's distraught," she reported, "and just wants to go to bed."

Well, it wasn't as if she had anywhere else she could go. Bryan wouldn't be driving back to the airport on a night like tonight, that much was certain.

Waldo Higgins and Audrey had gone upstairs. Once I'd returned to the kitchen, that left four of us there: me, Ellie, Bella, and Mika. The latter two had planned to leave at midnight, but now neither of them would agree to do it if Ellie and I had to stay.

"Not an option," said Mika very firmly as the clock on the mantel in the Cliff House parlor struck twelve.

"Sam's with the kids and your dad. I called and they're all fine," she went on. "So I'm staying here, even though—"

"Even though it is a little creepy," I finished for her.

Bella was blunter. "Ouija boards, hmph. Don't trouble trouble is my opinion on the matter. I had an ancestor who'd a-known what to do about this place," she uttered.

"What?" Ellie was half listening as she made up two plates of dessert leftovers and slid them into the new refrigerator.

"They'd-a burnt it down and salted the earth," Bella said darkly, and I saw the surprise on Ellie's face.

"You're just too good to know elemental evil when you see it," I teased her. But Mika had the last, most accurate word, or so I thought at the time.

"You want some elemental evil in your life, go try out those old cast-iron bathtubs upstairs."

I shuddered reflexively. We'd reconnoitered the bathrooms, of course, each a worse rust-streaked horror than the last.

She added spoons and napkins to a tray of cups, sugar packets, creamers, and the coffee carafe.

"And take these stuffed dates," Ellie added. She'd made them from things she'd found in that new refrigerator, which Bryan had stocked with enough food for a month.

"Maybe the dates will get stuck in people's teeth, they'll go upstairs to brush, and they'll decide to stay up there," she added hopefully.

"Who's the woman who didn't get all gussied up for this?" Bella asked suddenly.

Tilda, she meant, the unglamorous woman who looked like a "before" picture to the others' "after." I'd nearly spoken with her a few times during the evening, but I'd been busy, and anyway she'd looked neither welcoming nor particularly interesting.

Now suddenly Waldo Higgins was beside me again; the phrase "bad penny" sprang to mind. "I thought you'd gone to bed."

He shrugged. "Too quiet up there."

Yeah, that was one way of putting it. I took the dates from Ellie and he followed me back out to the parlor.

"So," he began. Earlier I'd heard him tell someone he was a casting director for TV commercials now, not acting in films himself anymore.

"Ingrid's got us here so she can show off this new place of hers," he said. "Couldn't even wait for the remodel."

I set the tray of dates on a coffee table.

In the dim-lit room, Waldo Higgins looked just as he had as a young film star: hound-dog face; sad, dark eyes; and a full, almost droopy lower lip.

"Or I assume that's it," he added. "Tell you the truth, I was surprised to be invited. I'm on her you-know-what list."

He gestured around at the falling plaster, faded paint, and the kind of old jalousie windows that if you don't replace them you might as well turn off the furnace and burn dollar bills in the fireplace instead.

"What was her hurry?" he wondered aloud.

Just then Ingrid Merryfield sat up from a high-backed chair

where we hadn't been able to see her, fluttering her pink-tipped fingers prettily at him in invitation.

He looked embarrassed by what he'd said about her house, but he joined her, and after they'd exchanged a few words he gulped the rest of his drink and went off to bed, this time for good, I hoped.

That left Audrey, she of the bonked head, plus the unglamorous brown-haired woman wearing tan pants and a shapeless green cardigan.

"Want to wrap it up?" said Ellie, appearing at my elbow.

Weariness washed over me. "Yeah, I don't care how late they stay up, but this shindig needs a last call."

So she got a glass and spoon from the kitchen cabinets and dinged the spoon on the glass a few times.

"Folks! We're shutting down for the night, so if any of you want a nightcap or snacks, they're in the kitchen and you can just—"

Help yourselves, she'd have said, I suppose, but just then the lights flickered. Once, twice . . .

"Drat," I heard Bella remark, and then the lights went out entirely.

"Maybe I should call Sam," Mika's voice came worriedly from somewhere behind me.

Worried was putting it mildly as far as I was concerned. "This isn't good," murmured Ellie, still right at my elbow.

A match flared, and candle flames began springing to life all around the parlor, setting orange flares and black shadows writhing on the walls.

"Nuts to this," said Bella, who was in the midst of going around lighting the candles.

Thunder crashed. "Yeah, Mika, maybe you'd better call—"

"I just tried," my daughter-in-law replied bleakly, holding her phone out to me. No bars showed on its screen.

"Oh," breathed Audrey Dalton unhappily, "I don't like this one bit."

Me neither. "Look," I told Mika, "we'll just get in Ellie's car, drive back into town, and get some help out here for these people. Even take them to the motel, maybe."

That is, if the lights didn't go on soon by themselves. But just as I thought this, a ferocious *rumbleTHUDBANG!* crashed through the night along with a bright-white flash of lightning.

Somebody moaned, but I didn't see who because I was busy nodding at the whiskey bottle Ellie had just handed me; oh, what a good idea.

But the booze wasn't for me, sadly. "Give them each a drink if they'll take one and get them to stay put if you can," she said quietly. "Then meet me in the kitchen."

I did as she asked. Nobody needed much persuading. "Just leave us the bottle," said Audrey, her dyed hair blood red in the candlelight.

"Here," said Ellie when I got to the kitchen, handing me a flashlight from the ones she'd brought along in her satchel; I blessed her "be prepared" habits silently.

Then she stood on tiptoe to squint out the kitchen window, with Bella pressed up beside her.

"He was there a second ago," said Ellie, "but—"

"Who?" I demanded, sliding in between them. "What's going on?"

All I could see out there was my flashlight's white beam turning the rain to sheets of silver.

Then a huge lightning bolt daggered its jagged way across the sky, now roiling with massive thunderclouds.

"There!" said Bella, pressing forward. "Did you see?"

More lightning lit the sky, turning the long, sloping lawn down to the cliff into a harsh black-and-white photograph.

With a figure in it. A moving figure . . . My breath caught in my throat as I spied, far down the lawn nearly at the cliff's edge . . . no, it was two figures down there.

The lightning flared once more. "Oh," Bella exhaled softly. "He was there, but now he's . . ."

Gone. Where two figures had been, now no shape hunched out there in the wind-driven rain. Then suddenly the lamp over the sink flared on and the patio lights outside the kitchen shone defiantly into the downpour.

But next came a flare of white light so explosively bright that it dazzled my eyes, followed by a boom of thunder that felt as if a meteor must've crashed in the driveway outside.

After that came a sharp *crack!* and a long *whoooosh* sound, ending with a *decisive* thud somewhere very nearby, and then the lights went out again. *THUD!*

Ellie's flashlight went on again. I looked around for Mika while Bella peered out the window.

But Mika wasn't there; not in the pantry or the parlor, either, or anywhere else downstairs.

"Bella, did Mika say she was going upstairs?" Bella just shook her head.

Then Ellie came back from delivering another bottle to the parlor. "Ellie, have you seen—"

"Oh. My. God." Bella turned, her eyes wide with shock.

"They were there again," she uttered shakily. "Two people. Men, I think. Or maybe one was a boy."

We hurried to join her at the window. The wind blew the rain sideways and lightning still flared sullenly.

I cupped my hands on the glass. A single figure now stood where I thought I'd glimpsed two, at the cliff's edge.

"Well, that doesn't look good," I said.

There's a big tree down, too," Ellie reported, "I saw it when I was in the parlor."

A sigh escaped me. "All right, that settles it. We should just take all these people to the Motel East."

It would take a while to get a tree cleared, and there'd be no lights, hot water, or even hot coffee until then.

Ellie looked unhappy. "Tree's blocking the driveway. I doubt any of these folks could climb over it, especially in the dark."

I doubted they'd even try. Strappy sandals with rhinestones on them, Italian loafers that looked soft as gloves, and suede Hush Puppies were their footwear of choice, from what I'd seen.

Tilda French, of course, had been wearing the Hush Puppies. "Look," Bella breathed from where she still stood at the window.

"Oh, come on," I said, "don't tell me you can see anything through—"

Bella adores being told she can't do what she's doing. She stepped back from the window. "Be my guest," she said, and of course she didn't add "you little know-it-all."

I pressed my face to the window. Then, "Holy crap," I breathed. The rain was slackening off but the lightning continued. And in the blue-white flares . . .

A hand flopped up over the cliff's edge and felt around as if trying to find something to grab on to, then slid on the muddy turf and fell back down out of sight once more.

We waited, but it didn't come back up.

Five

Ellie got there first, dropping to her knees to aim her flashlight over the edge.

Beside me as we followed her down the lawn, Bella made a sorrowful sound. "Oh, that's just terrible, who was that poor soul, d'you suppose?"

A mental picture of those pale, wet fingers clawing weakly for purchase in the moment before they slid out of sight froze my heart again.

"I don't know." And didn't want to, suddenly. This was way more than I'd signed up for. "Ellie!" I called as she aimed the flashlight down there once more.

Then she hopped to her feet; my heart only skipped a few beats as a wind-driven gust of rain shoved her a few uncertain steps back toward the cliff.

But she just ducked her head—in the murky wetness I had to imagine that stubborn chin of hers, jutting determinedly—and jogged uphill toward us.

"Couldn't see a thing," she gasped when she reached us. She shoved her wet hair back with her hand. "We've got to get hold of Bob Arnold."

"Fine idea. Got any suggestions for how?" I asked.

With our phones out and no landline set up in the house, an SOS by flashlight was the only method I could think of, and I was pretty sure Bob wasn't out there on the water where he could see the distress signal.

But then an amazing thing happened: my cell phone rang. Digging it frantically from my pocket, I thumbed the answer button hastily and felt a burst of relief when the Eastport police chief's voice came out of the device.

"Jake, you all okay out there?"

I said we were except that someone had gotten hit on the head and someone else either fell or got pushed off the cliff, and we didn't know who or by whom for either of them.

"What? Jake, I can barely hear you. Look, this thing blew up without anybody expecting it. Little squall, wasn't supposed to be anything, next thing you know, blammo."

I heard him take a breath. "The phone tower got hit by a big gust, did some damage. Back now, though."

I told him that we were trapped, that a big tree had come down on the driveway, and also that there was no power.

This time he did hear me. "Whoa. And you're there with a houseful?"

He knew we were. Well, not a houseful exactly, now that many of them had departed, but what we did still have, I told him, was plenty.

"Tell you what," he said, "we could come in with a boat, maybe. But we've got our hands full here in town and the state cops and sheriff's deputies are even more jammed up."

He went on to say that the storm on the mainland had been worse than here, with flooding and car accidents and so on.

"So unless somebody's bleeding to death I'm afraid you won't see us for a while. Is someone bleeding to death?"

"No," I admitted. Someone had drowned to death, I thought, but that unhappy event was over with by now, probably. Maine's not a place where you fall into rough water and come up smiling.

"Wade's out wrangling the *Star Verlanger*," Bob said.

"Wonderful." As Eastport's harbor pilot, my husband steered big freighters in through the tides, currents, and granite ledges with which our harbor was so plentifully furnished.

"Blowin' around like a beach ball," Bob said, meaning the freighter Wade was on.

"Coast Guard's gone over to Campobello to render aid," the police chief added. "They've got a yacht sinking over there, possible fatalities."

Double wonderful. All of that meant that for a while at least we were on our own, and so was whoever had gone over that cliff.

"Soon as it gets light enough for them to work, though, I'll send a crew out there, haul that tree aside," promised Bob.

"Thanks," I said, my heart sinking as we hung up.

The house loomed black in the pouring rain as we hurried toward it. Inside it was warmer and drier, but I grabbed another flashlight from a shelf in the kitchen and prepared to go back out again.

Mika came in from the parlor. "There you are!" I exclaimed, relieved.

"I was checking on the guests," she explained, coming in from the parlor, "to make sure they're all accounted for."

"Good." The way this night was going, any minute they'd start vanishing one by one.

"I can't seem to find Audrey Dalton, though, and she isn't upstairs," Mika went on.

"Well, she's around here somewhere." It had not, I felt sure, been a woman's shape toppling off that cliff. "Where'd you get to earlier, though?" I asked. "I looked for you."

"Oh, I was in the cellar," she replied, embarrassed. "I went to fetch a bag I left down there and the lights went out."

"So you . . . what, you just sat there? In the dark?"

She looked sideways at me, her look suggesting that creepy was one thing, real danger another. "Uncovered electric outlets scare me. Peanuts, marbles, things kids can choke on. I hate white vans, and I have a real horror of detergent pods, okay?"

Which was when I understood: a bump in the night was no problem unless it was the sound of her own kid's head hitting the floor. I'd felt that way once, too.

"Okay. Glad you're back, anyway. Listen, just hunt around a little more for Audrey, all right? Do me a favor and make sure everyone who *should* be here *is* here."

She nodded, a funny look coming onto her face. But I didn't think anything of it.

"And, Mika, be careful, okay?" I said as I went back out where the rain sloshed down onto the patio flagstones like somebody was hurling it from buckets.

Out on the patio, I muscled the kitchen door shut behind me, turned, and stepped back fast as a shape materialized in front of me.

My hand with the flashlight in it swung upward. "Don't you move an inch," I instructed.

"Okay," said a voice. A *familiar* voice . . .

Criminy, it was Bryan again. The guy was like a jack-in-the-box, always popping up where I didn't expect him.

I lowered the flashlight. "Can you just stop surprising me, please? I'm going to look over the cliff again. Somebody fell and I want to see if I can still spot whoever's down there."

I didn't really expect that I would see anyone, or know what I would do if I did. Throw a rope down or something, maybe.

But I had to at least look. "Cops can't get here tonight and the Coast Guard's jammed up with another problem," I added. "And in case you haven't seen it yet, there's a big tree down across the driveway; that's what took out the power."

I saw him absorbing this, shaking his head. Then all at once I was talking to his back as he strode away from me toward his rooms over the garage.

"There might be somebody we can rescue," I called after him, but he just waved dismissively without turning.

"I already looked. Just now." He reached the foot of the shiny black metal stairs and put a hand on the railing.

"You mean you saw—?"

"Yeah," he interrupted. "There's nothing down there but crazy rough water and big rocks."

He moved his arms in a big slamming-against-granite-cliffs gesture, and I already knew what he meant; a few minutes of that and not only were you done for, but it might not be immediately clear anymore just what species you belonged to, either.

The wind dropped off some, but that just meant I could hear the waves better. It was raining straight down, now, and I'm not sure it's possible to drown in a downpour but I certainly tested that notion as I left the patio and started toward the cliff.

"Wait," Bryan said. He'd set a battery lantern on the fire escape's step, and by its glow I saw his mashed face, creased even more by unhappy thoughts.

"You'd better come on upstairs," he said. "You won't find anyone to save down there, and we need to talk."

"It was Gilly Blaine who went over the cliff," said Bryan when I'd climbed those stairs and entered his small apartment.

"You saw him?" I repeated. "You know it was him?" But if he had, where was he when we'd been at the cliff's edge, I wondered.

"Did you see anyone else?" I asked. It did make sense that he'd made it to the cliff's edge before us, I guessed.

But to this he shook his head. "Not clearly."

Chilled and beginning to shiver, I moved toward the propane heater whose bars glowed orange in his apartment. He handed me a hot drink that I recognized wincingly as instant coffee, but I'd have swallowed used crankcase oil if it warmed me up.

"I passed you going toward the cliff as I was coming back, but in the dark and the storm I guess you didn't see me."

Beside him, Igor cocked his wiry gray head sympathetically. I was glad to see him here, where it was warm and dry.

"It happened so fast," Bryan said.

That's the way it had looked to me, too. "We saw some of what happened from the house," I agreed. "He was struggling with someone, but by the time we ran down there . . ."

Bryan interrupted. "Yeah, like I said, I saw you coming back up the lawn. But the other person you saw, could you tell who?"

"No. And I can't think why he or anyone else would be out there on a night like this."

I went on to repeat the rest of what Bob Arnold had said. "In a few hours, he'll be sending people," I said. "Before you know it, they'll have the tree hauled, power on, and cops all over the place."

Because there had been a murder here; it already seemed hard to believe, as if it had been a dream.

Bryan sighed heavily. "I told Ingrid that buying this house was crazy. This damned party she insisted on, too, it's all just nuts."

I sat on an orange upholstered sofa, a thrift store relic if I'd ever seen one, and we were silent a moment, listening to the hiss of the propane lantern in the kitchenette instead.

"She doesn't have family or friends here anymore," he said.

Had she ever? I wondered again, still not sure I believed that part of Ingrid Merryfield's story. But:

"Lots of people don't. People who move back here, I mean."

As I spoke, I looked around some more. The whole place was furnished with old things much like the ones in the big house: old wooden tables with elaborately carved feet, chairs covered in fringed brocade nailed on with decorative brass tacks.

"What I want to know, though, is why she's having a house party for these people, particularly. I'm not getting the sense that she likes any of them very much."

Ingrid had not, for instance, shown much concern for Audrey's bloody head injury, though she'd circulated among her guests in a hostessy enough manner to avoid criticism.

"Except you," I added.

He knew I'd seen him putting his arm around Ingrid Merryfield earlier, and now he spoke carefully.

"For a while Ingrid and I were an item. We're not, anymore. What you saw this evening was not what you thought you saw, and I've got no more insight into her thinking than anyone else."

He took a breath. "Although as far as I know there's no reason for her to be here at all, and especially not alone."

He was right; I hadn't thought of it before but once my crew and the remaining guests were gone, she'd be in that big old place all by herself.

Personally, I'd have chosen Bryan's apartment; there was nothing fancy about its varnished knotty pine–paneled walls and green linoleum–tiled floors, but the big uncurtained windows on three sides of the living-dining area made it feel pleasantly like a tree house, even at night.

"Once upon a time," he went on, taking a seat on one of the living-area chairs, "she took my advice on things."

He'd lit another propane lamp and set it on the divider between the kitchen and the living area. In its harsh light his face was full of yearning and regret, which vanished at once when he saw me noticing it.

Straightening, I pretended that I hadn't. "Why'd she need a bodyguard in the first place, though? I mean, that's how it must have started between you two, right?"

Across the driveway, dim lights flickering in the big house said they'd found more candles and lanterns over there, too. It made me realize that I'd been out for a while; I hoped Ellie and the others weren't worrying about me.

"She'd been getting threats," said Bryan.

"And once she'd hired you . . . ?"

He looked uncomfortable but he answered. "They shut off like a switch. I figure someone was watching her and when I came on board they decided it was easier to pick on someone else."

Igor got up, stretched, and walked into the kitchen, and I heard the sound of water being lapped up.

"Like I say, I don't know why she had to have a party right away. But she should've invited local people," Bryan said.

He drank some of the awful coffee. "So they could get to know her and find out she's not just a face on a movie screen."

Behind the smeary windows in the big house, some lights were brighter now, and moving around. Flashlights, maybe.

"But instead, for some reason she had to impress that bunch she had lounging around in there," he said, "even though they've all been complete jerks to her in the past."

"And let me guess, now they all want something from her? Did they even know what Cliff House is like?"

Old, poorly furnished, horrid bathing facilities . . . and now it was a murder scene, unless I missed my guess.

"Probably not," Bryan said. "I don't see why they would know the condition of an old Maine house, do you?"

Outside, rain still hammered down. "But it wouldn't much matter," Bryan went on, "because Audrey wants badly to write Ingrid's biography and Maud wants the lead part in the next Ingrid Merryfield film."

I must've looked puzzled. How could an Ingrid Merryfield film not have the famous star in it?

"Ingrid's too old to play the lead in romantic comedies,"

Bryan explained. "She'll be getting a producer credit on the new one, as a consolation prize."

He finished his coffee. "Maud's campaigning for Ingrid's approval in the new role, so she won't make a powerful enemy by moving in on the film franchise Ingrid created. And Tilda is Maud's assistant, so of course she's got to be here."

Setting down his cup, he added, "Audrey wants access, to get her book started. And if she'll cut back on her alcohol intake she might actually get it."

He got to his feet. "But I have no idea why Waldo Higgins is here. Free dinner, maybe."

Or possibly free cupcakes; Waldo, I'd noticed, had made quite a dent in our supply.

Igor came back and flopped down onto the linoleum again, reminding me of the time passing. With an effort I pushed myself up off of the sofa; I'd been away from the others long enough.

In the kitchen a dog's brushed aluminum water and food bowls stood side by side on the floor.

"As for the ones who came from Portland and Boston, I'm pretty sure they were just here for a story they could dine out on, tell people about the house party at Ingrid's. Plus they might make useful connections," he said.

I crossed the room to the door. The rain had stopped as suddenly as it had begun but everything still dripped.

"So why'd she invite them?" Waves crashed in the distance; I thought unhappily of Gilly Blaine being carried away by them.

"Oh, just for filler. To make it look as if her gatherings can still draw a crowd. Sad, huh?"

It was. But as I stepped outside onto the gleaming metal stairway landing, a new thought popped into my head.

"By the way, I looked Ingrid up online. Wikipedia articles and so on."

Because of course I had. "They say she was born in Omaha, not Eastport, Maine."

Ellie and I had puzzled over this the night before, bent together over Ellie's laptop. "You have any idea why?" I asked.

"Yeah. Like she said, she keeps her private information private. And if that means throwing snoops off the scent with a phony bio, that's okay with her."

And with him, his tone implied. "Okay, that makes sense," I replied. I turned away, then looked back.

"Listen, just one other thing. You haven't seen anyone else around here, have you? Not a guest. A kid on a bike, maybe?"

Bryan's gaze flattened. "What? No. And I've been keeping my eyes open, too."

Sure he had, what with him being the bodyguard, and all. "I see. Well, that's interesting. But—"

He narrowed his eyes further, not liking my inquiries. *What'd you think, Bryan, that I was just some dumb backwoods housewife with a baking hobby?*

Because for one thing, there are no dumb housewives in Maine. If there were, they'd get eaten by bears, poisoned by toadstools masquerading as mushrooms, or bled dry by mosquitoes so big they could stand flat-footed and look right over the barn at you.

"Bryan," I told him gently, "honestly, I really don't care what a hotshot driver or bodyguard you are."

His look grew puzzled. Helpfully, I enlightened him.

"You said you looked over the cliff and didn't see anyone down there."

He knew now where his mistake had come. He just didn't know what it was.

"But you can't see all the way down there like you said you did."

I'd been down there myself over the previous summer, in Ellie's boat. There was a dock in the cove below the cliff, old but serviceable, and precarious-looking hammered-together wooden stairs that led down to it.

I'd been on those, too; arguing and protesting, but at my adventurous friend Ellie's amused hectoring, I'd done it.

So I knew about one more thing, a feature that Bryan hadn't counted on. "A big granite outcropping partly blocks the line of sight from above," I said.

"Oh," Bryan countered gamely. "He must have bounced off and kept on falling, then. No wonder I couldn't see . . . ."

Yeah, maybe. One thing I knew for sure, though, was that we couldn't get to anyone who might still be down there right now. That cove's narrow beach was underwater presently, and if I remembered my tide tables—they printed one every week in the *Quoddy Tides*, and Wade used them regularly—that beach would stay submerged for another four hours.

By which time Gilly's body would be long gone, if it wasn't now. As I stood on the metal stairway landing, another tree went down somewhere nearby with a loud, drawn-out cracking sound, and then the kind of massive thud generally produced by tons of wood slamming to earth.

"Okay, Bryan," I said. "Thanks for the coffee." Hey, for all I knew, everything he'd told me was true.

I started down the metal stairs, then turned as Igor came sure-footedly down past me and trotted off into the shrubbery.

At the top, Bryan still stood watching, and something about the light from the doorway behind him lit up his face just right.

"Hey, Bryan. You ever work in film yourself at all or TV?" Because I'd suddenly realized that I'd seen him somewhere.

He laughed tiredly. "You've got a sharp eye."

Igor scuffled around in the bushes. "I had," Bryan said, "a few little jobs as child extra, years ago."

So that was it, then. "What'd you do after that?"

Bryan scanned the dark yard for the dog for a moment longer before he answered. "By the time I was twelve I was a pretty big kid, and older than I looked."

He looked down at me. "Famous people liked having me around in case they ran into any trouble."

He came halfway down the steps. "Let's just say I've been taking care of people all my life, one way or another."

Whatever else he'd said, this part sounded true.

"Sounds like you found your calling," I told him, and the sound he made in reply might've been a chuckle. I was about to ask more questions, but just then the dog appeared.

Bryan waited for the animal to gallop back; then they both went upstairs and inside while I crossed the white pea-gravel drive back to the main house.

Not much later I heard Igor whining outside the kitchen door.

"Come on in, buddy." The light at Bryan's was still on and from the bright slit running along the door's edge it looked as if the dog might've nosed it open and slipped out.

I brought him into the kitchen, where we four caterers had gathered by candlelight to put off going upstairs.

Three, rather. "Oh, he saw someone, all right," Bella was saying. She bit appreciatively into a roll stuffed with leftover sirloin tips.

"Now where's Mika gone again?" I asked, peering around.

"Out there by himself," Bella continued. She was talking about the victim who'd gone over the cliff, I realized; she didn't know yet that it was Gilly.

"That's the mistake people make, see, going places alone."

She was a horror film fan and knew just what activities the movie characters should avoid: going places alone, being around chain saws or bare hanging lightbulbs, hopping into bed with—

A face appeared in the kitchen doorway. "Is there any more wine?"

Waldo Higgins wore a black satin bathrobe with voluminous sleeves that in the dim candlelight made him resemble a hound-faced, hairy-legged bat.

"Wine," I repeated stupidly. It was two in the morning, the

house was quiet, and I was so tired that if I tried getting up I would probably fall right back down again.

Waldo beamed expectantly, rubbing his hands together like a child waiting to see which nice lady will give him a lollipop.

"Chablis?" he requested. "If you have it?"

Just then Mika appeared behind him, looking troubled.

"Or champagne," Waldo suggested on second thought, "if you have any of that left over."

There was plenty of wine, and champagne, too, but it was all down in the cellar in the large cooler that Bryan must have bought along with the new refrigerator. We'd thought that by morning they'd all be so hung over, they wouldn't even want to look at anything alcoholic.

But no; Waldo waited confidently. And he was a *polite* pest, his long, droopy face smiling pleasantly, so it was difficult to refuse him.

"I'll go," said Mika. "Me too," said Ellie, and even Bella hauled herself to her feet.

But Mika prevailed, grabbing a flashlight, and since she'd already been down there in pitch darkness and was fine with it, I figured she'd be okay.

Still, if I live to be a hundred years old I will never forgive myself for what happened next:

She started out all right. Faint scuffing sounds said she was descending the steps, then proceeding across the floor toward the cooler.

"You all right?" Bella called down after a few moments.

"Fine," she called back; I relaxed a little bit.

From below, Mika yelped startledly. Then something *thumped*.

Whereupon I was out of my chair and heading down those steps so fast, you'd have thought my hat was on fire and my backside was catching, as Bella would've put it.

"Mika? Mika, where are you, are you okay?" In a heartbeat I

was all the way down; Bella was in the doorway, above and behind me, aiming a flashlight past me.

I, by contrast, was not holding a flashlight, on account of my
having flown across the kitchen too fast to remember to take
one. So I mostly felt rather than saw the low shape trundle past
me: head down, elbows pumping.

One of them jabbed into my ribs wicked hard; then shoes
hammered the steps as whoever was in the shoes charged up
past Bella, knocking her aside.

Whoever. Or whatever. Although it was not—I can tell you
very surely from the way that elbow felt when it slammed into
my ribs—a ghost or anything like one.

"Ohh." A faint moan came from somewhere in the dark cellar.

"Mika!" I scrambled toward the sound. The gleam from her
flashlight shone weakly from under some fallen boxes.

"Ohh, what did I . . . ?" As Mika sat up, a dozen or so cans
of tuna rolled off her chest.

A shelf had collapsed. I aimed the flashlight. From the stained,
chewed appearance of the labels on the old cans—tuna, sardines—they'd been here a long time.

Mika craned her neck, rolled her shoulders, then rotated
each ankle in turn. "I'm okay. Who *was* that, did you see?"

"No idea." In the glow from the flashlight the dust smears
on her face looked like bruises, but fortunately they weren't.
Cautiously she hauled herself up and picked her way through
the tumbled cans and shelving material.

"Careful," I said as she kept clambering among the fallen
things: old cardboard boxes, bundles of venetian blinds, the
various other items that old cellars seem to fill up with.

But never mind, beyond the now-scattered stacks and heaps
of the stuff, a large arched opening yawned blackly.

"What's going on down there?" From the door at the top of
the stairs, Ellie and Bella peered down at me.

But I didn't answer because Mika was gone again; turning in fright, I opened my mouth to call her name.

Her dark head popped from between cardboard boxes that had broken open, spilling tins of Polish sausages.

"Here," she said, sounding shaken. "Someone's right here."

I hurried over with Ellie right behind me. Mika struggled up, her expression stunned.

Where she'd been, a hand lay motionless, sticking out of the jumble of fallen things.

I cleared cans and cardboard away until a snipped mop of dyed red hair appeared, and then I uncovered the face.

"Oh," Ellie breathed, sounding unhappy.

Me too. The woman in the rubble was Audrey Dalton, and she was dead.

"Come on," I told Mika and Ellie in the tough, *or else* voice that I hadn't used since Sam was thirteen, and we got back up to the kitchen, where Bella closed the cellar door firmly and braced it with a chair.

Meanwhile, Waldo Higgins had gone into the parlor to wait for his wine. When he heard us he returned to the kitchen, where Mika put two dusty bottles into his hands, along with a corkscrew.

Whereupon he had the gall to look disappointed. "Red wine?" He tried handing it back. "Because I was really hoping for—"

"Waldo? That's your name, right?" asked Ellie.

She gave him a smile that would've looked right at home on a tiger. "Take your wine, Waldo," she said gently.

Waldo's full-lipped mouth formed an O of surprise.

"Thanks," he managed, wisely backing away from her, and when he was gone we four women sat down together at the table again.

"Did you see who it was?" I asked Bella and Ellie, meaning

the figure who'd shot up out of the cellar at them, but they shook their heads.

"Going like he was shot out of a cannon," Bella reported. "I have his hat, though," she added. "It fell off as he ran by."

"Fine." I shrugged tiredly. So the guy dropped his hat. But as I got up to fetch the coffee carafe from the kitchen counter, she held up a brown tweed cap.

It was a newsboy's cap, brown tweed with a flattish top and a short, round brim, either the same one I'd seen on the bicycle kid at Bob Arnold's in Quoddy Village or one just like it.

A cold, swimmy feeling came over me. *How'd that get here?*

Bella peered suspiciously at me. "What's everyone not telling me?"

Reluctantly, I brought her up to date. Learning that we'd had two deaths didn't improve her mood.

"I found something else, though, too," Mika offered, in a bid to lighten the atmosphere, perhaps. "Maybe not what we need right this minute, but it's something, anyway."

The label on the jar she held out said that it contained a popular brand of chocolate-hazelnut spread. Bryan must've bought it along with the other supplies, I realized.

"Oh," said Ellie distractedly. "That's what I thought we'd use for the chocolate pizza."

The idea now seemed light-years distant. "Are there more of these?" I asked.

"A whole carton. Twelve, I think," Mika replied.

Maybe Bryan had a thing for the stuff and didn't want to share. By now I felt beaten up by waves of fatigue, my legs quivering bonelessly and my heart pattering in my chest.

"Jake?" Ellie looked alarmed, suddenly. "You okay?"

"Oh, I'm just ducky," I said, trying to sound convincing. From outside somewhere came a new sound, like an old outboard motor trying and failing to start.

Rrraghr, rrraghr—I stared dazedly through the kitchen's

open door into the pantry; the black and white floor tiles in there really were very *contrasty*, I recall thinking.

The sound, too, got more interesting. *Rrraghr . . . RRRAAAGHR!*

That's not an outboard, I realized, and then I got out of my chair—I don't know why.

The tiles rushed up to meet me.

Six

When I woke, they were already making the chocolate pizza, the gas oven's warmth radiating pleasantly in the candlelit kitchen. Stove burners were lit, too, and atop one of them a pan of milk steamed; fortunately, there were plenty of wooden matches in a box on the mantel over the stove.

I was propped in an armchair they'd apparently dragged in from the parlor. Bella poured some of the milk into a cup and handed it to me.

The hot, sweet liquid trickled down my throat. "Thank you," I managed.

"Hmph," she retorted. "Tell me, you eat or drink anything since . . ." She thought a moment. ". . . yesterday noon?"

Chagrined at a sudden realization, I fell back in my chair; oh, what a bush league blunder. Sure, I'd been busy, and too nerved up to eat much when we we'd all gone upstairs for dinner, earlier.

But busy was no excuse. Tired, hungry, and, worst of all, dehydrated . . .

"Sorry," I muttered, and drank more milk, meanwhile taking in the preparations busily going on around me.

The oven had been on all along, so it radiated pleasant waves of warmth. Chocolate-hazelnut spread melted gently in another saucepan. Dustings of flour on the countertop said the dough was rising; needing only flour, sugar, salt, olive oil, and yeast, with the addition of a little water, the stuff was ridiculously easy to make.

"How long was I passed out?" I climbed to my feet; the room made as if to start spinning, then settled.

"Few minutes." Bella stirred the chocolate mixture on the stove. "I dribbled some sugar water into your mouth," she added.

I took a few careful steps. The leg bones did seem reliably connected to the ankle bones, etcetera.

"So, I'm out cold, who knows if I've got brain damage, but you guys just decide to go ahead and make pizza?"

Bella turned with her spoon suspended over the saucepan in a way I'd come to recognize.

"It's not," she pronounced distinctly, "like we could call an ambulance."

And of course she had a point. My head ached dully; I drank more hot milk and put a hand to my eyebrow. "What's that noise?"

Outside, the racket from earlier still went on. It was a *familiar* racket. "And where's Mika and Ellie?"

"Upstairs, checking on the guests."

I picked up half of a sirloin tips sandwich she'd made for me. I still didn't feel hungry; in fact, I'd as soon have eaten a phone book, but I started on it, anyway, under Bella's watchful eye.

The roaring outside went on. Also, when I glanced at the kitchen window, a whitish glow kept flaring in it.

"Why," I asked carefully between bites, "did they go up to check on the guests? Did something else happen?"

Bella frowned as she stirred the chocolate. "Mika thought she heard something from upstairs, but no one else did."

On a coat that Bella had spread on the floor in the corner, Igor snored peacefully; it was Bella's own coat, I realized.

"Then Ellie thought she heard something."

"I get it." I poured more milk and drank it. Strong bones, as I used to tell Sam, were important, not to mention strong teeth, in case I ended up having to bite somebody.

"Finally we all heard," Bella continued, her spoon moving slowly through the melted chocolate. "Screaming," she finished.

She looked over at Igor, seeming to take comfort in the big dog's presence, and suddenly it hit me how pleased I was to have him here, too.

I mean, in case he had to bite someone, which was getting more likely by the minute, I thought.

"Screaming and screaming," said Bella with a glance at the window, where that odd white light still flared.

And I don't know whether that hot milk turned my lights on finally, or what, but all at once I knew what the glow was. The sound, too: that growling *rarrgh* was the sound of a gas-powered chain saw and the glow came from the kind of big floodlights Sam used when he got called out for emergency tree work at night.

And that meant—

"Screaming from upstairs," said Bella, who was obviously scared stiff. But being Bella, she'd refused to leave me alone.

A few hours in Cliff House was all that it took to wear most of the bloom off the rose, grand-old-house-wise. A lot of the original, elaborately milled trim was still there, and a good deal of the old wallpaper, some even in decent shape.

But upstairs, hideous red flocked material covered the old plaster, and the terrible vines twining through the hallway runner still seemed to writhe demonstratively.

"Hello?" Still no lights here; I aimed the flashlight beam

around, but the darkness seemed to soak it up. A few battery-powered emergency lights—the kind that go on automatically in a power outage—were in the baseboard outlets, though, and they made it possible to move forward.

More of Bryan's work, I thought appreciatively. Too bad the lights also created such weird, wavery shadows on the walls and ceilings.

On the other hand, now I knew that Sam was here. His crew probably, too, with their tools and equipment.

"Ellie?" I called out quietly; no answer.

The guests' rooms were at the hall's far end, the women sharing one rusty, tap-dripping bath and Waldo having the other to himself.

"Mika?" With my courage buoyed by the knowledge that my son and his helpers were outside, I peeked into the first inhabited bedchamber. It smelled like some astringently herbal soap.

Then, "Jake!" came a muffled whisper, but whose, and from which room?

I opened another door a crack, as silently as I could. Inside, someone's breathing was slow and regular; Maud's perfume hung cloyingly in the air.

The next few rooms were empty; I shone my flashlight's beam onto bureaus and old dressing tables whose mirrors reflected the light weirdly onto stained, outdated wallpaper.

Only one room remained. But this one I hardly even needed to look into; through the closed door the sounds from within included snuffling, snorting, and some really very energetic snoring.

Waldo, I thought, but just to be sure I stuck my head in, heard even louder snoring, and closed the door again. Then I crept back to the room that we catering ladies had chosen for ourselves and put my hand on the doorknob.

The door jerked suddenly inward. A hand grabbed me and

hauled me inside. Someone grabbed my flashlight, snapped it off. Angrily I lurched from between the hands gripping my shoulders, grabbed my flashlight back, and spun away in the darkness.

Then a match flared and a candle flame ignited.

"You!" I gasped, lowering the flashlight, which I had been planning to use as a bonking tool.

Ellie and Mika blinked in the sudden glare, both just as poised to attack as I'd been moments earlier.

"Oh, for Pete's sake," I said, as Mika lowered the heavy old book she held, and Ellie put down the china pitcher from the vintage washbasin set on the bureau.

"We didn't know who you were. I said we should get ready to bonk you," Ellie declared, stoutly accepting responsibility for what had very nearly happened to my poor noggin.

Relief squelched my temper. "Sam's here," I said. "That's his chainsaw you're hearing."

Then I stopped, not hearing it anymore, suddenly. "Maybe they're all done cutting," I theorized aloud.

But Mika and Ellie weren't worried about that, anyway. "If Sam's here, who's with the kids?" Mika wanted to know.

"And with your dad," Ellie added, pulling aside the shade they'd drawn to peek out the window.

"I'm sure Sam must have left them in good hands," I said, which they both knew as well as I did; they were just nervous, that was all.

"What about the screaming Bella told me about, though?" I asked. "Have you heard anything more?"

Two heads shook somberly in reply. Creeping around up here after what we'd just found in the cellar must have been a treat, I thought, what with all those ominously closed doors one after another like a corridor out of a bad dream.

Heck, being here gave me the creeping fantods and I hadn't even heard any screaming; I started to say so but before I could, a bloodcurdling howl shredded the silence and then my flashlight died.

"Well, darn!" I commented cheerfully, feeling that if I said anything else I might just start screaming myself. Also, just to make things more nerve-wrackingly challenging, the candle Ellie had found and lit chose that moment to sputter out.

"Okay, let's get out of here." I moved toward the door in the pitch darkness. Sadly, a footstool was in my path, so my next unbalanced, wildly careening steps were a little ungainly.

"Stick with me," said Mika, catching me and steadying me with a hand on my arm.

"Thanks. But what was that? Is it what you heard?"

"That's it, all right." Ellie's voice was grim. "But then we were downstairs, and now we're up here."

Yeah. Right here with it. "When this is all over," I said, "we're asking for—no, *demanding*—a bonus. And hazard pay."

They laughed; weakly, but they felt a little better, just as I'd hoped. Next, though my own fright felt like ice chips circulating in my veins, I stepped assertively past Ellie and Mika and yanked the door open.

"All right, dammit," I said into the hallway, and waited.

Nothing answered. Squaring my shoulders, I stepped into the hall, peering nervously around.

By the dim glow of the battery-powered lights along the baseboards the hall stretched away from us silently, the figures in the red flocked wallpaper capering and the carpet vines writhing like live things.

As we crept toward the stairs, a fat spider dropped down right in front of me from his ceiling web, his silk a silvery thread lit from below. Then a door slammed hard somewhere behind us; I nearly leapt out of my skin.

But at last we reached the stairwell door. Hope seized me; down the steps lickety-split and we'd be safe.

"Here goes." I looked over my shoulder. Two wide-eyed faces peered back. Snapping my failing flashlight back on, I aimed it down the steps just as a shape began scrambling up them.

A shape with *eyes* . . .

"Wuff," said the thing when it got to the top, and that's when I knew it was Igor, the God-forbid Irish wolfhound.

In response I didn't quite fall on that dog's neck and weep gratefully, but it was close. Instead I buried my face in his rough fur, an attention he accepted with impressive dignity, and then, feeling much happier overall, we returned to our task of getting downstairs. The dog, Igor, stayed right behind us.

And all went well at first. Being in the cramped stairwell was only slightly like being shut up in a coffin.

One step down, then another. "Careful," Ellie said as we all took care not to tumble.

But then from the darkness at the bottom came a warbling shriek. I didn't know what it was, but I knew I didn't like it.

To put it mildly, especially since Bella was still alone down there. "So," Ellie gasped, meanwhile flinging herself back up the steps with a frightened Igor scrambling ahead of her, "it *wasn't* the dog."

"Not," Mika agreed, hurling herself once again through the door to the upstairs hall, "unless he's in two places at once."

We got back to our room and crowded inside. I grabbed Igor and hauled him in, too; then Mika slammed the door and leaned against it, while Ellie relit the candle.

Soft light flickered from the bureau's top. No more sounds came from the hall. Even Igor lay down with his head between his massive paws.

Not for long, though, as now from the hall came a tapping sound, moving toward us.

"Ellie," I cautioned as she made for the door, and if she'd been coming for me with that look on her face I'd have run. She didn't get mad easily but when she did you should scram, was my experience.

"I don't care," she said grimly, her hand on the doorknob. "I don't know who's been yanking our chains here, or hurting people, either. But Bella's down there and I'm going to do something about it."

The door flew open, just missing Ellie before slamming into the wall behind it with a bang like a rifle shot.

Which made it feel appropriate that the man in the doorway held a gun. It was Bryan, the bodyguard/limousine driver. I could tell by the candle's gleam on his close-clipped silvery hair, and this time I was glad to see him.

That is, until I noticed that the weapon he held, an evil-looking little gunmetal gray pistol, was aimed straight at me.

"Come on, hurry." He gestured with the weapon.

I wasn't sure he recognized us. Or maybe he did, and a worm who'd seemed friendly had just turned for the worse.

Like into a rattlesnake, apparently. He lowered the gun apologetically, as if he'd forgotten it was in his hand.

"Sorry, I didn't know who was in here," he said, putting it away. "I was looking for Igor. I thought he might be over here."

And of course we all carry weapons when we're looking for our dogs, I thought sarcastically.

"Anyway, you'd better come on." He stood aside to let us out into the dim hall.

"There's been an accident," he said.

Downstairs, we found Bella on the floor with her head on a sofa cushion stolen from the parlor and her coat, no longer Igor's comfy bed, thrown over her legs. A bump already rising on her forehead said that whatever had happened wasn't much fun.

"They came up behind me." Her voice was steady; my heart rate dropped out of the red zone. "A reflection in the glass—" She gestured at the kitchen window. "It moved," she said, "and when I turned around to see, they were right behind me and they . . . whoever it was . . . *clobbered* me," she reported indignantly.

Mika got some ice, wrapped it in a towel, and touched it to Bella's head.

"Who?" I demanded, but she didn't answer.

"Ouch," she groused instead, then leaned back and let herself be tended to while I cornered Bryan, watching from across the room.

"You couldn't find somebody to stay with her?" I demanded, perhaps too aggressively seeing as I was the one who'd left her down here in the first place, and boy, was I ever kicking myself for it now.

"Hey, hey," he put a hand up defensively.

The other hand gripped the gun again. "What, I should've gotten Miss Merryfield to come and sit with her?"

Right, they were all still in bed, as I'd discovered for myself. The ones who were still alive, that is . . .

"Anyway, they all sleep with Prince Valium, to borrow a phrase," he added. And they'd all had drinks, too, so good luck waking them without coffee and a bullhorn.

But I wasn't done with Bryan. "So you came upstairs looking for us? That's why you were up there?"

"Of course. What else would I be doing?"

Mika began asking Bella questions: What's your name? What's today's date? And so on. To my relief, Bella knew the answers.

Then Bella got herself up off the floor, brushing away offers of help. After tottering to the sink, she splashed water on her face, wincing when she touched her forehead.

Meanwhile, I still didn't hear any more chain-sawing or see any more work lights.

"C'mere," I said, drawing Bryan into the dining room, where I pulled a chair out and waved him into it.

A dim triangle of lantern light from the kitchen lit his face. "We found Audrey Dalton in the cellar a little while ago," I said. "She's dead."

Bryan looked shocked. "How?"

"I don't know. That hit she took on the terrace could have done it, I suppose."

Brain surgeon ex-husband, remember? I used to hear all the time about people who came to the emergency room with head bumps from bicycle or car accidents. They'd be walking around fine, complaining about being there, then lose consciousness suddenly and end up in neurosurgery having a brain bleed drained.

So it could happen. But I thought it hadn't. "Bryan, could Miss Merryfield's stalker have followed her here?"

Because a lot of strange noises in a hallway was one thing, and a boy in odd, vintage-looking clothes riding a bicycle could be explained, too, probably.

But this pushing people off cliffs and bonking them in kitchens and on terraces had to stop, not to mention all the terrifying them in hallways and bashing them in basements.

Oh, did I ever want to get out of here. But I couldn't, not until that fallen tree was cleared.

In the half-light, Bryan shifted uneasily, frowning down at his shoes as if trying to decide whether or not to say what was on his mind.

"I haven't told anyone about this," he began slowly. "Not even her. But back home in California, I actually found Ingrid's stalker."

Silently, I awaited further illumination.

"See, I had friends with access to photographs," he said. "Those paparazzi she hates so much? They're not all creeps, and they've got lots of pictures, plenty of them with her fans in them. I'd gotten a glimpse of the guy once in real life, too."

Okay, now I knew where this was going. Like I said, back in the bad old days I worked for guys who could find you anywhere.

Bryan went on. "So I paid some of the photographers and went through a lot of photos, and I knew some cops, also, and they let me look at mug shots. Finally I ID'd him."

"So you went to see him." From the kitchen, the silence was as loud as a shout; of course they were listening.

"I went to the guy's place," Bryan agreed, "and I tried to use reason. When that didn't work I said I'd pay him, but that just made him mad."

He frowned again. "Look, the guy was crazy. I knew it the minute I saw the inside of his place. Full of all kinds of junk, and the walls plastered with her publicity stills."

The kitchen was as still as a held breath. "So?" I nudged.

He sighed heavily. "He had a knife, came at me with it. In the struggle I managed to turn it away. Then"—he made a sweeping motion with his foot—"I knocked him sideways. He fell on the knife."

A heavy sigh escaped Bryan. "After that, there was nothing that anyone could've done for him."

Yeah, not exactly first aid material, maybe. "So you got out of there without being seen and never told anyone, is that it? And that's how you know it's not him doing all this?"

He agreed ruefully, but I must've sounded just skeptical enough.

"He really was dead, though," Bryan added defensively. "I'm not a complete ass. I never would've left him that way if—"

"Yeah, fine. I get it, Bryan. The guy was a goner." We could argue about the morality of him not calling an ambulance—or the cops on himself—some other time.

He nodded. "So anyway, yeah, that's why it seems to me that whoever's up to something around here, it's someone who is here. Not secretly, I mean. One of us, or one of Ingrid's guests."

I waited. "Or," he finished reluctantly, "it's Ingrid, herself."

An unhappy suspicion struck me. He hadn't needed to confess that he'd killed Ingrid's stalker, even if accidentally. And I felt sure that unless he was under pressure, he wouldn't have.

I mean, who would blab something like that for no reason? "So, Bryan, how come you—?"

But he was already talking again. "You ever see anything really weird?" he asked quietly. "Like, impossible-type weird?"

I blinked at the change of subject, then realized he hadn't changed it.

"Because just now?" he went on. "Upstairs in the hallway where the bedrooms are?"

He bit his lip, hesitating. "Spill it," I ordered him, and for a wonder, he obeyed.

"I saw him. The guy I killed. It was him, no question."

No wonder Bryan had pulled his gun. I stared, but before I could process what he'd told me, Maud Bankersley stomped in, wearing a green silk dressing gown embroidered with moons and stars. She must've been listening from the staircase.

"What do you mean, one of us is up to something? Who are you to be saying a thing like that? Why, you're just a servant!"

I followed Maud back out to the kitchen, where Bella, seeming recovered from being clobbered, had caught the "servant" comment and glared daggers at Maud. But the angry young woman ignored this, yanking open the refrigerator to rummage inside.

"What was that god-awful scratching I heard upstairs?" Maud wanted to know as she dug around in there.

Ellie looked up. "Scratching? What kind of scratching?"

We hadn't heard any scratching. I looked at Igor, who'd followed us downstairs and now lay relaxed on the floor. Even from here I could see his black toenails, so short that they hadn't even clicked on the stairs. I doubted he'd been scratching anything with them.

"And the pounding," Maud complained. "Like a construction project was going on up there."

We hadn't heard any pounding, either. Just then Ingrid Merryfield came in through the dining room. "What's going on?"

Blinking sleepily, she had on the same kind of glamorous boudoir ensemble that she'd worn in all those romantic comedies she'd made: pink, gauzy, with clouds of dyed feathers down the front.

Pink satin slippers were on her feet. "Are you all here?" Her lips, shiny with rose-tinted lip gloss, moved faintly as she appeared to be doing a head count.

". . . me, Maud, and of course Bryan," she finished, turning to me in the candlelit kitchen. "And you ladies. But—"

Her forehead furrowed, which on her was quite a trick; the skin there was as smooth as a drumhead, pulled so tight that it was a wonder she could move it at all.

Bryan spoke quietly to her, possibly letting her know that Audrey and Gilly wouldn't be appearing anymore tonight. Not why, though; her look remained merely puzzled.

That's when I realized that even without knowing all that had happened here tonight, Ingrid Merryfield was right.

We'd lost Gilly Blaine, Audrey Dalton was still lying dead in the cellar, and now we were missing someone else.

"Where's Waldo?" she said.

Seven

We hurried upstairs and found the only occupied room whose door was still closed, other than our own. It was the one from which I'd heard loud snoring earlier.

No sound came from the darkened room now. "Oh, dear heaven," breathed Ingrid Merryfield from the hall as I stepped inside with a fresh flashlight from the kitchen.

It didn't take long for the beam to find just what I'd hoped it wouldn't. Somebody had hit a sleeping Waldo Higgins in the head with a hammer, multiple times.

He hadn't survived. No weapon was visible, but the room looked ransacked, every drawer dumped out and his things thrown around. The window was open, the draperies billowing; outside, the thunder of waves crashing distantly came from the darkness in the direction of the cliff.

"That window wasn't up before," I said.

At this, several suspicious faces turned toward me, like maybe I'd been cruising for unsecured jewelry or something.

"I was up here a little while ago, checking to be sure you were okay," I explained, figuring I'd leave the part about folks hearing screams for later.

"I opened the door, I stuck my head in," I said. "The window was closed; I'd have noticed, otherwise."

I crossed the room and pushed the blowing curtains aside to put my head out. Below, half surrounded by overgrown shrubbery, stood two huge, white propane tanks.

So there was nowhere to put a ladder. I looked around again in case some clue or other was right there in front of my nose, but nothing revelatory appeared.

"Okay," said Bryan, taking charge for the moment. "What do you say we lock up this room until help comes, and meanwhile, you all go back and try to get some sleep."

"Fat chance," said Maud, but she turned obediently from the door of Waldo's room, which not only was as cold as a mortuary but now actually had a dead body in it.

"Nightcaps for everyone," Maud declared as her silk robe swish-swished away.

I had to agree; if there's one thing that helps me perk up after finding a bashed-to-death person, it's a couple of stiff belts.

So I hurried behind Maud, but while Bryan was still busy locking the door to Waldo's room with a key Ingrid had given him, Ellie caught up with me.

"Quick," she whispered as we reached our own room. Her hand shot to the doorknob and moments later we were inside, where she relit the candle we'd blown out when we left, earlier, then turned urgently to me.

"Jake, we've got to get out of here."

"No kidding. Call us a helicopter, why don't you?" Because that was the only way we'd be leaving until Sam cut us free.

But when I bent to the window it was as quiet and dark as the inside of a coffin out there; no work lights glared, and no chainsaws roared, either.

"Maybe when it's lighter outside, we could try to get over the tree," I added doubtfully.

Very doubtfully; I'd glimpsed the massive old evergreen's fallen shape as I crossed the driveway from Bryan's place, earlier. Its trunk, lying horizontal across the gravel, was like something you'd attempt with alpine climbing gear.

Meanwhile, I didn't know why Sam's crew wasn't working out there anymore, and on top of all that, I sincerely didn't like the new sound coming from the hallway.

Scratching, just as Maud had said. Like claws. Ellie heard it, too.

"Jake, we have no idea what's going on here," she said urgently. "Trying to do something about it will be useless unless we get lucky."

Which we weren't getting so far. "And," she said, "whatever is going on, so far it's killed three people."

Gilly Blaine, Audrey Dalton, and Waldo Higgins; their names brought back my last sight of them.

"Someone's picking people off, Jake. And I'm starting to think we can't stop them, not without help. Eventually they'll get around to us and then . . . Jake, we've got to get out."

She had a point. "You and I might try it, I guess. Mika too, most likely. But what about Bella? She won't make it over the tree, and we can't leave her here alone."

Ellie's face said something new had occurred to her. "Mika could stay, too," she said. "She's resourceful. And Bella just doesn't have the stamina for anything like—"

She stopped, seeing my face. "Anything like what?" I asked suspiciously.

"Never mind, just take your bag," she said. "We might not get into this room again for a while."

I grabbed my satchel and jacket. Ellie crossed to the door. "Blow out the candle," she said.

So I did that, too, and we eased into the hall. I heard no more scratching but it was still just as dim and creepy as ever, now with the added, extra-creepy quality of there being a dead body behind one of the doors at the hall's far end.

Which for me, at least, was not nearly far enough. Ellie

yanked my sleeve, then guided me out of the room ahead of her. I fixed my gaze on her flashlight's glow shining out ahead of us, following it gratefully.

Ellie whispered. "Jake, do you see that?"

Ahead, a pale yellow beam bounced cheerfully, then paused as if waiting. I could see through it to the stairwell door.

"Jake?" Ellie's voice seemed to come from far away as the light seemed to wait patiently for me. I froze, not wanting to meet up with it even a little bit.

"*Jake!*" She seized my arm, muscling me along, hauled the stairwell door open and shoved me through, then hustled me down the steps ahead of her until halfway down them, I stopped again.

"What was it?" I looked back up the stairs to the top. The door was closed; I couldn't recall if we'd left it that way.

But as if in sly answer a gleam peeped through the gap at its bottom edge, fading and flaring.

"Yeah, that's enough of that," I said firmly, and from then on Ellie didn't have to hurry me down those stairs at all.

Down in the kitchen, Ellie scribbled a note on the back of a paper napkin and passed it to Mika, who was kneading another batch of dough. She read it, nodded, and stuffed the note into her apron pocket.

Then she returned to working the ball of dough. On the counter was another jar of chocolate spread, plus more nuts.

"Another chocolate pizza?" I asked, surprised.

The first was now in the oven, its smell so enticing you could've raised the dead with it. Mika nodded, her lightly oiled knuckles punching the pale, shiny new dough mound in the mixing bowl.

"We'll need to feed the ones who are left," she explained. We hadn't promised to, but I also hadn't seen much breakfast food in that refrigerator, and a hungry guest is a grouchy guest.

As for me, I was already grouchy. "They're in the parlor with coffee right now," said Mika.

Of course they were; who could sleep anymore tonight?

"You are a genius and a hero," I told her, noticing that she'd also gotten Bella back into the armchair we'd appropriated to use out here.

Now my beloved old stepmother-slash-housekeeper napped quietly with her arms crossed over her middle and her feet propped on a hassock that Mika must've dragged in here, too.

"But are you sure you're all right with what comes next?" I asked her in a low tone.

Leaving her and Bella here, I meant, while we fetched help. That's the plan that the note had outlined for Mika; I hadn't wanted to say it aloud, in case someone overheard.

"You'll be careful," I told my daughter-in-law. "You two will stay together. You'll never be—"

"Alone? Not a chance." Mika used the long-handled wooden pizza peel that we'd brought along with us to slide the plain baked crust out of the oven and onto a cutting board.

The crust had some darker bits in it. "Hazelnuts," she explained, "not just on top but in the dough, too."

"Brilliant," I said as Ellie sat and rummaged through her backpack.

Mika held up a full bottle of dessert wine. "And this with it, I thought?"

Perfect. We wanted them as comfortably sedated as possible.

"Like I said, brilliant," I told her affectionately, and just then Ellie held up some flashlight batteries from the backpack.

"Go on, though, both of you," said Mika quietly, waving at Bella. "Before she wakes up and insists on coming, too."

Ellie and I hustled out the kitchen door onto the patio. By now it was nearly dawn, a thin red line lying on the eastern horizon and the sky overhead fading to indigo.

Ellie crouched, rooting through her backpack some more. In

it were some flat orange things, pads an inch or so thick with wide black nylon panels linking the orange sections together.

It hit me all at once what those things were, and why there were two of them. "Ellie, please tell me we're not going to use those."

They were life jackets. "Can you think of another way?" She finished untangling the straps. "Put this on."

I complied. "I don't get it. We don't even have a boat. And where'd those life vests come from, anyway?"

And if we did have a boat, I wouldn't get into it, I thought but didn't add. The rain squall of the night before had long passed but a stiff wind still tossed in the treetops.

"Well, while you were with Bryan I sneaked out and did a little exploring in the old garage under his place," she said, "and guess what I found inside?"

She put her own vest on. "Besides these, there was a boat trailer. And this." She held up something small and shiny.

It was a key. "But no boat?" Not that a boat would help. The only way we could get it to the water would be to push it over the cliff.

Besides, a boat ride tonight was the fast route to Davey Jones's locker room, as Sam enjoyed putting it.

"I'm not completely sure we have a boat," Ellie admitted. "But remember the dock down there?" she said as we stepped off the patio onto the lawn.

I did. She meant the one we'd seen the previous summer, when we were visiting the cove below Cliff House in her boat. I'd been terrified, and now I remembered the dock on account of wanting badly to crawl onto it when I saw it. Bob Arnold's father had mentioned it to Bob a long time ago, too, I recalled.

So now I realized what Ellie meant to do if we could. "No," I said, stopping dead on the lawn. "Absolutely not."

Like I say, we'd seen the dock and the steep wooden steps down to it. But the environment here was so harsh, both were probably about as sturdy as Popsicle sticks. And that was still assuming that there was any boat to go with them.

Ellie dealt with my argument efficiently, by ignoring it. "Tide's going out," she said, listening. "You can tell when the waves start getting to sound farther away."

As if that might persuade me. "That water," I began as we started walking again, "is treacherous any time. And I still don't see why you think any boat is down there."

We reached the cliff's edge. She dropped nimbly to her knees and looked over. "See anything?"

I knelt grudgingly beside her, though the view past the wide granite overhang down to the roiling water nearly made me lose my lunch.

In the distance the horizon brightened to lipstick pink, color rippling on the water like spilled paint. Which meant we'd better move; soon they'd be able to see us from the house.

"I see more than I want to," I told Ellie. The rickety wooden steps that began just a few feet below us were so steep that they were nearly vertical, equipped with rotting risers and split or broken treads, and the whole thing was held to the cliff face with old iron spikes.

But by the time the full awfulness of the steps' unsafe condition sank into me, Ellie was on them. As she moved, the whole structure did, too, and this also did not inspire me.

"Jake!" she hissed up at me. In the brightening dawn her wavy, reddish blond hair was a fiery helmet.

"Come *on!*" she urged. "Hurry, before someone up there looks outside!"

"Just because that rickety mess of lumber and rusty nails can take *your* weight," I began, "doesn't mean it can take mine."

The unfortunate Gilly must've missed the steps on his way over, I realized. Ellie said nothing, just looked up at me.

"Oh, all right." I slid over the cliff's edge onto the top step. There were three flights in total, eight steps each, zigzagging down to what at low tide would be the beach.

And was now called "underwater." I didn't get it; what were we doing? Also, I saw no boat. But:

"Fine," I breathed, seizing the splintery wooden handrail, then freezing as with a *creak!* of protest the stairs pulled decisively away from the bolts holding them to the cliff face.

And then they *teetered.* The granite outcropping that stuck out halfway down the cliff looked attractive to me suddenly, but I couldn't quite reach it.

"Um, Ellie?" I gulped. By now she was two flights ahead of me, scampering toward solid ground even though at the moment it was still under several feet of ebbing tide.

"Ellie?" I whispered. It was all that I could force through my fear-squeezed voice box. The steps moved again as the iron spikes securing them to the cliff wall chose this morning of all possible mornings to begin failing one after another.

Creak. Groan. Pop. Most ominous were the snap-crackles of wooden sections warping and fracturing, readying themselves to collapse.

"Ellie? I really hate this," I squeaked.

No reply from Ellie. I tried looking down, but that was a big mistake, too. What with all the foaming and churning going on down there, it resembled a washing machine agitating a lot of ice-cold salt water.

But by now I'd somehow gotten down another whole flight, still cold, frightened, and not knowing at all how Ellie meant to get us out of here. It was too far to swim anywhere even without the icy-cold portion of the program, so without a boat, I didn't see how we could—

"Ack!" A too-fast move on my part sent my feet sliding on a wet step, which got the stairs swaying again. My arms flailed wildly as I swung first one way, then the other, gripping the railings but not feeling much confidence in them, or in those iron spikes anymore, either.

Finally I gave up and just started running down the steps,

taking them as fast as I could. The farther down I was when the whole thing collapsed and I fell, the better, I figured.

And then I was at the bottom, or nearly. Roaring white water slammed rocks while huge waves like great fists reared back and exploded with a sound like low thunder.

"Ellie!" Hunched a few feet above the surf on the lowest step, I scanned around for her. "*Ellie!*"

No Ellie. My eyes stung with salt as I went on desperately peering and calling. Finally her face appeared suddenly in the spray.

"Ellie!" She seemed to be floating, but that couldn't be. Then the enormous waves dropped for an instant and I saw what supported her: a boat.

An impossible boat. For one thing, how had someone gotten it to the water from the garage? But there it was, rocking and rolling in seas a good deal higher than it was built for; the broad-beamed, old wooden Chris-Craft runabout with its bright yellow cushions and mahogany decking was what my husband, Wade, called a lake boat, not meant to take an ocean's pounding.

Ellie motored the handsome old watercraft carefully nearer to the blackened, waterlogged wreckage that had been a dock. It didn't look sturdy enough to tie a boat to.

But I guessed it must have been; the pilings that held it up, anyway, if not the decking surface.

"Bob said they'd had a boat out here, but by now I'd thought it must be long gone," I said.

Ellie was fussing with something on the boat's console. Or dashboard, you'd say if it were a car.

"Um, Ellie?" My voice had returned now that I wasn't swinging precariously over a cliff. Yelling over the sound of wind and waves, I waved my arms around to indicate the watery doom we'd be risking if we did as she apparently planned. "This here is a little freshwater runabout, sixteen-footer, maybe."

From here, it looked even smaller than that. "And the water we're looking at is—"

A big wave churned in; I scampered backward. "—a little *choppy*," I finished.

Ellie just smiled determinedly, her hair frizzy with damp. "A little," she admitted. "But out there it'll be a lot calmer."

"That's what they all say." But even I could see, now, that out beyond the cove the waves were calming down; the wind, too.

"Get in," she said. "Seriously, I can tell this is a great little boat. You'll enjoy it."

They all say that, too. Also, she hadn't yet said how she'd known that the boat might be here.

I was almost as interested in that as I was in whether it would sink, emphasis on the *almost*. Meanwhile, Ellie edged the little vessel nearer to shore.

"Get *in*," she insisted, so finally I did, by the simple method of wading into the waves, crouching down into that ice-cold water as far as I could, then *jumping* up onto the boat's rail, sliding forward, and falling onto the deck.

All of it clumsily, by the way, and I landed on my face. But still, I was in. Also, there were plenty of places to hang on, which was lucky for me since Ellie immediately gunned the engine and we were off.

"Boat's in nice shape," I observed, mostly to keep myself from shouting with fright as she swerved us sharply away from the rocks, then shot us toward deeper water all in one swift, terrifyingly decisive operation.

Still, even I had to admit that it was thrilling in a what-the-hell, moments-before-certain-death way. The engine's snarl filled my ears and gasoline exhaust fumes reeked sweetly before blowing away on the spray the boat threw back at us.

"Woo-hoo!" Ellie exclaimed as we hit calmer water. Now that I wasn't in danger of being bounced overboard at any moment, I found an ancient pair of blue jeans and a moth-eaten sweater in one of the boat's storage bins; after stripping off my wet things, I pulled the musty-smelling but dry clothes on hastily.

Minutes later we'd motored through the whitecapped rough stuff off Buckman's Head, then rounded the red channel marker that told big freighters where to turn when they came into port.

"How'd you get on this thing, anyway?" I asked once I got my breath back.

She shrugged, slowing to maneuver us around some floating driftwood. "It was tied up to one of the dock pilings."

"So you what, scampered out to the dock?" Or what was left of it. A bird landing on it would've collapsed it.

"Yup." She turned to me. "The pilings got creosoted before they got put in; they last nearly forever."

She changed the subject. "Way to go, though, Jake, getting yourself down that cliff."

"Hey, nothing to it," I replied, and she grinned at me, unfooled.

Then she turned to the wheel again, gunning the engine once more for a run straight up the bay toward Eastport, with gulls rising and settling behind our churning wake and the sky above growing steadily lighter. The boat's engine ran pretty well, I thought, with only a few coughs and hiccups now and then; soon we were approaching the Eastport boat basin.

On Sea Street, the fish trucks on shore were lined up and waiting for the morning's catch to come in, while on the water beyond us fishing boats floated in silhouette against the dawn. Leaving them behind, Ellie eased the Chris-Craft between bobbing lobster buoys into the boat basin and then up to the breakwater.

"Ellie?" On Water Street nothing moved; it was too early.

"What?" The engine coughed again; she frowned at it, turned to maneuver us past tugboats tied up at the fish pier, then slipped us between an old wharf's half-fallen ruins and the dock.

"You were great, too," I said.

Her frown turned into a smile as our boat's rail thumped gently against a dock piling. Shakily I hopped out and fastened our lines. Finally, with a turn of the key she'd found, she shut down the engine. Around us, only the faint creak of other vessels rubbing against their piers broke the watery silence.

"But I still can't believe you just did that," I added.

"We did it," she corrected me generously. "You should've seen yourself getting into the boat, though."

"Very funny." But as we climbed the metal gangway up to the breakwater's paved upper deck, I couldn't help feeling a touch of pride at the way I'd handled myself.

By, for instance, not drowning or falling off a cliff.

Half an hour later at my house, I'd already tried calling Bob Arnold, texting him, and driving by his office in search of him, but hadn't found him. Even the dispatcher's help didn't help me; he was, she said over the phone, tied up at an accident on the causeway but had told her he'd be in the office again in half an hour.

And if mine had been an immediately life-threatening call— I mean, the kind where someone's bleeding to death—I'd have asked her to put me through to him right now, but it wasn't; not quite. So instead I tore off the old borrowed clothes I was wearing, showered fast, and pulled on some items that weren't full of moth holes and didn't smell like they'd been in a boat's storage bin for years.

In the kitchen, Wade was eating eggs, bacon, home fries, half a leftover baked apple, and toast. Coffee, too, and a big glass of juice; the elaborate meal meant he was going back on the water, where the refreshments consisted of sardine sandwiches washed down with bottled water, and he didn't like sardines.

"You mean you wanted out of there so badly you stole a boat?" he asked when I'd told him what had happened.

He knew we hadn't stolen it, precisely. But that wasn't the point.

"Wouldn't it have been better to just let Bob Arnold take care of this?" he asked.

Whatever *this* was. "Yes, but he doesn't know about all of it, yet." I reported my Bob-contacting efforts. "I'm going down to talk to him, though. He might even be back by the time I get to his office, and then he'll get right on it, I know he will."

Worry made me babble; I'd been sure I could reach Bob right away. Now on account of my anxiety over Bella and Mika still being out at Cliff House, I'd updated Wade more than I should have, I realized; real worry creased his face.

"Why didn't Bella and Mika just come along home with you?" he wanted to know.

"The, uh, steps down to the cove where the boat was tied up were way too steep for Bella," I replied. "And Mika wouldn't leave without her."

I poured coffee and gulped it. "But, Wade, I got them into this. Now I've got to do what I can to get them out."

His forehead remained creased but his sigh was resigned. "Oh," he said. "Sure. I get that, I guess."

And that's the thing about Wade, see; besides being big, broad-shouldered, and narrow-hipped, with a pale-stubbled jaw and gray-blue eyes whose gaze could knock you into next week—

Besides all that, he catches on fast; he knew there was more to the story. But he didn't press me on it.

"All right, then," he said reluctantly. He wasn't happy about the two who were still stranded, either, and Sam would like their current situation even less when he heard about it.

"You're right," Wade went on, "when Bob hears how bad things are, he'll do whatever he can. So once you've told him, you and Ellie just hang tight here in town while you wait, okay?"

I'm sure that most husbands would've said more; much

more, probably. But the thing was, mine was about to go out on a tugboat, practically out into the open sea, to where a huge freighter waited. He'd climb up an open steel ladder over cold, rolling waves onto the freighter's deck, then pilot her in through many watery hazards to Eastport's freight dock.

So when it came right down to it he didn't have a whole lot to say in the avoiding-danger department, fortunately for me.

He took his dishes to the sink. "In other news, Sam took the kids out to the new house last night," he said. "But your dad wouldn't go. He's still upstairs."

At my look Wade went on. "I tried, but he's a stubborn old coot. Said he'd enjoy the peace and quiet."

Great, I thought, now on top of all the rest I'd have to worry about my father. As I thought this, I heard the water go on upstairs; he was up and washing his face.

"Anyway, a neighbor in Quoddy Village is staying in the new house with the kids, someone Sam already knows out there."

Wade's words stuck blunt daggers in me. I'd been too busy lately to think much about the young family's new home. Still, I'd decided to be a grown-up about it, and I was going to be.

Starting now. "That's a good idea. Help them get used to the place," I managed.

But then: "Oh, Wade, what are we going to do without them?"

Wade came up behind me and wrapped his arms around me, his stubbly face buried in my neck. "We'll figure something out."

A laugh burst from me as I leaned against him. "No doubt."

"Besides, we're not really going to be without them," he said. "Not unless we're waiting for the shower or the washing machine, or I want to watch football instead of cartoons."

He let me go. "I mean it, Jake, it's not going to be so bad. For one thing, I firmly predict they'll all be at our house nearly as much as they were when they lived here."

All true, especially the part about them being here a lot. It was just that when they weren't, I would miss them so much.

"Anyway, I gotta go," Wade said. "Your dad's been fine so far, and the neighbor lady's staying for the day with the kids."

Mika would be glad when she heard all this; Bella not so much. But I could deal with that later. Now with his navy blue watch cap on his head, his duffel bag over his shoulder, and his boots on his feet, Wade was at the back door.

"Just don't do anything too crazy, all right?" he said.

I just smiled as he went out, glad he hadn't seen me on that cliff face, earlier. Or when I was finding Waldo Higgins's murdered body, for that matter.

Then, hoping my dad wouldn't get into too much trouble while enjoying his peace and quiet, I headed back downtown to find Bob Arnold.

Five minutes later, after checking to see that Ellie was still at the dock where I'd left her, doing something that looked urgent to her own boat, I pulled Bella's little sedan into the parking lot outside the Eastport Police Department.

I still felt sure Bob Arnold could help, and that he would; all I'd need to do was let him know. But as I crossed the parking lot toward the low, yellow-brick building that housed his office, I met Sam headed in the same direction.

Wearing jeans, work boots, and a bright red sweatshirt with a navy hoodie over it, he looked nearly as grim as I felt.

"I got a text message." He stuck out his phone.

The text was from Mika. **Get us out!** it read, and then came a notification: connection lost.

I hauled out my own phone; still no bars.

"They're still working on the tower, it's on and off, now," Sam explained. "Mom, what's going on out there? How'd you get back into town?"

"As for what's going on, I'm not sure. I left Mika there with Bella," I told him hastily.

Bob's car was in the parking lot. I turned to start toward the building, stopped as Sam's eyes darkened.

"Sam, she wanted to stay. Why'd you guys stop working on the tree?"

He grimaced, still not happy about Mika remaining at Cliff House. "Chain saw broke. Not big enough for the job. I've got a bigger one on its way. It should be arriving any minute."

But he'd come down here now because of the text message, of course. "What's she mean, Mom? Is something going really wrong out there?"

Drat, the dreaded direct question. Across the street, gulls rose and settled behind fishing boats heading out.

"Sam, it's not great," I admitted. "One of the guests is a little hostile. I'm hoping Bob can get in there, somehow."

Murderousness is hostile, so it wasn't a complete lie.

"Sam, could your guys maybe climb over the tree? Like with ropes, or something?" It was an object, for heaven's sake, even if a very large one.

Sam shook his head. "Tried. No luck. Tree was nearly dead in places, you drop a hook in the bark and chunks pull off."

From the boat basin a staticky bleat came from one of the boats' radios. Whoever was on it didn't sound happy. Also, I noticed that the Coast Guard boats weren't in their berths.

"Heck, there were hardly any roots left under the tree; that's why it went over so easy," said Sam.

Right, of course it would be an uncooperative tree. "All those old evergreens out there, the roots are so shallow and brittle I'm amazed they didn't all go over," he said.

Bob wouldn't be in his office forever. "Sam, I need you to leave all the other problems out there to me, okay? Mika's fine, you just get that tree out of the way so they can all . . ."

I'd been about to say "escape." ". . . get out of there," I said instead. "Now, I'm going to talk with Bob. He'll do what needs doing, you know he will."

Sam did know. But it was his wife we were talking about, and he didn't have Wade's all-in-a-day's-work attitude toward danger.

I walked Sam toward his pickup truck. "I'm sorry I got Mika into this job, though," I said, and that got a laugh out of him.

"Are you kidding? Have you ever tried keeping her out of anything she wanted to do? When she heard there'd be money in it to put toward our moving fund, wild horses couldn't have—"

"Okay. I get it," I said. "Let me go talk to Bob."

He gave in reluctantly, still wanting to go with me. "Yeah, okay. I'll go see if I can expedite that chain saw, then."

Minutes later Eastport's police chief, Bob Arnold, eyed me skeptically from behind his desk, an old gray metal number that probably dated from back when cop cars had stick shifts.

"You're sure about all this, are you?" he asked.

"Yes." I'd already summarized recent events at Cliff House for him, putting in a great deal more than I'd told my son.

The murders, for instance. "That's why I need you to help get Mika and Bella out of there," I added; I'd have said more but just then Sam came up behind me.

Correction: that's when I noticed him. From the look on his face, though, I knew he'd been outside Bob's office, listening.

And gosh, he was mad. "Came in to use the phone," he told me, holding up his cell. "These are out completely again."

Then, "Bob," he said, "you know Wade's got a lot of guns in the house."

Because Wade restored and repaired them, Sam meant, and collected high-quality weapons, too, many of them in excellent working condition. Due to Sam's kids living there, our house had more locks than the Panama Canal.

"And," Sam said to Bob, "I've got friends who know how to use them."

The guns, he meant. I felt my face go still; I hadn't even thought of taking a weapon with me.

But of course that was back when I thought Bob would be

handling this right away. Now his round, pink face flushed even pinker than usual. "Look, Sam, you can't just—"

"No, of course I can't," said Sam very reasonably. "For one thing, they're locked up and Wade has the only key. And I don't want to, either. That's why I want you to go out there right now and get Mika, Bella, and the rest of them out of that place."

I'd never heard him talk this way before: quiet, forceful. He really was an actual grown man now.

"It's also why you're going to believe my mother," he went on, "and not just ignore whatever's going on—"

He was still mad that I hadn't told him everything, but he was on my side, I could feel it.

"—just because it's hard to get at," he finished, then stood waiting for an answer, not backing off.

Bob sighed heavily. He believed what I'd told him, I knew that. He just couldn't summon anyone do much about it right this minute, and he couldn't go out there to do it himself, either.

I mean, if the young, fit guys on Sam's crew couldn't get over that tree trunk, Bob, with his shoulders that were narrower than his middle and his legs that were a little too short for his body, surely wouldn't be able to.

"Bob, can't the Coast Guard get out to the cliff area by boat?" I asked.

He shook his head. "They're all still out on calls for assistance on the water. Plenty of folks didn't expect such heavy weather last night."

Yeah, me among them. "And it's worse inland," he said. "We just caught the edge of the squall here, but they've got several big landslides on the mainland. Soil got loosened by that little quake yesterday, the rain muddied it up, and the dirt just took off downhill, buried a few houses, I hear."

Ouch. "Over there," Bob went on at my expression,

"they've got trees down, roofs half off, and the state cops've got their hands full with what's left on the roadway from wrecks on Route 9 last night. Couple people still trapped, I heard."

All of which meant we were far down the list of who would get help soon. At least we weren't trapped in a wrecked car, but this wasn't going at all the way I'd hoped.

I got up from the chair facing Bob Arnold's desk. "Power's still out in places," he finished, walking with me to the door. "I don't know when I've seen so many problems from one little squall, never even got forecast."

Sam came out into the building's lobby, too, his look disbelieving; like me, he'd been sure Bob would jump to our assistance.

"And there's nowhere to land a helicopter out there on that skinny little peninsula. But listen," Bob went on as we stepped outside, "I'm gonna call this guy I know, he works on a logging crew up north. He's got big tree machines."

To cut them down with, Bob meant. That this one lay flat already would make no difference to a logger.

"Just let me run home, get his number, the guy'll turn that tree to toothpicks," Bob finished.

"Great," Sam said, appeased for the moment; it was the best Bob could do.

"Tell him to get here as soon as he can, okay?" Sam said. "Right now I'm going back out there, myself."

He made a beeline for his truck. As I watched him go, a new thought hit me. "Bob, remember how you told me about that boat your dad said was out there?"

He got into his squad car, dug around in the console bin, and came up with something.

"Funny you should mention that. I was going through the notebook you saved out of the Quoddy Village house and found this."

He held out an aging black-and-white photograph. In it two men and a boy stood by a boat, the same little Chris-Craft that I'd just been in.

"They wintered it in the garage on a trailer," Bob said. "Had a dock built, too, so the Hollywood guy could go out for joy-rides."

"I've seen," I responded dryly, "the dock."

He didn't notice my tone as he resettled himself behind the car's steering wheel and tucked the snapshot away.

"But never mind my old memories, you and Ellie just wait here in town till I get the tree guy out there, okay?"

"Okay. We won't do anything without letting you know," I told him.

But I was crossing my fingers when I said it.

Eight

I wanted to go back to Cliff House about as much as I wanted an emergency root canal. But an hour later Ellie and I were on her boat, readying to do just that.

"So I guess we've really got to go," I grumbled. Anger felt better than the fright I was suppressing; this had not been in my plans.

Ellie had gone home to make sure everything was shipshape there, and it was; her daughter, Lee, was on a school trip and her husband, George, was working on a construction job in Bangor this week.

"You want to try telling Bella and Mika why we didn't come back?" she asked. "The idea was that Bob Arnold and however many cops he could find to bring along would be there soon, not that they'd be waiting all alone until whenever."

Clouds had pulled in once more, and without sunshine the dock area was as cold as a meat locker. Windy again, too.

"So, do you want to explain that to them?" Ellie asked again as she peered into the boat's oil reservoir.

"No," I said, shivering. But mostly I didn't want to try telling myself.

Ellie took the lines of her twenty-two-foot Bayliner off their cleats, leaving the Chris-Craft we'd pilfered from Cliff House tied up. For the trip back she wanted her own bigger, much more seaworthy vessel, with her own gear and instruments on it.

Emergency equipment, too. Flares, a signal horn, first aid stuff, tools, plus lots of towels and spare clothes in case of dunking incidents like the one I'd had earlier, all were neatly stowed in cubbies, bins, and compartments on the vessel.

The boat also had a big outboard engine with enough power to get out of any little hazards — riptides, rogue currents, whirlpools bent on sucking us straight down to the bowels of hell — that the water might try hurling at us.

"Everything okay at your place?" she asked as she tossed me a life jacket and put on her own.

"Yep. For the moment." My dad was a grown man, I assured myself again. As he'd insisted again when I'd returned to the house, he could handle a day alone.

"Good." She turned on the boat's battery, radio, GPS, and depth finder. She checked the oil and gas levels, trimmed the engine so the propeller eased all the way down into the water, and gave the black rubber fuel bulb a squeeze.

Then she returned to the helm and turned the ignition key. Nothing happened.

"No, no," she murmured, turning it again.

Same like before. "Okay," she uttered, returning to the boat's stern. "Give me a hand here, will you?"

We muscled the heavy cover off the big outboard engine and set it down on the deck. Ellie bent, scrutinizing the many wires, tubes, hoses, levers, belts, and other assorted parts of the outboard's insides.

"Darn." She stuck her hand in there, came out with her thumb and index finger pinching the stem of something.

Or . . . wait a minute, that wasn't a stem. It was the tail of something.

And the something was a dead rat. A few of the animals

dwelled in the rocks along the breakwater, playing hide-and-seek with the feral cats who also lived there.

Ellie pronounced a few words and short, pithy phrases that I won't repeat here, then flung the horrid thing over the stern into the water.

"Well, that's that." She sat back on her heels. "He got in when I had the cover off all day last Saturday, I imagine."

She'd changed some filters and a couple of fuel lines and foamed the whole engine down with some spray stuff that kept it dry.

"But now that he's out, we can go? It'll start now?" The closer I got to being back out at Cliff House, the more my worry about what I might find there increased.

"Nope." She held up a length of black tubing with ragged holes in it. "See this? The rat chewed it. We need a new one."

I took her word for this. "So? It's half a block to the marine store. Let's go get some."

"We will. In"—she checked her watch—"an hour and a half. They open later in the off-season, remember?"

Now I did. "You don't have a substitute we could use?"

She shook her head. "If it failed, we'd lose power and we wouldn't be able to steer."

Because boats don't turn in place, you see; you have to be moving to maneuver. "Why not take the other boat, the one we came here from Cliff House in?"

She looked up. "Because you know those little coughs and hesitations the engine on that boat was producing?"

Uh-oh.

"I've heard those before," she said, "and they mean that there's trouble somewhere. And I do not want to stall out on the water."

Yeah, me neither. But by now anxious impatience was making my heart pound and my throat feel tight. Maybe we should have tried getting Bella down that cliff. . . .

"Why don't you go back to your house?" Ellie added. "Once I get the hose, it'll only take ten minutes."

I grabbed my bag, with Bella's car keys in it. "Okay. I'll see you in a couple of hours, then," I said, and left her poking around in the engine's guts some more.

But I didn't go home. I was so nervous about Bella and Mika, I felt like a little bird was fluttering in my chest; the two of them weren't completely helpless, but still, no way could I just sit and wait when who knew what might be happening out there.

Besides, the rule about boat-turning applied to people, too, I thought.

You have to be moving if you want to maneuver.

So I did. Move, that is, and for once I knew just where I was going.

The house was a small, ranch-type affair at the end of a short driveway on Paul Street, a little side road that ran along the edge of Carryingplace Cove out beyond the airport.

Outside, the picket-fenced yard was ablaze with autumn flowers and fruit: echinacea, rose hips, lavender, burdock.

I opened the gate and stepped onto an old brick walkway laid out in the simple jack-on-jack pattern. On the back porch door of the small, shingle-sided cottage a sign said RING AND COME IN.

The bell didn't work but I went in anyway. Inside, dozens of blue glass pharmacy bottles with clear glass stoppers stood on unpainted pine plank shelves in the neat, bright kitchen.

The bottles bore handwritten labels inked in a clear hand: HOREHOUND, TANSY, WILLOW BARK.

Then Nanny Jackson bustled in, her white hair coiled in a coronet atop her head and her face suntanned

"Sit down, dear," she said, bustling around to clear a place at the plywood sheet on a quartet of sawhorses that she used as a table.

After what Ellie had said about Nanny Jackson's dislike of visitors, I wasn't expecting a welcome. Customers were another matter, though, apparently, and it seemed she thought I was one.

"You've arrived at the perfect moment," she said. She picked up a kitchen chair cushion, shook a small blizzard of dry leaf fragments and other items from it, then set it down again and waved me into the chair it belonged to.

Bills, a mortar and pestle, and a yellow cat who'd been aiming for the cushion were all swept aside; only the cat came back, settling in my lap.

"Now before you start on whatever you've come for, what do you think of this?" said the old herbalist, her gold-rimmed glasses perched halfway down her long, thin nose.

She set a steaming mug in front of me. The contents smelled amazing, like new green leaves on the first warm day in spring.

I sipped, considered, sipped again. "Licorice?" I guessed. "And what, coriander?"

She beamed. "Close enough. Tell me if you taste anything else, later. Or anything else you notice."

I set the mug down. "All right." I could taste-test for her, I supposed, though that "anything else you notice" part sounded a little ominous.

"But I'm not here for any remedies," I added.

Ointment jars, small corked vials, and baskets of sachets made from floral-printed cotton filled even more of the open-fronted kitchen shelves.

"I see." Nanny's bright, brown eyes regarded me calmly. They looked to me as if they'd seen plenty over the years, and from the reputation she had as a concocter of romance-related tinctures, especially, I thought they probably had.

"Why don't you tell me what the trouble is, then?" she invited, though I hadn't told her about any trouble.

In her long-sleeved plaid shirt, blue bib overalls, and a pair of bright yellow rubber clogs on her feet, she was an unlikely looking confidante. But the tea was so delightful, I took another sip, then looked up into her gently inquiring face.

"Go on," she invited. Her twinkling eyes reminded me of Glinda, the good witch from *The Wizard of Oz*.

A third sip, larger. Then: "Murder," I said unhappily. "Three so far." I was pretty sure Gilly was dead along with Waldo and Audrey, even though we hadn't found Gilly's body.

"And I don't know who's telling the truth," I added.

Her thin, white eyebrows arched amusedly. "Ah, yes, that's a common problem. Not the murders, so much."

She spooned some cat food onto a saucer on the floor. The cat sprang down for it.

"But the truth," she finished. "So, what did someone tell you that you think I might be able to confirm?"

The tea really was delicious once you got used to it. "Or," she added, "that I might contradict?"

The cat finished its food and meowed for more, twining around my legs. Outside, the flowers bobbed brilliantly.

But of course they weren't singing. I looked down into the teacup, which had somehow gotten empty.

"I want to know whether the movie star, Ingrid Merryfield, is from Eastport or not. I don't know if that's her real name, or if she uses a screen name, but if she is from here I thought you might know."

"Hmm." The eyebrows went up. "Merryfield . . . now where did I see something about . . ."

She fetched a thick book from one of the shelves not devoted to books about herbal preparations. When she opened it the sweet smell of lavender rose up from the pages.

". . . Minton, Minor . . . here it is, Merryfield."

She put a stained finger on the entry, which contained only the last name plus some letters and numbers.

"I keep a master book that says where each chart is," she said. "Born, married, children, their children . . . after a while a person can end up in a lot of family trees."

I nodded, opening my mouth to speak. But it seemed that my lips had gone numb, so I didn't. That tea, I thought.

"Here," said the elderly genealogist, turning a page in the book. "Martin, Marian, Micah, Michael . . . no Ingrid. Or Margaret, either."

She looked up. "These entries date back to the 1890s, and end in 1910," she said, closing the book.

"Nothing since; they might've all either died or moved away," the elderly herbalist added.

"Oh dear." I let a breath out, not disappointed, exactly, but a good deal more concerned than I'd been before.

It was a sort of *suspicions confirmed* feeling, reinforcing the general sense I'd had for a while now, that everyone—or almost everyone—at Cliff House had been lying to me.

"So there's nothing else about the Merryfields anywhere in Eastport? Old tax records, maybe an idea of where they went?"

The cat jumped back into my lap and began kneading my leg, pricking me with its sharp claws. But the small stabs didn't hurt; I blinked curiously at the animal.

"Nowhere but the cemetery," said Nanny Jackson, "and I don't know that for sure. I mean to note down where everyone's graves are, someday."

She waved the book. It probably had five hundred pages in it. "But it's a big job. Somebody younger should take it on."

She held the book out to me; I drew back, I hoped not with the amount of dismay I felt.

"Uh, no." I stood up. The room seemed to get larger and smaller, suddenly. It wasn't a bad sensation, just unfamiliar.

"Why don't you go splash your face with warm water?" she asked kindly, seeing my . . . well, not distress, exactly.

More like curiosity, or something. She waved at the narrow hall leading off the kitchen. "Use some of the geranium soap I made," she added. "You'll enjoy it."

Right, like that tea. Down the hall to the right I found the bathroom, neat and shiny and smelling not of herbs but of Comet cleanser.

Drink this, I groused mentally as water filled my cupped hands. When it hit my face it felt like spring rain pattering gently, and that couldn't be right, either, could it?

Still, it wasn't bad, exactly. I rinsed cat hair from my hands, then thought I might as well try the soap. As cheerful as I felt all of a sudden, by then I might've tried hang-gliding.

The small oval bar lathered richly; the pungent, energizing scent of crushed geranium leaves filled my head.

Or maybe it wasn't the soap that made me feel taller. And smarter. I wondered if she'd sell me some of the tea.

But then again, maybe that wasn't a good idea. Back in the kitchen, I got my bag and prepared to leave. Nanny Jackson was at the linoleum-topped kitchen counter, crushing something with the mortar and pestle.

"I have to go now. Thanks so much," I told her. But at the door I paused, struck by another question.

"Is there a way to find out where people's graves are?" I asked. "Without walking around to search them out, I mean."

"Oh, yes. You can talk to Pip Collins, he's in charge of the cemetery. And," she said approvingly, "he keeps a list."

She eyed me closely. "Feeling better, are you?"

The cat twined around my ankles. The flowers bobbed their heads. Above them, clouds tumbled over one another.

"I feel like a million bucks," I answered honestly. "What's in that tea, anyway?"

I figured it had to be illegal, since it made me feel so good. But: "Ginger, ginseng, parsley, rhubarb," she recited.

Uh-huh. And some secret ingredient, too, I was willing to bet. But let her have her secrets, I thought; I got the feeling she'd earned them, one way or another.

"Tell you what, if I sprout wings and fly I'll let you know," I said.

Then we laughed, the wrinkled old herbalist looking nearly as satisfied with her experiment as I was, and I departed, not the least bit unhappy at being the subject of the test.

But once I got into the car I wondered if maybe I shouldn't drive. Luckily just then Ellie strode up the street toward me, looking as if she was trying to walk off a lot of frustration.

"What?" I said, getting out from behind the steering wheel. "Why aren't you with the boat?"

By now at least an hour had passed here, somehow; that tea, I thought, could make even dentist visits go by faster.

It could set a kaleidoscopic swirl of bright, iridescent colors pinwheeling around behind my eyes, too. "You drive," I told Ellie, heading around to the car's passenger side.

She got in, took the key, and started it up. "So she just let you in? And talked to you?"

"I think I showed up just when she needed a test subject," I said as we drove away from Nanny's house. "Or maybe she thought I was a customer?"

If she sold what she'd given me, she'd have plenty of them.

I wondered if she did sell it, or if she only tried it on women who looked as if they really needed it.

Like me. "But she told me something interesting." I relayed Nanny Jackson's report on Merryfields in her records: nada.

"But why would Ingrid lie about it?" I wondered, not for the first time. "All she wanted was to hire dessert makers."

"If that's all she wanted," Ellie pointed out. "Because you're right, I don't see the benefit of lying about being from here un-less she had some other reason. What, I can't imagine."

She changed the subject. "Anyway, the hose size I need is al-ready on order at the marine store. I just went over there and they say it'll be here some time this morning, assuming the warehouse people remembered to put it on the truck."

In the distance, the clock on the old Presbyterian church struck nine. "Good, then we've got time for one more visit."

Ellie glanced at me. "Are you all right? I thought you were anxious to get back to Cliff House, to make sure Bella and Mika are okay."

She was correct; I just hadn't wanted to do it by boat. At the moment, however, I was pretty sure I could've just walked on the water.

"I'm fine," I said. All kinds of fine, actually, though the showier effects of Nanny Jackson's astonishing tea were start-ing to fade.

"And I do still want to get back. But we can't, yet."

The yards on Paul Street sported beehives, henhouses, and here and there an electric fence to keep the goats inside from wandering. Or the llamas; it was an interesting neighborhood.

"So we might as well keep busy," I finished.

Ellie kept her eyes on the road. "Which means what?"

In answer I reached over to flip the turn signal on. Paul Street dead-ended a block before it reached the cemetery. But Quarry Street didn't.

"Now," I said as we turned onto it, then passed a low, white shed whose hand-painted sign read MONUMENT ENGRAVING. Slabs of granite leaned against the shed, ready for the dearly de-parted's names and dates to be cut into them.

"Now," I said, "we're going to visit a gravedigger."

Pip Collins wasn't as famously antisocial as Nanny, but he was in a foul mood.

"Just look," he spat, waving at the hilly green expanse with the rows and rows of gravestones sticking up out of it.

Deep ruts savaged the neatly kept grass between the rows, long muddy trenches cut recently by, it looked like, a brigade of all-terrain vehicles.

Although probably it was only two. "Little bastids," Pip Collins grated out, stomping back over the cemetery office's gravel parking area to his work shack.

He had to be seventy years old at least, with his thin white hair, leathery face, and a pair of hearing aids in his ears. But in a denim jacket and jeans and with battered brown work boots on his feet, from behind he could've been fifty.

He went inside. Didn't come back out. After an uncertain moment we got out of the car and went into the shack, too.

"Mr. Collins?" I called. Inside, a woodstove made from a metal barrel and corrugated stovepipe sections crackled pleasantly.

"Hello?" Ellie ventured. A calendar hung from a nail in the plywood wall, which had been painted baby blue. On the battered old wooden desk, which looked to have been salvaged from a retired high school principal's office somewhere, another, larger calendar was neatly annotated.

He appeared from the shadows at the rear of the shack, where filing cabinets stood in rows. "What?"

Ellie stepped forward. "We'd just like some directions. There was a Merryfield family who lived here in Eastport a long time ago. Could you look up where they're buried, please?"

On our way up Quarry Street, I'd given Ellie the short version of why I thought we'd better check this out. Now:

"If there's a family plot, it would be in the old section," I blurted, and Pip Collins gave me a look that should've turned me to cinders.

"Oh, ye think so, do ye? Guess you're the sharpest hook in the tackle box, come up with a thing like that."

He stomped back to his desk, picked up an envelope, and flung it down again.

"Mr. Collins, if you could just look up the—"

"Don't need to look it up," he cut me off sharply. By now, the cinders would've been dust.

In the stove, a pocket of moisture buried deep in a stick of firewood exploded with a *pop!* I flinched and he noticed.

"Kinda jumpy, there, ain't you, girly?" He didn't look a bit sorry about this, and by now I'd had enough.

Also, I hate being called girly. "Look, if you don't want to find out for us where—"

"Didn't say that. Said I didn't have to."

He pulled a pipe out of a desk drawer, drew experimentally on it, and lit it. Rank smoke spiraled from the bowl and exited his mouth on either side of the stem.

"Just went out there a month ago, someone asked me the same thing," Pip Collins said. "So I already know. Could show you."

He drew on the pipe again. "But right now I'm on my coffee break."

He waved at the desk where a paper cup of coffee and a doughnut I recognized as being from the deli at the IGA waited.

"Half hour, this morning, 'cause I worked overtime a couple days ago," he said, and would not be budged from this even when Ellie implored him as prettily as she could.

Which, this being Ellie, was very prettily indeed: long-lashed violet eyes, wavy hair, smiling lips, etcetera.

Not to mention a manner so charming, it could tame a snake. But still no luck. Another *pop!* came from the stove; his eyes crinkled amusedly over his coffee container when I jumped again.

And that's when I got the brainstorm; that tea, maybe, had jostled it loose. "My son could fix those ruts for you."

He waved his pipe dismissively. "Yeah, sure he could. What, a kid with a rake? Take him a year."

"No, a man with a landscaping company. He'll drag the ruts flat, fill what's left with loam, seed it, feed it, and water it until it's established."

That was Sam's usual routine for a large lawn repair job, I happened to know. Hearing it, Pip narrowed his eyes.

"How much?" he demanded.

"Got a budget for it?" I countered. "From the city? Okay, then, he'll charge what they say you can spend for the project."

I felt comfortable promising this because I'd make up the difference myself if I had to. And when he still hesitated, Ellie chimed in, noting that her husband might also be able to help with a few things.

Getting that homemade woodstove up onto a pad of bricks, for instance, so if the bottom dropped out the fiery materials inside wouldn't burn right through the floor, and riveting the stovepipe pieces together, too.

By then Pip was looking at us both like we'd floated down on a pearl-pink cloud. "Let's have a look at that site," he said, upending his pipe bowl over an old china shaving mug he apparently kept for that purpose.

"See," I told Ellie as we followed Pip across the graveyard under gnarled maple trees and along worn, grassy lanes made for smaller automobiles than today's.

Black cast-iron fences with spiked tops surrounded a few old graves; passing them, I wondered whether the spikes were to keep the living out or make sure the dead stayed in.

"See, when you want something from someone, like for instance that they should just drop everything else and help you," I babbled, "I just think it's a good idea to—"

"Here it is," said Pip.

The gravestone, among a surviving sprinkle of others way out here in the cemetery's oldest section, was an ancient white marble slab with names cut into it in script. Father and Mother, it proclaimed, and under that a long list of children.

"Used to be some other Merryfields in Quoddy Village," Pip said, "but they're long gone. Don't know if they were related to these ones. None of 'em buried here, though, I know that."

I knelt by the stone. The letters incised in the marble were worn, with edges softened to near-illegible shallowness. But I could read enough to make out the name of the third child born to the original Merryfields nearly two centuries earlier.

"Inga," I said, reading the last name on the list of the Merryfields' unfortunate children. The infant's dates said she'd been two days old; possibly her life hadn't lasted even long enough for her to make it into Nanny Jackson's genealogy book.

I got up. "So someone else asked about this recently?"

"Ayuh." Pip stuck his hands in his jeans pockets. "I don't know who, it was my day off. Some kid the city hired was here filling in, but he didn't stick around long. Pal of his showed up, they lit out for California, what I heard."

He pulled his cold pipe from the breast pocket of his blue work shirt, put it back disappointed.

"Sorry you didn't find what you was lookin' for," he said, not realizing that I had.

"That's okay, Mr. Collins," I said. "Thanks a lot. Here's my card, you call me and I'll put you in touch with my son."

Pip looked doubtful. "This here's for a bakery."

He waved the card with our shop's chocolate moose depicted on it, googly eyes and all.

"Don't worry," Ellie reassured him. "Jake's son, Sam, will take care of you, and my husband, George, too. And if you ever want something better than a doughnut to go with your coffee, come and see us."

Now Pip was nodding. "Wait a minute, Sam Tiptree?"

His look brightened. My son's good reputation had pre-

ceded me, apparently; a little fireworks flare of happiness for
what he'd made of himself burst pleasantly in my heart.

"Well, all right, then," said Pip. "I hope you girls find what
you're looking for," he told us again.

Like I say, though, as far as I was concerned, we already had.
Or part of it, anyway.

Back at the boat dock, Ellie shoved the new length of hose
onto the engine. "You think Ingrid stole that baby's name?"

"Maybe. For now I just wanted to know if it was possible."

That despite her denial, at the start of her career Ingrid Merryfield had indeed taken a stage name from an old Eastport grave
marker, I meant.

Now I knew it could've happened. Still, why would she do
it? People stole dead infants' names to make fake IDs, I knew,
but not years in advance.

Mulling this, I helped Ellie get the engine cover back on and
latched.

"If she wanted to say she was from here and didn't want to
be contradicted," I began, and stopped.

She'd pick a family with a history here, but no living members, I'd have added, only that didn't make sense, either, because how would she know?

So the whole line of thought was a vicious circle and for now
I set it aside, turning instead to thoughts of our imminent journey: Life jacket, check. Iron grip on the rail, check.

Sincere act of contrition in case all other efforts failed, check.
I settled into the mate's chair and hung on as the engine va-
roomed to life and we backed away from the dock.

"Ellie," I said when we got out of the boat basin and away
from shore, "it's windier in this direction."

Spray flew, punched by gusts blowing out of the south. On
the way here those gusts had been at our back, a more conve-
nient arrangement. I leaned against the hatchway door, notic-

ing that the little screws holding the hinges up were loose; I made a mental note to tell Ellie about them.

"No kidding!" she called, taking an oblique angle toward the waves marching over the water. Soon we were speeding through the chop, thump-thump-thump; then she pushed the throttle, and we were skimming over it.

Ellie spotted a lobster buoy, veered around it. I hung on, plastering a smile to my face. But if people were meant to go bopping around in boats they'd have lungs on the outside for use as flotation devices, is my opinion on the matter.

Then: *Thunk!* I sat up fast at the sound and the feeling of having hit something semisolid.

"Easy does it," said Ellie calmly, idling the engine and stepping away from the helm. "Take the wheel."

"Do what?" Deep blue water stretched a mile on both sides of us, with Eastport resembling a toy town in the distance to our west and the Canadian island of Campobello lying east.

Ellie gave me a little nudge as she went by. "The wheel. Hold on to it. Don't run us onto rocks."

I'd have done that very thing if it got us to dry land any sooner. But Ellie had just had the boat's bottom redone, and the antifouling paint was so pricy, it could've been gold leaf.

Again, *thunk!* "We're bumping something," I said nervously.

Ellie stepped out onto the foredeck, leaned over the rail and with a big barb-tipped grappling hook caught hold of something that looked way too much like a body.

Not that I'd ever seen one just floating like this before. She hauled on the hook, drawing whatever it was back toward the rear deck, then muscled one end of it up over the rail.

Sagging, dripping . . . Suddenly it hit me that she really had pulled up a body. After laboriously hauling it inch by inch into the boat, she crouched by it, pulling seaweed from its face.

"Oh," she breathed unhappily, and let the kelp fall before I got too good a look. But there were a lot of sharp rocks at the bottom of that water, and from what I glimpsed it looked as if poor Gilly Blaine had hit most of them in his watery journey from the cove at Cliff House all the way out here into the bay.

Silently she rolled the body into a tarp and lashed the tarp to the rail. It looked much easier to roll than it had been to lift. Finally, she picked up fallen bits of shredded clothes up off the deck and tossed them into a bucket.

"Another twenty-four hours and he'd have had no clothes at all," she said.

"Or skin," I added. The poor guy's face was nearly unrecognizable already.

After that we continued our voyage in silence with Ellie back at the helm. Soon we were rounding the channel markers toward Buckman's Head again. Under a sky full of clouds once more threatening to rain, Cliff House perched darkly on its high bluff.

Ellie cut the engine as we approached the cove. The tide was only halfway out, which left enough depth to float in on, so she let our momentum carry us parallel to the broken-down dock.

Whereupon the ocean, being a sneaky bastard, flung a wave that washed us away again. But Ellie just waited for the next surge to wash us back, then threw the bowline at a blackened dock piling and nailed it.

"Hope that piling's not as rotted as it looks," I said as we clambered out of the boat. As she'd promised, the dock's gray, splintery decking supported me better than I expected.

Or at least I didn't fall through it, turning instead to survey the looming cliff. Something seemed different about it.

"Ellie?" We'd been paying attention to the wind, the water, and the granite ridges sticking up like dragons' teeth at the cove's entrance.

"Ellie," I said, "just look, and tell me if I'm—"

But she was still busy. I squinted again. Maybe the cliff just looked different from below. Certainly the sharp granite outcropping halfway up it didn't show itself the same way. But as far as I could tell, something had changed.

Something important. "Ellie? Um, Ellie, listen, I hate to say this but I think the steps that were here before are gone. The ones that we—"

Not just damaged. Gone. She got up from wrapping the bowline more securely after checking the dock piling's solidness by leaning on it, herself, which I thought took nerve.

Then she stood straight and dusted her hands together.

"Oh, come on," she breathed in annoyance as she stared at the cliff face where the steps had been. "How'd that happen, d'you think?"

"They were pretty rickety." I spotted the pieces of wood floating in the water. "Maybe a big wave?"

Heck, the way those steps had felt when I was on them, a bird's wing could've done it.

"Yeah, no." She stomped across the narrow beach, exposed now by the falling tide.

"Or, you know," I went on less happily, "I guess someone could've given the thing a hard shove."

Ellie scanned the beach. "Or a pull," she said, bending to retrieve a length of what looked like ordinary clothesline.

But it wasn't. "Ellie, that's strapping cord."

Sam used it to lash tools and landscaping equipment to his flatbed; light and flexible, it had an inner core of some high-tech synthetic as strong as steel.

You could buy it at the hardware store, I happened to know, and from the shreds of a familiar orange label still stuck onto this length of the stuff, it seemed that someone had.

"Wonder how it got here," Ellie said thoughtfully.

"Me too," I said, not liking the theory I was coming up with.

Behind us the wind off the bay puffed and gusted, nudging

me this way and that. A tide pool held ice-cold water that rose past my ankle.

Ellie thought the same. "Someone knew we got down here and how we did it, too."

"Yep." And they'd wanted to block our possible return. A good hard yank with a stout rope . . . "How'd they get back up?"

From where I stood, there were two possible routes, one of them vertical and without any steps to climb, and thus unusable. That left bushwhacking straight in off the beach through muck, sawgrass, half-rotted seaweed, and enough round, smooth rocks all slimy with algae to guarantee a skull fracture.

We'd still have to climb, of course; we were down here and the house was still up there. Also, we didn't know the way. But at least it wouldn't be straight up a cliff.

I hoped. "And if they knew we were gone," I said, "that means somebody was keeping an eye on us."

"Maybe," said Ellie, frowning at the beach and shoreline some more. Really, there wasn't much traversable landscape at all, only a few hundred feet of rock-strewn stones and sand.

The rest was kelp fields, uncrossable except on hands and knees. Kelp looks walkable, but it's as slick as ice.

Ellie strode thoughtfully away from me for a dozen yards, picking her way cautiously, then came back with her face saying that we were in trouble, and it was worse than I'd thought.

"You can get inland from this beach," she reported, "if you don't mind getting your feet wet. But past that there's a whole lot more swampy stuff and I can't tell how deep it might be."

She guided me back and pointed at the patch of black water, rotten stumps, masses of dark green vegetation, and many other decaying organic materials.

"And I have no idea what's behind that," she said.

I hate decaying organic materials, especially when I am up to my hips in them. Not only that, but the water's depth was a critical issue, also; once we ventured into the sullen-looking swamp there was nothing to stop it from pulling us down into itself, then closing over our heads.

Or we could climb straight up the cliff. I did not think I'd be doing this, however, despite all the times I'd seen it demonstrated in animated cartoons; even Ellie looked doubtful.

So we just stood thinking, hands stuffed in our pockets, while piping plovers with black beaks like sunflower seeds and scrawny orange legs trotted around, hunting for brunch items.

I pulled my cell phone out; still no bars. Then as the waves' foamy edges rolled nearer, Ellie looked more concerned.

Much nearer, actually; diurnal tides like the ones we had here in Eastport—two highs and two lows per twenty-four hours—move really fast.

"We should get off this beach," she said.

The boat was still right there, tied to a piling that at close range had in fact seemed reasonably sturdy despite its age. "Should we just get back in?" I suggested.

Ellie's assessment was correct; once the tide rose all the way, where we stood now would be submerged once more. She shook her head.

"We don't have time," she repeated, turning in frustration "We need to get up there, make sure Mika and Bella are okay, and then keep them that way until we can get them out."

Suddenly the urgency of what we were doing—not to mention the prospect of drowning if we didn't get out of this soon-to-be-underwater spot real soon—came over me again.

"Okay," I said, not wanting to think about the rotten tree stumps, decomposing creatures, and who knew what else was oozing into the black water in that swamp.

So I didn't. Think about them, that is. But I was still going to have to wade through them. As if to encourage me, Ellie lifted her chin, straightened her spine, and took a step.

I followed. Each time a wave rolled in, water covered the little beach stones we walked on, until soon they were entirely submerged and so were our sneakers. Leaving the water's edge to shove our way through stands of clumped grasses, we slogged our way toward what I knew was going to be an even worse misery.

"So you think past the bog we'll find a way up?" The trunk of a half-fallen willow tree blocked our way, suddenly, its thickly massed branches concealing the route ahead.

"There's got to be one," Ellie replied over her shoulder. "It's not just empty air between here and up there."

How steep was whatever did fill the between-space was my big question. Like, a climbable hill or another precipice?

We elbowed our way through the willow branches. Ahead, dark stagnant pools stretched. "I hope . . ." she began.

"We'll find out," I replied, not wanting to be a baby about this in front of Ellie.

Charging forward, I tried not to think about what sort of creatures might be living in the swamp, and whether or not they were hungry. Also, I tried not to notice that swamp rocks aren't all slimy; some feel like sharks' teeth trying to bite through the bottom of your shoe, and—

"Yearrgghh!" I said shudderingly as something clamped onto my sneaker.

"Ellie?" It wouldn't let go, and being grabbed by something lurking under the water was so ghastly, I could've flown across that swamp if only my foot would've come loose.

Which it wouldn't. Ellie planted her own feet and crouched, prying at whatever trapped me. "Lean on me," she instructed me finally. "Now give it a yank."

So I did. My shoe popped up with a mucky-sounding *blurp!* The gnarly root snag it was stuck in came up with it.

"Gah," I said, pulling the root mass off and flinging it away from me. Then I stepped forward again and promptly sank to my waist in the cold, unpleasant-smelling water.

Worse, my foot wasn't touching the bottom. "Ellie!" I cried as my whole right leg just kept sinking and sinking.

"All right, now," I heard Ellie tell the swamp sternly as she grabbed me. "I think we've had just about enough of this."

I doubted that the swamp was listening; if it was, we had a whole new problem. But it was nice to have somebody defending me as she dragged me out of the hole.

Horrid bubbles of some awful gas that smelled positively revolting glurped up from the depths and burst. Covering my face with one arm to block the stench, I felt my way blindly farther into the swamp with the other.

Not that I could've seen the even deeper hole just ahead of me, in any case. But it was there.

"Jake!" I heard Ellie through the stinking water. Frond-like things fondled my face and something else tried to go up my sleeve; also, there was the whole can't-breathe-water situation to deal with.

Because as it turns out, a life jacket won't float you if you've unfastened the darned thing, which I'd done somewhere along the line so I could move more freely. Instead, it slides up and floats all by itself, while you don't.

I couldn't even tell which way was up, and I dared not open my eyes to try orienting myself; *see frond-like things*, above.

Something long and thin found my armpit and poked me a few times, but I was too focused on my own growing oxygen deficit to pay it any attention. *Okay, now, if up into fresh air isn't that way or that way, then it's really got to be—*

"Jake!" Something grabbed my hair from above and pulled hard. First the hair and then my whole head came up into the air. The shiveringly, teeth-chatteringly cold air . . .

But I was pretty sure it had oxygen in it so I sucked some of it in. "Th-th-thanks," I managed, too chilled to say more.

Only about twenty yards more of mucky water remained to cross, but any minute I expected to see Swamp Thing rising out of it. Not that it mattered; long before we exited the flooded terrain, I'd be frozen solid.

And beyond the swamp I saw now, behind a sea of cattails and whippy willow saplings, rose yet another part of the cliff, gray and implacable.

"Okay," Ellie sighed, knowing a dead end when she saw one. She did, however, spy a way to reach the cove without recrossing the swamp; a narrow path around the edge of the mucky water.

I was so glad to see it that I didn't think about why it was there, or what we'd do when we did get back to the cove. Instead I waded toward the path and started down it toward the sound of crashing waves.

And as I'd hoped, it did lead to the shore. But when we got there, those wooden steps weren't the only things missing; now the beach wasn't there anymore, either.

A wave crashed in, and then another. The water was knee-deep where we'd stood earlier. We wouldn't be getting back onto the boat for a while, either. Every time a wave rolled in, it lifted the dock's planks from below, then slammed them down again; they'd have tossed us the way a bull tosses rodeo riders.

"Any ideas?" asked Ellie through lips blue with cold. It was fifty or so degrees out here, I guessed, but it felt more like thirty in our wet clothes, with a brisk onshore breeze.

"No," I replied grimly as a surge of frustration seized me and sent me stomping around yelling thwartedly. But that did about as much good as it ever does until finally I joined Ellie and we hunkered together miserably in a small as-yet-unflooded space at the foot of the cliff.

Around us a few last boards from the demolished steps floated, the rest already washed out past the jutting rocks guarding the mouth of the cove.

"I could try the swamp again," Ellie said. "Maybe there's a way up somewhere past it that we didn't see. If I got to the house, I could drop dry clothes down to you, and maybe a thermos of something hot."

I squinted at the encroaching waves, creeping nearer by the moment. "Better to drop a raft."

Which we'd need pretty soon, anyway. It was getting deep fast, and there was nothing here to cling on to. My only choice if she left me would be floating around in my life vest until somebody retrieved me.

Besides, she could get stuck somewhere as easily as I had, only there'd be no one there to help. I said as much, and Ellie nodded reluctantly.

"It's just not safe doing it alone, is it?" she admitted.

It wasn't safe doing it at all, I wanted to say. Even Wade would have had a fit if he knew about it. But I was shivering so hard, I could barely speak.

Then, "No," said someone from somewhere nearby.

I looked at Ellie. She looked at me.

Neither of us had said it.

Both of us looked up.

From up on the bluff's edge, a face peered down at us. I knew it at once; it was the kid I'd seen at Bob Arnold's old place out in Quoddy Village, the one on the bicycle that I'd also seen passing the shop the night Ingrid and Bryan arrived.

Although he wasn't a kid, I saw now. This was a man's face, observing us from above; something in his expression was too adult for it to belong to a youngster.

Also, I knew this guy from somewhere else. While I cudgeled my brain for when and how I'd seen him before, something rolled over the cliff's edge, lengthened as it fell, slid off the flat granite outcropping that jutted out halfway down, and dropped.

It was a rope ladder, old but intact-seeming, now fully extended with its bottom rung bouncing up and down a few inches off the deepening water.

Which was now *really deepening*. If Ellie and I didn't walk, climb, or otherwise make our way off this fast-flooding beach like right the heck now, we'd need to swim, and have I mentioned that I'm not the world's strongest swimmer even in warm water?

Meanwhile, Ellie frowned strenuously at the rope ladder as if, once she'd studied it intently enough, it might make sense.

"Who," she managed finally, "is that up there?"

The face at the top of the cliff—freckled cheeks, a rubbery-looking mouth with big teeth in it, sandy hair on top—kept grinning down at us and now I remembered where I'd seen him.

"That's Tink Markle. Used to be the star of a daytime TV show."

Back in the bad old days in the city, Sam and I used to watch the show in the afternoons instead of napping, Sam with his teething ring, me with my wine plus whatever new item of lacy black lingerie I'd found in my husband's coat pocket the night before.

"Fine, he's Tink Markle." Ellie was unimpressed, not being a TV watcher now or ever. "Any idea what he's doing here?"

"No," I sighed, "I don't. Or how he got here, either."

With the big tree still lying across the driveway, it must have been quite a trick. He heard me, though, and answered my implied question with one of his own:

"How d'you know I haven't been here all the while?"

Smart-ass. I'd have punched him but my arm wasn't long enough.

"Okay, let's try again," I called up to him, meanwhile restraining my temper. "What's the ladder secured to?"

"Couple of iron spikes driven into the rock. They've been here a while, it looks like," came the answer.

That was enough for Ellie, who promptly waded to the ladder through cold water up to her thighs. Grabbing one thick rung, putting a foot on another, she hoisted herself easily.

"Um, Ellie?" Ellie can shinny up a tree, creep out a long branch, grab a trapped cat, and shove it squalling and clawing into a burlap sack.

But I, to put it mildly, can't. Also, the ladder looked challenging even without all the wiggling and swaying it was doing while she climbed.

The part about sidling to one side of the outcropping like a skilled mountaineer seemed especially tricky. But once she was off and could lean over and encourage me, I would try climbing up, too, I decided, and I was feeling pretty darned virtuous about this until something small and hot zipped angrily past my face: *zzt!*

The gunshot's report came a millisecond later. I jumped back fast to scramble under the granite outcropping. Ellie was already at the ladder's top; quickly I started up behind her.

I had no choice: neither drowning nor getting shot were on my to-do list, so I had to get off that beach. On the other hand, if you want to be an easy target, suspending yourself on a rope ladder halfway up a cliff is a fine way to do it.

And where'd that shot come from, anyway? I could almost feel crosshairs centered on me. Then Tink Markle's ruddy face appeared above me again.

"Help a girl out, here?!" I yelled, and suddenly the whole ladder slid upward so fast that the rung I was standing on got yanked from beneath my feet. So there I clung, my hands already aching, desperately hanging on while kicking around frantically and ineffectually.

And uncontrollably; also terrifyingly. Losing my grip, I dropped abruptly four rungs, then grabbed on again, burning the skin off my palms as the rope slid through them. Next, I slammed bodily against the cliff face, got yanked up another six inches, and swung around to slam into the cliff once more.

Bottom line, if that cliff had been any higher, I'd have died from the blunt force trauma of getting pulled up it. But that wasn't the worst part.

Red ants boiled from crevices in the granite, swarming and gnashing their mouthparts together while marching right at me. Their bite was like an injection of red-hot battery acid, and as I hung there more of them appeared.

"You okay?" Ellie called down to me anxiously.

A great many spirited retorts sprang to mind. "Just ducky," I grated out instead, feeling another ant slip down my collar while a bunch more invaded my sleeve.

Finally, after I'd gotten enough itching, stinging ant bites to kill a horse, the ladder itself began rising again. Soon the rungs that I clung to reached the top of the cliff, where I swung first one leg and then the other over the edge.

After that I just wanted to lie there gasping for a while. But instead, "Are you guys nuts?" I demanded, sitting up fast; the world spun dizzily. "Didn't you hear that—?"

"Gunshot? That was just me," Tink Markle said, not sounding concerned.

But I still was. I got to my feet. "You . . . you *shot* at me?"

"Not *at* you." Below the brown corduroy pants he wore gray socks and scuffed brown loafers; above, a thin, brown belt, a black turtleneck sweater, and that familiar tweed jacket.

"*Near* you," he emphasized, retreating as I advanced on him, then continued, "and you have to admit, it got you moving."

So it had. A whizzing bullet will do that. But: "What," I demanded, "if you'd missed?"

As if in reply he pulled the gun out and fired again fast: *pow!* The flagpole ornament on Ellie's boat, thirty yards distant and no larger than a Ping-Pong ball atop the pole, exploded.

I stopped advancing; in fact, by then my body had decided on its own that it was time for some hasty backpedaling.

"Nice shooting," I admitted; it was an understatement.

Still, even *nearly* getting my head blown off irritates me.

"Thanks," he said, turning away. "As for how I got here, stick with me for a while, why don't you, and find out."

He'd had a running schtick on the show, firing a pistol at targets tossed up by audience members. Participants were chosen by a young lady in a swimsuit; that's the kind of show it was, and I'd thought the shooting routine must've been rigged.

Now Tink Markle knelt at the bluff's edge. "Come on," he muttered impatiently at the balky roller-and-crank contraption that brought the rope ladder back up, then abandoned the task and let the ladder fall again.

He'd found the ladder in the garden shed, he explained; he'd heard me yelling and looked there for anything he could find that might help.

"Thanks," I said, leaning back in the dry grass. All of my rope-climbing adrenaline had fled, leaving me feeling drained.

Also, by now the sky overhead was blue again, gauzy with a thin veil of fog, and in the distance I could hear chain saws again, too. It meant Sam and his crew were back, to my relief.

But as we made our way toward the white pea-gravel driveway by the house I got another look at the downed tree's trunk, its massive bulk still as huge as before, and whatever optimism I might've been feeling dissolved fast.

"Oh dear," murmured Ellie, who, like me, was seeing it for the first time in daylight.

Crashed to earth like some fallen behemoth, its rough, age-scarred trunk was much higher than Sam was tall. If you hollowed it out, you could park cars inside; crossways in the driveway it blocked car access completely and getting over it on foot was clearly impossible as well.

An excavator snarled to life beyond the tree trunk, taking a big rattle-and-crunch bite of earth. Then as we reached the upper part of the big house's backyard, Tink Markle turned and started up the stairs to Bryan's apartment over the garage.

I hurried after him. "Hey, you can't just—"

He waved unconcernedly, tried Bryan's doorknob, slipped inside, and closed the door behind him.

Ellie was right behind me. She stepped past me and went in behind Tink. Then her hand shot back out and grabbed my arm.

"What, you're waiting to be invited?" she said, and hauled me in there, too.

Minutes later, Tink Markle had Bryan's small propane heater blazing and his coffeemaker burbling, and was browsing through his music collection.

Ellie and I were in the bathroom toweling our wet hair. My own short, dark curls were nearly dry already; she'd wrapped hers in a towel.

The door flew open, startling us both so badly, we nearly leapt into each other's arms.

"Ladies," Markle said in the gravelly voice I recalled from his show. "I'm all for primping, but can we get down to brass tacks?"

"It's not primping," I snapped as I pushed out past him; gosh, he was on my last nerve.

Worse, the excavator I'd heard wasn't running anymore, and neither was the chain saw. Apparently the plan to get the tree guy from up north had gone south.

That's why a backup plan seemed ever more essential, but I hadn't been able to come up with one of those, either. And maybe whatever Tink Markle might tell us could help, but first he wanted answers from us.

"What do you know about what's going on here?" He was drinking brandy, but not from a snifter. It was a water glass of brown liquid filled right up to the top, and he was swallowing it in gulps. So I figured we should move the conversation along while we still could.

"We know Ingrid Merryfield bought the place sight un-seen," I said. "She got some friends here for a party, to see it."

"But," Ellie added, "I don't think they're really friends."

Tink barked out a laugh. "What gave you the clue?" He pulled a sandwich from his jacket pocket and bit into it while eyeing me like I was some mildly interesting species of bug.

"So you've been in the main house?" I asked. The sandwich was one that the caterers had left on a tray before their departure.

He pocketed it again, then got up and poured coffee for the three of us.

"Sure I've been inside," he said as he set out the cream and sugar. "Heck, I'm her friend, too."

He put a twist on the word *friend*. Meanwhile, all I wanted to know was whether he was mine; if not, it would be unwise of me to swallow any of the hot drink.

Still, he had dragged us up an entire cliff. "You brought the boat into town on the trailer, then motored back to the cove in it?" said Ellie, sounding sure of herself.

Markle drank more brandy, then nodded. "Right. Boat was in the garage. Someone winterized it and so on."

"But why bring it out here instead of leaving it at the dock in town?" I wanted to know.

The dock down in the cove was harder to get to, and on its last legs; town would've been safer. But before he could an-swer, a door slammed somewhere not far off.

I was certain it must be Bryan coming back to find us here in his place. But instead, from the window I caught a glimpse of him walking the other way, with Igor loping along beside him.

"Anyway, it's not really important that she's calling them her friends," Tink said, beginning to slur.

He was quite drunk already. "When the truth is, what she's really got over there"—he angled his head at the house—"is a nest of vipers."

I drank the rest of what had turned out to be strong Irish coffee; he wasn't greedy about his booze, anyway, I gathered.

And hey, a girl's got to get her nutrition somewhere. I prodded him with my foot.

"Mmphrgfgl," he muttered. I nudged him again. "Mmmph?" he asked irritably. He'd halfway passed out.

That's when I turned the sink sprayer on him. "Wake up. I'm not here for my health. I've got questions."

What he said as he jumped up and brushed frantically at himself isn't quotable here, but I enjoyed his indignant dance while he was saying it.

"How'd you get past that big fallen tree?" I demanded. "Why did you come here anyway, what's your interest, and what's with the bicycle I saw you on over in Quoddy Village, and in front of the bakery the other night, too?"

I wasn't fated to get an answer, though. "Hey, you guys?" Ellie said troubledly from the window.

I hurried over in time to see a man's shape vanish among low-hanging evergreen branches between the garage and the main house. Bryan was coming back.

"Jake, let's go," Ellie hissed urgently.

"Oh, you betcha," I agreed, just as Tink Markle lurched up out of his chair and came up behind us both, exhaling whiskey fumes. Now that he had his legs under him and had glimpsed this apartment's rightful tenant heading this way, though, I could see thoughts beginning to move in his alcohol-fogged brain.

"Come with me," he suggested, if you can call grabbing each of us by an arm and hustling us ahead of him a suggestion.

He kept the bottle and the glass he'd been drinking from and we each grabbed a coffee cup as we went by; I switched off the coffeemaker and propane heater. Nothing else betrayed our presence here as long as Bryan didn't notice the damp towels in the bathroom or touch the still-warm coffeepot.

That is, as long as he wasn't very observant. Unfortunately I suspected that he was, but it was too late to do much about it.

"Go," said Tink, yanking open a door I'd thought must lead to a closet, but didn't. Shoving us through, he followed and pulled it shut.

Steps led down steeply. I descended, aided by a flashlight Tink had produced. At the bottom, a stone-walled passageway led off into pitch-darkness.

I stopped. "Okay, what's the deal?" I demanded flatly. "Who are you really, and how'd you know all this was here?"

Whatever this was. "Keep your voice down," Tink admonished me as above a door slammed and footsteps moved across the floor over our heads.

Then the floor beneath us shivered; this was particularly unnerving since it was made of concrete. Crumbs of grit sifted down from the ceiling as the shaking lessened and stopped.

"I bet that's another little earthquake," Ellie diagnosed the shaking worriedly.

"Oh, come on," Tink Markle said as if this was the dumbest idea he'd ever heard. "Everyone knows Maine doesn't have—"

Another shake punctuated this remark. Tink shut up; it was heartwarming, really. But I didn't have time to gloat; besides, now that I'd had time to think about it I realized that we were headed exactly where I wanted to go.

So I let Tink Markle urge me and Ellie into the passageway, which have I mentioned yet how dark it was? I mean it was *really* dark, and also unless I'd just lost my sense of direction it was a tunnel between the garage building and Cliff House.

Then, once we were moving again: "Who are you?" I demanded, more quietly this time but no less insistently. "How'd you know—"

Because you have to admit, knowing about a tunnel under a place does belie some previous acquaintance with it. Like, *close* acquaintance.

"Yeah," Tink said, moving ahead of us with the flashlight aimed out in front of him.

He laughed unhappily. "That's a story, all right. Who I am, why I do things, how do I—"

Lights blazed on overhead. In the flash-lit gloom I hadn't seen the bulbs in their bare receptacles; now I nearly fainted.

"Motion sensors," he explained as the lights kept going on as we came alongside them and going out again once we'd passed.

"But they didn't even have motion sensors when the house was built, did they?" Ellie objected.

"Actually, they did," said Tink. "But you're right, these came later. Solar powered, there's panels on the garage roof."

Then, as we went on down the granite-walled passageway toward Cliff House, he told us the rest of the story.

Nine

"My great-grandfather built this house. He wanted a place where he could recover from the war. He had what they called shell shock, then."

Ellie looked back over her shoulder at Tink. "So you came here as a child?"

He nodded. "Few times. He was very old by then. It wasn't a childhood haven or anything like that."

To judge by his face, the memories he had made here weren't particularly happy, either.

He caught me looking. "What, you wanted a cozy bedtime story about sweet little Tinker and his beloved great-grandpa?"

Meanwhile, the tunnel went on; each time we got to where I thought it must be ending, it turned and another length of it stretched ahead.

"Almost there," said Tink, seeming to sense my unease, and now at the far end of the section we were in I spied a door.

Then: "My grandparents came here, though," he said. "And after my granddad died my parents inherited the place. Started fixing it up, found things he'd left behind. Not nice things."

Tink sighed heavily. "And after their discoveries, all they wanted to do with Cliff House was get rid of it."

We reached the door. Music played on the other side, a tune that I recognized from Sam's car radio.

"What about the stories, though?" I asked quietly. "Is that what the not-nice things were from, the murders and so on?"

I put my ear to the door. I wanted to know who'd be out there when I emerged, just in case they weren't friendly.

Tink laughed quietly, sounding less wise-ass than before. "Right, the murders," he confirmed my suspicion about what his folks had found. "That's what everyone wants to hear about."

He sucked in a breath. "My parents found remains. And other things. My granddad just hadn't been curious, I guess, or maybe he was just lazy. Left the place the way it had been."

Another big sigh. "It wasn't the war that damaged my great-grandfather, though, like people said. Even before, he'd been well known to girls in the movie business."

"Maybe the girls hoped they'd end up being his girlfriend? Or his next wife?" Ellie theorized.

On the other side of the door someone turned off the radio. "Yeah, probably. Or that he'd put them in movies."

"And your great-grandmother?" I asked.

"She took off from here, never heard from again." A bitter chuckle escaped him. "I guess she'd decided to scram before she ended up dead, too."

He shoved open the door and pushed through a curtain; I followed, emerging at the back of a pantry closet. Then Ellie and I stepped out of the closet into the pantry itself.

Morning light flooded through a small pantry window. Outside, dew glittered in the grass leading down to the bluff's edge. Igor was out there, nosing around.

I didn't see Bryan anywhere. "So," I asked Tink as I went on out into the kitchen, "how'd your murderous ancestor finally croak, anyway?"

Yeah, Bob had told me the old guy had hung himself, but I wanted to hear what Tink said about it. I turned to where he had stood by the stove just a moment ago.

But now he was gone.

Ellie tried the cellar door, just steps from where Tink Markle had been last time I'd seen him. But it was locked, and I was in no mood to delay any further. After searching downstairs without any result, we climbed to the second floor and found Mika and Bella in the bedroom we'd meant to stay the night in.

"We couldn't stand it anymore," Mika said once I'd brought her and Bella up to date on the state of things at home; that is, uneventful.

Or at least it was uneventful once I'd edited a few items out: my dad being on his own, for instance. Bella and Mika's time here without Ellie and me hadn't been, however.

"Howling, scratching, sounds out of a scary movie. Enough to put chills up and down your spine," Bella reported.

She straightened defiantly, glaring around the little bedroom; once dawn came she'd gotten her wind back, it seemed.

"But I ain't gettin' scared out of nowhere by spookity howls," she declared, and that stiffened my spine, too.

Sort of. "Listen," I said, "I'm sorry. I left you two here, and I apologize. Bella, I never even told you we were going, and I'm so glad you both survived."

That was putting it mildly; my heart rate might drop back to normal in a year or two, I expected. But neither seemed angry with me, I was relieved to see; instead they both seemed quite proud of themselves, and I thought they deserved to.

"But I think we'd better get out of here. Like, right now, immediately" I said.

All three looked queryingly at me. "I don't know what else somebody's got planned for us," I went on, "but it stands to reason it's got to happen before Sam and his guys get in here."

I squared my shoulders. "So let's just go. We'll get as close to the tree as we can and just start yelling for help. Now, everybody stay together. Down the stairs, out the door, down that driveway and nobody look back."

I didn't care anymore how Tink Markle had gotten in here; now that I thought of it, maybe he'd been here all along. But no matter; once we reached the fallen tree, we'd figure out what to do next, or better yet, the crew on the other side of it would.

Ow-ooooh! commented something from out in the hall.

"Ignore that," I snapped, waving toward the window, where the sound of the chain saws went on, and so did that excavator and maybe also a bulldozer, now, too.

I didn't know what the howling from the hall was; leaving it seemed more prudent by the minute, though, and Mika agreed.

"The sooner we leave Cliff House, the better, as far as I'm concerned," she said.

Ellie looked sharply at her. "Why, what's going on?"

Mika frowned. "Well, all the pizza got eaten and they were still looking around. I thought since I'm here I might as well cook them breakfast, too," she said. "Keep them happy."

The houseguests, she meant; the two who were still alive, anyway, plus Bryan and Ingrid. "Good plan," I commented.

"Maybe, but when Bella and I went to the cellar to get the eggs and the bacon that I'd seen in the cooler down there, I nearly tripped on this."

She held up a length of twine. "Stretched tight across one of the steps. It's perfect for tripping on and falling down the rest of them."

Ow-ooooh! the howl from the hall resumed lustily, whereupon Bella flung the door open and bellowed through it.

"You, there! Stop that caterwauling this minute!"

The howling shut off like a switch.

"There," she uttered. "Ghosts, my great-aunt Fanny."

"That's right," I pronounced firmly, though the prospect of

leaving this room remained daunting. All those closed, silent doors to pass, one with a body still behind it . . .

Also: *Ow-ooooh!* came another long howl, but I hustled the three of them out ahead of me, anyway.

"Keep together," advised Mika as we hurried along the faded red carpet to the back stairs.

"This is all so creepy," Ellie breathed, half-laughing with nervousness as I reached for the doorknob.

It was an old cut-crystal item that under normal conditions I'd have admired. They don't make doorknobs like that anymore.

But now all I wanted it to do was turn. And it wouldn't.

I rattled it hard. From behind us came scuffling sounds.

Elbowing me aside, Ellie *kicked* the door; it swung wide and we tumbled through. Then came slamming the door very hard behind us, clattering down the steps so fast it was a wonder nobody got killed, and falling into the kitchen, breathless.

Also, on my part there was a whole lot of praying that the door didn't drift back open again by itself. Or *not* by itself . . .

"Well!" said Ingrid Merryfield, looking up brightly from where she was pouring a cup of coffee at the kitchen counter. "I wondered where you all had gotten to. You slept well, I hope?"

We stopped. So much for the straight-out-the-door part of the plan. Also, it occurred to me that if I hadn't already known there were three dead bodies on the property—well, one was in a boat, but you know what I mean—I might feel happy, too.

But Ingrid Merryfield did know, and it was plain as well that not only were the deaths violent but also that someone had caused them. That someone *here with us* had caused them.

Yet she didn't seem a bit distressed about any of it; that is, until she saw my face.

"I suppose once the driveway is clear we'll have to call the police," she added, not sounding urgent about this.

She was heating the coffee in a saucepan on the gas stove;

with the power still out the electric percolator didn't work, of course.

"I already notified them," I told her. As far as I knew, no phones here worked yet; ours certainly didn't. But Ingrid Merryfield didn't ask about this.

"The crew out there is working to clear the tree as quickly as possible, and Eastport's police chief will be here as soon as he can," I said.

Now she looked thoughtful, but still not worried. It made me think she might not be the one behind all the current mayhem.

But at this point I wouldn't have bet against it, either. She'd gotten them here, after all, and according to Tink Markle they weren't such good pals as she'd made them out to be.

"Let's whip up a nice snack for people," I said, changing the subject while dispensing a trio of meaningful looks. "Mika, didn't you have an idea about that?"

She'd had no such thing, but Mika smiled sweetly at me in reply; like Bella, she caught on fast.

"Why, yes," she agreed, wrapping an apron around her slim middle. "Bella, would you like to help?"

Because we needed to be here in the kitchen, by the door. Once Miss Merryfield left the room we could all slip out fast, instead of trying to make it unseen down the front hall.

"And, Ellie, let's you and I check the cooler downstairs for some lunch fixings, shall we?" I added.

I wanted a look at where that twine had been strung across the steps, and sure enough, Ellie and I found the two small holes in the old plaster, freshly dug opposite one another. A tack or small nail had been pressed into each hole, it looked like, and the twine stretched between them.

Carrying a flashlight, I went the rest of the way down and crossed the concrete floor to where the cooler stood. Here the wall was built of granite chunks; their surfaces, whitewashed long ago, were now a scabrous bone white in the cellar's gloom.

Ellie squinted at them, aiming her own flashlight. "Jake, does part of the wall look funny to you?"

I'd seen it, too. "You mean newer? The paint's fresher?"

The patch she'd pointed out was about as high and as wide as a person, whitewashed like the rest but whiter, brighter.

I ran my hand over it. Smoothly, the newly painted section of wall swung inward, startling me more than somewhat.

"Oh, holy criminy," I breathed. Beyond the opening another tunnel stretched away from me. This, I thought, must be how Tink Markle had gotten in; there was an exit down there somewhere.

Ellie was already on her way in.

"Ellie!" I called after her. This passageway hadn't been modernized like the earlier one; no lights, for one thing, solar or otherwise. So a few feet of dim glow from our flashlights was followed by who knew how much more pitchy blackness.

But I couldn't very well let her go by herself, so I followed her. Then suddenly the blackness ahead was pierced by a whole lot of pairs of glowing red eyes, glaring malignantly and unblinkingly at us as they reflected the flashlights.

"Ellie?" I managed through my suddenly-tightened throat.

The eyes all winked out. Then, "Rats," Ellie whispered, and I realized she meant real ones. Not sweet little white lab rats, either; these, I imagined, would be the wild kind, iron gray with long, yellow incisors and evil tempers.

"Listen," I began, "maybe we'd better go back."

"Uh-uh," she replied firmly. "If this goes somewhere, we want to know about it. Maybe we could all get out this way," she echoed my earlier thought.

"Okay, but only a little farther. Then if it looks good we'll go back for Mika and Bella, and some more flashlights."

But just then the door behind us creaked as it swung shut, and try as we might we could not make it open again.

* * *

"Eek," I gulped quietly.

"No one will hear us from in here," Ellie said.

"Nope." Something tickled my cheek. "Besides, if this is a way out of here, we still want to know about it."

"Right." Even more, now. "But what if it isn't?"

"Hey, what's the point of a secret tunnel if it doesn't go anywhere?" I answered, trying to be encouraging.

Now if only someone would encourage me. Still, I took the flashlight and aimed it at the ceiling, discovering in the process that there must indeed be a way this passage led outside.

After all, how could all these bats have gotten in here, otherwise? Dozens of their small, furry bodies hung head down from the ceiling, packed side by side.

"Ellie," I said quietly.

"I see them." She took my hand. "They won't hurt you."

"Sure," I quavered, "but what if they want to—"

Just then they all opened their eyes at the same time and some of them stretched their wings lazily before settling again.

"—drink my *blood*?" I whispered, which was when they all dropped at once from the ceiling and flapped off down the tunnel in a squeaking cloud.

"Gah!" I exhaled, backing up very fast, but Ellie pulled me forward again.

"No exit in that direction," she reminded me, and that got me moving once more, at least. But now I kept having to brush small tickling things from my hair every few steps.

I didn't want to know what they were; if I did, I might run shrieking into the darkness. But they wanted to know what I was, and they took small, stinging nips at me every few seconds, to find out.

The darkness seemed to suck us forward, the walls pressing in on either side, and now one of the flashlights was failing.

"I keep thinking Tink Markle's going to pop up suddenly," I said, because, for one thing, where *had* he gotten to, anyway?

"Right," agreed Ellie, and then the floor shuddered.

"Another tremor," she said. "That, or something hit the ground really hard outside."

The flashlight flickered. "You think we might actually have a big earthquake?" I asked, and felt her shrug beside me.

"Don't know." It flickered again. "I suppose we could."

I supposed so, too, but I sure hoped we didn't. "It's bad enough being down here at all, without any shaking going on," I said.

To jack up the scared-out-of-my-mind quotient any further, I meant. Then after another thirty feet or so the passage turned left and light gleamed ahead.

The turn led into a large, well-lit room with . . . could those really be windows? Small glass panes gleamed high in one wall. Mid-morning light shone through them.

Also, I was pretty sure that our escape route had been identified; that swarm of bats had to be going somewhere. The air in here was fairly fresh, too, though the windows were all closed.

Faint hope arose in me. I stepped into the room. The windows were set in panels of three; each panel opened with a lever. I turned one experimentally and cringed as it let out a loud, metal-on-metal shriek.

"Jake!" Ellie shushed me. I stopped cranking.

But it was too late. A heavy, dragging sound now came from somewhere behind us in the passageway. It was the sound you'd hear if a giant was dragging the box of rocks that his leg-iron was chained to, dragging it toward you.

I grabbed the window crank again, since "out the window" is an escape route so well known that even I could think of it. But once the window panel was open, it was clear that to get through it I'd need to be cut into pieces.

And this, of course, was precisely the sort of thing I was trying to avoid. Also:

"Jake," said Ellie again.

"What?" Nothing good, I could tell by her tone.

The room was large, about twenty feet by twenty, redbrick walled on three sides and granite on the fourth. One end of it featured packed bookshelves, leather armchairs plus a few sturdy-looking wooden straight-backed ones, old rugs, and brass desk lamps with green glass shades.

But its other end, walled off by sliding glass panels, was set up as a spa with a now-empty soaking pool, a teakwood enclosure that I thought might be a sauna, and teak lounge chairs.

"Jake," Ellie repeated, beckoning to me. She'd opened the glass sliders and stood by the pool, looking into it.

I stepped up beside her, and immediately wished I hadn't. A body lay at the bottom of the shallow pool; from its clothing I thought it was a woman's body, though the aging fabric was in tatters.

She was dead, I knew that for sure on account of the dried, shriveled hands and withered face, and she'd been dead for a long time; decades, maybe.

The body lay near the pool's edge. Hesitantly, I knelt and reached down toward one of the dessicated hands, its long, thin index finger seeming to point accusingly at me. The nail at its end curved down clawlike, and the knucklebone was a yellowish lump.

My finger met the body's. At the touch, the body's finger fell off with a faint *crack!* I watched it roll down the gentle slope to the pool's blue-tiled bottom and lie there motionless. And now the dragging sound came from the passageway again, louder this time.

Whatever it was, it was fast, and it had already gotten too near the room's door for us to try getting out that way. I rushed back to the windows, but this time I didn't bother opening any of them. Instead dragged one of the straight-backed wooden chairs along with me, then climbed onto it.

Finally, ignoring the obvious hazards to life and limb that

my course of action presented, I gripped the chairback with one hand, then reared back and put my foot very forcefully into a whole panel of the windows.

My shoe bounced back so hard that I nearly kicked myself in the face, the impact slamming through my ankle, banging around inside my knee, and probably traveling on up through my hip bone and into my appendix.

Also, I fell off the chair.

"Ow," I said, grimacing, and by then I was so mad I yanked the chair upright, climbed back up onto it, and kicked the damned windows again, just for spite.

This time my foot smashed through glass, wood, and the caulking compound that joined them, all the way to the outside. Luckily the glass didn't sever anything important when I hauled my foot back in, although I did get scratched up a little. Fell off the chair again, too.

But I didn't care. "Ellie!" I cried in triumph, then noticed that she was staring at the doorway that led out into the passageway. Meanwhile the sound of something large being dragged along the floor out there continued.

Scra-a-ape-thump. Scra-a-

Ellie scampered toward me. Swiftly we set the chair up again, we both climbed onto it—and yes, this was a precarious operation, but we managed it—and finally I hoisted her up and out through the broken window, after which she hauled me out by my wrists.

Well, halfway out. Turns out being shoved from below isn't as helpful as being hauled from above, window-escape-wise. On top of which, Ellie was slimmer than I was.

"Stuck," I uttered grimly, and began wriggling and writhing, inching myself forward and cursing that second cream-filled cupcake that I'd eaten yesterday.

But at last I scraped through, jumped up, and crouched again. We were beneath the kitchen window; voices came from inside.

"Delicious!" said someone, "this stuff is perfectly . . ."

Divine; yes, it was. I told Ellie that Mika must've made yet another chocolate pizza.

"Good," she replied. "I could use a slice of it myself."

Me too. Even the body in the pool didn't distract me from what I recognized as hunger.

Meanwhile, I recalled that just under and to one side of that kitchen window was the spot on the kitchen counter where I imagined Mika might put the pizza after slicing it.

And that window was open. Cautiously, I eased my head up.

"Jake!" Ellie admonished me in a whisper, peering around anxiously.

I shooed her away. Up . . . up . . . I could see through onto the counter where, just as I'd hoped, a paper plate with four pizza slices on it sat.

Suddenly someone was right there at the kitchen counter; I ducked down hastily. ". . . just one more slice," said whoever stood by the counter. It was Ingrid Merryfield, I thought.

Drat. But then: "I'll get my coffee, first," said the voice, moving away.

I counted to five, straightened fast, shoved my hand in, and grabbed the plate with the pizza on it. After dumping the slices down into Ellie's waiting hands, I shoved the empty plate back in again.

And ducked down hastily once more. "Huh," said a woman's voice puzzledly from inside. "Who took my . . ."

Chocolate pizza, it turns out, is even more delicious when it's stolen; Ellie and I sat concealed by the shrubberies and flat out went to town on the food, and when we finished we got drinks of water from the garden hose spigot.

And that's when whatever had been behind us in the cellar began forcing its way out through the window hole I'd smashed open.

"Yeeks," said Ellie, scrambling up.

"No kidding." I pointed. "That way."

Without looking back we sprinted toward the corner of the house where the lawn ended and the wild-growing forest began. Once we got past one last clump of azaleas, we could melt into the undergrowth.

I'd just about made it when a hand caught my sleeve from behind. "Help me, please."

It was Maud Bankersley, who clearly hadn't been at Mika's pizza party just now. Her hair was in wild disarray, gray dust smudged her face, and her eyes looked panic stricken.

"Please," she said again, glancing fearfully around, "I've got Tink Markle down there in that awful cellar and I'm afraid he's dead."

"Bella wanted a bucket and some spray cleaner from the cleaning supplies closet. So I said I'd get them."

Great. Ellie and I needed a sidekick like we needed another head. Besides the one from the body in the pool, I mean; I dragged my mental gaze from the memory of her.

Meanwhile, we couldn't go back in through the house; the rest of them were in there, and the way I felt right then, if I ran into any of them, especially Ingrid Merryfield, who'd started all this, there might be another murder around here.

So I took out my frustration by kicking stray splinters and glass bits out of the window hole that led back into the cellar. Once I got them out, the hole was big enough to squirm through; I helped Maud and Ellie through it and then they helped me.

But when I got there, I wished they hadn't. Tink Markle lay facedown and motionless by the teakwood sauna.

Four down, how many to go? the thought popped unwanted into my head. *And would we be next?*

"So I came downstairs," Maud was saying, "and Igor just happened to be walking around and came along with me."

The dog was still down here; the window hole I'd opened was too high for him to jump out. Now he stood wagging his tail slowly at all of us as if unsure what his reaction should be.

"The next thing you know I heard a noise. Like, from *behind* the wall. Or *inside* it, like," Maud went on.

She wiggled her red-tipped fingers in the air, then pushed her hair back with them. "Like, it was *weird*."

I had no doubt of it. Everything here was. Still, she wasn't falling down in hysterics the way I might be after the experience she'd had.

"So I went over and leaned on the wall, like, trying to get my ear right up against it, you know? And I, like, *fell in*."

Igor strolled over to where Tink Markle sprawled and stuck his wet nose into Tink's ear.

He groaned. I had a feeling that bourbon must've hit him, and the dog wasn't helping.

"Oh good, he's not dead," Maud said, then went on. "So there he was on the floor just inside whatever this place is."

She glanced around in distaste. "I mean, really, that end looks like a bunch of stuffy old guys in tuxedoes ought to be standing around smoking cigars and drinking cognac."

I had to smile; she'd nailed it precisely. There was even a globe, and a dictionary stand with a thick, open book on it.

"And at the other end a swimming pool?" she said. "Someone had some seriously strange notions about interior design."

Oh, she had no idea. I reminded her about Tink Markle. "So what else happened after you found him?" I prodded gently.

"Well, I yelled but nobody heard me, I guess because once I went through the door it closed behind me. So I hauled him along behind me in case I found someone who could . . ."

Uh-huh. "But you must've heard us ahead of you, right?"

She nodded. "I heard you. But I didn't know who you were."

That made sense. Heck, I'd thought she was a giant with a boulder chained to his leg.

Tink Markle shoved himself up on one elbow. We all stared as he groggily massaged the bridge of his nose.

"For a while he was making this awful snorking sound," said Maud. "I thought for sure he must be—"

"Yeah." I sat her down on one of the leather-upholstered chairs at the library-ish end of the long chamber. Still no hysterics, but she looked sick and greenish now.

A delayed reaction, I figured. Tink Markle was no charmer when he was sober, and dragging what she'd feared might be his corpse had been no day at the beach, either, I guessed.

"Just wait here, okay?" I told her, then went back to the glassed-off pool-and-sauna end of the room and drew Ellie away from Markle.

"I guess he must have followed us in here, and then she accidentally followed *him* in." I theorized.

Ellie's lips pursed. "Maybe. But why didn't he hear us? We were making enough noise to wake the . . ."

Her voice trailed off. "I don't know," I said.

Tink was getting to his feet. "I'd love to ask him about it," I went on, "but for now let's just figure out what's next."

"I'm betting Maud's so glad to be with us, she'll go along with whatever we want," Ellie agreed.

In the getting-the-hell-out-of-here department, she meant, and this turned out to be true.

"Okay," Maud whispered when I'd confided what we planned: getting Bella and Mika, then clearing out of Cliff House however we could.

But Tink Markle was something else again. "I got down the cellar steps just in time to see the old tunnel door swing shut behind you," he said a few minutes later.

Now he sat with Maud in the books-and-leather part of the cellar chamber, with Igor lying by their feet. A decanter of golden liquid Tink had found in a desk drawer now stood on the blotter, half-empty.

"I know how the door works," said Tink, who was clearly

(a) still extremely thirsty and (b) no stranger to drinking out of bottles.

"I used to play down here when I was a kid," he said, "I knew you could get trapped. I followed you in, meaning to bring you out again."

"And then he passed out," said Maud scathingly. "So yeah, you were a big help."

Tink opened his mouth to retort; I cut in. "It doesn't matter. We're done here."

I turned, gesturing at Maud and then at Ellie to come with me; I wasn't sure where, but that window hole was looking pretty good to me again.

Tink Markle scrambled up, decanter in hand, and began striding around theatrically. "Done with us, all of us," he exclaimed. "Of course you are. We ought to be ashamed of—"

"Who is that guy, anyway?" Maud whispered. I guessed she wasn't a fan of old daytime TV. I didn't bother answering.

"Oh, can it," I snapped at Tink instead, and he did, but not because of me. He'd marched himself back into the spa area where the pool was, having produced his own flashlight.

The pool with the body in it. And this time he looked down.

His mouth opened again, but for once nothing came out. Maud hadn't seen the body yet, either, and now before I could stop her she was over there, too.

"I'd like to go now," she enunciated carefully after a moment. Again I had to give her credit; from her face I could see that she was working hard at staying calm.

But she was reaching her limit. "Girl's got a point," I said to Ellie. "The 'go' part, I mean."

"Yes, I think I'd like to, also," Ellie replied dryly. "But how do we deal with him?"

Weaving away from the pool with the body in it, Markle was still standing upright. The contents of the bottle he'd found had helped him, apparently.

But now he was so relaxed that if we took him with us, we would probably have to pour him out through the window hole.

I said so. He turned blearily as I gave Ellie a lift up. Then, seeing what I was doing, he scurried over, alarmed.

"Not that way," he hissed, and now I could hear them, too: people on the lawn. They were talking about quake tremors; I heard Ingrid wonder aloud to Bryan whether there'd be any more.

"Anyone's guess," he said as they moved from the window.

But not, I hoped, soon. "Where, then?" I demanded of Tink Markle, still wearing his brown tweed jacket and newsboy's cap.

"Where can we get out?" I repeated. "Because I told you, we're going, I don't care if I have to dig us out."

"Fine, but not that way. They'll see you. And if you go back up the cellar steps you'll be in the kitchen—is that what you want?"

He was no fool. He knew we were trying to escape without anyone knowing. And although he might not know all our reasons, seeing that very old dead body might've given him a clue.

Out on the lawn, Bryan and Ingrid still stood chatting, their tone turned confidential. But now I didn't dare get near enough to the window to hear their words.

"Right this way," said Markle, jerking his head toward the same dark tunnel that had brought us here in the first place.

I followed him to it, then realized that it didn't dead-end here in the room the way I'd thought. Instead it narrowed and turned in a way that was hard to spot.

He guided us around the turn. Once we were around it, a low brick archway opened. I shooed Ellie and Maud toward it and brought up the rear myself; Tink Markle was already way ahead of us.

The air here was dry and stale smelling, dust puffing up from beneath our feet with each step. Maud didn't have a flashlight but Ellie and I each still did, and between us we kept our footing all right and didn't walk into any walls.

"This way," Tink called back to us, his flashlight's beam stabbing the darkness ahead.

Above us, something hit the ground with a loud thud. That, or it was another small earthquake, I couldn't tell. Either way, though, grit sifted down from the passageway's low ceiling. I got some on my lips and then I felt it between my teeth: mortar dust, grains of sand, concrete chips, and something else, something tasting vegetation-y.

Moss, maybe. Or mold. "We're going to go home, take hot showers, wash our hair, have dinner," I told the others, trying to believe it.

Ahead, Tink Markle turned another corner I hadn't been expecting, into another passageway I hadn't known was there. I didn't trust him, and I didn't like him much, either, with his ruddy cheeks, a nose road-mapped by broken capillaries, and that knowing look in his eyes, as if your not-knowing was funny.

He looked like bad news, is what he looked like. But we had little choice but to follow him as more grit showers came down and the whole tunnel shifted a little. We heard rocks grinding against one another.

"Your great-granddad sure must've liked digging tunnels," I called ahead. "How much farther are we going?"

And to where, I might've added, but I was fairly sure I already knew. Somehow Tink Markle had gotten in here past the big fallen tree, and I was willing to bet that whatever we found where we were going, that was how he'd done it.

"A few hundred yards?" the answer came back. "And yeah, he did. Like digging, I mean, although mostly he hired other guys to do it."

We walked some more; here the blasted-out granite ended and actual excavating had begun. Big square timbers held back the earthen walls and kept the low ceiling from collapsing onto our heads.

More trudging, thudding, shaking, and spitting out of grit happened. Something big slammed to earth over our heads every so often; each time I waited to be buried, and wasn't.

So far. Igor padded behind us. "Not far now," said Tink.

"I hear machinery," said Ellie, and my heart leapt. "That must be Sam's crew cutting the tree and hauling the pieces."

Hauling was nearly as difficult as cutting, I knew; huge sections, each weighing a ton or more, got lifted out by bucket loader or, if even that wasn't big enough, in the massive metal jaws of an enormous tool called a logging grapple.

Thud. Thud. Big pieces of tree hit the ground outside. A pair of chain saws howled an angry duet and engines rumbled.

Ahead, the passage ended in a dirt wall with timbers braced up against it.

"The old steps leading out should be right around here," Tink said.

" 'Should be?' " I demanded. "You mean all this time we've been walking you haven't been sure there's still a way out?"

"I'm sure," he held both hands up defensively, "but it's not like I live down here. Got the landmarks in my head."

He aimed the flashlight around uncertainly. "Just give me a minute to get my bearings."

Maud spoke up. "You get us all down here to the end of this tunnel and now you say *maybe*?" she began.

But then she stopped, staring at the ugly little revolver he held. I was guessing that it still had ugly little bullets in it, too, the way it had when he'd fired it toward me earlier back when we were on the beach.

"So, why are you doing this?" I asked him.

Not that I cared, or at least not right this minute. The idea of keeping him talking just seemed good, that was all.

Still, his answer surprised me. "Ingrid promised me the

house. She doesn't want it. So if I just helped her do what she wanted to do here, she promised she'd deed it over to me."

Above us the heavy-equipment noise went on, the machinery howling and roaring and slamming the earth at regular intervals; a little extra shimmy now and then said the tremors continued, too.

I took a guess. "Tink, when your parents passed away did you expect to inherit Cliff House yourself?"

Because if it had been his great-grandfather's place, and then his grandfather's and his parents', Tink might've thought very reasonably that he'd get it next.

"My parents died years ago in a bus accident in Bolivia," he said. "World travelers, big spenders," he added snidely.

"And you're right if you're thinking that they didn't leave the house to me. They couldn't, they were too much in debt themselves."

His voice said there'd been more than money trouble between parents and son. But for now, money trouble was enough.

"Bank owned the place for a long time, drained what little was left in the estate for taxes and so on. But then some new guy took over managing the bank's real estate assets, and the house finally got put up for sale."

That made sense. "And Ingrid found out about it and bought it. Promised it to you if you'd help her. But help with what?"

The earth shook with more heavy thuds. "No!" Tink Markle shouted over them. "I got the notice from the bank and then told her about the house. But I had nothing to do with any of that other stuff. That wasn't in my plan at all."

Thud. Thud. Nothing to do with the murders, I imagined he meant, Waldo Higgins's and Audrey Dalton's; Gilly Blaine's, too, probably. I'd have questioned Tink more about them, but just then several things happened.

First, more crumbling ceiling bits rained down on us.

This time, though, it was a *lot* of ceiling bits. Next:

"Here!" cried Ellie, who'd been hunting around all this time with her flashlight for some sign of the steps Tink Markle had mentioned and at last had found them.

I peered where she pointed. A few stray light beams, each as thin as a hair, filtered sparsely down through what I guessed might be an old sheet of plywood up there at ground level.

"It's so rotten and crumbly, we can probably break through it," she said as Maud moved cautiously to join us.

"Oh no." Tink lifted his weapon again; we froze. "I'm so sorry, but I can't let you tell everyone what—"

Thud. He stepped toward us with that gun of his. As he did so, the ceiling caved in with a shuddering roar, burying him.

Instants later it buried us, too: me, Maud Bankersley, Ellie, and finally Igor, his doggy gaze the very last thing I saw before something hit me hard in the back of the head and I lost consciousness, myself.

Ten

When I came to, I was looking up into Wade's worried face, and watching the relief show up in his eyes.

I guessed he'd feel several more moments of this emotion before he got mad. *Really* mad, that is, just as I'd have been if I'd had to pull him out of a hole unconscious.

"What," he inquired mildly as he helped me to sit up, "were you doing down there?"

Hmm, I'd miscalculated. It seemed he was mad already. He wasn't saying any truly terrible swear words yet, but I could hear them in my head.

"I, uh, was trying to get out? And get Ellie out, too?"

I squinted around puzzledly, touched the back of my head wincingly, and finally realized that, somehow, Cliff House and I were on opposite sides of the fallen tree.

That meant the tunnel we'd been in must've led all the way out the driveway, ending beyond the downed behemoth. Then it hit me again, even more urgently this time: *Ellie.*

I scrambled up, shaking clods of earth, dried pine needles, concrete dust, and who knew how many insects, living or dead,

out of my hair. Behind me, big machines still worked at removing the fallen tree, but only one hunk of any appreciable size
had been taken away so far.

A shovel lay on the ground; I grabbed it. "Wade, come on,
we've got to dig. Ellie's down there."

He took the shovel from me. "She's not down there."

I thought he meant she was dead, so I grabbed back the tool.
"How do you *know*? We can't just leave her there."

"Jake." He grabbed my shoulders. "The phones are back.
She called me, I'd just gotten in from the freighter job. It's how
I knew to come over here and help dig you out."

"Oh," I said inadequately. He got the shovel away from me
and gestured for me to sit down on a nearby stump. I did,
mostly because I suddenly felt I might fall down: ears roaring,
cartoon tweety-birds circling my head, etcetera.

Also, there was the whole losing consciousness thing, which
always tends to make me feel as if I might lose my lunch. I put
my head between my knees.

"Jake, she's okay. She got back down the passageway you
guys were in and Mika finally heard her pounding and yelling,
and got that hidden door open for her."

He took a breath. "She says Bella and Mika are fine, too, and
they're all together inside, waiting."

I looked up in relief, letting the pale autumn sunshine bathe
my face. I'd been a little too busy to notice the weather for a
while, but now I breathed in the sharp smells of pine sap and
salt water gratefully.

Then I got up experimentally, drank from the water bottle
Wade handed me, and gave myself a hard mental shake.

Somehow, I wasn't hurt. "Thanks for unburying me," I said.

"Yeah, don't mention it." He didn't go on, his anger all dissolved now that he saw I was all right. Instead he slung an arm
around my shoulders as we looked down into the hole he'd
pulled me from.

"Ceiling caved in," I said, and his arm tightened.

"Yeah. Bob's friend from up north drove his tree harvester off the flatbed ramp a little crooked; it hit the ground hard. Couple-three tons, could've been what triggered the collapse."

Another tremor shuddered through the earth under our feet. It was the weirdest feeling, a quivery sensation so unfamiliar that I kept thinking there was something wrong with my legs.

"Or it could've been this," I said as the shaking increased briefly, then faded out altogether.

"Yup. That too. Geologists from U Maine were on the news again. They say these things could stop any time or go on for a week," Wade said.

I gazed at the depression in the earth where Wade had dug me out, although from the amount of dirt in my hair, eyes, and mouth I gathered I'd made it at least partway on my own.

"Yeah," he confirmed, trying and failing to repress a grin when I asked about this. "You were easy to find. Yelling, your head sort of sticking up. I'd called ahead so Sam and his guys were already digging when I got here."

I didn't remember; this was a good thing, probably. "You didn't see any steps or other construction down there?"

Tink Markle had said there were some. But Wade shook his head. "No. Nothing like that. And listen . . . you and Ellie are the only ones who got out. She said to tell you."

Igor . . . A pang of real grief for the big, shaggy dog struck me as I gazed at the spot where I'd been rescued.

"I can't get back in, can I? And the rest can't escape this way, either." It's why I'd followed Tink Markle at all, in hopes of finding us an exit.

Behind us the big machines still roared over the sounds of chain saws howling and the giant jaws of enormous grappling tools snapping shut. I put my face in my hands.

"No," said Wade. "I'm afraid now that you're out, you're out and that's it. I'm sorry."

"Tree was mostly dead when it fell," Wade commented after a few moments while I collected myself.

"But the parts that were alive are wet, and sometime a long while ago somebody wrapped barbed wire around it."

"So?" I walked in circles, flexing my fingers and rotating my neck, testing my knees and ankles.

"So now the tree's grown, wire's all embedded in the wood. Let's say a chain saw hits it." He made a kablooie gesture.

"Is Sam running a saw?"

"Nope. He's running the grapple." Wade took the water bottle and handed it to me again, and after I drank some more I splashed my face, neck, and hands.

"Ellie knows I'm okay?" The dazed feeling I'd had since Wade dug me out was fading enough now for me to notice Sam's pickup truck parked nearby.

"Ayuh," said Wade. "Sam called her. Why, what are you—?"

The pickup truck had a candy-apple-red paint job and custom pinstripes, funded by a wave of new business his landscaping service had done the previous year.

Behind it, Wade's old green Ford 150 sat. "You were going to drive me home?" I asked. Because he was indeed the most open-minded and understanding of men, but with him driving, there was no chance I'd be skipping a medical checkup.

Hey, I'd have felt the same. But I caught his glance at the unused chain saw lying in his truck's bed. He could use it or play chauffeur for me, obviously, but not both.

"I can drive," I said.

Wade looked skeptical. "I'll check on my dad, clean up a little, and get myself looked at if"—I left myself an out—"I can get a quick clinic appointment."

And another thing: by now my housekeeper-slash-stepmother would have figured out that Sam was no longer with my father.

"Let Bella know I'll do whatever my dad needs, will you?" I added.

Not that these were the only deeds I meant to accomplish. But they were the only ones I wanted to talk about.

"I'll just take Sam's truck," I said casually, strolling away toward it before Wade could object to any of this. Sam kept the keys in the console's cup holder, I thought I recalled.

I hopped in, felt around for the key fob.

Correctamundo, as he most certainly would have said.

"No worries," my dad told me cheerfully a little later, unfazed by another day of solitude.

He'd set up a sort of control center in the kitchen, with the phone, his laptop, a little TV, and wood in the woodbox for when he wanted the stove hotter.

"They're still all out at Cliff House," I told him when he asked about Bella and Mika. "They're fine," I added.

His bushy eyebrows, salt and pepper with glints of silver in them, went up and down. He knew I wasn't telling him everything; it was just that for now he'd decided to let it go.

"Dad, are you sure you wouldn't rather I drove you to the Community Center, you could see a few people, maybe play some cards?"

He gave me a look that said he loved me very dearly, but could I please stop saying silly stuff?

"I'll be fine, Jacobia," he said. "The kids are coming home in a little while, and the babysitter with them."

And I couldn't argue with that, so instead I made fresh coffee and a couple of cheese sandwiches with plenty of mustard, one for each of us.

Then when we finished eating I told him again that Bella was fine. I promised that I'd have her home along with Mika and Ellie in just a few more hours now. I'd said it all as calmly and convincingly as I could.

But he was a sharp old dude, and he didn't believe a word of it. I got up.

"Okay, look, the truth is that it's a complete mess, they're stuck there, and I'm doing the best I can to get them out," I said.

His expression cleared. The truth may hurt, but it also keeps you from imagining a lot of terrible untrue things.

"I could help," he suggested.

That's what I'd feared, that he'd hear the truth and want to do something about it, something physical if necessary.

Which it very well might be, but he didn't think he was too old for it. And I didn't want to tell him that he was.

"I'll be back soon," I said instead, and went out before he could start to argue with me.

Minutes later I pulled into a parking spot on Water Street outside The Chocolate Moose. I'd just run in and check the place quickly, I'd decided; Bob Arnold's car wasn't in the cop shop's parking lot, but if I knew him he'd be back.

The little silver bell over the door tinkled sweetly as I entered. Inside, the air was still and cool, and I longed to switch on the lights and the coffeemaker, turn the CLOSED sign to OPEN, and just go back to normal.

But my catering partners were waiting for me and trying not to get murdered; the thought sent yet another bolt of anxiety through me. Just one more thing:

On the shelf behind the counter sat a laptop computer we used for ordering supplies. I switched it on and waited for it to load, hoping the return of phone service meant Internet, too.

It did. I'd found Ingrid Merryfield here; now I looked up Tink Markle the same way, figuring there'd be plenty of info about the aging but once popular entertainer.

But, to my surprise, the entries about him were few; I'd

scanned most of them when a sound came from behind me: the shop bell tinkling.

Turning fast, I ran into a large blue shirt. The shirt had a man in it, and the man had a gun.

Luckily, the man was Bob Arnold. He'd lowered his duty weapon when he saw me; now he stowed it in its holster and snapped the safety strap.

Or maybe it wasn't so lucky; I could practically see steam puffing from his ears. "Come with me," he uttered.

Outside, he ushered me to his squad car. I cast a look back at Sam's truck, knowing he'd discover that it was missing very soon, but there was nothing I could do about it.

"I got a call," Bob said when I was in and buckled up.

He slammed the car into reverse, backed up, and threw it in drive.

"Caller said the Moose was being robbed, perp was armed."

So he wasn't mad at me. He was angry because he'd raced over here and charged into the Moose, then found out that it was nothing.

But the trouble he'd gone to wasn't the only thing he was steamed about. "So there I am," he went on, "wavin' around a goddam *deadly weapon*, when there is no, I repeat, no—"

Right. No robbery, no emergency. "Thank you," I said.

Bob took a right onto Shackford Street under the maples now stretching near-naked branches across the sky. Finally he slowed for a bunch of kids kicking through leaf piles.

"I mean it," I said. "I appreciate that you always come fast when people are in trouble." *When I'm in trouble*, I meant.

His eyes stayed on the road as he listened. "But this time I'm pretty sure someone just wanted you to be downtown," I said.

"Instead of where?"

"Your old place in Quoddy Village, is my guess."

It was just a guess. Or not even, really. One of those out-of-the-blue mental connections that often don't prove true. But I'd seen that odd bicycle guy twice, now: once very briefly in town the night Ingrid Merryfield and Bryan got here, and again the first time Bob and I visited his old house.

The bicycle guy had resembled Tink Markle—sandy hair, flat cap, tweed jacket—though I only saw him from a distance. And now, for no reason other than my sudden, urgent certainty, I'd have bet my last chocolate éclair that Markle hadn't died in that tunnel.

I didn't know it. Not for an actual fact. But I could feel it. And sometimes a girl's just gotta go with her gut, you know?

Anyway: Bob didn't say anything at first, just kept driving. He didn't know Ellie and I had gone back out to Cliff House, so he wasn't surprised I was here.

And he'd cooled down some now, too. He took the long curve headed out of town instead of turning around and going back. We were silent past the airport and the city yards, but on our way into Quoddy Village past the gravel pit and the recycling center, he spoke.

"You think someone's here? Or they were?" Bob's voice was mild as he turned into the warren of narrow, curving streets.

"Maybe." The false-alarm call hadn't happened by accident, I felt sure; it was too unusual, and way too specific.

And it had been Tink Markle riding around out here on that bike; the more I thought about it the more I was sure of it, now.

Maybe that tunnel cave-in hadn't buried him, after all. Maybe he'd just wanted us to think it had. As for why I thought he might be at Bob's now . . .

Well, he'd been there once and seen us. Maybe our presence had put a crimp in his plans, and he wanted to make sure he'd have privacy, this time.

Or maybe not. But: "Let's just get there," I said, and when we did reach Bob's old home, we found that someone had broken the front door in again. Not only was it off the wedge of shingles Bob had stuck under it, now it also dangled askew on one hinge as if someone had kicked it.

Bob followed me into the house, his hand on his sidearm. "Lots of memories here, I suppose," I said.

"Yeah." He frowned as if trying to repress one or more of them, then turned toward the door again, away from the falling plaster, curling wallpaper, and warped floors.

I wanted to let him go back outside but I couldn't. "Is there something else here someone might've wanted?"

He didn't answer. Maybe he needed a minute.

Or more. "Okay, just wait," I said, then went down a dark, hall off the front room to glance into the remaining ones.

Squirrel nests that had once been mattresses filled the bedrooms with the smell of animals and mildew. Someone had made a fire in the bathtub and tried to cook over it.

A dead mouse lay in the hall. "No," said Bob said when I came back, "there's nothing left here for anyone."

Maybe, but I still looked around some more. Moldy papers with faded typing on them, vintage record sleeves—*A Chipmunk Christmas* one of them proclaimed—and a few photo albums lay scattered around the living room floor.

Bob bent to one, flipped through it. But the pages were empty. "Unless they wanted this old stuff. But I don't see why anyone would."

He sighed. "My mom and her sister took hundreds of snapshots of us kids over the years. Used to have albums of them all over the house. Other kids would look through, pick out the ones they were in, and my mom would give 'em to the kids. Some of the poorer ones, that was a great gift for their moms."

Outside, a car went by, and then another. I envied the people in them, going about their daily activities. Meanwhile, back at Cliff House, most of my nearest and dearest were waiting for me to free them, and Sam was operating what his kids called ginormous machinery and I called dangerous.

Bob flipped through another one of the albums. This book was a blast from the past aimed straight at his heart; I could see that from his face.

"Moldy snapshots of someone else's family, though," he said, "why would anyone want those?"

I looked over his shoulder. The photographs were mostly unrecognizable. Except—

"Wait a minute, what's that?" I asked. One snapshot had slipped behind another under the clear plastic covering that held them all to their pages; he plucked it out.

The picture was stained and blurry, but you could still see a youngish woman and two little kids in it.

"Is one of them you?" I asked.

The maple tree in the yard had been smaller back then, and instead of a stack of concrete blocks the front door had boasted a doorstep, brick with black cast-iron railings.

Bob nodded. The kid he'd been wore a blue ball cap, a red shirt, and denim coveralls; red sneakers were on his feet.

"Yeah. And the woman, that's my mother." He almost smiled. "Avalon was her name."

The second child in the snapshot looked familiar, too. Sandy hair, lots of freckles . . . but then I had it, of course.

"That kid there, he just showed up one day," Bob said. "Hung around on the edges of things. Then one day he wasn't around; we never saw him anymore."

"Your mom was pretty."

The woman in the photo wore blue clamdiggers and a blue-and white-striped sailor shirt. She had wavy, brass-colored hair and red lipstick on a mouth that looked as if it laughed often.

"Yeah, she really was," said Bob, and made as if to tuck the photograph into his shirt pocket.

I stopped him. "Let me hold on to that a little while, will you? I might want to show it to someone, help identify the kid."

What I really wanted to do was shove the snapshot under Tink Markle's nose and demand the truth out of him. Because it was true, I thought, what Bob had said: Would you want ruined photos of other, long-ago people . . . unless you were in one of the pictures?

"You think this is what someone wanted?" he said as we made our way to the door.

Outside, the early afternoon air tasted like spring water after the smell inside the neglected dwelling. We crossed the leaf-covered lawn back to the car.

"Yeah, I do think so," I said finally as we got in and Bob settled himself behind the wheel. Around us in the quiet neighborhood, orange leaves twirled from the trees.

"And," I went on, "I have no idea why. Bob, did he have a bike with a horn on it? A squeeze-bulb horn that went 'ooh-gah ooh-gah'?" It had been part of Markle's act on TV.

"Yeah," Bob said, turning to squint at me, "he did. How'd you know about it?"

And for me that's when it all started to make sense.

"So his story was true," I said, mostly to myself, "or at least the part about him being here as a kid was."

Bob looked questioningly at me. "That kid," I explained, pointing at the shirt pocket where he'd slid the photo instead of giving it to me, "biked over here from Cliff House as a youngster."

Probably he'd just wanted other kids to hang out with. "I heard about him from someone who's there now," I said.

Which was at least true as far as it went. I didn't want to get too wound up in the details, though, when I didn't yet know what they meant myself.

"Bob, I think he went looking for that photo because it proves he came here as a boy. He wants that kept secret for some reason."

Wanted it enough to come back here and search again, on the bare chance that the photograph still existed, and the even smaller chance that somebody might recover it and know what it meant.

The reason: it would complicate the tale he'd tell once the murders began getting investigated:

That he knew nothing about the place. That he was merely a guest, like all the others.

That he hadn't killed them, by which I also mean us: me, Ellie, Bella, Mika.

"Then why did he tell you? And how'd he know about the photograph?" Bob asked reasonably.

The earth shook faintly beneath us again; gosh, I wished it would quit.

"He didn't expect me to live long enough to tell anyone else," I said. "Or that's my guess, anyway."

Tink might've known about the photograph because he'd been there when other kids picked out ones that they wanted. As for why he'd come back to get it at all—an obsessive, hyper-detail-oriented and possibly very risky maneuver . . .

Hey, people with murder on their conscience get nervous, you know? They want very desperately to cover all the bases, so that late at night while they stare sleeplessly at the ceiling, they can reassure themselves that they've done all they could. To avoid, I mean, being identified as a killer. I turned toward the busted front door.

"But whatever the reason, right now I need to get back to check on my dad."

I needed to know that Sam's children were home and that the babysitter was indeed still there with them, so he wasn't alone trying to take care of them.

I also wanted to know how Tink Markle had gotten here so fast when he was supposed to be dead in a collapsed tunnel.

But the main reason I had to get back to Eastport right now

was one I couldn't tell Bob Arnold. If I did, he'd be as against it as I was; it was so unsafe, no sane person would try it.

And this time, I'd be doing it by myself.

Well, almost by myself. "Dad, will you just get in the boat, please?" I said as I put out a hand for him to grab.

I'd known I was in trouble the minute I walked back into the house. My dad was still alone, and he'd gotten the martini-mixing kit out.

This was exactly what I'd have prescribed for myself if I could have; instead here we were at the dock.

"Dad," I repeated. Now he stood on the finger pier gazing around happily at the massive old fishing boats with names like *Pretty Girl* and *Daddy's Revenge II* painted on their sterns.

Gulls flapped overhead, and the chilly breeze felt bracing; he lifted his weathered old face into it before taking my hand.

"Okay, now," he muttered, stepping aboard with one leg, then swinging the other into the pretty little Chris-Craft lake boat that Ellie and I had left here earlier.

"There!" my dad said proudly, balancing on the deck, but just then a wave bounced us; he staggered and grabbed me.

"Sit," I told him, turning him to aim his backside at a seat cushion and placing him on it. "We've got to go."

By now it was well after noon, the tide long turned. "I wouldn't be in such a rush if you hadn't insisted on coming," I grumbled.

Battery, life jackets . . . what was I forgetting? I'd done all this with Ellie but not alone, and never in an unfamiliar boat. This one didn't even have an outboard engine; instead all the power was tucked away somewhere under the rear deck.

I put my hand on the old snapshot Bob had finally given me to make sure it was still there, and it was; I'd slid it into my back pants pocket. I checked that the inflatable vest I'd grabbed was zipped, then checked the nylon straps on the old-fashioned orange life jacket that my dad had put on.

Then I took a deep breath, screwed up my courage, and put my hand on the boat's ignition key. Here goes nothing.

"Jacobia?" My father's voice was still mellowed by the martini he'd had. "Thanks."

"You said if I didn't let you come, you'd call Wade," I retorted, meanwhile checking for the hundredth time that the lines were off and there was no one behind us in the channel.

When I got back to the house, I'd told my dad everything: where I was going, how I was getting there, what I meant to do when I arrived. That was the other reason, besides his own welfare, that I'd had to see him once more before I left: so somebody would know, if I went AWOL, where to look for me.

Whereupon he'd stationed himself in the doorway. "Jacobia, I'm coming with you."

And to my objections: "Look, even if I drown, it's not like I'm dying young," he'd told me, and finished with the kicker: the I'll-rat-you-out threat.

And by then with the tide on its way out I'd had no time for argument, so now here he was with his liver-spotted old face stretched in a grin and his eyes wide with delight under their bushy eyebrows.

As my dad watched, I started the Chris-Craft's engine by the simple method of pushing a button, shoving the throttle forward, and turning the key in such a way that when the engine fired, the wheel's hard lurch didn't break my hand.

Easy-peasy, I heard Ellie saying when the engine turned over and caught with a throaty rumble.

Last chance: I leaned across to my dad. "You're still sure you want to do this?"

He glanced sideways at me as all around him the life of the harbor went on. Smells of bait, seaweed, and fish guts mingled with the salt-tinctured fragrance of creosote and diesel.

"Jacobia, I wouldn't miss it for the world," he said.

A seagull flapped. A seal stuck its glossy wet head up.

"Hang on, then," I told him. "This might get a little rough."

I put the engine in reverse and the water slid by us on one side, the dock on the other. Turning the wheel, I let us drift a little, making sure we were in the channel.

Then a sneaky breeze kicked up suddenly. The boat's rear end rotated, aiming us toward deep water.

But we *kept* rotating, due to us still being in neutral. The boat didn't handle at all like Ellie's did, and it seemed no matter which way I turned the wheel, nothing happened.

Or nothing good, anyway. If Ellie were here, she'd have told me what to do. Instead we swung wildly toward large rocks in the front while our stern veered hard the other way, at a forest of wooden dock pilings.

"Jacobia."

"What?" I snapped; the dock pilings loomed. This whole boat that I was operating was about to become a salvage hull.

"Throttle," said my dad, rising in alarm. "Shove the throttle forward."

Of course; I smacked the heel of my hand to my forehead, too late remembering the first rule of boat-handling: you can't steer without power. So I gave it some, and—

Vroom. My dad sat back down hard and shot me a look. But as we motored out of the boat basin we were grinning like fools.

Out on the bay, our early success buoyed me; even when we hit rogue currents and shimmied hard, I gripped that wheel and rode the boat like a jet ski, feeling it rise up over a wave and smack down hard again, over and over.

Then at last we were through, heading into calm water. My dad turned, his eyes bright and the look on his face blissful.

"Jacobia," he said, "that was lovely. What's next?"

I eased us nearer to shore. Soon we'd need to keep our eyes peeled for rock-studded shallows, but not quite yet.

"Beats me," I said, and it was true; all I wanted was to find Ellie, Bella, and Mika and get them out of there, but the how of it was another story.

At the channel marker, we rounded Gay's Head; minutes later the cove we were aiming at came into view. In it, white-caps leapt between granite ledges now showing themselves at low tide.

"Dad? Better sit down." He was behind me now, inspecting everything on the rear deck curiously.

"Bella won't cut me any slack if I lose you overboard," I said, but he didn't seem to hear, picking up a ratty old black canvas bag curiously and putting it down again.

Abruptly we were in the turbulence, the boat bucking and jerking wildly. I gripped the wheel, half the time hanging on for dear life and the other half just struggling white-knuckled to maintain some sort of meaningful control.

"Dad?" I said as our prow lurched up so fast that he stumbled and nearly went overboard.

And then he did go. One instant he was there and the next he was in the water, clinging to the swim ladder at the boat's bouncing stern with both his gnarled, arthritic hands.

I stared back in horror as well as I could while also trying not to sink us or run us into any of those rocks. His fingers were loosening from the swim ladder, his grip slipping.

But I couldn't let go of the wheel to do anything about it.

Desperately I dropped the engine into neutral, looped a bungee cord from a bin of them shoved under the steering wheel console, then ran the cord through the wheel and around the stem of the compass mounted to the console, to keep the wheel from turning on its own.

I had no idea whether or not this was a smart move, but I also had no time to worry about it, so I left it and scrambled to the boat's stern.

"Dad!" When I reached him he was barely hanging on, the waves slapping his face and trying to shove him off the swim ladder. I leaned as far as I could over the transom, then crawled onto it, but his hold was so tenuous that if it failed before I grabbed him, I'd lose him completely.

Feeling around on the deck behind me, my fingers searched frantically for any tool I could find. Finally looked around and spotted a boat hook like the one Ellie had used to haul Gilly Blaine aboard, not as long or sharply barbed but still useful, I hoped.

"Jake," my dad whispered, spitting seawater.

"Hold still," I told him, then hurled myself back on deck, seized the boat hook and returned with it, and shoved the barbed end of the hook all the way down his back, inside his collar.

Turning it slightly, I felt the barb catch his belt. Then I pulled, lifted, and crawled backward off the transom all at the same time, which made me feel pretty good until I slipped, fell, and landed on the deck on my backside with the hook sliding away across the transom.

Gasping, I flung myself on the transom again, hoping that barbed hook wasn't taking out my father's appendix. Finally I hauled him in, dripping and sputtering.

"Sit, dammit," I said, then ran to the wheel, released it, and put us in gear just in time to not hit the *very big rock* looming in front of us. That meant other big rocks were all around us, just hidden under the water, and if I didn't want our boat's bottom torn out by them, I needed to do something.

Behind me, my dad lay flat on the deck, hacking up more salt water. I turned but he waved impatiently at me.

"Drive," he managed through another gargling cough, so I did, and at last we got out of the rocky shallows.

"Towels and clothes," I yelled to him through the waves' crash, "in the bin under the seat!"

That's where I'd found the musty stuff I'd put on earlier, and there'd been more; he nodded and found his way.

Soon he was reasonably dry again, looking around in wonder as we dropped the Chris-Craft's anchor in the cove directly below the Cliff House back lawn. The rope ladder Tink Markle had dropped to Ellie and me was still there, dangling over the cliff's edge.

"Good," my dad said when he saw it, and moved purposefully toward the stern. He meant to ease himself over it and slosh his way to shore, I supposed; there was no other choice.

But the water was still shoulder deep here; I grabbed a rope coil from the bin near the engine, then reached out to give him a hand while he was lowering himself to the water.

Which was when some fool up there started shooting again.

Eleven

Maybe he was an old guy but he could move pretty fast when he wanted to, and the gunshots made him want to. He hurled himself into the water like a man half his age, and I followed.

"Yeesh," I shuddered out past my clenched teeth, feeling the water's aching cold climb past my ankles to settle behind my kneecaps, then rise to engulf my hips.

Our feet barely touched bottom, waves punching us this way and that. "Here," I said, looping a length of the rope around his waist, then tying it around mine.

The rocks underfoot were slippery when we did manage to touch them, but we were well motivated and at last we hauled ourselves out of the waves; on land we tottered to a spot under the cliff's jutting overhang, out of sight for now.

But after that, there was only one possible direction to go. The rope ladder dangled in front of us; I couldn't believe I'd climbed it, and the idea that my dad might manage the thing didn't compute at all.

"Bella's up there," my dad reminded me.

Of course. He'd have walked on hot lava if it meant getting Bella out of danger.

"But how do we know when it's safe?" I asked. "We'll be like ducks in a shooting gallery."

Because naturally we couldn't just confront a steep cliff and a ladder that maybe the Flying Wallendas could've handled; there had to be gunfire, too.

"Don't worry about it, I'll go first," he said.

I felt my mouth open, ready to put the kibosh on this. But he was already scuttling out, yanking on the ladder to test it.

"Dad, you're not going to make yourself a target," I said.

"No more than I can help," he agreed. He put one foot on the bottom rung, then the other foot on the next.

From there, he was fully visible from the clifftop, but no shots rang out. When he'd gone up a few more rungs, I started up behind him, still linked to him by that length of rope.

And for a little while we made decent progress while not having any holes shot into us. But then the other thing that I'd feared would happen arrived suddenly, when we were halfway up; his spirit was willing, but the flesh needed a rest.

Craning my neck, I saw him gather himself, trying to lift his foot one more time, but to no avail; when his hand slipped, I forced myself upward a few more arduous, terrifying rungs so I could grab on to his belt.

"Hey," he protested, but when I began pulling upward on it, he quit grousing. After that our conversation consisted entirely of swear words and gasps of fright until finally, after several more heart-stopping moments, we reached the top.

But that was it. He flopped an arm up over the cliff's edge and stopped, worn out, and I just wasn't strong enough to push him the rest of the way. So there we dangled together, clinging to the rope ladder and each other like two stranded monkeys.

Until we fell, which was going to be the very next tune on today's hit parade unless I prevented it. But with what?

Then, *Wait a minute.* There, right in front of me.

"What?" my dad demanded as I reached past him. The iron spikes the ladder hung from still stuck up out of the granite.

"Okay, Dad, you're going to get lifted. Just go with it, okay? Crawl, scramble, whatever you need to do."

As I spoke, I checked that rope still fastened around his waist. Then I checked the one at my end, still securely fastened around my own middle. Luckily Ellie quizzed me regularly on my knot-tying skills; it was part of her long-term plan to turn me into a skilled mariner.

I reached past my dad again, looping the section of rope that was between us around one of the spikes. There was still plenty of rope remaining.

So now I had a pulley; if I went down, he would go up. But as I hung there, I noticed the ladder was fraying. Hemp fibers in the rung I gripped were stretching, unraveling, and parting rapidly, and have I mentioned that by now enough time had passed so the tide was coming in again?

Well, it was. Just not yet far enough. So if the ladder or the rope between my dad and me failed while I attempted this ridiculous stunt that was also our only salvation, our falls would be broken by a foot of cold water. And *then* we'd hit the skull-breakingly hard rocks.

"Jacobia?" My dad looked down at me.

"Yeah, just a second," I said, and jumped.

The result was gratifying, immediate, and painful. With my whole weight pulling down suddenly on him and the pulley stake holding firm, he practically flew over the cliff's edge while I dropped down six feet.

Stopping was interesting, and I don't believe either of my underarms will ever be the same, but I did it. Then, amazingly, the ladder itself began rising, clods of earth showering down on me as the rungs slid up and over the edge.

Not until I got to the top did I see who was pulling—Tink Markle—and by now I wasn't even surprised.

"You again," I said in disgust when I'd half-rolled, half-crawled up over the cliff's edge. "You're supposed to be dead."

"You're supposed to be dead, too," he replied.

"The world," I said as I got stiffly up off the grass, "is full of disappointments."

My dad sat nearby, untying the rope from his belt. He still looked tired but mostly he looked glad to be off the ladder.

I turned back to Markle, not caring how many cliffs he'd hauled me up and over.

"You were pointing a gun at us when it all went haywire down there in the tunnel," I reminded him. "And what about those gunshots we heard just *before* you pulled us up?"

"I never heard shots," Markle said; he was lying his face off, I could tell, and he didn't care if I knew it. "I heard your voices, came down here to see what was going on."

He spread his hands. In one of them was a square of paper. I grabbed at my back pocket; empty.

He had the snapshot that I'd found in Bob's old Quoddy Village home. Tink must've seen it sticking up out of my back pocket and plucked it out while I was busy struggling over the cliff's edge.

"Thanks," he said, tearing it up and releasing the pieces into a breeze that carried it over the water and out of sight.

The relief on his face was plain. It would never have caused him any harm, that snapshot; even if anyone ever found it, who would recognize him in it after all these years?

No one, probably. But when you're sleeplessly staring at the ceiling, worrying and wondering whether you've erased every possible clue to your guilt, 'probably' just doesn't cut it.

"And now, if you two happen to want to get back inside un-noticed . . . ," he began.

My dad turned, bristling. "Listen, Junior, thanks for the lift, but the day I need a twerp like you to get me in anywhere un-noticed is the day I'll just step in front of a freight train, okay?"

He stalked past Tink. "Not that I don't appreciate it," he said as he went by, but the rest of his monologue as he stomped away from us up the lawn included words like *snot-nosed* and *whippersnapper.*

He'd gotten his gumption back, I saw, noting his straight back and determined stride. Bemusedly, Markle watched him, too.

"So I gather the old guy's not, uh, senile or anything?"

My blood boiled, suddenly, and I swear it was a wonder I didn't just push him off the cliff right that minute. Meanwhile, my dad was halfway to the main house, approaching the steps leading onto the patio under the kitchen window.

"Yeah," I told Markle. "You gather right."

Nearing the house, my dad stayed in the lead, his stringy gray ponytail bouncing on his back as his stride gathered steam.

Congratulations, Jake, I berated myself silently as I followed him. *By risking your life and Dad's, you've put him and yourself right back into the trap you've just escaped.*

On the other hand, we hadn't drowned, we'd gotten off the beach, and we were at the house where I'd wanted to go in the first place.

So under the circumstances I figured I'd count it as a win. "How'd you know I was at The Chocolate Moose?" I asked Markle.

He'd put the gun away, assuming he'd ever had it out. Which I did assume, but obviously we wouldn't run; where would we go? And he could produce a weapon again any time, I reminded myself.

And then of course he did so, or I thought he did; my face must've shown alarm.

He stopped, shrugged, and pulled his phone out. The screen brightened into a picture of the Chocolate Moose's front door.

A *moving* picture; a pedestrian walked by. The screen was showing a live shot, happening now. He thumbed a button and the view switched to inside, where shadows moved in the afternoon sunlight shining onto the floor.

"You've been spying on us?" Street sounds muffled by the glass of our shop's window came from the phone.

So whatever he'd set up, it sent audio, too. Talks I'd had with Ellie, for instance, and with Bob Arnold. What we thought, how we'd felt.

"You can call me a control freak," he said. "Ingrid does. But the tiny little cameras I placed before she got into town sure came in handy eventually, didn't they?"

They sure had. With any luck at all—Tink's, not mine—Bob Arnold might've shot me by mistake on account of them, after Tink made the fake armed-robbery call to Bob. The cameras were how Tink had known where I was.

"Yeah, handy," I responded dryly.

We started walking again. "Why did you want the snapshot?" I asked him.

He shrugged. "Would you have left it? If you remembered it being taken, and you thought there was the slightest chance a bit of evidence like that could come back and spoil your story?"

He could tell people he'd never been here before, he meant, if no one could prove different. He could say he had no history whatsoever with this place.

That it was not, somehow, his motive for murder. Ahead, my dad waited on the patio. I tried again.

"You didn't cause the tunnel cave-in, though. Or know it would happen once you'd led us down there."

How could he, or anyone? Besides, I'd seen his face while it was happening. He'd been as frightened as the rest of us.

"Nope. That was luck," he confirmed. Good for him, bad for us. "I intended to do it another way entirely," he added.

Oh, terrific. "But how'd you get out?" Not up through the kitchen; people had been in it. And anyway he'd been on the far side of the cave-in, trapped there by the fallen earth; to get back to the main house at all, he'd have had to burrow through with his hands.

And even if *that* was physically possible, my mind went on relentlessly, his clothes were still clean and his hands showed no sign of digging.

Which meant there had to be another exit from the tunnel, one that didn't require any digging, returning, or explaining. I filed the information away for possible future use.

"Meanwhile, you're a famous comedian," I said. Hey, he was talking, and I wanted him to go on; who knew what fascinating tidbit he might drop?

"But you haven't worked in the entertainment business for years?" I needled him gently.

It's amazing what you can learn with just a few minutes' access to the Internet. This time his glance was annoyed, just as I'd hoped; a vexed man is a talkative man, in my experience.

"So? Show business is fickle. First you're hot, then you're not. I'll be back soon enough," he answered defensively.

"No, you won't." We were nearly to the house. At the yard's corner where bushes hid the masonry, a wooden Adirondack chair stood by a stone birdbath.

My dad was in the chair, resting quietly. Markle slowed, turning to me. "What do you mean by that?" he demanded.

I shrugged. "Something about felony drugs? Time in prison, stuff you were working on got cancelled, yada yada?"

The few entries there were about this washed-up old dope dealer had been very informative.

His hands balled into fists at his sides. "That was bogus. All of it, people were jealous."

He huffed out a breath. "Anyway, in a few more years I can get insured again and then I can work again."

The articles I'd read didn't seem to think so. The film business didn't hire people they thought might go to prison in the middle of production, apparently.

Or drop dead of an overdose. We reached the Adirondack chair, where my dad sat with his eyes closed and his knobby hands crossed over his chest.

"I'm fine," he said, not opening his eyes as I approached. "Just leave me here and I'll catch up."

The spot was secluded enough. And he did still look tired. "I should sit a minute," he said.

And I had things to do. "Okay, stay here. I'll come back. Don't go anywhere," I said, then saw what lay abandoned by his chair.

It was a dog's chew toy, gnawed to a lump at one end. *Igor . . .* A thump of sorrow hit me, followed by another surge of the fury I'd been shoving back all day.

Igor the God-forbid Irish wolfhound and Maud Bankersley were both dead or hopelessly trapped in that collapsed tunnel, and what I wanted to do was beat this jerk senseless.

But that would have to wait; I still had to get us out of here if I could, and for that I needed more info. A Coast Guard rescue helicopter would've been lovely, too, and it also was a thing that was not happening.

"Look, Tink. Just level with me, what's your deal here?"

By now we'd gotten around to the side of the house, seeing no one, and stopped under the portico. The roaring of chain saws and thundering of heavy machinery rose from beyond the big fallen tree's massive trunk.

Tink eyed me. "I don't know what you're talking about."

Sure, I thought, and moved away from him, toward the big front door. "Fine, whatever. I'm going in."

Which I did, not caring anymore who saw me. For one thing, I could smell fresh coffee brewing, and for another, once I'd had some I didn't intend to stay no matter what.

Markle followed me in. "Listen," he said urgently. "I didn't want to tell anyone. But I'm working for an agency, this private protection group I hooked up with out there."

I supposed he meant Los Angeles. He glanced around. "I'm keeping Ingrid Merryfield from getting murdered, or trying."

I nearly laughed out loud. "I'm supposed to believe that? And you were doing some protecting by trying to kill us because why, again?"

I stomped away without waiting for an answer; he stayed right behind me.

"Anyway, after I ran into problems . . ." The drug arrests, he meant. "Well, I was out of work and a guy I knew offered me a job doing protection for celebrities."

He didn't explain why this guy thought he might be good at it. I still had a lot of other questions for him, too, like where he was staying and why he'd felt entitled to barge into Bryan-the-limousine-driver's apartment.

Or where Bryan was right now, for that matter. I hadn't seen him for a while.

We were nearly to the kitchen door. "But don't tell Ingrid about me, okay?" Tink Markle pleaded. "She doesn't know that I'm here to watch over her."

Because it wasn't true, I was certain. He was making up this story about protecting Ingrid; otherwise why try killing us in the tunnel?

What a creep, I thought as we paused at the kitchen door. A murderous creep, with who knew what else up his sleeve . . .

I put my ear to the closed kitchen door. Someone in there had found the radio that the dinner cooks had been using that first night. Now it was tuned to the Shead High School station.

"Ingrid used to be married to a film studio bigwig," Tink whispered.

His breath smelled of brandy. "*Feelthy* rich," Tink spread his hands to show the size of Ingrid Merryfield's ex-husband's fortune.

The radio in the kitchen began playing Chet Atkins. "When they divorced, the prenup said she'd get security. She didn't want it, but he hired me, anyway," Tink said.

He named the film mogul. I wouldn't have known the name, and didn't. I kept on listening through the kitchen door, tuning out his voice and wishing he would shut up.

It was all lies, anyway. I didn't even know what he was trying to accomplish with them; I just knew he'd killed them all: Waldo, Audrey, Gilly, and Maud.

And Igor; I despised him the most for that. Liquid notes poured from the kitchen radio. Country music is not my jam; how many trucks, women, and dogs named Blue can a man lose, anyway, before he stops seeming unlucky and starts seeming careless?

But the sound covered the door's faint squeak as I eased it open and stuck my head in. Seeming to catch the movement from the corner of her eye, Ellie looked over from where she sat at the kitchen table and her eyes widened happily.

"Jake! You're back! Are you all right? What's happened?" the questions tumbled from her.

But if I answered them I'd be here all day, and we were in a hurry. Meanwhile, I'd lost track of where Tink had gone; he'd been right with me, but now he wasn't.

"Where is everyone?" I mouthed. If I had to, I'd decided, I'd carry Bella down that rope ladder myself. Ellie waved toward the parlor and now I could hear voices out there.

"Bella's keeping Ingrid busy," said Ellie. "Calming her down. When Ingrid figured out how many of her guests were dead, she got upset."

About time, I thought uncharitably. "Also, I haven't seen Bryan in a while," Ellie added, echoing my earlier thought.

Meanwhile, Mika stood quietly at the kitchen counter. In my absence she had constructed a pile of the sort of sandwiches that are possible if you've got half a leftover prime rib plus plenty of rolls, horseradish, and mayonnaise.

I grabbed one and bit into it famishedly. "You're soaking wet," Ellie pointed out.

So I was. But our duffel bags were all down here in the

kitchen now, I noticed, ready for the moment when the drive-way got opened up.

If we lived that long, which I feared we wouldn't; thus my plan. Thinking this I hauled dry clothes from my duffel, pulled my wet ones off and redressed, then looked around for something to give my dad.

"I talked to Sam," Mika said quietly, reminding me that the phones worked again.

"He says it'll be a little while yet," she said.

"All right," I told her, now digging through one duffel bag after another. "We'll just wait," I added, not wanting to say too much.

After all, who knew where Markle might've put more of those infernal cameras? I found a pair of jeans in Bella's bag, and since the two of them were equally skinny I thought they'd fit my dad, though he'd have to be content with an old red sweater of mine to go on top.

After gathering the clothes, another sandwich, and a bottle of water from the refrigerator, I took them all out the kitchen door to my dad, who still waited on the terrace.

"You all right?" I asked, but I didn't have to. He looked bright-eyed and bushy-tailed, as he'd have put it, taking the clothes eagerly and repairing to the privacy of the shrubberies to put them on, then returning.

Reassured, I let him bite hungrily into his sandwich while I moved toward the white gravel driveway and the garage building on the other side of it.

I glanced around. No one was in sight. I squinted in the direction of the fallen tree again, hoping maybe there really was some way around the thing and I'd just missed it somehow.

But it still lay across the driveway, too high to climb over, and as I'd thought I recalled, it blocked what little land lay at either end of it, too.

Try to get around it and we'd be over another cliff toot

sweet, as Sam would've said. And this time, there'd be no rope ladder to haul us up.

"Looking for someone?" My dad came up behind me, munching.

"Uh-huh." Because Ellie was right—Bryan hadn't been around for hours now, and if we were going to get out of here without trouble I needed to know where he was before we tried it.

Not that I suspected him of any of this. To me, he seemed pretty straightforward. But I didn't not suspect him, either.

By now I'd have suspected the angel Gabriel if he were around. Sucking in a breath, I got ready to make a dash across the driveway, to check Bryan's apartment.

But just then Ellie appeared beside me, wiping her hands on a dish towel. "So it's just us and them, now. Ingrid and Bryan."

"Not quite." Quickly I filled her in on the unexpected reappearance of Tink Markle. It seemed to me that someone else should still be around here somewhere, too, but I couldn't put my finger on why I felt that way.

When I finished, Ellie was looking puzzledly at me. But before she could say why, a new sound erupted from the area beyond the fallen tree, like a chain saw but louder. I put my hands over my ears, still gazing up at Bryan's apartment.

I didn't want to go up there. Last time, bad things had happened. But there was no point in procrastinating.

"Okay." I took off with Ellie right behind me. We hit the stairs leading to the apartment at a run and hustled up them.

If he was there, I'd say we'd come to let him know the sad news about Igor, I decided. Not that he'd seemed very attached to the animal, but it was the only excuse I had.

And I needed to know if he was going to be in our way when we were fleeing. Or if instead somebody'd already gotten in his way, as I'd begun suspecting.

We reached the landing outside his door. No tremors had

rattled the earth beneath us lately, but beyond the fallen tree some large item of machinery still slammed back and forth.

I pulled open the screen door, meaning to knock, but the inside door drifted open slowly when I touched it.

I hate it when that happens. "Bryan?"

Silence from inside. Then something hit the floor. I shoved the door wide open and paused, listening.

Nothing. After stepping inside I scampered quickly through the kitchen to the bedroom and bath: no one.

"Jake." Ellie's voice came from in the front room; her tone told me what she'd found. When I got there she was standing by the big uncurtained window, frowning down at the floor.

Correction: at someone on the floor. "Darn," I said at the sight of Bryan's slack, staring face.

He'd slid off the couch. A gun lay by his outstretched hand. I didn't know what kind, but I guessed it fired bullets, one of which had entered Bryan's skull.

Exited it, too, but I tried not to look too hard at that part. Overturned on the coffee table was the bottle of whiskey that I'd watched Tink Markle drink from earlier.

Outside, the light was sneaking out of the sky the way it did in autumn: gradually for a while, then suddenly.

"We don't have much time," I said. "In a couple of hours it will be dark again."

And although I'd already begun doubting that the tree crew would get us out of here today, now I was becoming sure of it.

"They're having trouble out there," I said, "something they didn't expect. They must be, that's why it's taking so long and why Sam told Mika to be patient."

"He didn't want to tell her how difficult it really is," Ellie agreed. "It would discourage her. But now what do we do?"

Good question. I grabbed Bryan's gun from the floor by his hand, the red plaid blanket draped over the back of the sofa, and, when I spied them, his keys from the coffee table.

Then I let Ellie out ahead of me, pulled the door firmly shut and locked it, and we went down and crossed the driveway once more.

Around back, my father seemed content, but as the afternoon waned it was getting colder out here so I threw Bryan's blanket over him, then went on with Ellie around to the front porch.

Inside it was even gloomier than out, shadows streaking the old hardwood floors and filling the out-of-the-way corners with sneaky little pockets of who knew what. The electricity hadn't come on yet, of course, and I hoped that if we were still here when it got darker, we wouldn't break our necks.

Although by now I was more worried that someone might try breaking them for us. Quietly we scurried to the kitchen, where Mika still waited and Bella had returned.

She was scrubbing the sink, her usual activity when stress made her want to muscle something, anything, into submission. I wished I could tell her my dad was here, but she'd have raised too big a fuss.

She'd find out soon enough, I hoped. Then Tilda French, the plain, dowdy woman I'd wondered about on our first night here, walked in and crossed to the refrigerator without a word. Her pale face bleached even more when the light from the window hit it, and her straight brown hair flopped lifelessly.

But that's not why I stared. I stared because I'd forgotten her. That's why I'd felt someone else must be here. Tilda hadn't been in any of the rooms we checked the night before, and what with all our recent boating and climbing and body-finding, and because she was in fact so quiet, so mousy and forgettable, I'd completely—

"Here you go, Tilda!" Mika called sweetly, turning from the stove, where she was putting the finishing touches on a fondue pot for the appetizer table she was setting up.

"Right, it's cocktail time!" I managed. Or near enough, considering how many of the potential imbibers were dead.

Tilda took the fondue tray from Mika. Her pallid expression

and hunched shoulders under a shapeless gray sweatshirt were no more memorable than ever.

Carrying the tray, she headed for the parlor. "Tilda, is Tink Markle in there?" I stopped her as she reached the doorway.

She shook her head, blinking nervously as if I might blame her for his absence even though, as far as I knew, she'd never known of his presence.

"And . . . Tilda? Listen, forgive my asking, but . . . how do you know Ingrid Merryfield, anyway?"

Why was Tilda here at all, I meant—Bryan had told me, but I wanted to know what she would say—and to her credit she took my meaning at once.

"I'm her personal assistant," Tilda replied. Then she went on into the parlor with the tray while Ellie sank into a kitchen chair again and Mika took her phone into the pantry to try getting Sam on the line again.

By now Bella had finished with the sink and started on the stovetop. "Next, those shelves," she said, shuddering in their direction. "They haven't been cleaned in years."

For Bella the correct shelf-cleaning interval was forty-eight hours. "And the *woodwork*," she added, shaking her head.

Cleaning hadn't been in our job description, but if she wanted to do it then I was all for it, I decided, and told her so just as Mika returned from the pantry looking disappointed.

"No answer," she reported unhappily. "I tried several times."

Ellie went over and patted her on the shoulder. "He just can't hear it with all the sawing and chopping going on," she told Mika comfortingly.

But my daughter-in-law was fading. "I miss my kids," she said.

"I know. We'll be out of here soon," I promised her. "But listen, let me just go check something," I said, and headed out the kitchen door to the patio again.

"Dad?" The chair he'd been in was empty. The blanket lay

draped across it. In the thick shrubbery I pushed aside balsam fronds, inhaling their sharp scent.

"Dad?" I returned to the patio. The chair faced away from me out toward the cliff's edge and the water beyond.

"Dad?" I said puzzledly to the chair again, but he didn't answer because he still wasn't there. Finally I stood squinting into the deepening shadows, not sure what to think.

"Dad?" I tried a last time. But he was gone, and inside I found that Tilda French and Ingrid Merryfield were gone, too.

"Ingrid said she wanted to see the cave-in," Mika reported.

And Tilda? What had she wanted? The more I thought about it, the more it seemed to me that looking harmless wasn't much of a character reference.

Maybe it was more like camouflage. "Now the cellar door's closed and we can't get it open," Mika said. The inside door, not the secret one in the cellar, she meant. "And when we call to them, no one answers."

Great. So now we were stuck here at Cliff House while the windows darkened, the rooms crept with shadows, and our hearts filled with dread of the coming night.

And my dad was missing.

"I'm going out to find him," said Bella not much later.

I'd had to tell her; she'd never forgive me if I didn't. Now her big grape-green eyes bulged with anxiety.

"I can't leave your father out there where it's—"

Cold. Dark, or nearly; the windows deepened to indigo.

"But if you can't see him and he doesn't answer . . ." I began. I'd searched inside, and down the driveway as far as the tree.

"I'll try again in a minute," I said as the tree-removal team worked on, floodlights blazing, heavy machinery roaring, chain saws howling ferociously.

"Let me just get my wits together, first," I added, like that was a possibility. Every time another chunk of fallen tree trunk got thrown down with a *thud!* Cliff House shuddered and I jumped.

But Bella couldn't wait. "Oh," she cried wretchedly as she ran for the kitchen door.

"No," I called after her as I hurried to grab one of the flashlights off the kitchen table. Ellie and Mika tried stopping her, too, but not until I'd wrapped my own arms tightly around her shoulders did she give in.

"Listen," I said. "You'd last about five minutes out there before something bad happened."

In the finding-her-way-around department she was about as useful as the compass from a box of Cracker Jacks.

"I'll go," I said, and at last she agreed unwillingly, still wringing her bony hands together.

"But you find him, d'you hear me?" she added as I closed the kitchen door behind me.

The night was cold, now, with a breeze whose razorish edge made me think of snow. A vee of geese arrowed over the full moon leering down from the sky.

"Dad?" Moonlight turned the lawn silvery, and now I saw footprints pressed into the grass. Anxiety pierced me, but when I got to the cliff's edge the rope ladder on which we'd climbed up here was still piled in the grass.

So he hadn't tried using it, anyway, I thought gratefully, and then without warning the whole cliff jerked and shuddered under my feet.

The tree crew, I thought distractedly. Then something touched me on the cheek and a thrill of fright went through me as I took several fast steps back.

"Who's that?" I whispered, glancing behind me, but no one was there. I crept to the cliff's edge once more, looked down fearfully.

Waves glimmered dully, the color of pewter. Straight down past the outcropping, white foam spread among the rocks.

"Psst." A whisper came from the darkness where the lawn's side edges ended and the softwood-and-saplings thickets began.

A *familiar* whisper . . . "Dad!" He seized my sleeve, drawing me into the shadows with him.

"I came to make sure Ellie's boat's still there," he said.

It was. Its white fiberglass hull floated sedately on the high tide, still tied to the dock where Ellie and I had left it.

I didn't see the Chris-Craft. It hit me that its anchor had probably lifted when the tide rose; that boat could be anywhere by now.

"Okay," I said, "but why?"

Thud. The earth shook beneath us again. And—had it moved?

"Did you feel that?" I asked, but he was already halfway back up the lawn, hurrying away with his head down.

Again: *thud.* He stopped midstride. The gritty soil under my feet seemed to shiver, and by the time I caught up to him it felt oddly mushy, too.

And then a big crack opened up in it. Yeeks. Zigzagging across the lawn, the sudden crack kept widening like a mouth slowly opening, as if the soil atop this whole section of the bluff behind the house had begun sliding.

Sliding toward the sea. "We need to get the people out of here," he called back to me as he hurried on.

More thuds plus new growling and grinding sounds filled the night air, rattling the patio chairs on their flagstones.

"This is all getting unstable," he said as he reached the kitchen door, then rushed inside, where I knew Bella would be as relieved to see him as I'd been.

But not about the news he'd delivered, because unless I was missing something, shaking the soil off the bluff meant shaking us off, as well.

And what had touched my face out there just now, anyway? Like a feather, or the caress of a soft-bristled brush.

Another thud came from beneath me. I aimed the flashlight at my sneakers just as a big chunk of lawn near the patio slid a few inches. Just . . . slid, and the patio shifted a little, too.

I aimed the light past the flagstones to light up the house foundation, built the old-fashioned way of granite and mortar. A crack ran through it, and I'm no geologist but I got the sense that my dad's old-fashioned horse sense had triumphed again.

As in, it was time to stampede. The crack in the foundation widened as I watched, as did the one behind me, in the lawn; it looked as if any minute the whole place—Cliff House, its lawn, trees, the garage, even the pea-gravel driveway glowing whitely in the moonlight—

It was all going to go downhill and us along with it, and as somebody famous once said about a similar thing, we needn't worry about drowning.

The fall was going to kill us.

Twelve

I sprinted down the lawn, hoping that the earth under my feet wouldn't slide away right this instant. At the cliff's edge, I looked out to where the moonlit sky met the water, as bright as aluminum foil.

Breathing in the fresh, salty air, I flexed every muscle I could find and raised up on tiptoe and down again a few times for good measure. Then I dropped into a crouch to reach over the cliff's edge and feel around for the iron spikes still sticking out of the granite.

They were good, solid handholds, the kind of thing a person could trust. But the rope ladder itself, piled nearby, was another story.

Maybe I could splice the frayed part somehow. As I thought this a flashlight beam appeared from uphill, near the house, and bobbed down the dark lawn toward me.

"Jake!" came a loud whisper. "Did you see the big crack opening up in the—"

It was Ellie. "I sure did, and it's getting worse," I said.

Then I started to tell her about the foundation crack and

about the patio's flagstones shifting. But a deep, grumbling rumble interrupted me, accompanied not by shuddering or tremors this time but by real, honest-to-gosh shaking.

A throb of sheer terror pulsed through me. It felt like the shaking might not stop at all, or that it might get worse. Then, after we'd scuttled up to the patio, where my dad was just then coming out the kitchen door, the shaking stopped.

"Huh," he said, looking around wonderingly. The sudden stillness felt shocking. "That's the first real earthquake I've ever felt."

And maybe the last, I thought, if I couldn't get us all out of here fast enough. The three of us hurried out the driveway until the fallen tree's massive carcass stopped us.

From the other side, the floodlights' bright white glow illuminated all the nearby branches from beneath. The earth shook again as the backhoe's creaking, groaning grapple hurled something that landed hard.

Suddenly the soil around my shoes slid liquidly. I stepped one way and then another, trying to stay upright as we made for the house once more.

I meant to get Bella and Mika and skedaddle; I just didn't know where to, yet. In the front hall, Tilda French hurried down the staircase with a white fur coat under one arm and a satchel gripped in her other hand.

After dumping them by the door, she trotted upstairs again; we went on to the kitchen.

"Where's Bella?" Ellie demanded, glancing around urgently.

Just then Bella returned, drying her hands on a paper towel and grousing loudly; that is, until she caught sight of my father.

"Oh," she uttered, her big green eyes softening as she hurtled into his embrace.

"There, there, old girl," he told her reassuringly; if I'd tried calling her that she'd have bitten my head off.

But never mind: "Where's Tink Markle?" I asked as now Ingrid Merryfield showed up, too, wanting to know what all this bustling around meant, and what was that shaking, and why didn't we all just stop and have a drink.

I explained briefly. "All the vibration from the tree work plus the earthquake activity that we've been having—"

She grimaced skeptically. "Earthquakes? Who says we've been having—"

"—has loosened the soil, I think, and now it's moving. Toward," I finished, "the cliff."

"No one told me about any of this," she said affrontedly, and it was all I could do not to tell her that as far as I knew, earthquakes didn't give a rat's ass about her information status.

"Seriously, we need to find Tink," I said. "I don't trust him and I don't want any surprises."

Ingrid scowled at that, too, but didn't say anything, lucky for her; not trusting my temper, I followed Tilda, who'd come into the kitchen behind Ingrid.

In the parlor the mousy young woman went straight for a magazine she'd apparently left on one of the aging sofas. But as she leaned to pick it up, she happened to glance over the back of the threadbare piece of furniture.

And stopped, eyeing what lay there. "He won't be surprising you," she said.

I hurried over. Tink Markle, I could tell right away, was a goner. His face didn't bear long inspection, so damaged by some hard, heavy object that it was practically caved in.

Another big shake made the chandelier sway and the fringe on the lampshades shimmy. A crack started up with a sound like a gunshot and traveled fast from the ceiling trim down alongside the stone chimney.

"Nuts to this," said Bella when I got back to the kitchen to report it all, and I heartily agreed. After we made our way to the front hall she yanked open the heavy old door and rushed out, with the rest of us following.

But outside, we faced the same problem as before—where to go?—plus the added utterly terrifying hilarity of old trees toppling all around, their shallow root systems freed up by the soil's vibrations. First one went and then the next, like very tall dominoes.

The popping apart of old roots and the splintering of branches sounded like gunfire. An enormous old evergreen keeled over onto the porch roof; snapped rafters flew.

"Come on," Ellie said, guiding us all around the side of the house toward the lawn where at least no big trees loomed.

But I hung back, unsure. Now that I'd seen her again, I knew there was no way Bella could manage that rope ladder, even if I got the frayed part mended somehow. My dad, either; just because he'd done it once didn't mean he could do it again.

For one thing, I wasn't about to try that pulley stunt a second time. Still, I couldn't think of anything else; in desperation I pulled out my phone to call Wade and tell him what was going on; maybe he'd have an idea.

Bars appeared on the phone's display and I started punching in numbers. But before I could finish, a hand reached out of the gloom and grabbed my arm.

I nearly screamed, it was so unexpected. "Who is that?" I demanded when I could breathe again. "And what are you—"

That's when I felt my mouth snap shut in astonishment, because standing there big as life right in front of me was Gilly Blaine, as slim, blond, and alive as ever.

Not drowned, I mean. Not hauled out of the water, dead.

"Yeah, no," he said, understanding my confusion. "As far as I can tell I'm still breathing and walking around."

Then I understood: the emergency that had kept the Coast Guard from coming to our assistance, that had involved several fatalities. The body Ellie and I had recovered must've been one of those. Gilly stuck what felt like a gun in my ribs.

This, I thought tiredly as the thing poked me again none too gently, *was supposed to be a nice, easy catering job.*

"Quiet," Gilly cautioned in a low tone.

A job that was supposed to have ended two days ago. "Yeah, yeah," I exhaled in disgust.

From the corner of my eye I glimpsed flashlights moving, as Mika, Bella, and my dad followed Ellie down the lawn.

"Just come with me," Gilly said softly, "and everything will be all right."

Yeah, sure it would. In reply it was all I could do not to fill up his mouth with my elbow and as much of the rest of my arm as I could jam in there. But considering how much I did not want a bullet shot into me I had little choice but to go along.

"Inside," he murmured as we reached the Cliff House front door.

He hauled it open one-handed and shoved me inside, across the hall past the staircase, then through the pantry and into the kitchen.

"Gilly, can I ask what you want out of all this? Because, I don't know, maybe we can make some kind of a deal or something."

His flashlight beam hit me in the face, blinding me. "I'm not interested in a deal."

So much for that idea. "Yeah, well, in that case we've got nothing to discuss and I should go join my friends, now."

Saying this, I turned hard away from him, then suddenly back at him again, surprising him. After yanking my arm from his startled grip, I ran, but he caught me easily, flinging his free arm around in front of my face.

That is, near my choppers. So I did what any red-blooded American girl would do: I bit down into his forearm so hard, I felt a tendon spasming frantically between my teeth.

He jerked away, howling, while I charged out the door and crossed the driveway into the shadows behind the garage.

Moments later I peeked out at the house just in time to spy a dark shape staggering out, cradling its arm.

He couldn't let me live, or the others, either. We'd be able to tell whodunnit, and he couldn't have that.

He started toward me, not knowing I was there.

Yet.

"Maybe I could let you and your friends get out of here," said Gilly, slowly advancing into the brushy area at the rear of the garage building.

It was the nearest dark place; of course I'd gone there. I eased back toward the fallen tree that the guys were still struggling to remove, the saws ear-splitting and the air so full of the smell of pine sap that it felt syrupy.

At least the tremors had eased off a little. "It's not like I've got anything against you," Gilly added, lying through his teeth; see *whodunnit*, above.

Then: "Gotcha!" His hands seized my shoulders from behind but my startled shudder wriggled me free. I backed away urgently through thorns, vines, and branches, then flailed my way around and shoved forward through more of them.

Finally my forehead collided with a low-hanging branch, I saw the kind of flickering stars that mean you have not quite knocked yourself unconscious, and sat down hard in a damp patch of leaf mold that felt very unpleasantly as if insects were scurrying in it.

Lots of them, and then they were scurrying on me; I got up so fast it was a wonder I didn't take flight, which would have helped me a great deal since it probably would've gotten me over the big tree trunk lying in front of me.

As it was, I swatted bugs off myself with one hand while getting the other one wrapped very tightly around a branch up there somewhere. After that, the pull-up that got me up onto the branch could've gotten me into the Olympics.

But there my good luck ended; I clambered higher and swung my legs up, too, just as Gilly's flashlight found me.

"Ha," he said, sounding pleased.

I was not pleased. Also, that's when I noticed that the spot where I perched was directly opposite the section of tree trunk now being chewed into by the crew's monstrous machinery. The noise and vibrations of the machinery should've alerted me, I suppose, but I'd been a little preoccupied by the task of not getting murdered.

Anyway, somehow I'd hauled myself up into the tangled branches of the very tree that blocked the driveway. Just not onto its trunk, but if I could clamber down, I might be able to . . . there, I'd made it. But then:

Chomp! The tree-cutting machine's biting mechanism closed on a chunk of tree trunk. The tree shrieked in protest, then gave up a ragged section of itself; a moment later the biting mechanism was back.

And its very next grab was going to seize me and munch me to bits, I could see by the size of the last bite it had taken. I scrambled quickly to a different handhold, but Gilly saw me there, too, and he'd have reached me if not for his bitten arm.

But he couldn't, not and hang on to the gun at the same time. From where I crouched above him, I watched while he tried, feeling a little smug.

Just not for long. He stuck the gun in his pocket, grabbed onto the branch above him with his good hand, and swung his leg up over it. That dancer's physique he had didn't just happen to him by accident, I gathered from this feat.

Fabulous; he was not only evil, he was also athletic, which at the moment was not my favorite combination.

"Could you at least tell me what all this is about?" I inquired, creeping farther from him and holding on tight each time the machine slammed into the tree again.

That got me away from Gilly, but it also put me farther from Sam and his team and deeper into the darkness outside the tree crew's floodlit work area.

"What it's about?" Gilly's laughing reply came at last, and it wasn't reassuring. "It's about survival, that's what it's about. Mine."

Ellie and the rest would've reached the cliff's edge by now, I thought. Maybe they'd even started down the rope ladder, the ones who could manage it, trying to outrun the shifting and shuddering of the earth.

Which had begun again after all, I realized; I'd just been too busy running for my life to notice. Anyway, even if they made it to the boat they'd have to get onto it, no easy task.

When I looked down, Gilly had the gun in his hand, again. Seeing it, I slipped, gasped as I nearly fell from my precarious perch, then grabbed on once more.

"Why?" I repeated, just wanting to keep him talking. "Why are you doing all this?"

"So she'll see," he said urgently. "I'm the only one who would do all this for her. They all *want* something, but I just want to protect her. Take care of her. I want . . ."

The truth hit me. "You're the stalker. Not some random fan and not the guy Bryan said he killed."

Gilly chuckled softly. "That was my roommate, actually. Bryan's not quite as sharp an investigator as he thinks; he got the address right but the face wrong."

Thump! The machinery tore gnashingly into the tree again.

"Pain in the ass, though," Gilly said. "I had to get rid of the body and find a new roommate."

A wide, pale gap had opened up in the tree's trunk. The glow from the big lights over there shone through, making Gilly's face look bloodless.

Mine too, I supposed, hoping this wasn't a sign of things to come. A low groan seemed to rise from within it; that, or I was hearing the whole back lawn sliding over the edge of the cliff.

"I see," I told Gilly. "A body would make people curious. The police, for instance?"

"Right." He eyed me resentfully. His bad arm made him unsteady when the tree and the ground beneath it moved again in a long, anxiety-provoking shiver.

But he didn't put the gun down. "She's had a feud at some time or another with everyone here," he said.

I looked around at the dark swathe of hardwoods and small trash trees surrounding the big fallen one. The whole area appeared about as welcoming as a bramble patch, probably because at ground level that's mostly what it was.

But maybe I could find a way down into it and run again.

"That didn't stop any of them from trying to get a piece of her, though," Gilly said. "Intros to casting directors, access for a biography, even Ingrid's own parts in the film franchises she invented. Can you imagine?"

He sucked in a breath. "But once she really knows just how devoted I am, that I'd do *anything* for her, she'll understand," he said.

The light from the other side caught his face again. Even in the harsh, bright-white glare it was clear that Gilly Blaine was at least thirty years younger than Ingrid Merryfield.

Gently, I suggested this. Gilly looked dumbfounded at the thought.

"You think I'm in love with Ingrid Merryfield? Like, in some silly little *romantic* way?"

He shook his head. "You don't get it. She's not just a movie star, she's a Hollywood icon. A treasure, a goddess!"

By now it had struck me that Gilly was several peas short of a pod, as Bella would've put it.

His voice turned bitter. "Anything she wanted, I would do. And this is how she repaid me."

I looked down. "For what? What did you do for her?" Kill the others, I was thinking. Because she asked him to do it.

But I was wrong. "All I was supposed to do was be here. Then at some point I'd hike into town, grab that little boat from the dock there, bring it back to the Cliff House dock, and take her away in it."

I could imagine why that plan would've appealed to him. The adoring fan rescuing the film goddess . . . yeah, it was right up this nutball's twisted alley.

"She didn't know? That you were her so-called stalker, all along?"

He snorted disdain. "Of course not. What, do you think I'm nuts?"

Better not answer that one, I thought, looking down. It was too far to jump. Also, Gilly was getting closer and he still had that gun.

"But, Gilly, she tried to kill you." It was a wild guess, just to distract him or slow him down, but I saw the comment hit home.

"She didn't mean to. It was a misunderstanding, that's all. She doesn't understand how devoted I am, that I'd do anything at all—"

Yeah, right. I'd heard love is blind but I'd never realized before how bone stupid it could be, too; she'd tried to murder him, for heaven's sake. Then another thought hit me.

"How did you survive going over that cliff, anyway?"

He made a *pfft* sound. "Landed on the ledge halfway down."

The granite outcropping, he meant. "Jumped over onto the wooden steps that were there."

But weren't, anymore. "Easy-peasy. Since then I've been in the garage, or once that other boat got here, on that."

Sure, Ellie's boat had a cozy sleeping space in the cabin, snacks and water, even blankets and a pillow.

"Anyway, she made a mistake. But she'll find out. When I take care of everything for her, when I've gotten the others to safety and she and I have escaped together."

His dramatic gesture took in the enormous wrecked tree, the shaking earth, the cliff and water waiting to smash us or drown us. "Just," he added deludedly, "like in the movies."

From beyond the tree trunk, power saws whined. A truck's engine roared and the crunch of huge tires running over fallen branches made a sound like bones being snapped.

"And now," Gilly Blaine said through the din, "it's almost time."

He didn't know about the others being dead, I realized suddenly. That's why he wasn't talking about them, or seeming shocked by their murders, or afraid of whoever might've committed them.

He just thought that Ingrid had meant to make a dramatic exit, not about the revenge she was planning to wreak on her gathered enemies. Or that she'd gotten it. "Gilly, do you want to know *why* she tried to kill you?"

Maybe I could shock some sense into him. But he just shook his head stubbornly.

"Like I said, it was a mistake. She and I will straighten it all out. I just need a chance to talk to her."

Right, so did I; there was that hazard pay we'd be needing to discuss. Mentally I doubled the amount I'd be demanding from her, assuming I got the chance.

Meanwhile, though: "So now you see," he said regretfully, "why I've got no choice in the matter."

His tone swung suddenly to one of fury. "I can't let her get away with disrespecting me, after all. Double-crossing me as if I'm no one. As if I'm *nothing*," he finished, his face now contorting with rage.

He was not, I gathered, emotionally stable. Or rational, either. As if to prove this, he raised the gun. He didn't need to get up into the tree branches where I clung, and he'd figured that out, finally. He meant to shoot me right here and now.

The gun barrel's dark O was like the mouth of a tunnel. I didn't want to slide down into it to my doom. So I did the only thing I could: I pushed off the branch I perched on, my legs stiff straight and my feet out in front of me, ready to *slam* them into his chest and take off running.

But then suddenly something else happened, only I couldn't see what. Gilly dropped his flashlight, I knew that much. But in its final moments of pale, tumbling glow his whole head was there: eyes, mouth, that wavy yellow hair—

And then it wasn't. His head, I mean.

It just wasn't there at all.

I hit the cold earth butt first after scraping my back on the fallen tree's bark and smacking my head on its rough trunk. I saw stars.

And then some jerk came along and roused me. "Up," said a voice I didn't recognize.

I stuck a hand out, grabbed the ankle attached to the foot that had just kicked me, and pulled.

"Oof!" The sound of someone else landing hard for a change was delightful. But I couldn't waste time enjoying it.

I jumped up. "Who the heck are you? And why did you—"

Gilly Blaine's body lay sprawled at my feet.

Rather, most of it did. Its head bone–neck bone link was out of service due to half of it being missing; I grabbed the dead man's flashlight and aimed it into the face of his killer.

But I wasn't prepared for what I saw. "Tilda?"

She had Gilly's gun. The dark eyes in her pallid face were like pushed-in raisins in risen dough as she looked down at him.

No remorse was in her expression, but she was trembling; the night was chilly, and besides, she'd just shot a guy's head off. And no matter how little feeling she might have about that, her body was reacting.

"This is good, though," she said as if trying to convince herself. "Now we can say he killed all of you. Only Ingrid and I survived," she added as if testing the idea.

"That's what you're going to tell the police?" She nodded, waved me ahead. I stepped forward obediently.

It didn't actually sound like that bad an idea. After all, no one would be around to say any different, would they?

We reached the driveway, then the back lawn. Behind us the sounds of the machinery faded; ahead, unseen waves hit the beach and spread hissing along the stones.

"Keep going," she said, and I had little choice. Overhead the full moon shone hazily; when we reached the cliff's edge, I could see that someone had thrown the rope ladder down over the drop-off again, likely without repairing it.

I tried to say so but Tilda cut me off, motioning sharply.

"I'm thinking that maybe we don't have a lot of time," she said, and the long, rolling tremor that rippled under our feet just then made me think so, too.

I glanced over the edge, past the dangling ladder to where white foam and surging waves roiled among rocks like jagged teeth, then jerked back dizzily.

None of the others were down there. "You're out of your mind," I declared, stepping back from the jutting-out-of-the-granite iron spikes that the ladder hung from.

The spikes seemed to be moving a little, too, I thought, and then a lot. I yelped, dropping to a crouch as clumps of grassy soil tumbled merrily away from me over the cliff, roots and all.

And since by now I was clutching frightenedly at this very grass, the whole thing just felt more and more inconvenient, not to mention potentially fatal.

"Go!" commanded Tilda sharply.

Below, rolling waves went on crashing enthusiastically. I leaned over the edge again as far as I dared. "Where are they?"

"On the boat." She was getting impatient. "You're going there, too. Too bad how it all turns out, though."

I thought so, too, and I didn't even know what she meant, yet. Through the waves and spray I glimpsed Ellie's boat now, somehow still tied up to the dilapidated old pier.

"You all tried getting back to Eastport on your own," said

Tilda. "It's what we'll say, Ingrid and I, that we tried getting you to stay until the tree got cleared, but the whole bunch of you insisted on leaving and your boat capsized."

I looked at her. "Are you nuts?"

Yeah, I know, dumb question. Still: "Tilda, that boat's not going to capsize."

Sure, the water was still choppy, but not much worse than earlier. Besides, there was fuel in the tank, a working radio. . . .

"Tilda, that's a fiberglass hull. To get it to sink you'd need to fill it with water, or drill holes in it, or put explosive charges on it, or . . ."

It occurred to me suddenly that I shouldn't tell her how to do this, so I changed the subject.

"Just out of curiosity, Tilda, what else have you done in LA besides work for Ingrid?"

Clumsy, but it was all I could think of. And as I'd hoped, she went for it.

"Lots of things," she replied with a proud little lift of her mouse-brown head. "Set construction, for one thing. Building fake storefronts and so on. I tried stunts, too, and did that a while. And finally special effects; that turned out to be fun and I got into a training internship."

Great. She might as well have gone to the Academy of Murder with a major in techniques and a minor in Getting Away with It.

"Impressive. And now you've already been on Ellie's boat?"

Her lips pressed into a thin, self-satisfied smirk. "To disable the radio, you mean?"

My heart sank. She waved the gun at me. "Now get down there," she said.

I peeked over the edge again. The view was the same as before: rocks, waves, the cliff face and the outcropping that jutted from it, all brightly moonlit and dizzying.

And one more thing, I suddenly recalled, though right now I spotted no evidence: that cliff face was *inhabited*.

Which gave me an idea. "Uh, could you possibly go first?" I simpered, pretending to be too scared to clamber onto the rope ladder dangling over the cliff.

"If you're on it when I climb on, it won't wiggle so much," I explained.

In the moonlight her eyes narrowed suspiciously. I held up the length of rope still lying there on the ground where I'd let it fall after coming up from the beach with it tied between me and my dad.

"If you're worried about me getting away somehow, you could tie this to me," I said.

It sounded right until you thought about it, but she was in a hurry now, so she didn't. The earth beneath us quivered again as she fastened the rope securely around my wrists, then climbed onto the ladder.

She was good at knot-tying, I noted unhappily; Ellie would have approved. What Tilda wasn't so good at just at the moment, though, was thinking; I might not have my hands free but I still had teeth, and I had that rope off my wrists in a few moments.

But what happened next was out of my control, and I hadn't expected it. "Hey! Let go of me!" Tilda yelled. "Who . . . what're you . . . let go!"

It was no laughing matter but I couldn't help giggling as Tilda went on shouting many of the things you might expect from a woman who's had her ankle grabbed onto by an invisible—until that moment, at any rate—old man.

"I've got a gun," she hollered furiously. As if to prove this she fired off a shot; the report echoed off the granite with a bang loud enough to blow my hair back. Then:

"Oh!" Something metallic clanked down there somewhere on the beach rocks. I guessed Tilda's gun-wielding strategy was *kaput.*

On account, I mean, of her no longer having a gun. So I

risked peering over the cliff's edge once more, and there was my dad, crouched on the cliff's stone outcropping.

Its surface was flat, and from what I could see of his face in the gloom I thought he looked delighted, gripping Tilda's ankle in one hand and holding on to the ledge's rough edge with the other.

Meanwhile, from Tilda came an absolute torrent of some of the most creative profanity I'd ever heard. She couldn't go up, she couldn't go down, and she couldn't quite get at my dad since if she let go of the rope ladder she would fall.

Still she kept trying, shifting her weight back and forth to get a pendulum effect going. And every time she did that . . .

Horror surged through me. Every time Tilda made the rope ladder swing, the raggedy section just above her frayed more.

"Tilda," I said. "Listen, honey, the ladder's breaking, you need to climb back up here right away so you don't fall."

The tide was rising fast again, the surging water below rising farther onto the beach with each white-topped wave that hurled itself onto the rocks.

Tilda paused in her effort. "You lie." Her upturned face, bone pale in the moonlight, was flat with disbelief.

I reached down. She could just about reach me from where she was on the rope ladder. Just one hand clasped to mine would do it; she could still hang on to the ladder with the other.

"Tilda, come on. It's breaking," I said, and then it did, the fraying fibers letting go all at once.

The good news was that only one side of the ladder broke, the whole thing lurching downward and sideways very sharply but the unbroken side hanging on.

The bad news was that now my dad was almost over onto the ladder. Not looking anymore at what was happening above him, he'd slid over to the outcropping's edge and was about to put a foot on a lower rung.

"Dad!" I yelled, but the waves' crash overpowered my voice.

And with his weight added, that ladder was going down for sure.

"Tilda, climb," I pleaded, thinking that my only hope now was to get some of the strain off the thing. Maybe if he was the only one on it, it would hold long enough.

"Tilda. Come on, now." I flopped onto my belly and reached down to help her once more. I nearly touched her.

But she drew back snarlingly. Then the rest of the ladder's strands parted and her face fell away from me, suddenly.

My dad had let go of Tilda's ankle. Now his arm shot out reflexively to stop her fall.

My heart stopped; she'd take him along with her. But he couldn't reach far enough and she fell right past him.

No scream. No nothing. "Dad?" I uttered quietly. Everything else was quiet, too, suddenly. Even the waves' roar seemed to fade.

"I'm here, Jacobia." In the distance on the other side of the house, the tree crew's machinery started up again. "Jacobia?"

"Yes, Dad?" I leaned over. The ladder, of course, was gone.

He was on his feet, hanging on to the granite outcropping one-handed.

A rumble shuddered through the earth. I picked up the rope that I'd untied from around my wrists and showed it to him.

"Maybe," I began, "I could—" But then I stopped, not knowing *what* I could do. If anything.

Fortunately, though, my dad did seem to know. "Jacobia," he said firmly, "I want you to take that rope right now and do just what I say with it, understand?"

I didn't, but I got ready to obey, anyway. Might as well—I was out of ideas; out of energy, too.

And after all, this was my dad talking to me, here.

* * *

I dropped one end of the rope to him and he put it through his belt and knotted it. At his direction I tied my end in a slip knot around one of the iron spikes still embedded in the granite.

So far, so good. But then as a shiver rattled the soil and grass beneath me again, he began *climbing*.

I'd thought by now he would be making his way down to the beach, before whatever the earth was still doing all around us either buried us or stopped doing it.

But he wasn't. His arms flopped up over the top. I hauled him the rest of the way and he got up, shakily, but he did it, and along with him came what remained of the rope ladder.

Which turned out to be most of it; the break had come near the top.

"She let go of it on her way down and I just grabbed for it as it went by," he explained, "and I got lucky."

"Dad," I exhaled as I flung my arms around him, not knowing whether I ought to be grateful or furious. But it didn't matter; he gave me no time for either.

"Look." He threw the ladder to the ground. In the moonlight the rope sections were clearly visible.

"We can cut off the bad part, use the rest of it."

He was right, and he still had his jackknife, too; when we were done, we hung what remained over the iron spikes again.

"Go," he instructed. "I'll be right behind you."

I wanted to argue. But he was cold, wet, and tired, and I didn't know how much more of this he could take. So I did it: I knelt with my back to what felt like a dark, sucking void, and stuck my leg out over the cliff and down onto the ladder's rung.

My foot slipped. Suddenly my whole lower body extended itself with nothing beneath it, my right foot searching but not finding anything except thin air. I was hanging by my hands.

"Jacobia, draw your leg back in toward you slowly."

Breathe. Breathe. My hands burned, my knuckles ached, and my terrified heartbeat thudded deafeningly in my ears.

Gah. My foot drew in, found the ladder's rung, and settled on it.

"Ayuh," said my dad from above. "Go on, now. When you get down there, you can hold it steady for me."

That motivated me, and so did the knowledge that if a rope ladder can break once, it can probably break twice; I moved fast, and by the time my feet touched down my legs were rubbery. I staggered, rubbing the feeling back into my knotted hands.

But moments later I was steadying the ladder's quivering ropes while he stepped off. In the moon's bluish glimmer he was already frowning around puzzledly.

Then I remembered: Tilda. Her body wasn't anywhere on the rocks that I could see, and I didn't spot it floating.

The bigger problem now, though, was that I didn't spot the boat. From where we stood, almost all the old, broken-down dock was clearly visible but now nothing was tied to it.

Glumly I sank my tired backside onto one of the few rocks that wasn't yet awash in ice-cold seawater.

"Jake," said my dad. He was starting to shiver. "I hate to say it, but maybe we'd better—"

"Yeah," I cut him off. "I know. We need to try to find a way back up there again."

It was a terrible realization. Everything in me wanted to find Ellie, Bella, and Mika, and get them out of whatever was happening to them if I still could.

On top of which, the very idea of tackling that cliff once more made me want to throw up. But the beach was now shrinking so fast that soon the spot where I sat would be under water, and I had to get my dad out of the cold, as well.

Besides, I'd just patted my back pants pocket but no phone was in it. Maybe it had come out when I was in the tree, or while I was climbing down the cliff.

"I'm sorry I brought you here," I told my dad as a sob swelled my throat; gosh, but this was a mess.

"I didn't exactly give you a choice," he reminded me.

"There's that. And I am really glad you're with me."

He slung an arm around my head and pulled it tightly to him. "I'm glad I'm here with you, too, Jacobia," he said.

But this is still all my fault, I thought miserably. Then something cold and wet invaded my ear.

"Hey!" I jumped up. The water was around my ankles now, and my first startled thought was that something had snaked up onto me from it.

Instead, right there wagging his tail, was a dog. "Igor!"

I reached out and seized him by his warm, bristly cheeks, and smooched him on the snout. "Igor, you're alive!"

The dog wriggled happily as my dad sloshed over, grinning. Me too, not only because the dog was alive but also because if Igor could get down here we could find a way up.

How the poor thing got out of the collapsed tunnel at all was a mystery I could solve later, I decided.

"You think somehow her body got washed away?" my dad asked a few minutes later.

Tilda's, he meant. By now we'd followed Igor back to the dismal swamp where Ellie and I had gotten discouraged and turned around, earlier.

"I don't know what to think." The dog moved sure-footedly ahead of us, but I slipped repeatedly on the slick rocks and my dad scrabbled stubbornly forward on his hands and knees in some places.

Still, we were moving uphill, and sooner than I expected we were on the grassy path leading around the swamp.

Which, as I wished very much I had thought of the first time I'd seen it, might lead in the other direction back up to the house, too.

"Okay," I gasped after we'd hurried along for a little while longer. "Once we get back to the house, you're going to sit and rest. I'll find a phone; somebody must've left one."

In Maud's room, maybe, or perhaps Waldo's. "I'll call Bob Arnold and tell him they've got to get us out of here, fast."

I didn't know how. As Bob had pointed out, there wasn't a spot to land a helicopter even if the state cops brought one. And there was still no sign of the Coast Guard.

Still: "I got a good look at the fallen tree a little while ago, and the crew was getting through it, finally. If we can't get cops, maybe Sam's crew can extend a bucket loader to us and we can ride over the tree."

But even if this was possible, a final obstacle lay between us and trying it. The wide swathes of sawgrass, pale gold in the moonlight, had blades like . . . well, like blades, actually.

Only that wasn't right. "Dad?" I called ahead to him.

I didn't remember any sawgrass from the last time I was here. None of this looked familiar, in fact; we were uphill from the beach but not in the direction I'd thought.

We'd gotten turned around somehow. "Put your arms up over your face, keep walking straight," I told my dad, "so the grass doesn't cut you up."

He obeyed and began moving forward again with Igor right behind him. Beyond the tall grass we could rest, I thought, then head toward the distant roar of the tree-clearing machines.

But instead, with my own arms up over my face and covering my eyes, I walked blindly into someone.

"Oh!" I staggered back. It was Ingrid Merryfield, and she'd traded her usual glamorous getup for canvas pants, a heavy sweatshirt, and a black knitted cap pulled down tightly over her spun-glass blond hair.

"You people all keep popping up everywhere like the nasty surprises you are," I complained, rubbing my bumped nose.

L.L.Bean rubber shoes like the kind Wade and Sam wore for duck hunting were on her feet. So all this had been planned, I thought; not the exact details, since who could stage-manage a night like tonight in advance?

But something like it. That's why she had the outfit for it. As I thought this, she produced the sweetest little pistol I'd ever seen. Pearl-handled revolvers can kill you just as well as howitzers, though, I thought as she urged us uphill with it.

"Where's Mika and Bella," I demanded, "and where's Ellie? What've you done with—"

She replied serenely, "I'm so sorry about all this."

She didn't look sorry. "But your friends are on the boat, and once they were secured there I'm afraid I took the liberty of removing the boat's . . . tell me, do you call that thing I made Ellie take out a stopper, or a plug?"

It's called a plug, and it gets removed at the end of each boating season to drain the hull for winter storage. But if you pull the plug with the boat still in the water, you flood and sink it.

"Move along, now," she instructed us briskly. "We'll need to hurry, if there's going to be time for you two to join the others."

"Oh, you did no such thing, you liar," the words I'd been too shocked to say burst out of me at last. "You couldn't find a boat plug with both hands and a road map."

But then I stopped, because (a) how did I know that? and (b) she hadn't had to find it, had she? Ellie knew, and if, for instance, Ingrid threatened to hurt Bella or Mika, then Ellie would tell.

Still, I couldn't believe the coldness of it. "So you're sinking them?" I demanded, looking back at Ingrid.

My dad marched behind me, too, just ahead of her. His face went still as he listened to her, his eyes like flat stones in the moonlight and his lips a thin, straight line.

"Bella," he repeated, "and Mika. And Ellie, they're all on that vessel?" he asked.

Leaning one-handed on a stout stick he'd found somewhere and with his stringy gray hair flying around frazzledly in the

sea breeze, he looked like a storybook wizard about to summon up some big-time reinforcements.

Too bad there weren't any. "That's right," Ingrid replied
smugly, "and in a minute you're both getting onto it, too."

"It's my wife down there," he said, "and my granddaughter-
in-law, and our friend. . . ."

His voice turned confidential. "And we're all reasonable
people, here, so what if you simply let them go?"

Reasonable, my aunt Fanny. "Ha," she uttered, proving my
point.

"So when the police come, you'll say Tink Markle killed us,
and you killed him?" I said.

"Got it in one," she congratulated me, and I saw my dad
carefully refrain from hitting her over the head with his stick.

"Yes, I think blaming poor old Tink will work," she went on
thoughtfully as we struggled the last few steps up the path.

"Actually I'd been planning to blame Gilly Blaine. Tink might
still have come in handy," she added.

I struggled up the path's last few feet only to find that we'd
returned nearly to where we started. "Well, here we are," I told
no one in particular. "Back on the clifftop."

"Tink probably inherited his murderous tendencies from his
grandfather," Ingrid Merryfield was saying, possibly rehears-
ing what she'd say to the police.

At least she pronounced it theatrically, with gestures and ex-
pressions I guessed she'd learned from acting in films. Taking a
well-placed step toward us, turning her pretty head just so—

It was while she was showing off that smooth, swanlike neck
of hers that my dad launched himself at her.

Thirteen

There were two ways off that cliff, straight down and nearly straight down, and by now you probably know enough about my dad to know which way he chose.

Well, not *straight* down, exactly. We'd come out in a spot just above where the cliff's flat granite outcropping broke the otherwise sheer descent.

Still, watching them hurtle off the edge together turned my blood to ice. The two of them hit the overhang; then, tumbling and bouncing on the lichen-covered granite, they hit a patch of loose gravel and slid sideways out of my line of sight.

"Dad!" I galloped back down the path we'd just been on, shoved through the sawgrass, skidded over the slick rocks, and raced out onto the beach.

"Dad?" He sprawled facedown and motionless on a flat, pebbly patch just below the outcropping. When I got to him he was still out cold, but he was breathing.

"Jake!" A cry came from somewhere on the water. It was Ellie's voice; when I looked up, her boat sat fifty yards or so straight out from me, in what I guessed was maybe six feet of water.

Confused, I looked back again toward the old dock. The boat hadn't been there when I looked earlier. Now the dock wasn't there, either, not even the pilings, one of which the boat had been tied to.

The boat itself sat aslant, not moving with the water at all, which meant it must be resting on the bottom. Usually the tide refloats grounded boats, and the tide was coming in, but Ellie's wasn't rising with it; instead the water rose up around it.

That drain plug, I realized. Ingrid really had pulled it.

My dad groaned as the encroaching water lapped around him. Gasping, I hauled him by his shoulders onto the highest rock I could find, rolled him over so if he upchucked he wouldn't choke, and left him.

"Jake!" Ellie's voice came again, urgently. The boat she was trapped on creaked painfully as a wave slammed it sideways.

It was a good boat, but it wasn't going to take a lot of knocking around on rocks. "Jake, she's got us—"

I didn't hear the rest on account of the earth's lurching and jolting, suddenly. Dropping to a crouch, cursing silently on account of not having enough breath to do it out loud, I waited until the shaking was over, I hoped, and then I waded in through water so cold all it needed was a few icebergs.

But if Ingrid Merryfield had done what she claimed, I had only minutes to get people off that boat before they drowned.

Halfway to where the vessel sat firmly lodged among sharp rocks, the ragged part of the rope ladder that my dad had cut off floated in front of me; I grabbed it.

Ellie must've glimpsed me. "Jake, are you wearing—?"

Her voice cut off midyell. I didn't like it a bit. But I knew what she was trying to remind me about.

I put a hand to my chest and felt it still resting there: the inflatable life vest that I'd put on when my dad and I left the dock in Eastport.

I hoped I wouldn't need it. But just as I thought this, my hand snagged on the life vest's ripcord.

Bang! The damned thing inflated explosively with a sound like a gun fired near my head.

Also: *Pow, right in the kisser!* The blown-up vest chucked me hard under the chin as it expanded; the impact threw my head back so fast I felt my eyes bouncing around.

I staggered and sat without wanting to. The water would've closed over my head, but the vest floated me.

The impact must've also knocked an idea loose: I could swim with the vest on.

"Ellie!" I yelled. Still atop the cliff, Igor heard me and barked as if cheering me on. I paddled faster.

"Ellie, here I come!" I cried desperately, then swam face-first into the floating body of Ingrid Merryfield.

Her hair spread on the water like some bleached-out aquarium specimen. A face glared from its center, wide eyed and open mouthed. With a shudder I pushed past the horrid thing.

"Ellie!" Waves rolled in, ready to drown me, but I had a secret weapon.

"Ha," I said grimly, pleased with the life vest as I reached the boat's slanting side. Its waterline was submerged, and if it was going to float, it would have done it by now.

That meant the water was going to rise up over it instead. And that's what Ingrid Merryfield had counted on.

"Ellie! Can you still hear me?"

A cold wave slapped my face and filled my mouth. I gagged and just about ruptured a gut, as Sam would've put it, coughing the water out.

Then, "Ellie!" Still no answer. I reached the stern, hauled myself up over the transom and past the outboard engine, and fell onto the deck.

Nothing moved, but from the small cabin below came urgent thumping and bumping. I crawled to the hatchway door.

Locked. And the toolbox, of course, was in the cabin. There

was, however, that wickedly barbed boat hook still lying out on the deck, and the hatchway latch was still loose.

I smacked the latch handle with the end of the boat hook, smacked it again, and on the third try it let go, the screws holding it to the bulkhead popping out and flying as the door fell open.

"Ellie?" I grabbed the flashlight from the console and snapped it on. Pale, scared faces appeared: Bella, Mika, Ellie.

And Tilda. My jaw dropped; I'd seen her go over that cliff. But clearly she hadn't died at the bottom of it.

"It's not like I'm clumsy, you know," she said, seeing my surprise. "I know how to take a fall. And the rope ladder caught on some rocks partway down, so I didn't land so hard."

Right. *Stunt work*, she said she'd done, and I guessed now that she really had. Ingrid Merryfield must've found her on the beach and persuaded her onto Ellie's boat.

Probably by convincing her that they were still a team, I guessed; Ingrid was good at that.

Had been good at that. "The old man's just lucky he didn't catch me," Tilda added, and of course I didn't just climb right down there and punch her in the face.

I wanted to. But I had other fish to fry. And there'd be time; she couldn't get far with her wrists and ankles bound the way they were. It looked as if Ingrid had used clothesline; there'd been a coil of something that looked like it in a bin under the seat cushions, I recalled.

"Hey, Ellie?" I aimed the flashlight around. Now half hidden in the gloom, she lay against a heap of life jackets.

She wasn't answering, and she didn't move, either; I half-fell down the cabin's step and hurled myself at her.

"Ellie!" She roused, blinking groggily at me. One of her eyes was swollen half shut, the skin around it purpling.

"Too noisy," Tilda said. I glanced at her knuckles, which were swollen; she'd punched Ellie to stop her yelling to me, probably.

I supposed I wouldn't be in a good mood, either, in her situation. But that didn't make the coal of anger in my heart burn any less furiously.

"You know, Tilda," I said evenly, moistening the corner of a towel with the water now soaking the floor because the drain plug was out and the boat was filling up, "I do plan to get everyone out of here."

As I spoke, I dabbed Ellie's face clean of blood from a ragged cut that Tilda's knuckles had opened in her cheek.

"But I'll make an exception for you, Tilda," I finished, "if you don't shut up and do just exactly as I say, capisce?"

"Oh," Ellie breathed, blinking. "Ouch." But she seemed to be coming to herself a little more now.

I bent to examine the rope more closely, thinking now that maybe it would be fastest to just cut them all loose myself. But on closer examination, I found that it wasn't clothesline at all.

A lot of metallic-looking threads ran through it. I held the loose end up questioningly.

"Oh, gosh," said Ellie, recognizing it. "That's the mooring line I just bought. You can't cut it with anything short of . . ."

"A hatchet?" I asked. Because we had one, in the emergency kit.

"Yeah, no." She got to her feet, her hands still bound and her ankles linked to her neighbors' ankles, chain gang style.

"A blowtorch, maybe," she said, just as the boat groaned and pitched to the side suddenly.

Alarm pierced me; water through the floor was one thing, but once it rose to the level of the deck it would pour into the cabin. And because I had not brought an acetylene torch with me, I had two choices: I could let all the tied-together prisoners stay down here where they would drown. Or I could get them all up on deck somehow and force them overboard, to battle the tide and waves.

Where they would also drown, probably; tied-together people are notoriously poor swimmers and Bella couldn't swim at all. Quickly I wrestled my life jacket off and wrapped it around her middle, but of course I couldn't get her arms through the arm holds or fasten it very well, either, so it wasn't going to be much help to her. What I really needed was a way to get water flowing out of the boat.

"Ellie? Will the pumps still work, you think?"

Not waiting for an answer, I rushed back up onto the deck and tried the switches. In answer the boat's pumps started up with a low hum and water began gurgling out the hull's drain port.

What I would do when the tide covered the deck and filled the cabin—we were still missing a drainage plug, so even with the pumps on we couldn't float ourselves—remained to be seen.

Perch them all on the foredeck, maybe? The highest spot would be the last place to submerge. "Everyone okay so far?" I asked, not wanting them to see my fright.

Bella nodded, sitting quietly with her eyes closed and her hands in her lap. She might have been praying; Mika definitely was, her lips moving fervently and silently. And Ellie—

"Hmm," Ellie said troubledly. She was fully awake now and knew as well as I did that we were in bad trouble.

"I don't hear the chain saws," Mika said, looking up suddenly. "Do you still hear them?"

I listened, knowing she still hoped that somehow Sam would manage to save us. "No," I had to tell her. All the machinery's howling and rumbling had stopped.

But not the thudding from somewhere. "What's that, then?" Mika asked, and as if to answer the whole boat shifted sideways and an ominous sloshing came from the bilge tanks; the pumps were barely keeping up, their hum now more like a labored whine.

"We need to get up on deck," I said, thinking that at this point all we needed was a rain of fire and possibly a plague of locusts to make the whole situation complete.

Thud. Jolt. Sway. Slosh. "See, if we stay down here it's going to fill up with water," I went on.

Tilda French jumped up, yanking Mika up on one side of her and Bella on the other. So it wouldn't be too hard to herd them up on deck, I thought.

Just one problem, though. "Jake?" Mika was closest to the cabin's tiny porthole. "We're kind of stuck. I am, anyway."

"What?" I snapped, then saw what she meant and just about lost it.

"Damn, how'd she do that?" I demanded, but it was obvious. I hadn't noticed before, but the high-tech mooring line Ingrid Merryfield had used to tie them all together snaked out the porthole and then back in again.

I looked out. With no engine to charge them, the batteries had begun failing, so the deck lights were dim. But I could see the line wrapped twice around a cleat bolted to the rail.

After that, someone had tightened a hose clamp around the returning strands; the clamps had been in a paper bag here in the cabin after Ellie used some on the fuel pump hose repair.

"She tossed the screwdriver overboard once she'd tightened the clamp with it," Tilda said, meaning Ingrid Merryfield.

Great. I'd never get that hose clamp loose. "So when did you figure out you weren't leaving here?" I asked her, figuring she deserved the jab.

She grimaced in reply. I guess knowing she'd dug her own watery grave was bad enough without me taunting her about it.

Correction: our grave. I scanned the cabin. "What about power tools?" I asked Ellie. "Any of them aboard?"

Because our situation was simple, really: instead of being floated by the rising tide, the boat sat on the bottom with water coming in the drain hole. Soon the tide would rise over the deck and then everything in the cabin would be submerged.

Including the three people I wanted to free and one I didn't want to but would probably have to.

"Skilsaw," said Ellie. "Aft bin, port side."

The words shot me up, out, and across the deck toward the engine; by the time I got there the wind had nearly frozen me solid and my wet clothes felt deadly, as if they were sucking what remained of any warmth out of me.

But it could get worse, I reminded myself, and it would if something didn't change soon.

The thought shoved me along urgently. In the aft bin I rummaged hastily past a quart of oil, a plastic funnel, a roll of paper towels . . . and there it was, the small, orange-handled battery tool with the slim, sharp-toothed blade.

Back in the cabin I dragged the blade over the line a few inches from where it encircled Mika's wrists.

Some strands of the line parted. Many more didn't. Then just to make the whole thing even more enjoyably challenging, water droplets started dripping down the back of my neck.

I stuck my head up through the hatch again. On the deck, water slopped over the rail with every new wave and streamed toward the cabin.

An icicle of fright impaled me; the water was here, and so was the terrible decision I'd been trying not to think about:

"Jake. Listen. You'll have to go." It was Ellie, saying what we both understood.

That I wasn't tied here, unable to escape. Only they were. Mika bit her lip, white faced. Bella gazed stoically at nothing.

"Mom," said Mika. She'd never called me that, before. A sob escaped me, one I tried not to let them hear as even more water poured down into the cabin.

Much more. Swiftly, it had deepened to about six inches around our feet; in half an hour it would be over their heads, and there was nothing I could do about it.

Nothing except leave them to drown, but I couldn't do that. I waded over to sit beside Bella, who was beckoning to me.

"Now you listen," Bella said quietly when I got there. Her rawboned face looked like something carved out of driftwood.

"We're going to count you down. Three, two, one, and you're out of here. Understand?"

Me, she meant; not them. "No, I . . ."

Ellie leaned past Bella. "She's right, Jake, it's too late for anything else."

I thought that when the water reached their chins they'd change their tunes, but I didn't say so. "Go," whispered Mika.

"I can't," I told Mika. "I can't just go and leave you."

"Try again," Tilda demanded of me, angling her head sharply at the Skilsaw.

The boat shifted judderingly, and this time its agonized creaks and groans ended in an ominous-sounding crack! Then somewhere a rivet popped out—*bang!*—followed by a whole row of them: *powpowpow!*

Suddenly the water rose and spread scary fast across their laps. A fat wave flowed straight over the deck and slammed the hatchway door, jamming it shut.

"Hey," said Ellie quietly, tipping her head. She'd never been one to panic, but now she sounded super calm.

Deadly calm. "What?" I demanded, then realized that she was listening to something, and now so was I.

Rough, juddering vibration rattled loudly just outside the cabin. If I hadn't known better, I'd have thought the sound was another chain saw. Then several amazing things happened:

A chain saw's whirring blade broke through the cabin's wall just under the porthole, making Mika leap back with a shriek.

The blade went on cutting right on down in a straight line past the seat cushions, stopping somewhere below the floor, then came back up again.

All this happened fast. Then the hatch door flew open and more water poured in from the deck; the tide had risen nearly to the level of the porthole, now, and spurted in through the cuts someone had made below it.

But there in the doorway, wet and determined-looking, stood my son, Sam. With the chain saw.

"Sam!" Mika cried, her face suddenly luminous.

"Yeah, let's get you out of there," he told her, wasting no time before pulling the saw's cord so the tool roared to life again. "Once I get this thing free," he began over the racket.

But just at that moment came the hardest lurch yet, a jolt that knocked Sam half off his feet while the saw's running blade hit the hatchway's metal-reinforced doorframe and the saw careened from his grip, right down through the hatchway's opening at me. Luckily, the chain saw had stalled by the time I caught it, snatching the grip by pure reflex as it went by. It nearly broke my arm and I'd be sore for weeks, but there it was in my hand.

"How?" I gasped to Sam, who'd flung himself into the cabin after the saw.

"Sam!" Mika cried joyfully again. He lunged for her, kissed her thoroughly, then turned away to take the saw and pull its starter cord once more.

"How'd you know we were here?!" I yelled.

By now Bella's and Ellie's faces had lit with hope and even Tilda looked cautiously optimistic. But we weren't out of here by a long shot; not yet.

"Gramps told me," Sam said, and while I was still digesting this notion the boat leaned hard once more. The sudden movement knocked my feet from beneath me and the next thing I knew, I was underwater.

There was, after all, a lot of it in the cabin; worse, I couldn't find which way was up. Then my hair got yanked hard from above, my face emerged, and I could breathe once more.

"Don't do that again," Sam said. Then he turned back to his task of finishing the hole he was cutting in the side of the boat.

"Uh, Sam?" The saw's howl went on. He touched its whirling chain to the metal-reinforced rope that held everyone down here.

Everyone but me. Sparks flew and the saw stalled; my heart stuttered. He pulled the starter cord again, it caught, and he went back to what he'd been doing before: cutting the hole.

Meanwhile, through the swamped hatchway door, a large wave slopped every half minute. The water level in the cabin where we huddled rose steadily; now it had reached our chests.

Where Sam was cutting more water poured in, the saw's howl filling the cabin.

"Get ready! Ma, I cut the rail loose from outside."

The rail that the cable had been tied to, he meant. "In a minute I'll kick this porthole out; the chunk of rail will fit through it."

He caught his breath. "When it comes in," he went on, "you just grab it all and go!" he shouted. "All of you, follow her!"

He gestured commandingly to us, and in that moment I really believed we could do it.

Or anyway I did until the hole he was cutting exploded in at us suddenly, followed by a massive surge of cold salt water.

"Go!" he yelled again as the mooring cable and the chunk of the boat's rail tumbled in.

Then everything was chaos, all screaming and scrambling. I backed fast up through the open hatch, hurled myself toward the base of the captain's chair at the helm, and wrapped my arms around it, clinging to it.

Tilda was right behind me, grabbing greedily at the other chair's base. Next came Ellie, coughing and gagging as her face popped up from under the water; she half-swam, half-floundered to me and clung to my leg.

And then came Mika, gasping but looking not too bad; that is, until some terrible realization hit her. Before I could stop her she turned, pinched her nose shut, and plunged back down.

"Mika!" I shouted, and let go of the chair, but by the time I reached the hatch she was up again with Bella under one arm.

"Here," she gasped, and we got Bella up into the chair I'd clung to. She leaned over and upchucked a lot of seawater, then leaned back tiredly.

"Okay," she breathed. "Okay, we're all right." But now the saw had stopped.

"Sam?" I said anxiously, and then, "*Sam?*"

No Sam.

By now the sun had peeked over the horizon, spreading pink light across the waves' tops. No one was in sight. We were fifty yards from shore, too far to swim. And Sam still hadn't come up.

"Sam!" The boat rocked hard yet again, sending me sprawling. The deck was awash; I let a wave carry me toward the hatchway, and when I got there, I kept going.

Sam . . . The murky water in the flooded cabin tasted like engine oil. I felt around blindly; he had to be here somewhere.

Something seized my ankle. I yanked it back but whoever it was—or, dear God, *whatever*—wouldn't let go.

"*No!*" The shout escaped me in a cloud of bubbles as a pair of hands began hauling me out of the cabin, back onto the deck.

Struggling all the way. "Let me go, I've got to—"

"Jake?" Ellie shook me by the shoulders. "Jake, look!"

She turned me and pointed at the water. "See? It's—"

It was Sam's head, and as far as I could tell Sam's body was still attached to it. He reached the foundering boat's stern and hotfooted it up the swim ladder.

Grinning. "I went out the hole," he explained. "Once the water quit pouring in, it was easy."

Yeah, easy for you, I thought, and of course I didn't swat him for half-scaring me to death, either. For one thing, he'd saved our lives, and for another, I didn't have the strength.

He looked around. Collapsed on the deck where the water around them kept deepening, the others shivered visibly.

"Yeah," I began, "we've got to get them to shore."

As if in agreement, the boat rocked as if it wanted to shake us off. It didn't quite succeed, but it could capsize any time, and when it did some or all of us would drown.

"Sam," I began, but before I could say more a boat appeared at the cove's entrance. Lights blazed from it, from its comms gear way up top to the blazing-white search lights crossing and recrossing the water.

I couldn't believe it. A voice out there called out some orders, sounding as if its owner was accustomed to those orders being obeyed.

Then came the loud, obnoxious *whonnnk!* of an air horn. A *Coast Guard* air horn, I recognized the sound, and the boat was their orange rubber Zodiac.

I turned to Sam, whose lips were a deep shade of blue. Like my own, I guessed; just then a Popsicle wouldn't have melted in my mouth.

"Oh, come on," he answered before I could ask, "you didn't think I'd just swim out here alone and not tell anyone first, did you?"

Before I could answer, the Zodiac pulled alongside us and the crew threw Sam a line. Beyond the Zodiac, something white floated; it was the big cooler we'd brought to keep the whipping cream and the chocolate chip cupcakes cold, I realized.

Sam had put his chain saw in it and floated it here; oh, what a good, outside-the-box-thinking boy I'd raised.

Then a sudden thought struck fear into me and I was peering around frantically again. "Where's your grandfather?"

I'd have thought of it earlier but I hadn't had time, what with nearly drowning and all. But Sam's reply reassured me.

Sort of. "Bob Arnold tossed him in the squad car as soon as he saw him," Sam said, "and then headed for the hospital. Pretty banged up."

Guilt raked me again; I should never have agreed to let him come no matter how much he insisted.

One of the Coasties hopped nimbly aboard our boat and

began fitting life vests onto us. Another had set up what looked like a sort of zip line between us and the Zodiac.

It all looked efficient and professional and as if we might live through this, after all; still, I didn't want to jinx it.

"But, Sam"—I looked away from the Coasties—"how'd he get to you? Your grandfather . . . had you guys gotten through by then?"

Because when I'd seen it last, the white gravel driveway in front of Cliff House had still been blocked.

"Uh-uh." Sam moved to help three uniformed young men and women get Bella onto the zip line. From the way she squawked, I thought maybe she was surviving all right, too.

"That guy that Bob Arnold called? His big saw broke. But the tree's still there," Sam called back to me.

Just then Bella, buckled into a sort of harness contraption that lifted her off the deck, sailed away down the zip line. The Zodiac's crew caught her and sent the harness back to us.

"Now we're waiting for the guy to fix the saw," Sam added as he approached me.

"Bottom line, I don't know how Gramps got to us," he said, bending to me. "But when I heard him say what was going on over here, I had to do something."

He was holding Bella's harness. "Did someone out here have a dog, by the way?" he asked.

I told him that someone had, that its name was Igor, and he smiled; I guessed Igor must've made a good impression despite his enormous size.

"Anyway, I made them put me in the bucket loader and sort of catapult me over," Sam said, "and then the dog found me and started leading me down a path."

The one with the sawgrass, slipperiness, and lurking swamp creatures, I recalled only too well.

Another smile from Sam. "He was pretty insistent about it. Here, put this on."

"What?" I drew back. "Sam, I don't need to be next, let Mika or Ellie go."

But by now they stood behind him, working to keep their balance in the water sloshing around their knees, but looking adamant nonetheless.

"Put it on," said Ellie, and that was when I noticed all the warm stuff running down the side of my face.

I touched it curiously, inspected my hand. *Blood.* A fair lot of it. *That wild shot Tilda fired,* I realized.

I hadn't felt it. But it had felt me; somewhat forcefully, it seemed. It would've been a lot more noticeable to everyone else if I hadn't been spending so much time under water, lately.

"Ma," Sam said gently, "I hate to tell you, but it looks like you've been shot. Now get on that Coast Guard boat or I'll put you in the water and swim you over to it, myself."

He made as if to grab me and in escaping him I found myself backing into the Coasties and being seized by them.

Click! went the harness's clip, and I was flying, hearing the *zzzt!* as the clip slid down the line with me dangling from it and carefully not screaming.

At the other end, more Coasties caught me, steadied me, and set my feet carefully down on their boat's deck.

Where I promptly collapsed.

Fourteen

Those fresh-faced young Coast Guard men and women all looked about as forceful as puppies, but they knew how to move me along to where they wanted me to go. On their boat, the last person I saw before the youthful mariners hustled me below was Sam, sprinting back uphill through the sawgrass with Igor loping behind him.

Above, Cliff House loomed with dawn light glittering in its windows. I shuddered, turning away as one of the Coasties threw a blanket around my shoulders.

"Everybody okay for now?" she asked as she helped me into a cabin where the others already gathered.

"Anyway, sorry we took so long," the young crew member went on. "We just got called off a recovery search or we'd have been here sooner."

Ellie's gaze met mine, from where she sat on the cabin's bench seat. A recovery was what they called it when no rescue was likely possible, we both knew.

"Back on the boat in the cove," I managed through teeth chattering like castanets. "In a tarp."

If we hadn't hauled that body out of the drink, the Coast Guard might've found it sooner, and rescued us sooner, too.

But it was in the past, now; all of it, I sincerely hoped. Thinking this, I joined the others who hunched in the cramped cabin, shivering under their own blankets.

Hot drinks were in their hands; I saw Bella sip from hers all on her own, and I relaxed a little. But Tilda was in the cabin, too, and she was my last chance at finding out what the heck I was doing here at all; I mean *specifically* what.

And I wasn't about to waste it; this had been all my idea, after all, and I owed that much to the others.

So I plopped down beside Tilda. She glanced over at me and flinched.

"Oh, poor baby, are you bothered by the sight of blood?" I asked, not sparing the sarcasm.

Big engines rumbled to life and the boat took off, throwing me backward before I could wrap my fingers around her throat.

Luckily for me; if I strangled her, I couldn't interrogate her. So I stifled my fury. "You know, Tilda, I could tell Bob Arnold the truth about you."

She looked alarmed, as well she should have. She'd survived while Ingrid Merryfield hadn't; that meant there was nobody left for her to testify against, to try to save her own skin.

"Or I could tell him you want to talk to him, tell him the truth about what happened. That you'll cooperate, maybe even that you helped us. But first you have to talk to me."

She looked cautiously interested; I would have, too. Six people were dead—seven, counting Ingrid—and Tilda was the only one still alive who'd helped make them that way.

"Who was in on it? Tell me," I warned, "and fast."

Five minutes, tops, and we'd be at the dock in Eastport. I wouldn't have any access to her after that; no doubt Bob Arnold would be there when we arrived.

"Bryan," she said grudgingly. "And Tink Markle. Gilly was in on it for a little while, but he didn't know much."

She put a look of appeal into her eyes. "But it was all Ingrid's idea, we never wanted to—"

"Shut up. The idea was to kill the others, then: Audrey, Maud, and Waldo. But why? And why'd you go along with it?"

She eyed me flatly. "She knew Bryan killed that guy, that stalker who'd been hassling her. He'd talked about it, hoping it would make her want to get back with him."

The boat hit the turbulent currents around Gay's Head. I gripped a stout canvas loop hung from an overhead strut in the small cabin.

"But she threatened to tell the cops," I guessed, "unless he did it again? Only she'd pick the victims, this time?"

Tilda nodded, biting her lip. Of course Ingrid hadn't done the murders herself. Just as I'd thought when I'd first met her, she had people for that.

"And Tink, how'd she convince him?"

Tilda leaned back tiredly, closing her eyes. "Drugs. He'd been using again—she found out about it—and if anyone else knew it, he'd really never get any more work."

Because he couldn't be insured, of course. Nobody wants a guy who might pass out on set, or worse, die of an overdose and ruin the whole production.

"And there was something she said about him ending up with the house. I didn't understand it, but he seemed to think it was his and she made him feel like she could make that happen for real; I don't know how."

Probably we'd never know exactly what she'd told him—not unless we fired up that Ouija board and it worked, anyway—but whatever it was, apparently he'd believed it.

"He did the scary sound effects?" I asked. "All the scratching and howling and so on?"

Another nod. "After he couldn't get hired anymore in the

film business, he did a lot of things so he could eat. One of them was sound effects for a rock band called the Haunteds."

Oh, for Pete's sake. Sam liked the Haunteds. On stage, they dressed up as ghosts and wailed like banshees.

"Okay, that leaves you and Gilly. I know Gilly would have done just about anything for her, but what turned you into a killer, Tilda?"

She opened her eyes. Ellie, Mika, and Bella all gazed flat-faced at her, listening.

She closed them again tiredly. "I thought it was all just talk. That we might scare them."

A shiver went through her. "But then we got here and Waldo died, and after that poor Gilly did."

The engines slowed and the chop beneath us smoothed out. We were nearing the Eastport dock.

"Gilly wasn't really in it," Tilda went on. "He was only sup-posed to bring the boat back to Cliff House so we could leave when it was time. Ingrid said she had plane tickets to a place she knew in France."

Why she'd thought extradition wouldn't work there I had no idea. But it didn't matter, I supposed; if Ingrid Merryfield's plan had worked the way she meant it to, there'd be no coming back for Tilda with or without a warrant.

"So *she* said," Tilda finished bitterly, meaning the place in France. "I thought I was helping her, that we were a team, right up until she tied me up, too."

Meanwhile, the familiar clanking and creaking of the old wooden docks in the Eastport boat basin said we'd arrived.

The Coast Guard crew began moving on the deck as brisk orders got called out and docking routines were followed.

"Just one more thing," I said. "Ingrid meant to kill off three enemies: Waldo, Audrey, and Maud. The rest of you were just witnesses she had to get rid of afterward."

Tilda winced and her eyes popped open again as the boat

thumped the dock. The engine noise dropped to a liquid grumble, and I heard the unmistakable brief whoop of a squad car's siren from up on the breakwater.

"But why?" I persisted. "Why'd she kill those three?"

I wanted to know why we'd been put through all this, sure, but mostly I wanted to hear it so that I could testify to it, in case she changed her story later.

Across from me, Ellie got up and helped Bella to her feet. Shakily, Mika followed them out into the narrow corridor.

Tilda stared at nothing. "Maud got the part that Ingrid expected in the new film," she replied, "and on top of that, Maud let it be known that it was because Ingrid was too old."

She took a breath. "And Audrey was dating Ingrid's filthy-rich ex-husband. Not many people know it. She thought Ingrid didn't know it. She thought she could write Ingrid's biography, anyway, that Ingrid wouldn't find out. Or wouldn't care."

Tilda took a breath. "But she did care."

I got up. Those Coasties could count; soon they'd be down here to fetch their remaining two rescued persons.

"And Ingrid wanted him back? But I thought—"

"No. She hated him," said Tilda. "She just didn't want anyone else to have what's hers. Or was ever hers."

A man's ruined face rose awfully in my mind's eye at last. "And what about Waldo, what'd he do to her?"

Tilda got off the bench seat. "Nothing. He was camouflage, that's all. She said if someone she didn't have anything against were to die, too, then she wouldn't be suspected."

That wasn't true. The cops would've figured it out. It's not like in the movies where the killer is always smarter; no one's smarter than a police forensics lab, anymore.

"I guess it's hard to understand," Tilda said. "She had so much. Money, freedom."

She turned to me, her expression defeated. The Coasties were coming for us; I heard their boots in the passageway.

"But she was losing it all. Just . . . time passes, you know? She blamed them, though, and she was obsessed over it. Thought about it every minute, hating them for having what she didn't."

A fresh young face atop an energetic young body in a blue Coast Guard uniform appeared in the cabin's doorway. "Time to go. Can I help you ladies ashore?"

Oh, yes indeed, good old dry land, and once I got there I planned never leaving it again. But first:

"I guess," Tilda finished brokenly, "it was easier for her to despise them than to accept things for what they were."

She sighed. "That it wasn't their fault, any of it. That her glory days, the fame and the money and power, were going away all by themselves, and no one could stop them."

Right. And now they were gone. Tilda's, too, and her face told me that she knew it.

She let the young crew member help her out of the cabin and I followed.

To the east, the sun hovered over the water, igniting the autumn foliage on Campobello. "You might want to get that head looked at," said the young man who handed me over onto the dock.

Up on the breakwater, Wade jumped out of Bob's squad car and ran toward me while Bob drove toward me; they reached me at the same time

"She confessed," I told Bob through the car window, waving tiredly at the dazed-looking woman now walking away alone. "Not to the whole thing, but to enough."

Bob let the squad car roll slowly in Tilda's direction, but I didn't see what happened next because then Wade reached me and his arms wrapped around me.

"So, listen," I managed into his jacket-front. It smelled faintly of the nasty stuff he cleaned gun barrels with.

But right then I'd never inhaled anything so wonderful in my life. "Things got a little out of hand," I said.

Behind him the sun lit the windows on Water Street, turning

them to mirrors. "Out of hand," he repeated. "Yeah, you think?" Then before I could ask:

"Your dad's okay. They looked him over in the ER, decided to admit him anyway. He's tired, scratched up, couple bruises and he's dehydrated. But he's old, you know, and he'll be there for a day or so, they said."

Relief coursed through me. "And Sam?"

Ellie's husband, George, arrived, his pickup truck slamming to a halt. An instant later he got out and swept her into an embrace.

"Sam's back at the job," Wade said. "I ran some dry clothes and shoes out to him just now, and some food. He's got a real tree-harvesting machine on site there, now."

A machine, Wade meant, that could eat through a twelve-foot tree trunk lickety-split and wouldn't break in the process.

He gripped my shoulders and held me away from him, examining me. From his expression, I gathered that he found all the blood in my hair and eyebrows particularly interesting.

In the boat basin, the fishing boats' engines rumbled to life. Gulls flapped around the departing vessels, crying.

"You," Wade pronounced, drawing me near again, "need your head examined."

So we went and did that.

Three days after the incident at Cliff House came to an end, I was seated in the parlor at home in a lounge chair that Sam had set up for me. A blanket was draped over my lap and a small fire snapped pleasantly on the hearth.

"I could get used to this napping in the morning stuff," I said.

Well, except for the part about seeing Ingrid Merryfield's drowned face every time I closed my eyes.

"Drink up, now, it's almost time to go," Ellie urged me as she delivered a cup of coffee to me.

Sam and Wade had set up a card table with my phone and a

laptop and an iPod of Sam's that he'd loaded with music for me. Mozart and Sondheim weren't his favorites, I knew.

But they were mine, and he'd put them on it. "To make you feel," he'd said, "like living."

Not that there was any big question about that. I was fine, just skull-thumped by a bullet that had dug a shallow groove in my scalp. It had been a close call, but I had no brain damage, or as Bella had said dryly, no more than I'd started out with.

I could do without all this sitting around, but it was doctor's orders for a few days more, anyway, so I put up with it. Now I got out of the lounge chair and followed Ellie to the kitchen, where Bella was putting cupcakes on a tray.

Chocolate chip and cream-filled, of course; I filched one. The cream still liquefied eventually, even cold, but none were ever left over.

"You look great," I told Bella. Navy slacks, white blouse, and tan LifeStride sandals with a short, stacked heel.

Even her frizzy red hair was tied back in a plaid scrunchy, and her big grape-green eyes sparkled nicely with some Vaseline smoothed onto their lids. "Bella, is that lipstick?"

It was. Light pink; she harrumphed a little. But my dad was coming home from the hospital today, so she was all snazzed up, as she put it, and not about to take any teasing about it.

Ellie brought my jacket from the hall. "Come on, ladies, we've been invited for lunch and it's eleven-thirty right now."

At Sam's new home in Quoddy Village, she meant. Except for a carefully managed, Jake's-still-an-invalid visit to my dad in the hospital, it was my first venture out of the house since having my hair parted nearly down to my skull bone.

Or, at any rate, it was the first venture that anyone else knew about.

"I'll be there in a sec," I said, and they went out, each with a tray of cupcakes, but I stayed behind for a moment to look around the kitchen with its high, bare windows; wooden wainscoting; and the big round table with the red-checked cloth on it monopolizing most of the room.

I could hear the clock ticking in the hall, it was so quiet suddenly. And we wouldn't be needing that enormous table anymore, would we? When Sam and his young family came to visit, we'd just use the dining room.

They weren't going far, I knew. Still, after today nothing would be the same. I went outside and closed the door behind me.

"Big day," said Ellie sympathetically when I'd gotten into her car; Bella was in the backseat.

"Right," I managed, not trusting my voice; so much was ending.

"It's going to be fine, you'll see," she reassured me, and a few minutes later we were pulling up in front of Sam and Mika's house in Quoddy Village.

"So that movie star woman was behind the whole thing, all along? That Ingrid Merryfield person?"

"'Fraid so," I told the bearded young man in the vintage Iron Maiden T-shirt.

"Her and her three helpers," I said. "But of those three, Bryan Dwyer, Tink Markle, and Tilda French, only Tilda is still alive to talk about it."

I didn't count Gilly, dead or alive. Maybe I should have. He was in on it, all right, but not in a guilty way, just a stupid one. Meanwhile, Tilda had told Bob Arnold all that she'd told me, and more: Ingrid's vengefulness, Tilda's fear of her employer. I supposed it was Tilda's only hope of minimizing her punishment, the idea that she had been forced to do what she'd done.

That when she killed Waldo Higgins, for instance, with a claw hammer that Bryan had found lying rusty and forgotten in the old garage, Tilda hadn't had a choice.

Yeah, right, I thought, putting down my sandwich and picking up my glass of apple juice. Approximately the last thing I wanted to talk about was murder, and the last thing I wanted was apple juice, too.

A nice dry martini, up with a twist the way my dad made them, would've gone down real well with the lovely chicken salad that Mika had made for lunch. But the pills I was taking against the headache I still felt made having one a big nope.

"Come on, there's got to be more. What else happened?" the question broke into my thoughts.

My questioner, a fellow about Sam's age whom I gathered was one of Sam's new neighbors, eyed me as if he were a crow and I was a shiny aluminum pop-top. The other guests listened, too: more new neighbors, my whole family, and of course Bob Arnold, enjoying the chicken salad and pleased that for once he didn't have to do all the explaining.

Well, I guessed that was fair enough. "Gather round, children," he intoned, and I began:

"Ingrid Merryfield was a real old-fashioned movie star, the kind with a mansion, designer gowns, and fabulous jewelry. She married well, too: a Hollywood businessman, wealthy and powerful, and through him, naturally, she got even more money and influence."

Sipping my apple juice, I glanced around. Sam's new home was cozy and neat with new curtains and cushion covers made by Mika plus a great many hand-me-down rugs, potted plants, and a collection of elegantly framed black-and-white photographs on the walls.

"You'll be snug as a bug in a rug, here," I said, grabbing Sam's toddler son, Ephraim, to nuzzle his sweet-smelling neck, then hauling him into my lap, where he promptly fell asleep.

"But Ingrid made enemies along the way," I went on to the still-attentive group. "Two in particular. And there was a third."

Mika brought in a tray of cupcakes and—surprise!—a chocolate pizza, fresh from the oven and sliced into small, easy-to-handle squares.

I bit into one: heaven. Ellie had been right; we'd sell heaps of these, no problem.

"One of Ingrid's guests had Ingrid's ex-husband. Another had a part in the kind of film Ingrid used to star in herself."

I took a breath. "And the third," I went on, "an aging performer himself, wasn't an enemy at all. She just killed him to divert suspicion from herself."

Assuming that the running-away-to-France plan didn't work and she needed one; a diversion, that is.

"Bottom line, Ingrid Merryfield was accustomed to getting exactly what she wanted," I said. "And when she didn't, things went poorly."

T-shirt guy's eyes were as wide as dinner plates. "Man, I guess so, huh? I'm glad I never had anything she wanted."

The T-shirt was ghastly but I loved the guy already for the post holes he was helping Sam to dig. It seemed Sam had gotten some good neighbors.

"Right," I told him. "I'm glad, too." Besides everything else, the kid had a knockout smile.

"Her plan didn't include that tree falling, though," Bob put in. "Or the ground moving under her feet like it was trying to shake her off."

All the little earthquakes had shut off like a switch by the time the Coast Guard boat with us on it had reached Eastport. Naturally I didn't think the ending of the events at Cliff House had anything to do with that.

Of course not. "But Ingrid adapted," Bob went on. "She must've figured that if she was the only survivor, she could say what she liked and have a good chance of being believed."

Right, I thought, even though with every breath she'd taken she'd been lying through her teeth. Even the story that Tilda had told me about the plane tickets wasn't true; the star had a secret hideaway in France, all right, and a whole new identity waiting there for her so she wouldn't be found and extradited.

But according to the one-way ticket she'd bought without telling anyone, not even Tilda, Miss Merryfield had planned to be traveling alone.

"What about the baby?" asked Mika.

I'd told her about my visit to Nanny Jackson, and then to the graveyard. But I hadn't yet told her that the interesting old herbalist had called me soon after we all got home. She'd done a little more research, she'd told me, but not in genealogy books. She'd tracked down the fellow who'd showed two mysterious male visitors to the Merryfield plot in Eastport's old graveyard, and asked him a few questions.

Like, what had the visitors actually looked like, and after hearing the descriptions he'd reported to our town's venerable old historian and herbalist, I'd put together the rest.

"Ingrid Merryfield lied about not taking a stage name. Her real name, which she'd managed to get wiped out of any online references to her—"

"One of those fix-your-reputation services?" Mika put in acutely, and I nodded agreement as I went on.

"Her real name was Helen Jones." The state police had dug this information up and told Bob Arnold, and Bob had told me.

"Anyway, the baby in the grave had nothing to do with her plot to get revenge and get away with it," I said.

Ellie's eyebrows went up. I hadn't told her about this yet, either; we'd been too busy deciding just exactly how we were going to portion out the pay we'd earned by catering the Cliff House party.

The enormous checks that Ingrid Merryfield had given us had cleared; we could keep The Chocolate Moose's doors open all winter, no problem.

Now all we needed to do was figure out one more thing: should we start selling the chocolate pizzas now, or save them for later in the winter when front porch plow-watching started seeming attractive again?

"She wasn't from here, but she wanted to say she was. She was smart enough to know it would ingratiate her even more with people here, if she could."

Anything to further eliminate all chance of later suspicion falling on her would've been welcome, of course.

"So she sent Tink and Bryan to see if there was any chance of this—"

"And by luck they hit pay dirt?" Mika, again.

"Yup. Not only had there been a Merryfield family here long ago, but they'd had a dead child named Inga. To her it must've felt like a sign."

I mean, assuming she'd still believed in such things; on second thought, I suspected she didn't.

Pip Collins, the cemetery supervisor had called me, right after Nanny Jackson did; word of what had happened had gotten around town, of course.

There was room in the Merryfield plot, he'd said, and city funds available for indigent burial. But I'd told Pip not to worry about that, that Miss Merryfield's estate would cover the costs eventually and I'd cover them meanwhile.

I didn't owe it to her. And I didn't feel particularly sorry for her, either; why should I?

But I did feel pity for her, and besides, maybe if I buried her I'd stop seeing her face glaring up through the seawater at me every time I closed my eyes.

"So no ghosts?" my earlier questioner asked. "At Cliff House, I mean. Because I always heard the place was—"

Haunted. "Yeah, no ghosts." Hey, the kid might be excellent as one of Sam's new neighbors but he didn't have to know every little thing, did he? "Sorry," I said.

Earlier, Mika had showed me two bright, cheerful-looking

bedrooms, each furnished for a child. One had a crib in it, the other a brand-new big-boy's bed.

I glanced over at Sam, who stood surveying the scene and looking like he'd just swallowed the canary; big boy, indeed, I thought, and felt better about his moving. I mean, I loved them all, of course, but my house had been so overfull that it was a wonder we didn't fight like cats and dogs.

The front door opened and Bob Arnold came in; he'd gone out without my noticing. Then an actual dog shoved in past him.

"Igor!" He'd been boarding at our local veterinarian's kennel; now he bounced around happily greeting everyone, then made a beeline for Bella and dropped his shaggy head in her lap.

"Wait a minute," I said, "what's he doing here? I thought he was going to be offered for adoption."

Sam knelt by Igor, not answering. Or at least not answering me: "It's not going to be all fun and games," he warned the dog, who grinned at the news.

Oh yes, it is, Igor's expression promised, and as I figured out who must be adopting the animal I thought the dog was right.

"Wuff," said Igor, dropping into a play bow.

No kidding; the dog had a new home, a young family to play with him. . . . They should change his name to Lucky, I thought.

"Jake." Bella's voice came from the corner, where she sat by my dad, who was smiling delightedly at the company and his grandchildren but still had the hospital ID band fastened on his wrist.

While he was at the hospital, I'd tried replicating his astonishing feat of climbing over the big fallen tree. That was the trip outside that I'd taken that nobody else knew about, and there had been enough of the old tree trunk still on-site to make the experiment realistic.

But I'd gotten only about halfway over it before I gave up.

What he'd done for us, however he'd managed it, was more than heroic. It was practically miraculous.

I got up. More young people were arriving, some of them Sam's friends, some Mika's, and all with young children in tow.

"Time to go," I said when the decibel level in the house could've drowned out a chain saw. Sam and Mika wrapped their arms around me while Wade and Bella helped my dad negotiate the front steps.

"Ma," Sam said, "thanks."

It seemed like only a moment ago that he'd been a rigid-with-misery twelve-year-old, slamming himself into every bad habit he could find in hopes of finding one that made him feel anything.

And then he'd found Eastport and become who he was, now.

"No, Sam. Thank *you*," I said, then followed my dad down the steps and across the front lawn of my son's new home.

"It's going to be awfully quiet around here," Wade said later that evening.

"Except for the parrot," I replied. Upstairs in its big wire enclosure with the swing, the mirror, the bell, and the door wide open, the big green bird was singing "Take Me Out to the Ball Game" in a Bronx-accented falsetto.

We sat in front of the parlor fireplace, side by side on the settee. On the coffee table in their glass tank, neon tetras flashed brilliantly around the red plastic diver who bobbed up and down blowing bubbles.

I settled against Wade. "Having to be rescued, though," I sighed, "so embarrassing."

He drew back, looking at me like he couldn't believe what he'd just heard. "I wouldn't say you were exactly rescued."

He curved his arm around my shoulder again. "Look, you raised that kid from a sprout and here's what you produced: a man, one who would help you, could help you, and did help you."

On the hearth, flames licked hungrily at the logs, curling their splinters to frizzled wisps.

"Now I know a lot of that is probably due to his inborn temperament. But you might just entertain the notion, Jake, that some of it is due to you."

". . . take me out wit' da crowds," the parrot sang lustily.

"Think of it," Wade said, "as an investment, all that you did. And what Sam gets out of it now is being a real, no-kidding hero, to his mom and to his wife."

I stared into the fire, listening, not having thought of it at all that way, before.

"Tell you the truth, I'm feeling pretty affectionate toward the kid right now myself," said Wade.

He pulled me against him. "And if I were you," he finished gently, "I might just leave it at that."

"Huh." I thought about it. "You know, it's possible you have a point there," I said finally.

Bob Arnold had stopped by after the party at Sam's so I could tell him for sure where all the bodies were; the homicide cops wanted to be sure they accounted for everyone, including the mummified remains of the woman in the pool in the cellar.

"The police think the oldest body belonged to Tink's great-grandmother," I told Wade now. "Bob thought she might've gotten away from the house and her awful husband all those years ago."

A sigh escaped me. "But I guess she didn't," I finished.

"Was she there all that time? In the pool?" Wade wanted to know. I shook my head.

"I think maybe she'd been in the cooler. Or . . . I don't know. Wherever she was, Tink moved her so we wouldn't find her, I'm guessing."

I looked up. "But don't tell Mika. If it was the cooler she'll be horrified at what was in there before the bacon and eggs."

How Tink had linked up with Bryan, and through him with

Ingrid Merryfield, was a story of its own. They'd met as child performers, stayed in touch afterward, and voila!

Or viola, as Sam would've said. "Tilda told Bob that Tink and Bryan had been doing bad deeds together for years," I said.

As for Tilda herself, no personal history had been offered to minimize or excuse what she'd done on her employer's behalf.

"Pretty exciting, being part of a plot like that," Wade theorized. "If you're a certain kind of person, that is."

Indeed. The kind with no life of her own, who liked killing people. Because maybe it had all been Ingrid's idea, like Tilda said, but the only one I knew for sure Tilda hadn't killed was poor Maud Bankersley, still buried in the collapsed tunnel.

By now it was getting dark outside, the sky's last light draining away and the moon not yet risen. A branch scraped at the parlor window as if tapping out a message.

"Wade," I said, trying to get up, "I need to go check on my dad and Bella."

They'd gone upstairs early, pleading fatigue, which was probably true. But they also wanted to give me and Wade some time alone.

They were like that. But: "Oh no you don't," Wade said, pulling me down again. "They're fine."

His eyes reflected the dancing firelight. "So what happened out there that you haven't told me about?"

I sat up fast. "How did you know?"

Out in the hall, the old grandfather clock ticked hollowly.

"Call it a hunch," he said. So I told him:

"Ingrid Merryfield set up the whole haunted house schtick, with Tink Markle to help her. He came in advance, that's why the special effects equipment was already there and set up when Ingrid and Bryan arrived."

Set up and ready to scare Ellie and me right off the bat, I meant. And it had worked.

"Yeah, Bob told me the state cops have been through the

house. Said you could've made the whole place whistle 'Dixie,' it was so wired up for sound," Wade replied.

The howls and scratching, footsteps and weird lights . . . like Waldo Higgins's death, all of it was meant just to muddy the waters, to make what was happening seem complicated and strange.

Even Bryan the driver-slash-bodyguard's visit to Bob had been just a smokescreen, I realized now, to make it seem to Bob that Bryan was a stand-up guy.

In case, I mean, any little questions should develop on that topic, Bryan got out ahead of them. But never mind that:

"Wade, do you believe in ghosts?"

He chuckled at the question, then saw that I was serious. "Not sure. Why?"

"Well," I said slowly, still not sure I wanted to tell this part, "when I visited my dad in the hospital, I asked him how he got over that tree."

An elderly man, not terribly strong and by then exhausted, he'd somehow made his way back up the lawn, down the gravel driveway, and then through thick brush, finally to a monstrously large fallen tree trunk that he'd had to climb over.

Which he had. It was that last part I hadn't been able to fathom. "And when I asked him how he did it, he said someone helped him, shoving him up and forward from behind, he said. He felt it, and heard someone urging him on. A woman, he said."

He'd said he'd looked at her, too, at her hand pushing him. He'd said the woman's index finger was missing.

Like it was broken off, he'd said.

Wade sighed. "Jake, your dad's a very old man. He could've imagined it or misinterpreted something."

"I know that. I know he could have. He didn't imagine climbing over that tree, though, did he?"

I'd have said it was impossible. I'd never know for sure what really happened, I supposed.

Not for sure. "Want to go for a walk?" Wade asked, getting up. I joined him, and we headed downtown under the maple trees fluttering their yellow leaves.

"At least now I know why Ingrid Merryfield came right to us," I said as we walked.

Among Bryan's things in the Cliff House garage apartment, the police had found a *Bangor Daily News* clipping about us, The Chocolate Moose, and our history of sticking our noses into matters less attractive—and more dangerous—than chocolate.

"She wanted our catering, of course," I said.

That's one thing Ellie and I wouldn't be doing anymore: catering house parties for strangers. "But I'm pretty sure she also wanted the town snoops out there with her, too," I said.

Because, as I'd learned from my bad-to-the-bone employers back in my city days, the best way to keep somebody from interfering in your business is to involve them in it.

On Water Street, the closed and silent shops basked in the bluish light of a just-risen moon. Across the dark water, cars' distant headlights pricked the night on Campobello.

"Look," said Wade as we walked out onto the fish pier.

The dark shapes of south-flying Canada geese passed over our heads, their wings whooshing softly. Wade put his arm around me just as my phone pinged.

I dug it out and it was Sam. "Ma, come on out here, will you? I mean, if you feel like it. The kids are asking for you."

"Oh," I breathed, pleased, and of course a little while later Wade and I did go, still with that hazy autumn moon in our rearview mirror.

"I'm going to miss him," I said, meaning my dad.

He'd had a martini when we got home from the party, and eaten a good dinner. But I couldn't help worrying that this all might've been his last hurrah: that at his great age he was with us and not with us, staying and going, all at the same time.

Wade understood. "We'll all miss him," he said as we pulled up in front of Sam's house.

A lamp glowed warmly in the window and the porch light was on. We walked up the path to the doorstep, where Mika had set out red potted chrysanthemums.

"But not yet," Wade said reassuringly. "Not today."

The door opened and Sam was there, welcoming us in.

Chocolate Pizza

Chocolate pizza is so easy to make, you'll be wondering why you didn't try it before!

Start with a 12-inch plain pizza crust. You can make your own, with these ingredients:

2 cups flour
1 tsp sugar
$^3/_4$ tsp salt
$^3/_4$ cup warm water
1 envelope dry yeast
3 Tbsp olive oil

For the toppings:

Bits of white chocolate, milk chocolate, semi-sweet chocolate
Chocolate-hazelnut spread
Chopped nuts (optional)

Dissolve the yeast in the warm water. Mix together the flour, sugar, and salt. Add the dissolved yeast and warm water. Add the olive oil. Mix it all together until it forms a dough. Dump the dough out onto a floured surface. Knead until the dough is soft, adding more flour to the kneading surface if needed.

Put the dough in an olive-oiled bowl and let it rise in a warm place until it doubles in size—45 minutes or so.

Then punch it down in the bowl, cover, and refrigerate. When it's time to use it, punch it down again and turn it out onto a 16-inch square piece of parchment paper. Let it rest for 10 minutes and then use a rolling pin to roll it out into a 12-inch circle.

Slide the crust, paper and all, onto a pizza stone (or a cookie sheet). Bake for about 20 minutes in a preheated 450 degree oven. The time is approximate, though—you want it browned, not burned, so check it starting at about 15 minutes.

Cool the baked crust until it is just warm, then spread with chocolate-hazelnut spread. Top with bits of white, dark, and milk chocolate plus chopped nuts if you like them (salted nuts are great on this!).

Slide the pizza back into the oven until the chocolate bits melt slightly, remove from the oven, cut into slices, and enjoy!

DEATH BY CHOCOLATE RASPBERRY SCONE

Summer guests are eager to sink their teeth into tantalizing desserts at The Chocolate Moose, Jacobia "Jake" Tiptree and Ellie White's bakeshop in the island village of Eastport, Maine. But attracting the wrong kind of attention can be deadly. . . .

With the August heat strong enough to melt solid chocolate into syrup, Jake and Ellie crave a break from the bakery ovens, despite tourist season promising a sweet payday. But they never envisioned spending the last weeks of summer drifting around Passamaquoddy Bay searching for pirate's treasure—and a dead body.

Sally Coates believes her husband was murdered off the coast, and begs Ellie, a trusted childhood friend, to locate his remains. It's unusual that a skilled fisherman would vanish along with the gold doubloon he inherited from his grandfather. And Sally isn't the only one coveting the valuable heirloom for her own.

As Jake and Ellie island-hop for answers, they find themselves caught between hungry sharks and hungrier suspects. Can the duo tempt fate and dodge danger before there's blood in the water—or are they destined to fall into the jaws of a killer's trap?

One

"Standing in front of a hot oven during a heat wave is not what I signed up for," I complained, sliding another batch of chocolate chip cookies onto a platter.

"You could stand over there by the hot cash register," my friend, Ellie White, replied, waving the knife she'd been using to smooth frosting onto a cupcake. "Or the hot display case, or . . ."

Ellie and I owned and ran a small, chocolate-themed bakery, The Chocolate Moose, on Water Street in the island village of Eastport, Maine. Ocean breezes usually cooled us here, or anyway, they had until recently. But outside our shop windows now, heat shimmered under a mercilessly blue sky.

"Even the walk-in freezer is starting to look good to me," I said, spray-rinsing soapsuds off the baking sheets I'd just scrubbed. "I mean as a place to sleep."

It was August, the height of Eastport's tourist season, with a high pressure system lodged stubbornly over us rocketing the thermometer above ninety for five days, now. And we weren't the only ones; just two miles across Passamaquoddy Bay from our fair city, the Canadian island of Campobello lay sweltering under a sun so cruelly bright, even the seagulls should've been wearing sunglasses.

Ellie finished frosting the cupcakes and offered one to me. "Chocolate cherry. Lots on top, just the way you like it."

But the only kind of cupcake I wanted was frozen and had a gin-and-tonic wrapped around it. "Thanks. Better put them in the cooler before they melt."

Then the little silver bell over the shop's front door jingled and a half-dozen tourists came in. In their L.L. Bean summer garb they all looked adorable, but also as if they were sweating to death.

"No air conditioning?" one of them inquired disappointedly, dragging the back of his sunburned arm across his forehead.

We did have a big AC unit in the kitchen window, but with the oven on it didn't help much. Our century-old building's vintage paddle-bladed fans turned steadily overhead, too, and a portable electric fan in the open back door kept the air moving.

But it was still hot air. The newly arrived tourists looked around uncertainly as if they might leave until Ellie rushed out and cajoled them to a table by the front window; iced coffees and slices of ice-cream–topped chocolate cake followed swiftly, and soon all was well again.

Past them through the window I caught sight of a blue-and-white power boat motoring into the harbor across the street. Two people stepped up onto the pier, each lugging one end of a long black bag.

The third person off the boat was a woman who even at this distance looked vaguely familiar, but I couldn't quite place her and anyway it was the bag that interested me. While the tourists chatted happily over their refreshments, I followed Ellie back out to the kitchen.

"Hey, somebody just brought in a body bag. With, I'm pretty sure, a body in it."

Not that we hadn't been expecting this; Paul Coates's boat, *Sally Ann,* had been found by the Coast Guard running in circles way out past Cherry Island, two days earlier.

Coates hadn't been aboard, nor in the water nearby. But now he'd been found floating or washed up on shore, I supposed.

"Sally will be relieved," Ellie said.

Paul's widow, she meant. It seemed to me a strange kind of relief, although I guessed it might help to put a stop to the worst of the bereaved woman's imaginings. Still, the reality was bad, too: cold salt water, fast currents, sharp rocks . . .

"Not the cheeriest thing for a new top cop's first morning on the job," I said.

Eastport's new chief of police was supposed to start work today, and amazingly for Ellie and me, we didn't even know his name, yet. The Moose had been madly busy this summer and we'd had other things going on, too, that had kept us hopping. So all we did know was that the new chief had a strong recommendation from our previous one, Bob Arnold.

And since Bob had been caring, thoroughly competent, and a good friend, besides, we figured that was enough. Ellie rinsed and dried her mixing bowl and utensils, then turned to the big butcher-block worktable in the center of the kitchen.

"All right, now," she said determinedly, eyeing the ever-present 'To Bake' list taped to the refrigerator, "what's next on the hit parade?"

But then the bell over the shop door rang energetically again, signaling the start of the midmorning rush. That was when people—even sun-hammered tourists—began feeling that they might just possibly eat a little something: a fudge-frosted brownie topped with a scoop of vanilla, say, or a chocolate cannoli stuffed full of cream with cinnamon, cocoa powder and powdered sugar lightly sprinkled onto the top.

You know, something light. "I'll go wait on them," said Ellie. "And how about you run up to the bank, meanwhile, and get us some change?"

I'd have hit the bank earlier, but major construction was under way at my house (see *things going on,* above) and talking to building contractors always makes me too crazy to be able to count money correctly.

"Fine," I said, grabbing the cupcake that Ellie had offered me earlier. The mingled flavors of dark chocolate and cherries hit my brain as I stepped out into the shop area; by the time I reached the counter, my face must've looked like it belonged on a saint being drawn bodily up into heaven.

"Ellie'll be out in just a minute," I began, and then I saw who the customer was.

"Hi, Jake," said the woman at the counter. "How are you?"

"Hi, Lizzie," I managed. She had short, spiky, black hair, blood-red nails that matched her vivid lipstick, and smoky-dark eye makeup applied skillfully and with a feather-light hand.

"I'm fine, how are you?" I added inanely. She was wearing dark blue tailored Bermuda shorts and a black, short-sleeved T-shirt whose snug fit flattered her arms and shoulders. A badge was on her belt, a holster with a .38 auto nestled in it was on her hip, and she was, I suddenly understood, Eastport's brand-new police chief.

"Congratulations," I said calmly, just as if her sudden reappearance in Eastport hadn't knocked me for a loop.

But it had.

**Don't miss the previous Death by Chocolate
mystery novels by Sarah Graves!**

DEATH BY CHOCOLATE MARSHMALLOW PIE

The island village of Eastport, Maine, is full of delights—including the delicious treats sold at The Chocolate Moose, the waterfront bakery run by Jacobia "Jake" Tiptree and Ellie White. But a new bakery in town is proving that you can *have too much of a good thing . . .*

Summer in Eastport means lobsters and blueberries, though tourists and locals alike always leave a little room for baked goods from The Chocolate Moose. This year's arts fair, featuring food, games, and rollicking local musicians, means even more sweet-toothed customers. But it's also bringing competition from a new rival, Choco's, that's trying to slice into the action.

Choco's owner, Brad Fairway, is pulling sneaky stunts to divert Moose patrons to his own shop, and Ellie finally confronts him about his tactics. But when Brad is found dead the next day—and the weapon is a gun that belongs to Ellie—it's only a matter of time before she is charged with the crime.

Sifting through the victim's connections, Jake and Ellie sense they're getting close to the real culprit—a little *too* close. Can they serve up the solution before the killer dishes up another helping of murder?

*Available from Kensington Publishing Corp. wherever
books are sold.*

DEATH BY CHOCOLATE SNICKERDOODLE

Jake Tiptree and Ellie White are fired up for Eastport, Maine's annual cookie-baking contest, but when a cunning killer and a devastating fire threaten to ravage the quaint island town, Jake and Ellie must dip into another homemade homicide investigation before all they love goes up in smoke . . .

As co-owners of Eastport's beloved waterfront bakery, The Chocolate Moose, Jake and Ellie know their customers expect them to cream the competition. But they're really just in it for fun, hoping to get Jake's daughter-in-law baking again. Those plans collapse when fearsome local curmudgeon Alvin Carter is murdered, and every crumb of evidence points to Tiptree family friend—and all-around sweet guy—Billy Breyer.

Billy's sisters beg Jake and Ellie to prove his innocence. After all, lots of folks had gone sour on Alvin, whose popularity ranked somewhere between a toothache and the plague. But just as the ladies begin sifting through the suspects, a series of grass fires blaze across the island, threatening catastrophe. Could someone be trying to hide the truth about Alvin's murder?

Now, Jake and Ellie will need all their courage—and an extra dash of that Down East Maine stubbornness—to sniff out the real killer before anyone else gets burned . . .

Available from Kensington Publishing Corp. wherever books are sold.

DEATH BY CHOCOLATE FROSTED DOUGHNUT

When a pirate festival blows into their small town, bakeshop owners Jacobia "Jake" Tiptree and her best friend, Ellie White, expect they'll be busy baking up a storm, but instead they find themselves marooned in a new murder investigation after someone kills a well-known food writer and TV personality . . .

Everything is shipshape at Jake and Ellie's new waterfront bakery, The Chocolate Moose, especially now that the annual Pirate Festival is dropping anchor in their quaint island village of Eastport, Maine. Jake and Ellie are ready for the bounty of tourists sure to flood their shop. But their plans quickly sink when the body of celebrity foodie, Henry Hadlyme, is discovered in the Moose's basement.

Jake and Ellie are horrified, but their shock turns to dismay when Jake is pegged for the murder. Now, to clear Jake's name and save the shop, Jake and Ellie must swashbuckle down and figure out who among Henry's numerous enemies scuttled him in the cellar. Was it a long-ago jilted sweetheart's vengeful relative? His long-suffering personal assistant? Or perhaps some bitter-as-dark-chocolate unknown enemy, now aboard the mysterious ship lurking in Eastport's harbor?

Alas, dead men tell no tales, so Jake and Ellie will have to get to the bottom of the case on their own and find the real killer before anyone else is forced to walk the plank . . .

Available from Kensington Publishing Corp. wherever books are sold.

DEATH BY CHOCOLATE MALTED MILKSHAKE

The island fishing village of Eastport, Maine, has plenty of salty local character. It also has a sweet side, thanks to Jacobia "Jake" Tiptree, her best friend, Ellie, and their waterfront bake shop, The Chocolate Moose. But when island life is disrupted by the occasional killer, Jake and Ellie put their chocolate treats aside to make sure justice is served.

This summer, Eastport's favorite lovebirds, kindergarten teacher Sharon Sweetwater and Coast Guard Captain Andy Devine, are getting married. The gala reception is sure to be the fête of the season, especially with a wedding-cake–sized whoopie pie courtesy of The Chocolate Moose. For Jake and Ellie, the custom-ordered confection will finally reel in some much-needed profits. But the celebratory air, and sweet smell of success, are ruined by foul murder.

When Sharon's bitter ex-boyfriend, Toby, is murdered with a poisoned milkshake, Andy is jailed as the prime suspect and the wedding is canceled, whoopie pie and all. Then Sharon makes a shocking confession—one that sounds like a fishy attempt to get Andy off the hook. Now both the bride and groom are behind bars. And with the fate of The Chocolate Moose at stake, it's up to Jake and Ellie to catch a poisonous predator before someone else sips their last dessert.

*Available from Kensington Publishing Corp.
wherever books are sold.*

DEATH BY CHOCOLATE CHERRY CHEESECAKE

*Life just got a little sweeter in the island fishing village of
Eastport, Maine. Jacobia "Jake" Tiptree and her best friend,
Ellie, are opening a waterfront bake shop, The Chocolate
Moose, where their tasty treats pair perfectly with the salty
ocean breeze. But while Jake has moved on from fixing up
houses, she still can't resist the urge to snoop into the
occasional murder.*

Jake and Ellie have been through a lot together, from home
repair to homicide investigation. So when they decide to open
a chocolate-themed bakery, they figure it'll be a piece of cake.
With Ellie's old family recipes luring in customers, they expect
to make plenty of dough this Fourth of July weekend. Having
family home for the holiday only sweetens the deal for Jake—
until the ill wind of an early-season hurricane blows up her
plans. When the storm hits, Jake's grown son, Sam, is stranded
in a Boston bus station, and her husband, Wade, is stuck on a
cargo ship. But as bitter as the storm is, something even more
sinister is brewing in the kitchen of The Chocolate Moose—
where health inspector Matt Muldoon is found murdered.

Ellie never made a secret of her distaste for Matt, who had
been raining on their parade with bogus talk of health code
violations. Now, with no alibi for the night of the murder,
she's in a sticky situation with the police—and it's up to
Jake to catch the real killer and keep Ellie living in the land
of the free.

*Available from Kensington Publishing Corp.
wherever books are sold.*

Visit our website at
KensingtonBooks.com
to sign up for our newsletters, read
more from your favorite authors, see
books by series, view reading group
guides, and more!

Become a Part of Our
Between the Chapters Book Club
Community and Join the Conversation

Betweenthechapters.net

Submit your book review for a chance to win exclusive
Between the Chapters swag you can't get anywhere else!
https://www.kensingtonbooks.com/pages/review/